Thornhill Trilogy 1

ENTRANCE

By J. J. Sorel

AUTHOR'S NOTE

All the characters in this fairy-tale romance are consenting adults. For those readers who like their romance novels peppered with descriptive sex scenes, then this is for you. However, for those disinclined towards steamy boudoir scenes I suggest you either approach this with an open mind, or just pass it on to someone looking for an escape in the arms of a sexy read.

Table of Contents

CHAPTER ONE

The secluded mansion was a rare jewel that hugged the cliff perilously.

It wouldn't take much for a landslide.

I peered up at my imposing destination as my sticky palms steered the car along the snaky coastal highway.

Pushing down on the accelerator, I turned onto a steep road leading up to the estate. My old car was weak and churlish, the gears struggling. My heart palpitated. *What if I stall and roll back?* I took a deep breath and gritted my teeth. This was hardly the time for a panic attack.

After conquering the incline, I passed a fortress of whitewashed walls.

"Where the hell's the entrance?" I mumbled, scolding myself for not getting properly acquainted with technology.

I rummaged in my bag and dragged out a scribbled note that instructed me to swing right after passing the front entrance.

Okay, there was the entrance. I expelled a slow breath. My chest relaxed for the first time since I'd raced out of my apartment forty-five minutes earlier.

I pulled up close to the intercom, and stretched my arm out to push on the buzzer.

"Yes," a baritone echoed.

Craning my neck, I responded, "I'm here for the interview."

"Name?"

"Clarissa Moone."

"Take a left turn past the gate, and you will come to the visitors' car park."

The tall iron gates yawned open, and I drove into the estate.

As the car slowed to a crawl, my jaw dropped. My flesh tingled at the splendor before me. A pre-war era mansion came into view behind a flourishing garden, resembling an Italian villa in Lake Como.

Focus, Clarissa!

I looked ahead. There stood a tall, well-built man in black clothes and sunglasses. He waved for me to park amongst shiny, latest-model cars. I gulped. The poor old clunker would seem so alien. Was that a contemptuous expression behind his dark glasses?

Sweat dripped down my arms as I stepped out of my car. Despite the day being hot, I would have to keep my cardigan on to hide the wet patches.

Wiping my brow, I followed the enormous man along a cobbled path. The air, redolent of salt, flowers, and earth, was uplifting. Blood flowed to my face. I couldn't believe I was heading for a job interview. At least the aesthetic distractions helped me forget my anxiety.

I wasn't watching my step, and my heel got caught in a crack. I twisted my shoe sending a twinge of pain up the side of my calf. Luckily, I adjusted my weight in time and avoided a fall. Coming to my aid, the security guard stretched his arm out to support me.

"Are you okay, ma'am?"

"I'm good, thanks," I said, blushing.

Eyes down this time, I started moving again as we continued on. He walked so quickly I struggled to keep up. Being a flat-pumps girl, I was not well practiced at walking in heels.

We passed through an archway of creamy, chiseled columns that led us to the portico. I climbed the stairs with care, watching every step I took. Mr. Security opened a stained-glass double door so mind-blowing in design that I uttered a quiet "Wow."

The interior didn't disappoint, either. It resembled a nineteenth-century museum. The yellow walls were covered by gilt-framed art, pearly marble goddesses stood on a black-and-white checked floor.

Could this be the home of one of America's most eligible billionaires? I'd pictured something modern, minimal, white, and boxy. Just as in the movies.

We then entered a teal-colored room. Watercolor seascapes hung in profusion. Were they by Turner? *Not possible. He'd have to be a trillionaire.*

Having majored in art history, I had to ogle. One thing was for certain: this mysterious tycoon had impeccable taste. I found myself warming to him.

Although the agency had kept his name a secret, Ellen mentioned that he was an eligible bachelor. I didn't quite know why I needed to hear that. But I gathered from her higher-than-normal pitch that she was rather pleased to be dealing with such an illustrious client.

She also revealed that she was sending a dozen girls to the interview, and the only reason she'd considered me was that her client had asked specifically for someone cultured and well versed in the fine arts. It was nice to know that my major had given me an advantage even though I'd chosen it for loftier reasons than becoming a PA to a billionaire, married or single.

But then, I had no ambition. I just loved looking at beautiful things. I needed a job desperately. And so there I was.

My God, Louis XIV armchairs! I stroked the silky mint-green damask. *Probably a reproduction.* I sighed so loudly that the security guard looked at me. A faint smirk appeared, and then his blank inscrutability returned. I supposed appearing disinterested was part of his job.

He pointed to an adjoining room. "In there, ma'am."

A room full of hopefuls sat waiting. Wearing low-cut blouses and tight skirts, they looked more like super-models than personal assistants. Their heavily made-up eyes peered up simultaneously, starting at my T-bar shoes and settling on my bare face. Pouty and plumped up, their lips curled mockingly all at the same time. I nearly laughed.

Still, I'm sure I appeared rather outlandish wearing a 1960s pencil-skirt inherited from my late mother. A white, button down shirt hid my larger-than- normal breasts. *What possessed me to wear the green cardigan?* Nevertheless, I needed a job, not a husband unlike the rest, with their hungry, seeking-a-billionaire vibe. My maxed-out credit card meant that Tabitha, my roommate, would need to cover our rent again.

A throbbing spasm at the side of my neck and damp palms spoke of stress. I hoped he wouldn't shake my hand. To add to my discomfort, the mélange of celebrity-endorsed perfumes tickling my nasal passages was making me sneeze.

I could also feel my heavy bun threatening to sag. I tucked a stray strand behind my ear. Thick and long, my untamable hair needed hairspray. I shouldn't have washed it. It never behaved. I always complained about my waist-length hair, much to Tabitha's chagrin. But I couldn't bring myself to cut it. My mother had shared the same black mane. I had many wonderful photos of her looking chic with her stacked-up bun and eyeliner. Despite inheriting her features, I was more like my father: shy, awkward and a dreamer.

For the umpteenth time, I recrossed my legs. I was clearly the attraction, with everyone's unwavering attention directed at my green cardigan, purchased from my favorite vintage store. *Were they rolling their eyes?*

Finally, an older lady came out. Much to my relief, she looked drabber than me. Maybe she was being replaced. In either case, I was the closest in clothing choice. I fantasized poking my tongue at the room full of catty girls.

"Good morning, ladies. My name's Greta Thornhill." There was a sudden rustle amongst the girls. "You're required to answer one question. You have five minutes to do so. Clipboards with paper and pens are here." She pointed to a table. "I'll be back in five minutes to collect your responses."

As we gathered to collect our clipboards, I overheard two girls whispering, "Oh my God, it's Aidan Thornhill."

I'd heard the name before but couldn't place it. Not one for celebrity gossip, I had no idea who the most eligible billionaire in town was. My aspirations were not that high. And although I loved the idea of a boyfriend, I had met none I liked. Apart from some heavy petting, I'd never gone all the way. Tabitha couldn't believe I was still a virgin at twenty-one.

The question read: "If you received one million dollars with only one day to spend it, how would you use it?" Good. No trick questions. No esoteric math. This shouldn't tax my overwrought brain too much.

I wrote, "Buy my father, a professor of English literature, a fully furnished cottage in England with an extensive library. Buy an airline ticket and car for him. Stock his cupboards with enough food to last years." (I left out the lifetime supply of single malt whisky.) "Then I would donate to the homeless shelter and the lost-dogs' home. With any leftover, I'd buy myself a ticket to Paris and visit the Louvre." I put down my pen and relaxed.

A few minutes later, Greta Thornhill entered. "Time's up, ladies."

Frustrated sighs filtered through the room. *How hard could it be?* I did a subtle eye-roll.

When I presented my clipboard, I noticed her cool blue eyes studying me closely.

"Thank you, ladies. We'll be in touch."

CHAPTER TWO

Tabitha opened the door just as I entered, causing me to stumble. "How did you do? Did you find out who it was?" she asked, her wide green eyes brimming with impatience.

Parched after the long drive, I headed for the fridge and grabbed a juice, gulping it in one thirsty mouthful.

With hands on hips, she followed me into the kitchen. As always, Tabitha looked stunning in tight white jeans and a floral blouse. Her long blond hair framed her pretty features.

We were an odd pairing. While she was stylish and outgoing, I was old-fashioned and introverted. Joined at the hip since the age of five, we grew up in the same apartment block, both of us raised by widowed fathers.

I poured myself another glass of juice. "Not sure how it went."

"Did you get to see him? Is there a name?"

"I only met an older woman. But I did hear the name Aidan Thornhill being whispered about."

"Seriously? You're kidding me…" she screeched. "My God, Aidan Thornhill."

I shook my head. "Who's that?"

Her stretched gaze nearly ate me alive. "Shit, Clary, he's only the sexiest and most eligible billionaire in LA." Without a moment to lose, she sprang up and tapped away on her laptop. "Come and have a look. Shit, he's hot."

Aidan Thornhill was indeed very good-looking. "He appears glum in every shot," I said.

Tabitha leaned on her elbows and peered into the screen. "Hmm…the broody type. That makes him even sexier. Wow, imagine if you get the job."

"I haven't got it yet, Tabs," I said.

"But you might. That's the exciting bit."

I sighed. "Let's not jinx it. It's better that way."

"Don't be so negative, Clary. Remember that seminar we attended. If one projects positive thoughts, life will deliver."

"That's new-age claptrap and a recipe for disappointment. At least this way, I'll be ecstatic if I get it." Standing over Tabi's shoulder, I checked the images of my potential boss. In each photo, he appeared with different women, never the same one twice. "He's got a thing for blondes."

"But wait till he sees you in a bikini." Tabitha's voice had gone up a decibel.

"Now you're being crazy. I'll be working as a PA, not a model. I don't even own a bikini. And if I did, I wouldn't be wearing it to work." I tilted my head. Tabitha's mouth curled into a wide, contagious grin. Imagining me at a computer in a bikini made us giggle.

The sound of "La Marseillaise" blaring startled both of us. *I must change that ringtone.*

While I searched for my phone in my handbag, Tabitha was close at my heels like an eager puppy dog. Taking a deep breath, I pressed the button. "Hello."

An unfamiliar voice asked, "Is that Clarissa Moone?"

"Yes."

"This is Ellen Shelton from the agency."

"How are you?" I asked with a thin and high-pitched voice.

"Great, thank you. I've got pleasing news for you. You've got the job."

"Really?" My eyes widened in disbelief.

"Don't sound so shocked. You impressed them."

"I didn't do that much," I said.

"Whatever you did was more than enough. I just spoke to Greta Thornhill. She requested that you go in tomorrow to discuss your role and sign a contract. Can you be there 9:30a.m.?"

I clutched the phone with a tight grip. "Yes, of course," I exclaimed. "Thanks so much."

"The pleasure is mine. They've been interviewing for quite some time. Well done."

CHAPTER THREE

It was 9:20a.m. when I headed towards the regal entrance to the Thornhill estate. Once again, my tummy was tight with nerves. But with time on my side I ambled along taking in the charming sights while drawing in the salty sea air.

Out of nowhere, a dog suddenly raced up and pounced upon me in a friendly manner. Not the typical canine of a billionaire, I thought. I would have expected a poodle or a designer breed. This wild fellow, a white-chested black cattle dog, resembled one I'd grown up with, making our meeting rather heart-warming.

"Rocket!" a tall man in a baseball cap and sunglasses called out, running to rescue me from the dog's enthusiastic embrace. I patted the keen canine and spoke in a childish doggy voice. His brown affectionate eyes, helping me to relax, filled me with joy.

"I'm sorry about that," the owner said, panting.

"Oh, he's such a sweetie," I said, rubbing Rocket's back. The dog, in response jumped up and placed his paws on my thighs.

The man made a command and the obedient animal sat. "I'm so sorry." He pointed at my skirt, which was now covered in paw prints.

Frowning, I bit my lip. *Damn!*

"I'll get someone to wipe it for you," he said in a deep drawl. Before I could respond, he had disappeared.

I tried to brush the stain with my hand, but to no avail. *Good start, a stained skirt!*

Heavy-hearted, I walked up the stairs to the entrance. The door opened just as I touched the bell. Before me stood the security guard I'd met the day before. He pointed up the stairs. "First room on the left, ma'am."

I nodded and gripped the smooth wooden bannister. The lacework staircase was so grand I pictured Scarlett O'Hara descending in her bouncy ball-gown. Taking careful steps, I ascended the staircase. Stern, judgmental stares from the portraits on the wall followed me. All historical figures, the original occupants I assumed.

I knew they couldn't be related to Aidan Thornhill, however, because Tabi's relentless googling revealed that he had been a ranger with the Special Forces in Afghanistan. Unless he was some kind of adrenaline junkie, I couldn't imagine a billionaire from established wealth doing that. We also discovered he'd built his empire from playing the stock-market. There was nothing about his family.

Lost in the deep, rich colors of the still-life before me, trying to determine whether it was an original *Brueghel,* I didn't notice Greta Thornhill waiting for me. When I turned and saw her within a few inches of my face, an embarrassing squawk left my lips.

Clasping a damp cloth, she remained expressionless. "I heard you had an accident courtesy of Rocket." She stared down at my skirt.

"Yes, I did. I'm sorry about that. Not that it worries me or anything."

Greta handed me the wet cloth.

"Thanks." I took the cloth and proceeded to rub it into the stains. "I think it should be okay now." I held onto the damp fabric unsure of what to do with it.

Taking it from my hand, Greta said, "Here, give that to me."

As we continued down the long hallway laden with jaw-dropping artwork, Greta said, "We'll first pay a visit to your new office. And then the cottage."

I stopped walking. "Excuse me. Cottage?"

Greta frowned. "Didn't the agency tell you? We expect you to live here during the weekdays."

"No, they didn't," I said.

"Will that be a problem for you, Miss Moone?"

I shook my head. "Please call me Clarissa." I imagined going to the beach after work, walks in the flourishing gardens, the sketches I could do. "I won't need to commute daily. Can I leave on the weekends?"

Greta touched her graying French-roll. She reminded me of a school principal from the 1960's. "You can come and go as you please. We prefer our staff to be housed here in case the need to work late arises. Your primary task will be to manage the gala nights and to attend them on a monthly basis. They take place on a Saturday evening."

"That suits me fine," I said, flashing my biggest and brightest smile.

As with every room I'd visited so far, my new office was astonishing. The pink silk damask wallpaper and contrasting crisp white cornices stole my breath away. "It's simply stunning." I sighed.

Greta's lips twitched.

Unable to stay focused in one spot, my eyes moved from the antique mahogany desk to the paintings landing on a *Kandinsky*, at which point I exhaled audibly.

"Aidan's an avid art collector," said Greta, noticing my flushed surprise. "He was impressed by your education in art history."

"Will I be advising him on acquisitions?" I asked, trying to remain cool while my mind popped a champagne cork at that thought.

"No. He doesn't need advice. Aidan's very particular when it comes to art."

I nodded. "From what I've seen, he has excellent taste."

"I'm sure your views will please him," she said with a tight smile. Greta pointed to the desk. "You should have everything you require here. You'll report solely to me."

"Yes, Miss Thornhill."

"Call me Greta, please," she said. "I'm Aidan's aunt."

"I see," I said, my eyes landing on the view of the sea outside the window.

"I'll take you to the cottage now," said Greta, directing me out of the room.

At the end of the hallway, towards the back of the house, we descended a set of stairs, taking us into a massive, industrial-sized kitchen decked in stainless steel. A large man, who I assumed was the chef, and a younger woman moved about the space. We then entered a dining area. From there, a door led us outside into a courtyard with table and chairs for dining alfresco.

As we moved along the cobbled path surrounded by terracotta pots filled with exotic flourishing plants, Greta pointed to a charming cottage with a porch.

Stepping through French doors, I was met by a cozy environment. No expense had been spared. I gushed, "This is such an inviting room."

"We've tried to make it as comfortable as possible," said Greta.

After being given a tour of my new home, I wanted to ask what happened to the last personal assistant, but I didn't wish to pry. *Why would anybody want to leave this?*

"Your predecessor got married," said Greta, seemingly reading my mind. "You're free to come and go as you please. You are required to sign a privacy clause, and visitors are not allowed in the main residence. There's a separate entrance at the back of the estate."

"That sounds more than reasonable. Apart from my father and my roommate, I'm unlikely to entertain," I said.

"As you wish," she said, directing me out of the cottage. "I've drawn up a contract which I'll give to you in a moment. Please read it with care. You'll see what's expected of you. It's vital you pay attention to clause seven."

I followed Greta back into the dining area. She pointed to a chair. "I'll bring the contract. Melanie will look after you for tea or coffee. Baked daily, our cakes and muffins are always on offer."

"Thanks," I said.

"I'll leave you to it," said Greta.

Served with cream, the coffee was so delicious I had two cups. The aroma of the chocolate cake made my stomach rumble, I ended up polishing the plate.

Buzzing, not only from the sugar hit but from what had just taken place, I stared at the contract: "Hours 9:30 a.m. to 6:00 p.m., Mon.–Fri. Breaks for coffee, morning and afternoon, and lunch. One Saturday a month, you are to attend the charity gala event held at the Thornhill Estate. You will sometimes be required to work late. After a probationary period of six months, provided you perform your tasks satisfactorily, this contract will be extended."

Clause seven read, "Under no circumstances are photos of the estate or dealings therein to be divulged through social media or any other outlets, i.e., magazines, newspaper columns etcetera. Visitors are not allowed in the main house unless invited to do so."

That seemed reasonable enough, I thought as Greta crept back into the room. "Is that all in order?" Watching me rummage in my bag, she passed me a pen. "Here you are."

"Thanks." I accepted the pen and held it over the document.

"Have you any questions?" she asked.

I shook my head. "No, it's easy to follow. Thank you."

"Right, then. That's it for today. Can you start tomorrow?"

"Yes," I replied with enthusiasm.

She clapped her hands together. "Good. The gala fundraiser is only two weeks away, and we have much to do." Her eyes ran up and down my body. "You'll be requiring six ball gowns. In this envelope is a credit card with a generous limit." She placed it on the table. "If you prefer, a stylist can select your gowns. It's up to you. Aidan stipulates we look our best. He's very strict when it comes to his staff's appearance. No casual clothes. You can charge your work clothes to the account."

I was still getting my mind around the six ball gowns. *Do I get to keep them?*

"The clothes will be yours to keep," said Greta, once again reading my mind.

CHAPTER FOUR

"You're back? So soon," Tabitha said. I nearly fell into her arms. She had an annoying habit of opening the door just as I was entering.

I headed to the fridge for a juice. Tabitha followed at my heels. "So, are you going to tell me what happened? Did you meet him?"

With a thirst equally as impatient as Tabitha, I fell onto the sofa and emptied my glass. "I signed a contract and was taken to a charming little cottage where I'm expected to live during weekdays."

Tabitha knitted her thin, well-plucked eyebrows. "You're moving out?"

"No, I just won't be here weeknights. But I'll be back weekends." I touched her hand.

"Oh..." Tabitha reflected. "It will be lonesome without you here."

"You can visit, you know. I am allowed to have visitors."

A smile dissolved her frown. "Seriously? Does that mean I can stay?"

"I can't see why not." I dragged the contract out of my bag. "Here, read this. It will answer everything. I have to pack. Then I've got to go shopping."

Tabitha gaped at me. "Shopping?"

"I need to buy work clothes. I have a charge account," I said, keeping a straight face, unlike Tabitha, whose eyes were bulging out of their sockets. "Greta gave it to me."

Tabitha's mouth fell open. "Are you kidding me? A charge account so soon? I mean, you haven't even worked there yet. What "Thanks for the vote of confidence, friend."

She tilted her head and smirked.

Placing the contract down, Tabitha screamed. "Oh my God, Clary. Six ball gowns, and designer, I bet. Fuck. You've won the lottery."

"It certainly feels that way," I said with a permanent grin that was making my jaw ache. "Do you want to come?"

"Who else is going to advise you?" said Tabitha springing up off the sofa.

"Let's do lunch first. I'm starving, and it's on me," I said, upbeat and buoyant.

Grabbing my arm, Tabitha trilled, "This is so exciting."

That was us. With a tendency to share in each other's highs and lows, we were more like sisters than friends.

****

"Oh my God, Clary, a $10,000 limit," crooned Tabitha.

"It must be for the formalwear and work clothing combined," I said, equally stunned.

"They don't expect you to buy the gowns today, do they?" Tabitha asked as we sprinted towards the fashion district.

"I doubt it. Let's focus on office clothes for now. Not that I'm sure what to buy," I said, happy to have my fashion-savvy friend in tow.

"Leave it to me, Clary. We'll have you looking sexy and professional in no time." She looped her arm in mine and was all bouncy.

"Not sexy, only professional," I said.

"Don't lay that virgin crap on me. You're working for the hottest guy in town," she blurted so loudly people's heads turned.

"Tell the whole of LA, why don't you?" I snapped.

"You've got a figure to die for and a face like Natalie Wood's," Tabitha said, dragging me along by my hand.

"Tabs, need I keep reminding you that I'm employed as a PA?"

"I know, I know. But there's no harm in making the most of your assets," she said, sounding more like an ambitious mother by the minute.

We passed "Yesterday's Child" my favorite vintage shop. Instincts fully aroused, I headed for the doorway. Tabitha pulled me back. "No vintage, Clary, only contemporary, stylish, and sexy."

"Vintage can be super classy and fashionable," I argued. Although she was right, I had a pathological addiction to 1960s clothes. Tabitha said it was because I was trying to emulate my late mother. I couldn't disagree. My mother and I were so alike in build that I still wore her clothes. It was an obsession that had caused much trouble at college, at least until vintage became fashion. Then the bullies suddenly regarded my Mondrian-inspired mini worn over white patent-leather boots with envy.

"Let's go there." Tabitha pointed to an enormous department store. I followed along submissively.

Inside, there were racks everywhere. I frowned. "Where should we start?"

"Isn't this fantastic?" Tabitha was in her element. "Let's begin with shirts." She selected a cream-colored cotton fitted shirt. "This is a flattering shape." She held it against me. "Three in varying shades should do it. That way, you can mix and match."

"It's very fitted. Couldn't we go more for this?" I pointed to a silk, loose-fitting shirt with a necktie.

"Clarissa, you're going all vintage again," Tabitha sang, selecting three more of the fitted variety. "These are just right. They'll look swish— trust me."

"I don't know, Tabs. I think I'd prefer loose."

"Stop being so damn bashful. You've got nice big boobs."

"I don't want to look cheap, Tabs. Greta made it clear they expect modest and professional-looking clothing."

"Hello. A high-waisted pencil skirt with a crisp cotton, well-tailored shirt is hardly skank-wear." Tabitha pulled one of her many silly faces, making me giggle.

"Okay, then, but I'm taking one of those." I selected a loose silk shirt with tiny pale-pink polka dots. The price-tag read $500. "Shit, this is pricey."

"Classy means expensive, Clarissa." Grabbing me by the hand, Tabitha led me to the skirts. "This is cool." Tabitha held one with a slit to the thigh.

"I'm not going there to perform an Apache dance, you know where I leap from my desk and end up in the splits on the floor," I said with a chuckle.

Tabitha laughed. "You're a nut-job."

After we settled for three skirts, Tabitha dragged me over to a rack of short sheath dresses.

"I can see what you're doing, Tabs. You're dressing me in alluring clothes. These are hardly professional," I said.

"Hello. One can be sexy and professional. You have a stunning figure and dancer's legs. You should show them off."

"Yes. But not at work."

Ignoring me, Tabitha flicked through a rack of knee-length sheath dresses, selecting a red one. She placed it on my body. "Hmm, yes. Red's your color."

More mother than friend, Tabitha was bossy. But then, considering my incurable indecisiveness, it was a practical arrangement.

Without waiting for my approval, she popped the dress in the shopping cart.

"Now for some nylons." Stroking a silk camisole, Tabitha purred with delight.

"I'll get you one," I said.

Her face lit up. "Really?"

"Why not? Pick two. If they complain, I can always pay it back. I'm about to be properly waged," I said, lifting my sternum with pride.

While Tabitha chose cream and pale pink, falling for the irresistible feel of silk, I selected two as well.

"Shit, suspenders?" I exclaimed as she dangled a lacy ensemble in front of me.

"Coming from a girl who's still living in the sixties."

"Mm...point taken," I said, watching her pop it into the shopping cart.

"We need to buy some shoes," Tabitha said, extracting most of the joy from our expedition.

"What's wrong with my new Mary-Janes?" I asked.

"Nothing, I guess. But we need some heels, sexy spiky ones."

"I won't wear those during the day. They're hard enough at night."

"Come on," she said, stubborn as always. "Your Mary-Janes make you look like a spinster."

"Does anyone even use that word anymore?" I asked, rolling my eyes.

"Whatever. You need spiky heels. Not too high, but stiletto-thin. Come on." She dragged me off to the Shoe Emporium. Half an hour later, we walked out with three boxes.

CHAPTER FIVE

Stocked with everything I needed and much more, the pantry was full. For someone accustomed to lonesome cans of beans and half-empty boxes of cereal, this was novel. There was enough food for a year. I was well prepared for a catastrophe. The fridge, likewise, was filled with all the yummy food one would pine for, especially late at night while lazing about on the sofa. Then there were the staples: milk, juice, cheese, ham, and even olives. I couldn't believe how generous my new employers were. Not only was I being paid a decent higher-than-expected wage, but my clothes and my personal needs were being seen to as well.

A knock came at the door. Greta stood before me, wearing a whisper of a smile. It was the warmest I'd seen from her to date, not that she gave me a bad vibe.

"Good morning, Greta," I said, all smiles.

"Good morning."

I stepped away so she could enter.

Greta looked about the room. "I trust Linus helped you with your cases."

"He was extremely helpful, thank you," I said, recalling him carrying everything from my car to the cottage. "I also discovered that you filled the cupboards. It's such a generous gesture and most unexpected."

"Stores are far from here," she replied in her usual cool tone. Her eyes did a quick sweep of my outfit and settled on my French roll.

"I hope this is suitable," I said, touching my bun.

"It's fine. Is your hair long?"

"Ah, yes, it is. Is that a problem?" I asked with a lopsided grin.

"Not at all." She shook her head. "I was just curious. Most girls go for the shorter styles these days. I prefer longer hair myself. It's easier to style."

"That it is. My friend helped me this morning. She's rather adept at styling hair. I'm more of a ponytail girl. Will that be acceptable?" I could feel a little drip down my arms. All the scrutiny was making me uneasy.

"You can wear it how you like."

She looked at my suitcase lying on the floor unopened. "Are you ready to start?"

"Yes… raring to go." I nearly saluted, but deeming it too clichéd, I resisted the urge.

The aroma of baking, as I passed through the kitchen, was so alluring my stomach grumbled.

"Have you eaten?" Greta asked. Her ability to read my mind was starting to freak me out.

"No, only coffee, I'll make up for it at lunch."

"We have freshly baked muffins. I'll get Melanie to bring you one, along with some brewed coffee. How do you have it?"

"Milk and two sugars, thanks."

I'd forgotten how sensory commanding my new office was. I sighed silently as I stepped into the pink haven.

With ocean views and artwork all vying for my attention, I had to concentrate hard as Greta instructed me. My first task was to process guests' payments and email receipts. Noting my bewilderment at the $1000 price tag, Greta said, "These events are very popular. With only five hundred tickets, they get snapped up quickly."

"I see," I said, reading the list of charities that Thornhill Holdings ran. There were seven in total. Amongst those were foundations for retired members of the armed forces, homeless shelters for women and children, and even dog shelters. I formed a favorable impression of my elusive, generous boss.

"Once you've done that, you need to study the spreadsheet to ensure it tallies with that figure."

Although I was kept very busy, the work was simple to grasp.

"I'm ready for the next task," I said as Greta re-entered the office.

"Excellent. You've exceeded expectations. After lunch, we'll go over entertainment and catering."

"I can grab a sandwich and keep working if you like."

She studied me with her cool blue eyes. "No, you've made exceptional progress. I expected this to take a full day. There's no need. Melanie will get you some lunch. You can either eat in the dining area, or outside."

I looked out the window and opted for eating outdoors. Tranquil, inviting, and kissed by a hot sun, the sea glistened. I promised myself a swim after work.

"We like to feed our staff. There are always plenty of leftovers to take home should you wish. While you're here working, lunch, coffee, and cakes are on us."

"That's very generous," I said, smiling so much my face hurt. I'd grown awfully fond of Greta.

The steak sandwich had my tummy groaning with delight. I had never tasted anything so delicious. The meat was so tender it melted in my mouth.

I felt as if I was in Southern Europe as I sat under the old willow outside my cottage. A soft breeze swaying the wispy branches worked as a fan. My legs were stretched out on a chair, giving my feet respite from my new spiked heels.

The sun caressed my face as I closed my eyes. I never wanted to leave. For once in my life, luck had touched me.

A puffing sound roused me. I looked up, and there was Rocket, his hungry eyes on my lunch. I gave him my leftovers, and within a blink they'd gone. To show his gratitude he licked my hand.

"You're such a glutton, like all doggies," I said, patting him. "Such a cute boy, though."

"Rocket!" hollered a deep, husky voice.

I turned and saw the tall man from the day before standing close by.

"I'm sorry about this. He doesn't normally do this." He pushed back his collar-length hair, and immediately, my skin tingled. "He's taken a liking to you, which is rather unusual."

He was dressed in a t-shirt, and his broad shoulders and shapely biceps were impossible to ignore. Although sunglasses and a baseball cap obscured his face, I sensed he was hot. He had a towel draped over his shoulder and wore shorts that hung loosely over his athletic thighs.

"That's okay," I replied, putting on my best smile. "I love dogs. I had one just like him growing up. They're such great companions."

He glanced at my discarded shoes.

"New shoes," I said with a goofy smile. *Will I ever learn to act dignified around good-looking men?*

He nodded, lingering. *Hmm…is he checking me out?* "Anyway, sorry about Rocket."

"Not an issue. I could walk him after work," I said, giving Rocket a farewell pat.

"I'll bear that in mind. Thanks for the offer." He hovered again. I sensed he might have been staring into my eyes, but I wasn't sure because he wore sunglasses.

Is there a spark? Or is that just wishful thinking?

Elegant and self-assured, he had an easy stride that made it hard for me to look away. Perhaps he was the gardener. His light-brown, wind-tousled hair was streaked gold in the sunlight. I fanned my face. I had developed an instant crush.

Hot and flooded with raging hormones, I returned to work despite taking only thirty minutes for lunch. There was much to do. And I wanted to make a good impression. There was no doubt Mr. Sexy Gardener had affected me. The pleasant throb between my sticky thighs was evidence enough. *Now, why didn't I meet guys like him back in the city?*

As I passed through the kitchen, I caught sight of Melanie. "Do you want a slice of cake? It's chocolate."

This is cake city.

"Sure, why not? Thanks. The food is extremely yummy."

"Would you like coffee as well? I can bring it up for you, if you like."

"That would be amazing. I can make it if you're busy," I said.

She frowned, shaking her head vehemently. "No way. I wouldn't dream of it. That's part of my job. Just press the green button on your phone anytime, for anything: juice, coffee, food, or cake."

My jaw-dropped. "I can't believe this setup."

"It's great, isn't it? The Thornhills are really generous."

"Are there just two of them here?" I asked.

"Yep. Greta's Aidan's aunt. She's more like a mother to him, even though he's still got one." A weird expression coated her dark eyes. It seemed as if she'd revealed something she shouldn't have.

"Aha. Well, it's fantastic being here." The desire to ask more questions was so great I had to work overtime not to.

"Have you met Aidan yet?" Melanie asked.

"No," I replied.

"A word of advice: don't fall in love with him."

What?

"I'm not planning to," I replied meekly.

"Then you'll stay on longer than the others."

I was about to respond when Greta entered the room. "Thanks," was all I could utter. *How many have there been?* Maybe that was why the contract stipulated that I wear modest clothing. I was suddenly glad I hadn't worn a fitted shirt.

Although Tabitha saw my D-cups as a blessing, I didn't. Tight blouses drew too much unwanted attention. I wouldn't have minded, of course, if it came from men like the sexy gardener, however.

"You can take your full lunch break. There's still thirty minutes," said Greta, glancing over at the florid French clock—one of the many objects I'd been admiring all morning.

"No, it's okay. The gala's only two weeks away," I said.

Greta's eyes rested on my chocolate cake.

I asked, "Is it okay having this here while I work?"

"Of course it is. Grab anything that takes your fancy. And there are always leftovers. Make sure you help yourself when you leave this afternoon. It will save you the need to cook."

"You're really generous. I'm touched." Oh no, tears threatened. With my period due, my mood was sensitive. Not one to miss much, Greta cast me a sympathetic smile.

I breezed through my first day at work. I suggested a string quartet in the garden for twilight cocktails, followed by a band playing jazz classics for dinner in the ballroom. Greta loved the ideas, much to my delight. From PA to event manager, I loved this role so much that when five o'clock came around, Greta had to push me out of the office.

The first thing I did when entering the cottage was to change into a loose cotton skirt. My legs were pleased to be naked and stocking free. I shouldn't have allowed Tabitha to talk me into them—they were really uncomfortable. Speaking of the devil, I had to return her calls. She'd already called me twice.

"At last. I've being dying to speak to you," said Tabitha over the phone, all high-pitched and excitable.

"I've only just finished now," I said, putting my feet up on the coffee table.

"How was it? Did you meet him?"

"No, I didn't. The work's easy. The food's amazing, and my cottage is very comfortable. But I have to get Dad's car back to him. He called and said he needed it."

"What are you up to?"

"I'll drive it over now and get him to drop me back," I said, my shoulders sagging at the thought of a longish drive.

"Then you can drop in," said Tabitha.

"I won't have the time, sweetie."

"Steve's coming over later," she said with a thin voice.

"I suppose he's left his wife again?"

"This time, he's promised to."

"If only I had a dollar for each time he's said that," I said.

Steve had been Tabitha's boss when she waitressed. She was only eighteen when they first got together. I disliked him. But according to Tabitha, he was super in bed and had an enormous penis. One thing was for sure: I wouldn't miss the stomach-churning moans and the vibration of Tabitha's bed against the wall.

"Don't be like that, Clary. He's in love with me."

"Whatever. If you want, you can pop over for dinner on Thursday. The food's amazing here. How's that sound?"

"That sounds exciting. I guess I can wait till Thursday," said Tabitha, sighing.

"Enjoy your booty call," I said, checking the time.

"Don't call it that," Tabitha snapped. "I'm needy at the moment. My best friend's left me."

"Come on, Tabs. Don't do that."

CHAPTER SIX

When we drove into the car park, my father whistled. "This is rather opulent."

"Do you want to see the cottage? There's plenty to eat. Too much for me." I missed my father, and I was dying for him to see my new home.

He removed his glasses and rubbed his eyes. "Why not? But I can't stay too long. I've got to meet a potential publisher tomorrow, early."

"You didn't tell me about that."

"I didn't wish to give you false hope. The eternal pessimist—that's me," he said, chuckling.

"So that's where I get it from," I said, taking his hand.

"How marvelously old-world," he said as we traipsed along the cobbled path. The grounds were lit up with charming Victorian lamps.

"Here we are," I said, pointing to the cottage.

I turned on the outside light so that my father could admire my friendly willow. He tapped the fat trunk. "My, he's a beauty."

"Isn't he? And there's a cute dog named Rocket. He looks just like Huxley."

"Is that right? I look forward to meeting him," he crooned, eyes all wistful. He'd never gotten over the death of our beloved dog.

I placed roast beef, potato salad, coleslaw, and pasta salad on the outside table. The night was warm, so a cold supper, alfresco, was ideal.

"Do you want wine or beer?"

"You have beer?" My father's bewilderment made me giggle.

"Amazing, isn't it? They stocked the fridge and cupboards with everything and more, including liquor. Mind you, the beer is for you. I can't stomach it, as you well know. I much prefer wine."

"This is fabulous, Clarissa," he said, following me back into the cottage and looking about. His eyes landed on an original landscape. "Is that a Constable?"

"No, but it's damn good, isn't it? You should see the art inside the house. They've got a *Breughel*. And I'm sure it's an original."

He raised his eyebrows looking impressed.

We stepped outside with drinks in hand.

"There's a charming moon. After my stuffy apartment, the sea air is a real godsend," said my father, peering up at the sky.

"You can come over whenever you like, Daddy. There's even a spare room so you can stay over sometimes," I said, filling his plate with food. "Is that enough?" I placed the plate in front of him.

"It's a veritable banquet, sweetheart."

My father and I were like two peas in a pod. We shared a penchant for history and classical aesthetics. As we sat at the latticed iron table, we took to the delicious food with the hunger of people who'd subsisted on a bland, frugal diet.

"This meat is mouthwateringly tender. Absolutely delicious," my father said, taking a sip of his beer. "Mm…" He studied the exotic label and smiled. "And this sure beats the cheap stuff I've got back in the fridge at home."

Greta stepped out of the kitchen door and lit a cigarette. How odd—she was the last person I expected would smoke. Her hair was out. And dressed in a cotton floral shift and flat sandals, she looked very retro.

"Hi, Greta. It's a delightful evening."

"That it is." Her eyes drifted over to my father.

"This is my father, Julian," I said.

Greta's eyes landed on my father's face and lingered. There was a soft, feminine glow emanating from her blue eyes. Her long, light-brown hair, which she wore loose, was speckled in gray.

My father, likewise, brightened. I hadn't witnessed that before. *Wow, they are attracted to each other.*

"Pleased to meet you. I am Greta Thornhill," she said, offering her hand.

My father took it. "Pleased to meet you."

Oh my God. They are really having a moment.

I felt like an intruder suddenly. "Dad and I share a car. He just dropped me back. There were so many leftovers. I hope you don't mind."

"Better it gets eaten than tossed out, which is what generally happens," Greta said in a matter-of-fact tone. The cigarette remained between her fingers. I could tell she was sensitive about smoking around others.

"Why don't you join us?" said my father. "There's beer, wine or juice."

Once again, their eyes met for longer than usual. "Sure," said Greta. "I'll put this out."

She was about to get up when my father said, "No need, please. Keep smoking. You don't happen to have one?" He smiled charmingly. In his mid-fifties, my father was still handsome. He was a Jeremy Irons look-alike with his graying dark hair, expressive brown eyes, and slender, tall frame.

"Dad, you promised me you'd kicked the habit," I said.

He flashed a smile at Greta. "Oh my, how the tables have turned. In my late youth, it was my mother scolding me for smoking, and now it's my beloved daughter." He gave a husky, contagious chuckle.

"Can I offer you a glass of the wine or beer you so considerately placed in the fridge?" I asked.

Greta demonstrated a small amount with her fingers. "Just a tiny glass of wine, then." She flashed a shy smile at my father again. "It's such a pleasant night."

"Isn't it?" he chimed. "The moon is full." He opened his arms out. "It's delightfully continental here, and there's this charming fellow." He tapped the trunk of the tree. My father and I had a thing for old trees. "Tell me, how old is the house?"

"I'm told it was built around 1910."

"Italianate classical. Very nice indeed," he said, casting his eyes on the stuccoed walls.

When I returned with Greta's wine, I found them sharing a laugh. It was the first time she'd looked so relaxed. And my dad was in his element.

"You are more than welcome to come anytime and visit the house," said Greta, nodding as I handed her the glass.

"I'd like that. Clarissa informs me that there are impressive artworks," he said.

"There's also a library with an extensive collection of first editions. I believe you're into English literature."

"That I am indeed," he said, casting me a side-glance.

"How did you know that?" I asked.

"You spoke of your father in our recruitment test." Greta finished off her wine, and she rose. "I'd best be getting back." She looked at my father and smiled. "Lovely meeting you, Julian, please feel free to pop in and visit Clarissa whenever you like. This is her home now." She glanced at our empty plates. "And our leftovers are always on offer."

"It's been an honor meeting my daughter's employer. You are most generous," my father said, standing and taking her hand.

"See you in the morning," I said.

"Greta's nice," said my father when she was out of earshot.

"She certainly took a shine to you." I placed my arm around him.

"Really?" He had a shy glint in his eyes.

I nodded. "Greta's an attractive woman."

"Yes, that she is," he replied. "Say, those first editions sound like they're worth investigating."

"Probably American literature, that's not your cup of tea, is it?"

"I wouldn't say that. I'm rather fond of Mark Twain. Then there's Steinbeck—he was a giant. Nathaniel Hawthorne, Poe, and let's not overlook Henry James."

"You've changed your tune, Daddy. I recall you turning your nose up at James."

"I've softened in my old age, Princess."

CHAPTER SEVEN

The following day, Greta asked that I visit one of their charities.

"We normally allow them to run themselves," said Greta, showing me the spreadsheets. "But the RSHC has become too overdrawn to ignore."

"I see," I said, studying the procedure that I was expected to implement. Although not my strong point, I had adequate math skills. And it did seem straightforward enough.

"I'll need you to drive out there in the morning and introduce yourself to Bryce. He's the director and has been told that you're coming. You're to show him how to record his personal expenses."

I nodded. *How will I get there?*

"You can take one of our cars," said Greta, reading my mind as always. "I'll need your license for insurance purposes. After lunch, I'll get Linus to show you a car. The fleet is electric. You should familiarize yourself with the vehicle. Linus will help with that." Greta hovered. I sensed she wanted to ask me something. "It will be your car, to do as you wish, during your time with us."

My car to use as I wish?

"Can I use it on weekends, as well?"

She nodded. "You'll have to charge it here. It does one hundred miles per charge." Her face softened. "I take it your father enjoyed his time here last night." Her tone had shifted from professional to familiar.

"Dad loved it. He was taken aback by your generosity, as I am, of course."

She nodded. "Yes, Aidan is a kind soul, sometimes too kind for his own good."

I couldn't help but wonder what she meant by that.

The entire morning was spent arranging the entertainment for the ball. Just as I wrapped up for lunch, Greta asked, "Do you want to select your outfit for the ball, or would you prefer our personal stylist to do it? That being the case, she'll require your measurements."

Clueless on what to wear, I agreed to the stylist option. Butterflies flooded my tummy. Excitement had finally hit me. I'd never attended an event of such magnitude.

"I spoke to the agent. Both the string quartet and band have made themselves available," I said, placing some paperwork in my tray.

Greta looked pleased. "Good. I like the idea of a string quartet as people are entering. And I'm sure Aidan will be delighted with the band. He's got a thing for jazz classics."

"I see," I replied, increasingly intrigued by this mysterious boss. So far, I'd established that Aidan Thornhill was benevolent and had excellent taste in art and an interest in jazz. I couldn't help but like the guy even if he did appear aloof and earnest in the pictures I'd seen online.

After work, I decided to go for a swim. I changed into my one-piece, which Tabitha referred to as a spinster swimsuit. This was often followed by me arguing that I couldn't wear a bikini because it offered no support. Tabitha would then point a finger, calling me a prude.

Under the shade of trees, bright-pink bougainvillea hugged the weathered rock wall, making for a picturesque descent. The steep stairs leading down to the beach seemed interminable. They were carved in stone, transporting me back in time, and like everything else at the estate, the setting reminded me of Southern Europe. The closer I got, the saltier the air became. Having always loved the sea, I was excited by the thought of a swim.

A jetty came into view. I removed my sandals to indulge in the pleasant squelching sand which was warm and massaging. Impressive-looking speedboats came into view, no doubt my boss's toys. Out in the distance, an impressive yacht sat alone, swaying gently. With its white sail fluttering and dark wood, the handsome vessel screamed of money.

I had never visited a private beach before. The pristine, tranquil bay was flat, ideal for swimming. I could have even skinny-dipped. Perhaps when Tabitha visited we would do that together. She'd be into it without a doubt. But for the moment, I'd stick to my one-piece.

I undid my sarong and went straight in. Despite the hot afternoon sun, a shiver ran through me as my white feet touched the chilly water. I acclimatized to the coolness and then dived under.

It was so exhilarating I cried out. The beauty of being alone was that I could do that. The sea always brought out the wild child in me.

My body cried out for a workout to atone for all the creamy cakes. At first, I swam breaststroke, then freestyle and backstroke, and then I floated on my back for respite. Once my breath regulated, I repeated it over again.

All puffed out I fell onto my towel, stretching out like a lazy cat, my skin puckered with delight as the sun dried my soaked flesh. The straps of my swimsuit dug in. I looked about to make sure no-one was around and then pulled my swim-suit down to my waist.

Ah... how delightful. The sun wove its magical warmth through my flesh.

I opened my book and drifted off to old France when I heard puffing. A dribble of fluid on my leg followed, and I looked up. There was Rocket. His tongue hung, and his large, friendly eyes filled with joy.

I sprang up and grabbed my sarong. Rocket, meanwhile, shook out his wet hair all over me. "You little shit!" I exclaimed, clutching the sarong around my breasts. Next minute, the sexy gardener was there by my side, inscrutable as usual in baseball cap and dark glasses. This time he was bare-chested, setting off a warm pulse below. He was so hot my breath hitched. Speechless, I clutched onto my sarong.

He appeared a giant compared to my five-foot-two frame. My eyes drank him like ambrosia. In the sun, the dusting of hair on his firm, rippling chest shimmered. Droplets of water, which I suddenly thirsted for, settled on the puckered flesh of his tanned, shapely biceps. His wet shorts hugged his muscular thighs. I nearly swooned when I noticed a considerable bulge clinging to his drenched shorts. *Is that an erection?*

Reminded I was topless beneath my slightly see-through sarong, I tightened my grip. The heat raging through me was intense. My nipples, with a mind of their own, pierced through the thin fabric.

I couldn't see where his eyes were behind those dark glasses. But I felt his gaze burning into me anyway. With no idea how long I'd been staring, my senses scattered.

At last, the god spoke. "I'm sorry about that. He's taken a shine to you, which is unusual for Rocket. He's generally reserved, bordering on anti-social." A deep, sexy voice accompanied his scrumptious physique, which was fortunate. A high-pitched voice would have been heart-breaking.

"That's unusual. Most cattle dogs I've known are friendly and smart. That's why I love them," I said, bending down to pat Rocket with my one free hand.

"He likes you." His sculpted, fleshy lips curled up at one end. It was the closest to a smile I'd seen. "He came from a shelter and had a rough start. Most of the time, he either ignores people or growls at them. I've never seen him like this before."

He bent down to pick up my book, which had been disturbed by Rocket's excitable greeting. Badly timed, I also went to pick it up, and to avert a collision, I fell backwards. Not only did I appear clumsy, but my sarong flew off, and I was topless.

Shit.

I grabbed my sarong, and an embarrassing squawk left my mouth. Before I could help myself, he had lifted me. For a moment, I was in his arms, rendered senseless by the smell of sea and male oozing off him. My gaze fell on him. I wanted to remove those glasses. I was desperate to see his face. He'd seen my breasts. It was an intimate moment.

Why wasn't I confident and experienced?

A blaze had been set off between my thighs. I was soaking wet, and it was not from the sea.

Back to reality, I quickly covered myself and sat on my towel, biting my lip and lost for anything to say that could relieve the tension.

Meanwhile, he held my novel in his large hand, reading the cover. "Scarlet and Black," he said with his killer husk. "I take it this is a classic?"

"Yes, nineteenth-century French. It's my second reading. It's one of my favorites," I said, taking the book from him.

"I read *Les Misérables* last year," he said.

"Victor Hugo. A masterpiece."

He nodded slowly. "I thought so. It made me question morality and what makes a decent person and how redemption should be part of that equation, especially when poverty pushes one over the edge. He redeemed himself by becoming a model citizen, and then along came this twisted, unwavering cop. It should be made compulsory reading."

"I couldn't agree with you more," I murmured, nodding longer than was natural.

My God, I was in love. I wished I had the courage to remove that damn cap and those glasses. I was suddenly imagining holding his longish hair in my fist as his full lips ate me alive.

By the way he lingered I could tell he was equally shy. "Well, I better leave you to it, then."

Before I could respond, he'd vanished. All I had was a view of his perfect butt and a stride that was mouth-watering like the rest of him. Phew!

A dip was called for. I had to douse the fire somehow. When I sprang up from a dive, I saw him in the distance. He'd been watching me at play in the sea. The next time I looked, he was gone.

Flooded with hormones and drugged on pheromones I bounded up the stairs. My stomach rumbled. The beach always made me hungry. And with each famished step, I became increasingly grateful that Melanie had, earlier, placed a plateful of leftovers in my hand. God, I loved my job.

CHAPTER EIGHT

The Veterans' Health Center, or VHC as it was known, was indeed a remarkable place. Fitted with a gymnasium, swimming pool, bar, billiard parlor, and a restaurant offering inexpensive meals, I could see the benefits it offered to its members. In addition, there were psychiatrists, psychologists, and doctors who offered their services for free. The generosity of Aidan Thornhill saw no boundaries.

My first impression of Bryce Beaumont was that he was a sleazy, self-entitled brat. Tall and well-built with dark eyes and hair, he was good-looking. Even so, he was more Tabitha's type than mine. His ogling made my skin crawl. Patently, he'd mistaken my breasts for my face. Ick.

Earlier that morning, I'd set off in the company electric car. The engine was very quiet and the car was so effortless to drive that I found the whole experience novel. Although normally not fond of driving, I actually enjoyed it for once.

One of the pricklier aspects to this dream job, however, was visiting the facility in order to go over expenses. Peeved and blustery, Bryce Beaumont didn't hide his annoyance.

"How about we grab a drink at the bar?" Before I could respond, Bryce led me out of his office.

"We service the needs of retired defense personnel. We have fifty thousand registered." We entered the bar. "What's your poison?" he asked, chuckling.

I noted a look of disappointment in his piercing eyes when I asked for a coffee. Did he expect to seduce me? Eek. Not a chance.

The more I grew acquainted with Bryce, the more I disliked him. To ward off the unease, I thought about the sexy gardener. I even dreamed about him the previous night—his impatient hands unbuttoning my shirt. I woke up hot and sticky, something I hadn't experienced since Ian Wilson fondled me at school when I was sixteen. I still recall my broken heart when he left. After that, no-one affected me that way until the sexy gardener. I smiled to myself, acknowledging that he might not even be that. But with that strong, hard body of his, being a gardener would have suited him. Predictably, he kept intruding on my thoughts. Since that steamy encounter on the beach earlier, he was constantly there. He even made a star appearance while Toy Boy, my trusty vibrator, tickled me senseless.

"So, Clarissa, do you enjoy working for Aidan Thornhill?"

"I haven't actually met him. But I do love my new job. Everyone's so kind. Greta is thorough, patient, and helpful."

Bryce smirked while running his hands through his short, wavy black hair, his lips wide and suggestively carnal. He had chiseled features, and I imagined Tabitha purring at the sight of him. Of a solid frame, his legs struggling for comfort in tight-fitting jeans. I even made the mistake of glancing down, where his bulge was impossible to miss. *Hell.*

"She's his aunt." Catching my accidental glance at his hard-on, Bryce grinned lasciviously.

"Yes, um, Melanie told me," I said, crossing my arms. The cold air-conditioning had my nipples pushing against my cotton shirt. *Shit. That's why he has an erection. I wish I'd worn a sweater.*

"Watch that Melanie. She's got a big mouth." He sneered. "She's a gossip and a troublemaker. Don't believe everything she tells you." He ordered another drink. "Are you sure I can't offer you something harder?"

I shook my head. *Oh my God, was that a double entendre?* I wanted to run. And we hadn't even looked at the reporting program yet.

By the way Bryce knocked back his liquor, I imagined he did everything to excess.

"Mr. Beaumont—" My voice was thin.

"Call me Bryce."

"Bryce, I've got to get back." I studied my watch. "Greta has asked me to show you a new accounting system…"

His body slumped, his face contorted with impatience. "Not another damn accounting system. What's up? They don't trust me." His irascible tone went up a decibel. He'd become scarier.

Bryce must have read my fear, because his hard stare softened. "Okay, then, let's get back to my office so that you can show me." He raised an eyebrow.

Hell, what is he going to do to me?

When we got back to the office, he stood at the doorway and waved me through. "After you."

To get through, I had to suck my bottom in tight, just missing his protrusion. Droplets of sweat dripped between my shoulder blades.

He approached his desk and placed a chair by his side, tapping it. "Come sit here, then."

I placed the USB stick into the computer. We were seated too close for comfort. The whole while, his eyes were pitched at my breasts. It was so awful I nearly bolted.

Half an hour later, I stood at my car. Despite the fact I told him there was no need, Bryce had tagged along, all the way to the bitter end. Just as I was leaving, he said, "I'll see you at the ball next week, then."

I fumbled in my bag, searching for my keys. I regarded his smarmy face, realizing my sense of unease was lost on him. He was either a sociopath or dim-witted.

Blowing out a tense breath, I felt my chest finally expand as I drove into the sanctuary of Thornhill Estate. After leaving the car with Linus to recharge, I rushed back to the cottage for a cold shower. My underwear was drenched, not from arousal but from fear and loathing.

I changed and headed for the kitchen, where Melanie carved up roast beef.

"Are you hungry?" she asked, her face cheery as usual.

"That I am. It's been quite a morning." I sighed, refreshed after my shower.

"Roast beef, potatoes, pumpkin, and broccoli. How's that sound?"

"Yummy. Thanks, Melanie. You're really kind," I said, recalling Bryce's scathing remarks about her.

She passed me a plate filled to the brim. I smiled with gratitude and ate with the gusto of someone who'd been through a trial.

"I met Bryce Beaumont this morning," I said, chewing away.

Her mouth contorted. "I bet he tried to hit on you."

Nodding, I pulled a face of dread.

"He's a nasty son-of-a-bitch," she said.

"Does he always act this way with the female staff?"

Melanie nodded. "Amy, the PA before Cherie—the one you replaced— was loose, so to speak." She raised an eyebrow. "She liked to drink, and I'm sure she had a fling with Bryce. But then, she had issues."

"What do you mean?"

"She had it bad for Aidan, which mind you, isn't hard to imagine. He's strikingly handsome, you know." Her eyes twinkled. "Anyway, one night at the ball, she got so drunk she jumped all over Aidan. After that, they fired her."

"So why do they keep Bryce on?"

"Good question. I wouldn't even be surprised if he's stealing from them."

"Then why persist with him?" I asked.

"Bryce and Aidan were in the services together. I've heard a whisper that he's got something on Aidan." She lowered her voice.

"How do you know all this, Melanie?"

"I've been here from the beginning and"—she shrugged her shoulders—"one hears things."

When I returned to the office, I found Greta waiting for me. "I trust you travelled well?"

"I explained the new program," I said, keeping it vague.

"Good." She moved away, and my breath returned. Then, catching me unawares, she turned. "Did he come on to you?"

I swallowed. My voice croaked. "Ah... not really."

"Not really?" She knitted her brows. "You can tell me." Her attitude towards me had changed since meeting my father.

"Well, he did appear overconfident, and I suppose he was forward, but I handled it." I stared down at my hands as my armpits dampened.

"How did he react to the new system? Was there any resistance?"

"Some. But he agreed to co-operate." My wavering voice betrayed me. Watching her eyes narrow, I could tell that Greta was unconvinced.

"Okay, then." She stared out the window, ruminating.

"It's such an impressive organization. The foundation does such great work," I added with enthusiasm. "I've read that many returning soldiers suffer."

My attempt at brightening the situation worked. Greta had swapped her concerned frown for a soft and respectful expression. "Yes, Aidan has a kind heart. He works tirelessly to ensure that everyone's taken care of."

After Greta left, curiosity had me visiting Thornhill Holdings' charities. An impressive website, if not vague, given that it contained no photos of Aidan or information about him. Still, I admired someone who didn't blow his own trumpet, another fine point for my elusive boss.

As I kept reading, I learnt that apart from the health services to returned members of the military, Thornhill charities included: shelters for abused children and women, rehabilitation facilities for liquor and drug addicts from impoverished backgrounds, lost-dog homes, protection for endangered wildlife, college scholarships for underprivileged children, and free renewable energy for the poor. That last one was left of center. I clicked on it and discovered that Aidan was building wind-farms and solar energy farms throughout the country. They'd be designed to feed into poor households and not-for-profit charities. *I worked for one of the nicest guys on the planet!*

CHAPTER NINE

My muscles unwound in the salt water as I floated on my back. White gulls glided above in the cloudless blue sky, the breeze sending them on a journey to wherever. Weightlessly, I soared along with them.

Vigorous splashing suddenly woke me out of my meditation. I stood up in the water and spied Rocket chasing a ball. In his signature baseball cap and dark glasses, the sexy gardener was waist-high in the water.

As I made my way out, Rocket pounced on me to say hello, his paw leaving a scratch on my thigh. His master ran towards us. For some twisted reason, my eyes went to his wet shorts. That bulge was on full display and was impossible to miss. I immediately averted my eyes while heat engulfed me. Dripping wet, I remained frozen, pining for sunglasses. *Can he read my attraction?*

"I am very sorry about that. Did he scratch you?" he asked.

I checked the scratch on my thigh. It did sting a little, but I remained stoical. "It's nothing. Don't worry— the salt water should disinfect it." My heart was in my mouth, and I could barely utter a clear word. He just got hotter and hotter.

"You may need it bandaged. There's a first aid kit in one of the boats," he said in that clit-swelling husk.

"No, that's fine," I said, smiling awkwardly. I really wanted to say yes, imagining his fingers visiting my injured thigh and beyond.

How stupidly bashful can one be?

Rocket stood by my side, sincere apology written in his large, soulful eyes.

He shook his head. "Boy, he likes you," he said, patting the dog.

"He's a cute dog."

Although he was mysterious as ever in those dark glasses, I still sensed his gaze burning into me.

"Well, then, I'd best leave you to it," he said, lingering. Like me, he seemed unsure. Cold comfort, really. Two shy people resulted in frustration. And frustrated was certainly how I felt watching him turn away. His butt looked delightfully squeezable. I swallowed hard as I watched his strong, athletic calf muscles flex on the soft sand.

After I returned from my little swim, I was so ravished by fantasies that I needed a session with Toy Boy. When Tabitha gave her vibrator that name, we laughed our heads off. From that moment on, I referred to my trusty, battery-operated friend as Toy Boy too.

I lay there alone in the dark. The image of his hungry hands all over me, and his big hungry penis, sent a delicious ache, making my orgasm more intense than usual. As I panted on my back, an inner voice screamed, *you must find a man*.

I plotted to get drunk and hunt down Mr. Sexy Gardener. While I cooked up ways to seduce him, I did wonder why he hadn't introduced himself or even tried to hit on me. Could he be gay? Now, that would be tragic and grossly unfair, for women at least.

One thing was for sure: he had stirred something in me.

Despite raging, out-of-control hormones, I craved more than a one-night stand. Was that too much to ask? One thing I knew well about myself: I was not cut from the same fabric as Tabitha, whose desperate need for a man meant she ended up with jerks.

****

It was the week leading up to the gala ball. Brimming with anticipation I found it hard to sleep. As the event manager, I'd designed the ballroom, booked the entertainment, and arranged the catering. Too busy to indulge in anxiety, I spent most of the time on the phone, ensuring that everything about the event flowed. My contract renewal depended on it.

Amid this flurry of activity, I needed a gown fitting. And when Greta handed me a voucher for hair styling and make-up for the morning of the ball, butterflies migrated into my belly. I even passed on a batch of hot donuts that Melanie offered for morning tea, which was a first.

The thought of a lavish gown was too exciting. My only other experience with formal wear had been at the debs' ball, and that didn't go down too well. I'd worn a vintage dress owned by my late mother. I could still hear the snickering.

The only thing I knew about my gown was the color I'd chosen to suit my black hair. I gritted my teeth, hoping I wouldn't hate it. Now, that would be a come-down after the shrill-filled speculation generated mainly by Tabitha.

When the gown finally arrived the day before the ball, I whisked a photo off to Tabitha, who purred with approval at the other end. It was silk, no less, and a breathtaking sky-blue color. The layered gown fell languidly to the floor, and although the bodice was fitted at the waist, it had a modest neckline. No cleavage would be revealed, much to Tabitha's disappointment.

This friend of mine was on a mission to see me in the arms of a rich man. Despite hissing at her inflated ambition, I loved her for it. After all, Tabitha only wanted happiness for me—and of course, gossip fodder to keep her stimulated.

It was the morning of the ball. Too excited to eat, I drank my coffee and headed over for a final tour of the ballroom.

I walked about the grand room to make sure everything was correct. With all the tables and chairs in their rightful positions, the lighting rigged, and the stage dressed with red-velvet drapery, I was satisfied— if not ecstatic with the result.

I was astonished by the room's sheer opulence. White, detailed cornices with carved angels' faces contrasted pale, green-blue damask wallpaper. The gigantic fireplace of opalescent marble, held up by goddesses, was startling.

Glass doors opened out onto the terrace, making the room seem immense. A swimming pool positioned in front of the sea added to its boundlessness.

However, nothing staggered me more than the artwork. There were paintings by Alma-Tadema that rendered me speechless. The sublime works all featured nymphs on marble seats with a rich turquoise sea in the background. The neo-classical paintings all carried the same theme: languid women dressed in flowing robes by the sea. My favorite was the Godward showing a woman with long black hair reclining.

One thing was for certain: Aidan Thornhill loved beauty.

When asked to design the room, I'd envisioned something French from the late 1890's. After all, I had a decent budget to work with, and my directive was to create a stylish and unique event.

Greta entered the room, nodding with approval. "This is fantastic, Clarissa."

I sighed silently in relief. "That's music to my ears. I wanted to recreate a scene from a Parisian café, inspired by the paintings in the room." I pointed to the image over the fireplace. "They are a remarkable collection. Did Mr. Thornhill select them?"

"He did. Aidan spent a long time in Europe. Needless to say, he loves antiques."

I nodded, in awe of my mysterious boss.

CHAPTER TEN

"Greta, I love that dress. Is it original sixties?" I asked, touching the soft pink floral gown.

"Yes, it's one I've held onto. Not that I'm on a budget. But I do like that era."

"Me too," I said, bubbling over. "I can't get enough of the sixties. I still wear my late mother's clothes whenever possible."

"I've noticed," she said with a wry grin. "It looks wonderful out here, Clarissa. I'm sure Aidan will be pleased with the quartet. It's an inspired choice."

I had to agree. The quartet musicians, as per my request, were dressed in the style of Louis XIV. The men wore satin breeches, white ruffled shirts, and high-heeled buckled shoes that I would've walked over hot embers to own. The women, dressed in low-cut bodices, hooped gowns, and an effervescence of curls sculpted up high, looked like they just stepped out of the Palace of Versailles.

As a backdrop, and looking surreal in the dusk, the sculptures on the grounds were lit up. Strangled by creepers, they appeared animated.

The damp air— a heady mix of flower, sea and earth—filtered through, adding to the intoxicating allure of the setting. My eyes travelled over to the colored lanterns set up throughout the grounds, and I noticed how, almost like magic, the trees had metamorphosed into a kaleidoscope of color.

A satisfied breath escaped my lips. My flesh puckered with pride as I feasted on the result of my imagination. Mindful of my professional make-up job, I had to fight to suppress tears.

Earlier, in my cottage, while twirling and delighting in the floaty silk layers of my dress, I studied myself in the mirror. I saw my late mother. The transformation was so extraordinary that I took a selfie and sent it to Tabitha and my father.

Tabitha gushed, "Clarissa, you look beautiful."

While my father, finding it hard to speak, muttered something about how much I resembled my mother.

"Do you mind if I film this for our records, Greta?" I asked.

She nodded slowly. "I can't see why not."

"I thought I could create a collage of images from the night. I could upload it onto the Thornhill website."

She knitted her brows, mulling over my suggestion. "Mm, I like that idea." She added, "I will have to run it by Aidan first."

"Oh yes, of course. Will he be joining us this evening?" I asked.

Greta studied me closely. "He should be down soon."

The guests arrived as the plaintive strains of Pachelbel's Canon caressed the air. Although not French, it was still a fitting choice and so moving that goose-bumps kept prickling my arms.

As I watched the waiters offer champagne to the guests, I craved a glass but wasn't sure if I was allowed, so I held back.

"This is working very well, Clarissa," said Greta, praising me yet again.

"Thanks. I've loved doing it. And now that it's in full swing, I'm over the moon," I said.

Designer gowns floated by. Flesh was out in abundance—low-cut backs, necklines that plunged almost to the naval, and slits up to the thighs. The style seemed to be the less fabric, the better. Apart from Greta and a handful of older guests, I had the most fabric on my body. Not that it worried me. My main concern had become balancing on my stilt-like shoes. I did not need gaping, out-of-control cleavage.

"There are so many women," I said to Greta, who stood by my side as the parade of guests flowed in.

"They've all come for Aidan," she said soberly.

"I see. It must be gratifying to have so many striking women around, I suppose."

"No. For Aidan, it's a nuisance. But they pay. This event is to raise money, not to socialize."

"He doesn't enjoy that part?" I asked.

"No. He's a private man."

The garden had filled quickly with people. Although most were young, beautiful women, a few attractive young men had come along as well. But it was the older, more distinguished guests who really stood out.

As I studied them, Greta said, "They're regulars. Old money. They bring class to these events."

A parting of bodies occurred as the crowd's focus moved to the portico. And to the uplifting strains of Boccherini's Minuet, my boss made his entrance.

My heart raced with anticipation. Finally, I would see this mysterious man. I reminded myself that I had nothing to worry about and that everything was going smoothly. But nothing, except champagne, would quell my nerves. I must have had longing etched into my eyes for the waiter came straight over to me with a glistening tray of glasses.

I looked over at Greta, who had just taken one. There was no mention of not being allowed to drink champagne in my contract, so I took one.

I'd never had champagne of that caliber before—crisp and cool on the tongue. As it slid down my parched throat, I reminded myself to take little feminine sips, especially since I had a propensity to gulp when nervous.

Although he was far away, I recognized Aidan Thornhill from the celebrity pictures that Tabitha had shown me. Dressed in a black tuxedo, bow tie, and white shirt, even from far back he cut a strikingly handsome figure. His light-brown hair, sitting on his collar, was pomaded stylishly. He carried himself with a graceful and easy stride.

As I observed my boss gliding along, greeting the guests, there was something familiar about him. I was thinking about that when a deep voice from behind, so close I felt his breath on my neck, uttered, "Miss Moone."

I turned and discovered Bryce Beaumont sporting a greasy grin.

Dressed in a tuxedo, he scrubbed up well. But those undressing eyes pausing on my breasts made me squirm.

"You look stunning, just like a goddess," he said loudly. Such was his boom that guests looked in my direction.

"Thanks," I said, shrinking from the sudden attention. He stood closer than I cared for. All the while, I plotted an escape, and forgetting to sip, I quaffed my champagne.

Greta came to my rescue. "Bryce, how are you this evening?"

"Well, thanks. This looks sensational."

"Yes, Clarissa has done well," said Greta stretching out her arm. "Come and sample the canapés."

As he followed her, he turned and flashed me a creepy smile. *Ick!*

Mingling amongst strangers was not my thing, so I sat on a bench under a tree. The waiter, nevertheless, noticed me. And making the journey with tray in hand, he offered me another glass of champagne. I gratefully accepted.

Bryce was joking with a trio of blondes. What a relief he'd lost interest in me. I imagined most of the willowy, attractive women there were eligible, if not husband seeking. And putting aside Bryce's unpleasant attributes, I imagined he could be seen as a potential partner.

CHAPTER ELEVEN

Having finished my second glass of champagne, and pleasantly relaxed as a result, I decided to check that everything was going according to plan in the ballroom.

Reluctant to walk through the crowd, I opted for the kitchen entrance instead. This proved a very bad idea. As I traversed the grass, my spiked heels kept sinking in the muddy ground. Just my luck, it had rained overnight.

I sloshed along, muttering expletives. I even contemplated removing the shoes, but then my nylons would have muddied. I hurried along assuming illogically that it would minimize the damage. From graceful princess to clumsy Clarissa in one stroke—my pathetic attempt at walking would've had a spectator squealing with laughter. I reminded myself that I was alone and surrendered into the sodden ground, my feet becoming heavier with each step.

I expelled a long, slow breath of relief when I finally hit the path. Bending down to survey the damage, an exasperated "Fuck!" issued from my lips like a missile through the air. My obscenely expensive nude heels were covered in mud.

As I searched hastily for a tissue in my purse, a familiar deep voice resonated over my shoulder. "Do you need a hand?"

I looked up, expecting it to be someone else. Such was my bewilderment I lost my balance and fell onto my bottom. My gown ended up around my thighs showing off my stocking clasps.

What a sight I must have made. Did he think I was drunk? Oh God, it got worse with every second. I was sure I was the color of beetroot, because my face was on fire.

It all happened so quickly that I didn't have time to collect my wit. And before I'd even attempted to stand, I was floating in the air like a ballerina. Having lifted me effortlessly, he placed me upright on earth.

All the while, his deep-blue eyes remained glued to my face. Hypnotized, I opened my mouth, but no words came out. Time stretched. Everything was going in slow motion—just like in a romance movie, but without the build-up music and heavy breathing.

As my body rested in his strong arms, a heady mix of cologne, body wash, and masculinity travelled up my nostrils and straight to my nipples, which, with a mind of their own, pierced the silk fabric. Much later, when I was reliving that moment over and over again, I wondered whether his hand may have accidentally brushed them.

His mesmerizing blue eyes remained focused on my eyes. I had to look away in order to gather my senses, but I still felt his searing gaze burning into me—like a naked flame, but instead of bright specks, his blue eyes became the after-burn.

Not helped by my skyscraper heels, my legs wobbled, as he continued to hold me up. "I'm sorry. I'm not used to these heels. I'm more of a sensible-shoes-girl." My attempt at a chuckle was thin-if not-pathetic.

Aidan Thornhill's well-sculptured lips twitched into a faint smile. "I don't know how you manage to walk in them. It strikes me as a difficult unnatural feat."

Should I giggle? Was that a pun? I checked out his expression, which was suddenly earnest, just like the photos. Or was he one of those dry-delivery guys? My face cracked into an awkward smile nevertheless.

With equilibrium restored, physically speaking, I pulled away reluctantly from his grasp and smoothed down my gown. I brushed the back of the dress, praying it had not been ruined.

I needed a bathroom to regain composure and fix my outfit. But Aidan was so arresting I couldn't move. I feared falling, this time from swooning, not from my shoes.

How could a girl not swoon? That tuxedo showed off his broad-shouldered, manly physique, in one mouth-watering package.

"How's that scratch?" His deep voice vibrated through my ribcage and travelled down to that tender spot. Those ridiculously deep-blue eyes had stolen my senses.

"Scratch?" My brows drew together in one sharp motion. *Freaking Hell.* I tapped my forehead. Aidan Thornhill was the sexy gardener I'd been fantasizing over these past nights.

"Oh… you were with Rocket. I'm so sorry. I didn't recognize you without the cap and glasses," I trilled.

"There's no need to apologize. I should've introduced myself." Aidan's voice was so seductive he could have read the phone directory, and I'd still salivate.

"I love what you've done here tonight. Greta has spoken highly of you. Now I can see why." One side of his mouth curled slightly. Smiling didn't come naturally to him. I sensed shyness.

"That's so kind of you. Everybody's been generous. The cottage is heaven. The gardens, the beach—I feel blessed," I said, hoping that I wasn't blabbering. "I'm sorry. I must be holding you up from your guests. I was heading for the ballroom to check on things."

"I'll leave you to it, then. I look forward to hearing the band in the ball-room. I'm fond of jazz. Good choice. And the quartet are superb, they look and sound fabulous in the garden," said Aidan.

His lingering gaze was spellbinding. My core tightened. I was almost hyperventilating from lack of air.

I watched him move off. There was that unmistakable relaxed, manly stride that I'd already lost my head over. Phew. I leaned against a wall for a moment. Taking a deep breath, I gave my heart a chance to steady.

CHAPTER TWELVE

Much to my relief, the dress was unstained. Despite a flushed face, my make-up was still where it should've been too. Electricity from Aidan still buzzed through me as I patted my bun gently. There was so much hairspray that my normally untamable mane was going nowhere.

When I entered the ballroom, the band was tuning up, and the staff was racing about putting finishing touches to the tables. Drifting through the air was an appetite-inducing aroma coming from the kitchen, which reminded me that I hadn't eaten all day.

Having discovered the virtues of expensive champagne, I helped myself to another glass and headed for the kitchen where I found Melanie sharing a laugh with a waiter.

She turned, and her face brightened. "You look so amazing in that blue dress," she gushed, touching the fabric of my gown.

"Thanks, Melanie. That's kind of you to say. Can I help with anything?"

"No, babes, just enjoy yourself. And keep looking beautiful. I take it you've met Aidan?" she asked, her gray eyes flickering with curiosity.

Why was she giving me that look? Was I giving something away? Were my flushed cheeks that obvious, or was desire oozing out of me?

"I have," I said, keeping it brief, a technique I'd adopted when talking to Melanie. It was easy to stoke the fire with her. A slight hint and she would be ablaze with all kinds of speculation, just like Tabitha.

"Well, then, don't keep me in suspense. What do you think of him?"

I bit my bottom lip. What was I to say—that a mere whiff of him had sent my juices flowing with wild abandon? That his blue eyes undressed my soul, and his six foot two of sheer masculine perfection had unleashed an agonizing and addictive ache throughout my body?

"He's nice," I said weakly. "A good person, I believe." *Oh damn. I stuttered.*

Alarmingly perceptive, Melanie sang, "Why, Miss Moone, I think you're blushing." She elbowed me with a cheeky smirk.

"I'm not," I said, drawing away from her. "Better go and check on things."

She remained with her arms on her hips, her head tilted. Stamped on her face was *I-can-tell-you're-smitten*. Or was I just imagining that?

I'd booked a jazz band with two singers. Having been brought up on jazz standards, I went with that. Greta had intimated in her own subtle way that the last ball was a disaster. One of my predecessors—the purported drunken floozy who had hit on Aidan—had arranged a DJ. The music was rap and hip-hop. Evidently all the guests, apart from the younger cohort, had left in haste after dinner.

I'd checked out the jazz band on YouTube before booking them. I loved that they had a male and female singer. I also chose them because the chanteuse wore a vintage slinky gown, therefore fitted into the 1920's theme.

Dressed in white suits, the male members of the band looked the part. They certainly stood out against the rich red-velvet drapes. And the lighting made the brass instruments shine.

The African-American singer meandered towards me. I held out my hand. "Devina Velvet?"

The statuesque woman, of a slinky sensuality most befitting a cabaret singer, cast me a wide smile. "Nice to finally put a face to the voice, Miss Moone." Her large, dark eyes swept the room. "The stage looks heavenly." She stretched her vowels with a seductive southern twang. "This is Marcus."

He shook my hand. "Thank you for having us. It's wonderful to be part of such a classy affair."

"We're so pleased to have you," I said. "Come, I'll show you your dressing rooms. There are refreshments in there, and if you need anything just call out. We've set a table for you and the band for dinner during your break."

"That sounds super," purred Devina.

****

Relaxed jazz filled the ballroom as the guests entered. It was splendid, just as I'd imagined. I was profoundly fulfilled, my delight made sweeter by the sighs of approval that hummed through the air as guests entered. Pitched against a wall, I indulged myself in the animated expressions of delight emanating from the guests. I had to keep pinching myself. If someone had told me a month earlier that I would become an event organizer for a big-hearted boss, who happened to be hot and unaffected, I would have thought them mad.

Greta approached me. "It looks fabulous, Clarissa. You have exceeded all expectations." This was a different Greta to the daily one. She'd been drinking and was more open and cheerier than usual. Not that I minded the more serious Greta. I'd grown fond of her. She was like a kind aunt who economized on smiles. I imagined this trait ran in the family, because I had yet to see Aidan flash his teeth. The most I'd garnered was a slight curve of that shapely mouth, which was enough to weaken my knees.

The single women huddled together. Their high-pitched cackles pierced the air. Standing within earshot, I heard, "They're no longer together. He called it off, and she's left town to get over him."

It was safe to assume they meant Aidan given that their attention was directed at him.

Aidan, meanwhile, ignoring the glamorous set, seemed more interested in the older guests, giving them his undivided attention. Not much had left his lips.

From the little I'd observed, he struck me as the quiet type. My thighs grew stickier at that thought. What was it about brooding men that drove me to distraction? I suppose I could blame it on Tabitha's penchant for dramatic romances.

She was not a good influence, that best friend of mine. And this predilection was not practical, given that quiet men were less likely to initiate intimacy. For someone as timid as I, that could only end in a solitary life with vibrator in hand. I expelled a long, frustrated breath.

Waiters had started directing everybody to their seats. Dinner was being served. Not sure where I belonged, I was just about to make a quick dash to the kitchen when Bryce tapped me on the shoulder. *Hell.*

I was sure my eyes gave that "stay away" vibe. But being seriously insensitive, he was only interested in getting his own way. Tight-lipped, I tried to put him off by remaining mute. I intuited that he enjoyed the sport of seduction. The harder the prey, the more persistent he became.

"So, Clarissa, may I escort you to your seat?" he asked, with that slippery smile travelling up to his twinkling brown eyes.

I wondered if I should say that I had leprosy or an incurable disease communicable by breathing. As my brain worked on a more plausible excuse, I sensed someone standing close by.

I turned and met Aidan's hypnotic blue gaze. Had he come to my rescue?

"Miss Moone, may I request that you join us?" My mouth opened, but words got stuck at the back of my throat. My face was on fire.

"I thought I might grab something in the kitchen," I said, my voice pathetic and weak. *Please let me crawl under a rock.*

Alone on a beach with an affectionate dog, I could talk to him. But with a whole audience of salivating supermodels watching on, that was beyond me. *Oh no.* My nipples hardened, and before I could cross my arms to hide them, that slippery snake Bryce gaped salaciously at me. *Err!*

Aidan pointed to the table. "There's a place for you next to Greta." His lips drew a tight, reassuring smile.

I assented, of course, and wobbled in front of him as Aidan rather unfairly— although unintentionally I'm sure—got me to lead the way. High heels and dizzying attraction were a dangerous mix. A graceful glide was out of the question. I would have needed a month of walking with a book on my head for that.

Greta sat by Aidan's side. I saw by the way they interacted that they were close. She was maternal and protective towards him. On the other side of Aidan was a young woman, giggling and flirting with him. I didn't see his lips curve ever. He did nod on occasion, but I could tell that he wasn't that interested. Or was I just hoping? She was blond, blue-eyed, and leggy. I supposed she was a model or an actress like all the girls who were there that evening.

He did, however, throw a glance my way more than once. Each time, his expression was deep and raw, turning me upside down. I shifted about, the swelling between my thighs intensifying with each gaze.

When the attractive blonde bent in towards him, I wondered how her breasts stayed in place with that slit down to her tummy. If I wore that outfit, my D cups would spill into the soup in no time. It was, nevertheless, a popular look that evening. By comparison, my elegant sky-blue silk dress was almost nun-like. Having always been self-conscious of my larger-than-usual chest, I didn't mind.

Aidan Thornhill was doing things to me that I'd never experienced before. How could one glance from those blue eyes bring me to the brink of an orgasm? Even the creamy mushroom soup seemed erotic as it slithered down my throat.

"I'm enjoying the music, Clarissa," said Greta.

"It sits well in this room, doesn't it?" I smiled. "I'm looking forward to hearing Devina Velvet. She's got such a wonderful voice."

Aidan shifted his attention back towards me. His dazzling eyes held me again, like blinding light. My lips drew a tight, awkward smile. I had to look down back to my soup, which I took care not to slurp.

One of the older guests, a distinguished man in his fifties who reminded me a little of my father, said, "I love that you've lit up the paintings. It suggests an art gallery, Aidan."

Aidan tilted his head in my direction. "That is Miss Moone's doing. She designed this event."

Saved by deft application of napkin, I avoided a dribble of soup. I acknowledged the compliment with a modest, tight smile.

"It's a triumph, dear girl," the gentleman said, holding up his glass in my honor.

"The pictures are pretty in an old-fashioned kind of way," said Miss Pumped-Up-Lips.

"I like them," replied Aidan, curt and clipped.

Her mouth opened to respond, but she said nothing.

"All Alma-Tadema's, no less," said the gentleman's wife.

"Is he famous?" Miss Pouty asked, in her high-pitched drawl.

Aidan turned and regarded me again. *Oh no, please don't ask me to talk about art.* I cringed.

"Miss Moone's the authority amongst us," he said.

The older gentleman regarded me. "A Victorian artist, I believe?"

His wife nodded with ebullience. She focused on me. "They're so beautiful."

I wiped my lips. "Yes, he was a superb exemplar of the style from that period."

"Was he a Pre-Raphaelite?" the gentleman asked.

"No. Alma-Tadema came later. He was part of the neo-classical movement, despite being recognized as a symbolist in the vein of Gustav Klimt, who he greatly admired. Who wouldn't?" I chuckled. I waited for someone to jump in, but instead, I had everyone's undivided attention. *Shit. They wanted more?* "Inspired by the Pre-Raphaelites," I said, acknowledging the gentleman's earlier comment. "He picked up where they left off."

"The other paintings are by him, I see," the wife said, pointing.

"No, they're not entirely," interjected Aidan, "as I'm sure Miss Moone will be aware of." His eyes softened as he regarded me. We were alone suddenly. *If only.*

I took a deep breath. "They're by John William Godward, a contemporary of Alma-Tadema. Their styles are so alike that it's hard to tell them apart, especially their compositions featuring languid women by the sea." Pausing for a sip of wine, I hoped that no more questions would come my way.

"She's not just a pretty face," said Bryce.

Aidan cast a sideways, censuring glance at him.

Course number two came around, and all were now focused on eating except for Aidan, who kept visiting me with that intense gaze. I looked down at my seafood cocktail to hide my swirling emotions. I concentrated on the appetizingly fresh food. I'd never had anything like it before.

CHAPTER THIRTEEN

Devina Velvet, having gone burlesque, wore a slinky gold gown with a slit, revealing a long, dark, shapely thigh. She had her back to the audience. Gloved arms up in the air, she swayed sinuously to a moody saxophone solo.

With the grace of a trained dancer she turned and sang "My Funny Valentine." Living up to her name, her husky voice had a velvety sheen. Her act was so emotive that hairs stood up on my arms. Everybody stopped eating for a moment. She'd captured the whole room—such was her charisma.

The music fitted the evening magically. A consummate performer, Devina had the audience enthralled. When she finished with the song "Summertime," chills moved up my spine. It was by far one of my favorite songs from that era, and suited the slinky chanteuse's impressive range.

The word "sexy" escaped Bryce's lips as he worked his sleazy charm on the woman, who, having given up on aloof Aidan, flirted openly with muscle-headed Bryce instead.

Aidan watched the stage. I was grateful for a break from his burning attention.

Greta leaned in and whispered, "This is one of my favorite tunes."

"Mine too," I replied. "It's what sold me. After I googled them, I clicked on one of their YouTube clips, and this song came up."

"There's also a male singer, I believe?" asked Greta.

"Yes, he does the dance set. Sinatra-style," I said, pushing my plate aside.

"Is the food not to your liking?" she asked.

"It's delicious. I'm just not used to eating this much," I said, rubbing my tummy.

"Make sure you leave room for dessert. These caterers make the best sweets."

While the band was on a break, I spied Aidan chatting with the guitarist. He appeared interested in his guitar.

I decided to stretch my legs and headed over to the quieter side of the terrace. As I perched against a wall, high-pitched voices of the supermodels floated my way. There was talk of visiting a nightclub. With a cigar in his mouth, Bryce had joined them.

Greta, meanwhile, stood close by with a cigarette. I approached her. "Do you mind if I call it a night?"

She frowned. "But you haven't had dessert yet."

"I'll grab some in the kitchen for breakfast," I said.

In the distance, Aidan had been drawn into the group of supermodels. By his side, Bryce placed his arm around one while pinching the bottom of another. *Gross.*

"Have Monday off. We love what you've done here tonight. Many of the patrons have commented that it's the best one by far," said Greta, smiling warmly. "And I agree with them."

Aidan came and joined us. "Who do you agree with?" He flashed me a rare smile. My legs went to jelly as I fell under his spell again.

"I was just telling Clarissa that the guests are raving about the evening," said Greta.

"I agree, it's the best by far. I love the band. The crooner has got a Sinatra quality, which is saying something." He hadn't taken his eyes off me even though he spoke to both of us.

"Are you into Sinatra, Miss Moone?"

"Please call me Clarissa." Greta snuck off, and we became the only two people in the universe again. "Yes, I do. My father was a keen fan. I grew up with his music."

Butterflies churned through my meal. How could some-one be so handsome? Aidan Thornhill had a chiseled jawline, high cheekbones, an adorable cleft chin, and full, sensuous lips. He also had a small bump on his otherwise regular nose, which only added to his masculine perfection. But it was those eyes that changed from dark blue to the most dazzling sky shade that ravaged my senses. *Phew.* I imagined fanning my face. If only this was Jane Austen's time, I could hold a fan and flick it gracefully. I'd be able to hide the blush and dry the sweaty brow in one coquettish wave.

Bryce stumbled over. He was clearly drunk.

"You've had too much, Bryce," said Aidan coldly.

"I'm having a fun night." He directed his attention to me. "Look at this little beauty." Before I could move away, he grabbed my arm and drew me in close.

Aidan's brow went into battle mode, his eyes dark and threatening. "Let go of her, Bryce."

I pulled away from his grasp as Aidan pushed Bryce off me. Drunk and disordered, Bryce stumbled and fell.

"I think you should leave now, Bryce." Aidan bent down and picked up the heavy man effortlessly, showing his incredible strength.

Bryce shrugged Aidan off. "Fuck you, Mr. Perfect."

Unsteady on his feet, Bryce went to swing at Aidan, who moved away, and Bryce fell onto the ground.

The women around the pool covered their mouths. Shocked expressions painted their faces. Some were even laughing, which made me angry, on behalf of Aidan, who held Bryce in a headlock.

Bryce's face remained red with rage as he struggled in Aidan's hold. My suspicions that he was dangerous were confirmed by that fierce display of belligerence.

My loathing for Bryce went up a notch. Not only did he treat women as sex toys, but he also took money from Aidan's charity to fund his own lavish lifestyle. Something I'd discovered while going through the accounts of the Veterans' Health Center.

Greta led me away by the arm as a mother would. "He always drinks too much. Bryce is such a brute. I don't know why Aidan puts up with him."

"Why does he?" I asked.

About to respond, Greta was distracted by the scene playing out in front of us. Linus was there. The burly man took a hold of Bryce as one would a child and dragged him away.

"I won't forget this, Thornhill," bellowed Bryce, thrashing about like a wild beast.

Aidan smoothed back his hair, focusing on me all the while. His once easy stride had become urgent and edgy. And—oh my, could it be possible— he was even sexier. Perhaps his battle-ready hormones were gushing up my nose, because my panties were as sticky as my throat.

"I'm sorry you had to see that." Aidan's eyes had gone so dark blue and serious they resembled the night. It was a different face—still alluring, if not more so.

Greta stood by his side. "Are you okay?"

"I'm good." Aidan glanced down at his Rolex. "I'm off. Can you deal with the guests?" Before leaving, he turned towards me again. Was he trying to say something? With Greta there, I returned his gaze. Uncertain whether to smile or look earnest, my face remained blank.

He nodded then left.

When we were alone in the kitchen, Greta pointed to a plate of food and cakes that Melanie had made up for me.

"Why does Aidan put up with Bryce?" I asked.

Busy selecting sweets for her plate, Greta replied, "That's a question I've been asking Aidan for as long as I've known Bryce. They were in Afghanistan together. That's always his response." She took a bottle of mineral water from the fridge. "I can't stand the brute. And next time you'll take someone with you to VHC. Aidan doesn't want him coming near you alone again."

At that point, I had to admit, I'd fallen into the grip of Aidan's spell. Recalling Melanie's warning not to fall in love with him, I wanted my job more than I wanted my handsome boss. Or did I?

With those thoughts fighting for space in my tired brain, I traipsed back to my cottage barefoot. My expensive shoes dangled in one hand, while a plate of leftovers, enough for a week, balanced in the other.

That night, I dreamt of Aidan, his roaming hands undoing my dress. With a silken touch, he slid down my tingling flesh. I woke to such a profound throbbing that my fingers had to finish off what my overactive imagination had started. The fantasy came to an explosive conclusion when my handsome boss entered me with his large, thick cock, and the orgasm roared through me. I tumbled about in warm, gooey splendor for longer than I'd ever experienced before. Awake or asleep, Aidan had gotten under my skin.

CHAPTER FOURTEEN

The next morning, while drinking my third cup of coffee outside on my charming porch, I realized that for the first time in weeks, I could be idle. It had been a hectic few weeks. And although I loved Tabitha to pieces, I was not up for an inquisition. I put off talking to her about Aidan till later. Otherwise, I'd never hear the end of it.

Since arriving at this fairy-land, I'd been itching to stroll about the grounds and find an appealing scene to draw. More than anything, I loved to draw and paint. It had always been part of my life back at home with my father. My desk had been a makeshift easel. Watercolors and ink my preferred medium.

After coffee and a hard-to-resist slice of cake from the ball, I gathered my sketchpad and pencils and set off for the rose garden, which was ensconced in a curvy, wrought-iron enclosure.

As I entered the temple-like dome, a statue of Venus rising out of her shell captured my interest. How could it not? Modelled on Botticelli's painting, a fountain cascaded at her feet. Roses were trained to grow around her body, adding to its charm. They also crept over the archways and around the domed structure. I loved walking through there late afternoons when the damp air captured the heady floral aroma.

I settled on a marble bench shaded by a languid willow. For my subject, I decided on the rose-laden structure. If that went well, I would then tackle Venus.

Losing all sense of time, I paused to study my sketch. It was such a sticky hot day. I had to keep wiping my brow. A gentle breeze gifted me with an intoxicating scent of roses. As I inhaled the perfume I gave in to a moment of reverie.

The sudden sound of footsteps brought me back down to earth.

"I told you to stay away from her." It was Aidan's voice. He sounded agitated. Hearing no other voice, I guessed he was on the phone.

"I don't give a fuck about your threats. You're not to go near her."

I wondered if I should let Aidan know I was there. But curiosity got the better of me and kept me put.

"I've warned you. Another stunt like last night and you're out…" His voice had such a threatening rasp I gulped. My mind cast back to Aidan's physical handling of Bryce the previous night.

"It's none of your business what I think of her, you fucker. You're to stay away from her."

Hmm…was that me he referred to?

I was about to move, but he'd caught sight of me as he passed the willow. I quickly looked down at my sketch, pretending to be absorbed in my work. I peered up. And channeling what little acting skill I possessed, I raised my eyebrows in surprise.

"I've got to go," he said abruptly. He tucked his phone into the pocket of his knee-length shorts and approached me. His intensity dissolved, and a charming smile brightened his handsome face. "Miss Moone."

He stood so close he stole my breath. I snapped my sketchpad shut, and squinted in the sunlight. "Please call me Clarissa. I would prefer that."

Aidan's focus shifted to my sketch pad. "You're drawing, I see."

"I'm trying," I said in a nervous warble. "It's so magical out here. The rose enclosure is my favorite part of the garden."

"I like it as well. It's one reason I bought the house. The rest of the grounds are also impressive. I've had the botany society here on the odd occasion," he said, looking pleased.

If he was trying to impress me, it was working.

"They're a fascinating, eccentric bunch. If I'm here, I join them. They're like walking encyclopedias."

For some reason, the idea of Aidan ambling along with a bunch of spectacled professors amused me. "I haven't had a chance to walk the grounds entirely."

"Then why don't I show you around?" he asked charmingly.

I took my time in answering, not by design but because he had this uncanny ability to rob me of my senses. "Why not, then? The only plan I have is to swim."

Dressed in shorts, a loose T-shirt, and flip-flops, I regretted not wearing a summery dress.

"I'd love to check out what you've been doing," Aidan said, staring at the sketch pad in my hands.

I squirmed. "It's not very good."

His lips curved up at one end. "I'm sure it's better than anything I could do."

"I'm out of practice." I hoped he'd give up, but he remained standing there, obstinately so, with his strong arms crossed. Giving in, I passed it over to him. Aidan studied the drawing for a long while.

"It's beautiful—so pure," Aidan said almost to himself. "You undersell yourself." Aidan had removed his sunglasses. A hint of tenderness reflected back from those undressing eyes of his. "Clarissa, something tells me you have many talents." His lips curled divinely, and he stretched out his arm. "Come, let me show you something. It's hidden. Nobody knows of its existence."

"Okay, then," I said.

After depositing the sketch pad on a table by the swimming pool, we headed to the mysterious destination. I so wanted to engage in conversation, but assaulted by his alluring masculinity and not well-practiced at banter, I could barely walk let alone talk.

We finally arrived to a natural rock wall in an overgrown and untouched part of the grounds. "This has a very different aspect than the garden," I said, admiring the vista of the wild scrub against the ocean background.

"Doesn't it? So untamed, just as nature should be, wouldn't you agree, Clarissa?"

He spoke with such a deep, seductive voice he made my name sound erotic.

Struggling to string together a coherent sentence, I settled for a nod.

"This is what I'd like to show you," he said, pointing to the cave. I poked my head in, and a statue of the Madonna with candles at her feet came into view.

"Oh, a holy grotto," I said.

"Are you religious?"

Was that a trick question? "Not…in the traditional sense," I replied tentatively. I prayed he wasn't a devout Christian and wished I'd come up with something more opened-ended like, *I believe in a god, but don't go to church.*

"Are you a Buddhist, or something more esoteric?" He removed his sunglasses. I wished he hadn't. His eyes were so impossibly blue, almost turquoise, that I had to fight hard to concentrate.

"No, I'm not, although I am fascinated by some of the rituals associated with religion. This, for instance, is moving." I pointed to the icon in front of me.

"I agree. I often come here and light candles. When…" His voice drifted off.

"When?" I had to ask.

"A few troubled memories." Aidan shrugged. "I wasn't brought up in a religious house, but many of the neighbors were religious. Before joining the forces, I tried to keep an open mind." He reflected. "Afghanistan changed me. I saw things that made me question religion. You know?"

I nodded. "I know." *Don't I just.* When my mother died so suddenly, I decided, at the tender age of eight, that a god would not do that—take a loving mother away.

His eyes drank me in. "I often come here to contemplate. I always leave calmer."

"Yes, that's one thing religion does, it offers hope and a sense of peace. On that front alone, it has an important role to play in society," I said, directing my focus back to the Madonna.

"I agree. But I must admit I'm riddled with conflict, having witnessed the damage done to some of the guys in the force. There were some who joined to suicide for a cause." Aidan's tone was somber.

I frowned. "Martyrdom you mean?" A shiver ran up my spine, more from the chill in his face than his words.

He nodded. "Mainly those born homeless, who, as orphans, were placed in institutions run by the church. Many were abused. I soon learnt to recognize the look in their eyes—you know, like they'd seen the devil. One of them was my best friend." He was staring at his feet.

"I take it he passed away," I said softly.

He nodded, raising his face to mine. The pain in his face was profound. "Yes, in my arms. He took a bullet meant for me. Pushed me out of the way and wore it instead." Aidan brushed his hair away from his face. "I'm sorry. This is getting a little heavy. I didn't mean it to go there. It's just that you have a calming way about you. That's rare in the women I meet."

Our connection had just deepened. "That's touching." My voice cracked. One could almost cut the frisson with a knife.

"We should go back, I suppose." Aidan sounded uncertain as he regarded me.

As we walked back, Aidan asked, "And what are your plans for today?"

"Just a swim at the beach." I wiped my brow. "It's quite hot." Especially around him.

"I had the same idea. Rocket's hankering for a walk."

Was that an invitation?

"He's an adorable dog."

"He's aloof. Like his owner," he said, grinning.

"You don't strike me as that aloof," I said in my thin uncertain voice.

"Depends on the company… I like talking to you." Aidan stopped walking and faced me. "Very much."

I could not find a fitting response instead my face burnt.

Aidan's lips curled into a faint smile. "A swim it is, then. I'll get Rocket, and we'll go down."

"I'll see you there," I said.

"I hope so." Aidan tilted his head—a new gesture, but adorable nonetheless.

I was about to bound off when Aidan pointed to my sketch pad on the table. "Don't forget your drawing, Clarissa. I won't. I'm looking forward to seeing it in its completed form."

I smiled tightly and floated off.

CHAPTER FIFTEEN

Staring down at my boring one-piece, I regretted not listening to Tabitha and buying a bikini.

My mind swam in all directions. On the one hand, I imagined losing my job if I fell into Aidan's irresistible arms, while on the other, I sensed his attraction. Or was he just as attentive and suggestive with every woman he spoke to?

I changed into my don't-touch-me-I'm-a-virgin swimsuit. Moving my head from side to side, I studied myself in the mirror—longish, dancer-shaped legs that Tabitha had always envied, and a thin waist that accentuated my curvy thighs and heavy breasts. I supposed they suited me.

After tying a sarong around my waist, I grabbed a towel, my sunglasses, and hat. Impatient, I decided to do sunscreen at the beach in front of Aidan. My overactive imagination suddenly painted a scene of him rubbing cream on my back while my straps hung dangerously low. Heat gushed up my legs at the thought. It fulfilled one of my sexual fantasies—being fucked by a handsome stranger after he offered to rub sunscreen on my inner thighs.

Aidan had fueled such insatiable desires that I had to be LA's horniest—and only sex-addicted—virgin. What would he say if he knew I was untouched?

As I lifted my heavy bag I realized there were enough supplies in case of a shipwreck. Now, that would be sensational: marooned with Aidan all alone—a fantasy I filed away for later.

****

Floating on my back, I was off with the fairies when I heard a bark and a splash. I looked up and Rocket was swimming towards me, his tongue hanging out.

"Hello, cheeky boy." I patted Rocket, who was treading vigorously. Aidan, meanwhile, sprang up from under the water and stood by my side.

"That feels amazing," he said, his beautiful face dripping in water. "Have you been in long?" He pushed back his hair. His eyes, bluer against the sea, were twinkling.

"Only a few minutes," I replied.

He tossed a ball to Rocket, who swam back within seconds with the ball in his mouth. Aidan then tossed it to me. And before I knew it, we were playing ball. It was such fun. I giggled raucously, which helped me focus on something other than Aidan's curvy biceps, his firm, well-defined abs and rippling chest.

When Aidan moved to knee-high water, his trunks bunched around his manhood. I was grateful that Rocket was there to take my focus.

Aidan laughed at his dog's sheer tenacity. The canine demonstrated extraordinary stamina as he swam tirelessly for the ball. It was the first time I'd seen my boss so relaxed.

Being the first to step out of the water, I ran to my towel. Rocket and his yummy master followed along.

"Now, that feels better. I'm almost back to normal. I drank a little too much last night," Aidan said, drying his face and his firm stomach. Boy, how I envied that towel.

Watching me squeeze excess water from my hair, Aidan said, "I didn't realize you had such long hair."

"I can't bring myself to cut it. It's annoying after swimming, though," I said with a weak giggle.

"Don't ever cut it. It's beautiful hair," he said seriously. "You remind me of the reclining woman over the fireplace." Aidan's gaze penetrated deep.

"Oh, the Godward piece. I think it's titled *When the Heart is Young*." The compliment was not lost on me, given that the girl in the painting was beautiful.

Aidan nodded. "I'm in awe of your knowledge, Clarissa." My name flicked off his tongue so suggestively. "I picked it up at Sotheby's last year. Soon as I saw it, I had to have it. I wanted to put it in my bedroom, but it suited the Alma-Tadema works." Aidan sat on his towel while keeping an eye on Rocket, who was playing down in the shallows.

"It's the ideal place for it. All the art I've seen so far is amazing. You have impeccable taste, Mr. Thornhill."

"Please call me Aidan. Today, I'm not your boss," he said with a divine, bone-melting smile.

I grabbed my sunscreen and applied it onto my arms and décolletage. As I tried to reach for my back, Aidan said, "Here, I'll pop some on your shoulders if you like."

Taking the tube from me, Aidan lifted my heavy wet hair and dried my shoulders. As he touched me, my skin prickled. His manly hands were on me at last.

Because I'd been sitting on my calves, I had pins and needles. As I went to adjust my position, I lost my balance and fell into his arms. There I remained, and Aidan wasn't going anywhere. He just kept holding me. With my heart in my mouth, I pulled away.

"I'm sorry. I'm nervous." Turning to face him, I bit my lip.

He shook his handsome head slowly. "You have nothing to be nervous about. Here, I haven't finished yet." Aidan squeezed more cream on his fingers and rubbed it into my back. I wanted to drift off and enjoy his touch, but my heart was beating like mad.

When he passed the tube back to me, I was disappointed he'd stopped.

"Do you mind rubbing some onto my shoulders and upper back?" He raised his eyebrows and cocked his head.

With tube in hand I rubbed the cream into his well-built, tanned shoulders. He smelt of sea, and virility. I was so inebriated I couldn't speak.

"Done," I said. My mind was relieved. My hands, however, wanted to continue and travel south.

He stood up and shook the sand from his shorts. "Do you feel like a walk?"

"Sure," I replied, getting up.

My nose reached his shoulder as I walked by his side with Rocket close at my heels.

"I'm sorry about Bryce's brutish behavior last night. It added a sour note to an otherwise perfect night," said Aidan, turning to look at me.

"It's not your fault. He seems troubled," I said, staring down at his bare feet splashing along.

"Troubled is an understatement. He's getting worse." He stopped walking again. Intensity had returned to his face. "I'm pissed that he's coming on strong towards you. He's a ladies' man, and a sleazy one at that. I sense you're not that way inclined. That's why…" He stopped all of a sudden.

I shook my head. "That's why…?"

"That's why I hired you," he said with a serious note.

"Why did you hire me?" I asked.

"Where do I start?" Even though he wore dark glasses, I sensed his eyes stripping me bare again. "I liked your green cardigan." He grinned.

My brows squeezed together. "But you weren't there, or at least I don't recall seeing you."

"I saw everyone," he said soberly.

My eyes widened. "You were watching us?"

"Yes. Does that sound creepy?"

"Kind of."

"I hope you won't hold that against me," he said. It was hard to tell if he was playing or serious.

"How can I? I ended up getting the job of the century. But why hide?"

"I decided against a conventional interview. I wanted to treat this process in a different fashion than the past interviews. And as it transpired, I got it right for a change."

"For a change?" I asked.

"You're the sixth in so many months."

"Wow." A frown rippled through my brow. "I don't get it. It's not that difficult."

"For you it might be easy. But not for the others, as it turned out. You're the brightest, the most cultured, and well-mannered we've had to date. Both Greta and I feel blessed."

"I'm the one that's blessed," I said almost to myself. "It's like I've won the lottery."

Aidan chuckled.

"So was it the green cardigan that scored me the job?" I had to know whether he was joking. Aidan was so dry in his delivery.

"No. Although green is your color." His gaze lingered. "No, it was what you wrote. Your answer was the most selfless. I wanted someone whose heart was in the right place. And I liked that you put the needs of others ahead of you, namely your father and the dog shelter and also…" He stopped himself again.

"And also?" I asked, hanging onto every word.

He stopped walking. He turned to face me. His hand brushed my cheek, leaving a fiery imprint. "Your breathtaking beauty." He took a strand of my hair and twirled it in his fingers.

My throat was dry. My mouth fell open but nothing came out.

"I shouldn't have admitted that. I know it seems wrong." He returned my wide-eyed stare with a slight, uncertain smile.

"What are you doing now?" He stopped to turn back.

"I have no plans."

"I've arranged for Will to prepare fresh fish caught this morning, here in these waters." He pointed to the yacht anchored about two hundred meters away. "Dinner on my yacht. What do you think?"

I glanced over at the impressive vessel. "I'd love to, but…"

"But?"

My voice cracked. "I love my job here, Mr. Thornhill."

"Please call me Aidan. And what has your visiting my yacht got to do with your employment here?"

"I was just warned not to…" I stammered.

"Not to hang out with the boss?"

"Kind of." I sighed.

"I hired you, Clarissa Moone. I'm the only one that decides who comes and goes."

"I suppose when you put it that way…" Riddled with uncertainty, all I could do was press my lips into a faint smile.

Aidan's features softened. He removed his glasses. If only he hadn't. Starved of air, I fell deep into his gaze. "What do you think? It will be a warm evening. The sky will be amazing. And it's magical out there. I'm off to New York in the morning. It may be some time until…" There was something deep in those eyes, remote and hard to decipher.

I shook my head "Until?" His inability to finish sentences had become frustrating.

"I'll be away for two weeks. What do you think?" He cocked his head.

We arrived back at my towel. Rocket came running towards us with something in his mouth. "What's that you've got?" asked Aidan, grabbing the dog by the collar. He dragged out what looked like a decayed fish bone. "Bad boy." Aidan tossed the fish away then returned his attention to me. "I'm still waiting for your answer."

"I don't want Will to see me," I said in one quick breath.

His eyebrows drew in. "Why?"

"He'll tell Melanie, and she'll tell Greta. And it will make me out to be, you know…" I bit my lower lip.

He held my gaze again. "Melanie's a gossip." He collected his towel. "I'll instruct Will to keep it to himself. He's been with me since the beginning. He's a discreet man. I'm sure you'll have nothing to worry about there."

The wind was blowing my dried hair all over my face. I pulled it back and tied it in a knot. "All right then. Should I go back and change?" I asked, wrapping the sarong around my hips.

"There's no need. I'm still in my shorts. And I have a pullover if you feel cool, which I doubt, we're in for a hot night." We started to head for the jetty. "That's unless, of course, you want to change." He stopped and faced me again. His eyes full of suggestion caused my body, naval down, to tingle with anticipation.

"No, I'm happy as I am."

CHAPTER SIXTEEN

The interior of the large yacht was mainly dark, glistening wood, with a scattering of fine leather furnishings.

Aidan took me up the stairs to a living room area. Decked with cane furniture and white leather cushions, it was very opulent. There was a stocked bar. In an adjacent room, I saw a well-equipped kitchen, and to the other side a glassed-off deck for cooler weather.

I fell into the comfortable leather cushion of the outer exposed deck. Surrounded by nothing but the sky and deep-teal sea, it was like heaven.

Aidan brought back a bowl of water and placed it on the ground for Rocket, who slurped the lot, making a mess of the polished floorboards. He then went into the fridge and brought out a large bone. The eager dog took it in his mouth and hid in a corner to munch in private.

While my boss busied himself at the bar, I stretched my arms out, giving into the pleasant sensation of being surrounded by nothing but sky and sea.

"I've got some chilled Pinot Grigio." He held the wine up.

I nodded. "Thanks. That would be great." My, did I need a drink. I didn't recognize that wine. But being an any-wine-will-do sort of girl, I was sure it would be heavenly. Just like the man balancing the bottle in his hand.

The gentle swaying of the craft was so relaxing that I almost lost all the tightness in my body. With a horizon filled with nothing but rippling variegated oceanic blues, and a sky promising a sunset to die for, I was floating in paradise.

Predictably, the wine was crisp, cold, and complex in flavor, as only fine wine could be. I had to remind myself to sip for it didn't take me much to get drunk. Nevertheless, I needed it around my captivating boss, who had settled over at the seat on the other side. His long legs stretched out in front of him. He was earthier than I would have expected for someone so super rich.

"Have you travelled very far in this?" I asked.

"Not that far, only around the West Coast."

I walked over to the barrier and stared down into the deep water. "Seeing the world in this would be amazing. Has it got many bedrooms?"

"How many would you need?" A mischievous glow came to his eyes.

My face reddened. "No, I didn't mean it that way..."

"Just playing with you. Come," he said, leading the way with his arm. "I'll show you around if you like."

I followed along like a child at a theme park. He showed me the kitchen and dining area, which reminded me of an intimate restaurant. Decked out in dark wood and rich burgundy velvet, it had a classic design. There were stained-glass Tiffany lamps and panoramic windows.

"It's the size of a house," I exclaimed.

"This is an average size for a motor yacht. Some are like mansions. In any case, this is adequate for me. I rarely entertain."

"Will you travel the world in it?" I asked, walking up the stairs to the outer deck.

"I'd like to one day, when I meet the right travelling partner." His gaze lingered.

Hmm.

Aidan pointed. "Here we have the upper deck as you can see."

My eyes did a quick sweep. There was more cane furniture and another bar. In the corner stood a Jacuzzi and deck chairs, upon which I visualized lazing about with a book.

We went down the stairs to the main living area and bedrooms. "This is bigger than my apartment," I said, my jaw dropping at the sheer size of the bedroom. Oil paintings of nudes filled the walls. The women were all brunettes, which I thought was interesting. Not a blonde in sight. Aidan watched as I walked from one to another.

"All modern painters?" I asked, unable to recognize any of the artists' names.

"Yes, twentieth century. I have a thing for the nude," he said, lifting a brow. "I hope that's not too sleazy."

My focus remained on the paintings. I chose my preferred: a long-haired woman against an oriental backdrop. I shook my head. "They're sensual and far from tacky. Appropriate for a boudoir," I said, studying the brush strokes, "and well done. All of them."

Aidan, meanwhile, held onto his elbow and balanced his chin in his hand. His eyes shone with the admiration he had whenever I spoke of art.

I fell into his eyes. Time stood still. I wasn't sure how long we remained that way. Redirecting my focus to more material matters, as difficult as that was, I said, "It has such a relaxing ambience." I stroked the lush velvet cushions and silk drapes.

"Doesn't it? I loved it at first sight. Earlier, you mentioned the word boudoir. I bought the yacht from a French family. It came furnished, except for the paintings, which are from my collection. The original owner made his money from wine. When he died, he left his offspring with debt, so I became the proud owner of the boat."

"Has it got a name?"

"It has," he said, looking boyish.

"May I ask what it's called?" I asked as we entered the top deck again.

"Scorpio," he said, grabbing wine from the fridge. "Can I offer you more?"

"Yes, please. Are you a Scorpio?" I wasn't a follower of astrology, but Tabitha was crazy about it. And knowing her, she'd be asking for Aidan's birthdate and study his chart.

"I am," he said, filling my glass.

He stood at the edge, glancing over at the horizon. The sun was starting its fiery descent towards the darkened sea. "Are you into astrology?" he asked with a hint of a smile.

I shook my head. "I'm not, but my friend Tabitha is. She's told me a little about my sign."

"What are you? If you don't mind me asking."

"I'm a Pisces."

"You seem to love the water," he said, sitting across from me again.

"I do. The little I've read seems accurate I must admit." I shifted my weight. "And are you true to your sign?"

His deep-blue eyes impaled me. "I'm apparently meant to be powerful, jealous, possessive, dangerous…"

"Whoa… that's intense. Is that accurate?"

"Perhaps. I can be a prick when pushed." Aidan's eyes softened. "I hope you don't mind me being coarse."

"Of course not, you're the boss. You can say whatever you like." I giggled.

"I'm not your boss now. We're equals. I hope you realize that." Aidan had become serious again.

My mouth opened, and I was about to respond when my phone buzzed. The Marseillaise pierced the air. I rummaged through my bag. "I'm so sorry," I said, going red. Noticing it was Tabitha calling I turned my phone off.

Aidan chuckled. "Mm, that reminds me of Bastille Day celebrations in Nice, five years ago."

"Oh, you've been to France. I'm envious," I gushed.

"I remember reading in your application that you wished to go to Paris."

"I love most things French, from a historical perspective, that is—the literature, art, everything."

"There's much to love about France. I admired it. But then I loved Italy and Spain too." Aidan ambled off, my eyes drinking in his masculine agility.

He returned wearing a blue worn-out T-shirt. Blue was definitely his color with those air-robbing blue eyes of his.

"Have you travelled the world?" I asked.

"Only Europe— nowhere else. I spent a year travelling around." He combed back his thick, light-brown hair with his hands. "I was never the same after that trip. It nourished me."

"You mean through culture and knowledge?"

"Most definitely," Aidan said. "I found it healing. After Afghanistan, my world view was pessimistic if not narrow." He drew a tight line with his lips. "It wasn't until I visited places like Paris, Madrid, and Rome that I learnt that the true power of human endeavor was not through weaponry and brutality but intellect and creativity."

Well said!

"But they had both, didn't they?" I said.

Aidan, whose focus was out to sea, regarded me. "What do you mean?" His brow creased.

"Europe's history is covered in blood, especially ancient Rome. Their war strategies were adopted by Bonaparte and beyond. Art and intellect developed against a backdrop of brutality. They coexisted."

"That's true. But we've come a long way. When one reflects back, it's art and sheer human ingenuity that stand out. Not the crazed cruelty of war. With the benefit of hindsight, all one can do is question why so many people had to die, you know? What was the cause? In America it was the constitution, but Vietnam, Iraq—what was that about?"

"I've had these conversations with my father again and again. We always arrive at the same conclusion: humankind is both creative and destructive."

Aidan nodded with a wistful glint. "That they are."

"Afghanistan must've been harsh. I imagine you were young," I said.

He nodded slowly, his eyes remote.

"I can't express the sadness I feel for the plight of soldiers."

"It's not a subject I enjoy. But I try to help out where I can."

"I was so moved by the health center. I told my father about it. He was as taken by your benevolence as I am."

"It's not that much, really. I'm very wealthy," he said without affectation.

"I disagree. It's substantial what you do. Some of my father's friends, including my uncle, fought in Vietnam."

"He's that age group, isn't he? I'd like to meet him," said Aidan. Our gaze lingered again. The wine and the conversation had relaxed me. I could've sat there forever. "Greta mentioned she met him. She liked him. And that's saying something. My aunt's one tough operator." He chuckled.

"I've noticed. I like her, though. Her heart's in the right place. My father loved the little he saw of the estate. He adored the cottage, as do I." I peered up and gave him a little smile.

"That pleases me to no end. I want you to feel at home and comfortable." Aidan stretched his powerful arms. "You'll have to invite him over. He can stay for as long as he likes. We have lots of vacant rooms in the house. And there's the library. He's more than welcome to hang out there. In fact, I need someone to catalogue the books. That's if he's interested in a job."

"Oh, really?" I shook my head in disbelief. "It would be a labor of love for my father."

"The offer's there. I will insist on paying him. He's a man of learning. I respect that. I have a high regard for educated folk. You, Clarissa Moone, included." Aidan stood up. I was about to comment, but he disappeared.

I headed to the barrier to catch the sun sinking into the sea. A red-and-orange streak of color rippled along a path in the dark-green water.

Aidan returned. "I called Will. He's on his way now. Dinner shouldn't take too long." He held a bottle of wine. "Another?"

"Why not," I said with a smile. "I'm a little tipsy. I'll have to be careful."

"I like you tipsy. You're easier to chat with. I can see you're shy." He pulled an irresistible half-smile. "Mind you, I do like women who are sensitive. Not like the society girls there last night."

"They were all very beautiful," I said.

Aidan scrunched his nose. "Only if one's into confected beauty." He stood by my side, taking a strand of hair that had come loose from my knotted bun and tucked it behind my ear. Aidan's touch sent heat racing up the side of my neck. "I like natural beauty. I'm also very fond of long dark hair and big brown eyes." His eyes had darkened.

Words remained stuck at the back of my throat.

His lustful glint intensified. "Do you have Southern European in your family?"

I swallowed. "Umm…my grandmother—my late mother's mother—was Spanish. I take after her, I imagine."

He stood so close that his legs brushed against mine. My nipples, erect and crying for his lips, gave my arousal away.

The sound of a boat arriving stopped us. I had even licked my lips in readiness. Aidan's eyes lingering on them reflected the same urge.

I broke away first. "We have a visitor."

"Yes, it's Will," he said, not hiding his disappointment. "I tell you what." He contemplated for a moment. "Let's do this. I'll get him to unload the food and to take Rocket back. Then I can do the rest. That way, he doesn't hang around. Are you okay with that?"

I returned a slow nod. "That's so considerate. I'd also like it if he didn't see me. Do you mind if I hide?"

He gestured with his finger for me to follow him. "He's discreet. But I do understand. I'm also very private. I respect your need for it." Aidan's voice was so deep and suggestive. It was him I wanted to eat, not food.

"There are refreshments in the fridge. You can play music. There's plenty of reading material. We won't be long. I'll see to it," Aidan said with a smile that robbed me of air. He touched my cheek. "Hey, I'm so glad you decided to join me."

"I'm glad you asked me." Channeling the tipsy coquette, I gave as good as I got, returning his stare with heavy eyelids and a slight curl of my lips.

CHAPTER SEVENTEEN

With time on my hands, I called Tabitha. She answered against a background of noise. "At last, you've remembered me."

"Where are you? Can you move somewhere quiet? I don't want to yell," I said, trying to keep my voice down.

"Hang on, I'll just step outside," she yelled.

When the line grew quiet, I said, "That's better. Where are you?"

"I'm at Regina's, that new swanky bar that's just opened."

"Who are you there with?" I hoped it wasn't cheating Steve.

"Josh. He's this new guy I've met." She sounded overexcited. I'd been there before. Tabitha was frequently convinced she'd met the love of her life.

"How did you meet?" I settled onto the bed and propped myself up against the velvet cushions.

"We met at the supermarket of all places. Isn't that weird? He's so cute. We've been together all week. We haven't had a minute apart."

"Doesn't he have a job?"

Tabitha laughed. "He does. He's an actor."

"Shit, Tabs. Not an actor. Remember the last actor you were with— what was his name, Jamie—the egomaniac?"

"Josh is different. And anyway, he's got stamina." She crooned.

"You're wicked, Tabs. But I do need some of your badness." I sighed.

"Why? What's happened? Damn it, Clary. I need to see you!"

"Tomorrow for breakfast. Afterwards, we'll go shopping. I'll buy you those jeans you've been salivating over all month."

"Oh my God, seriously? Aren't you meant to be working? And how can you afford them, anyway?"

"I've just received a bonus. It's substantial and generous, most unexpected," I said, expelling a deep breath. "It's hard to process this luck. And then there's Aidan."

"Mr. Hottie. Tell me, has he tried to hit on you?"

"It seems to be going that way."

"Yay. I want details," said Tabitha.

"Well, for starters, I'm on his yacht as we speak." I paused to give Tabitha time to overreact. Sure enough, one loud scream followed. I held the phone away from my ear.

"In his yacht? Fuck, has he tried to kiss you?"

"We've come close. It may happen. I hope so," I said, barely able to hide my excitement, my heart beating madly.

"Where's he now?"

"He's arranging dinner. I'm in hiding."

"In hiding? Clary that sounds seedy," she exclaimed.

"Coming from the queen of seed," I said, laughing.

"So anyway, are you going to let him, you know… it's about time, and having someone so sexy for your first time. Although it might hurt if he's…"

That was why I'd called my best friend and sex advisor: I needed to know what to expect. I was nervous. "What were you going to say?"

"It will hurt if he's well-endowed. It's always painful the first time. After that, it's divine." She stretched her vowels, and her voice was breathy again.

"I don't know if he has, although I suspect so. After swimming his shorts were wet, and, you know..."

"Oh, lucky girl! Okay, make sure he makes you come beforehand so you're all nice and wet. It will slide in easier that way."

Eek! "I guess I'm not so worried about the pain. I'm just embarrassed about being a virgin. What if he mistakes me for someone who won't have sex until she's married? And we're forgetting that I work for him. He's my boss, for God's sake. I shouldn't go there. It will get messy."

"Have you finished?" she said, sounding annoyed. "How do you know? It might be true love. And I'm sure you're grown-up enough to manage if it's just a fling. Now, listen: make sure he takes it real slow. By the morning, you'll never want him to stop. Trust me." She laughed.

"Tabs, you're such a slut," I said, giggling.

"Oh, and make sure he wears protection. Tomorrow, we'll talk about getting you on the pill. Boyfriends like skin to skin. So do girlfriends." She giggled.

I was all hot and bothered. Sweat poured from my armpits. "He may not even want to. He may be gay," I said although unconvinced of that after what had just transpired between us.

"Don't talk silly nonsense, Clarissa Moone. You're one hot babe. Just those boobies alone will have him shooting a load."

"You're talking gutter again."

Aidan had just entered the room. "I've got to go. Speak to you in the morning." I turned the phone off abruptly.

He leaned against the doorway. "Speaking to your boyfriend?"

"No. I don't have one of those," I said, stepping out of the bedroom.

His gaze held mine again. A slight smile touched his lips and travelled all the way to his heavy-lidded eyes, drugging me again.

"Dinner's ready. I've sent Will off, so the coast is clear," he said with a wicked grin.

My tummy was so knotted, I didn't feel like eating. But then I smelt the grilled fish. My stomach relaxed and even rumbled. "Mm... that smells very appetizing," I said, sitting in the chair that Aidan held out for me.

"We have salads. I thought that would suit such a hot night." He pointed to the potato salad, coleslaw, and green salad.

He picked up the platter and served me one whole fish. "Will that do?"

"It's really too much," I said, staring down at my plate, which was taken up by the fish.

"Eat what you can. They had a decent catch this morning. There's plenty where that came from," he said, taking a seat.

The food went down well. I only got through half the fish which Aidan had removed the bone from the center for me.

"Do you fish?" I asked, pushing my plate aside.

"On occasion. I didn't fish this morning, though. Will's the keen angler. He takes the boat out most mornings." Aidan stretched his arms. He had polished off his fish and much of the salad. "The sea makes me hungry. And I do like to eat a lot."

"It doesn't show. I mean you're not over-weight at all. Do you work out?"

"No gym. But I swim, play tennis. I trained hard in the army. I have some muscles left from that," Aidan said.

He had more than some muscles left. That was for sure.

I followed Aidan back to the upper deck. The sea mirrored the sky in an alluring shade of orange-pink. "That's spectacular," I exclaimed, looking out to the horizon.

"It doesn't get much better." Aidan looked up and pointed. "And we have a full moon. How magical is that?"

The pearly orb looked gigantic against a backdrop of fiery reds and deep blue. Warm and balmy, nature had delivered well.

"How do you spend your leisure time, Clarissa?"

"I like to draw, read."

"Do you socialize much?" Striding over to the bar, he held up the wine. "Can I top you off?"

"Why not," I replied. "I've got a day off tomorrow."

"What do you do for a Saturday night?"

"I don't hang out in one place. But I go to Sammy's, which is a bar my best friend's brother works at."

"A boyfriend?" He stood so close his breath was on my neck.

"No, I don't have a boyfriend," I said, taking a sip of wine.

"You're incredibly beautiful, Clarissa Moone." His hooded eyes held me. Low and seductive, his voice penetrated through me.

I didn't know quite how it happened, but I fell into his arms. He held me tight. His heart beat hard against mine. "I have wanted to do this from the moment I saw you."

Even though my body craved his touch, I had to pull away. "I love my job."

"Clarissa"—he stroked my hair— "you're way too talented. Thornhill Holdings won't let you go."

"It's not that so much. I'm just sensitive," I said. Aidan stood so close he made me tremble. The chemistry between us was so palpable that sparks seemed to fly off us.

"That's what attracts me to you." His expression turned dark. He pulled away. "Maybe you're right. This is crazy."

He sat down. His eyes remained fixed on me.

My body screamed, while my mind and heart squabbled. "I know nothing about you," I said, clearing my throat.

He rose and sat close enough to me that my pulse raced again.

"What do you wish to know?" He asked, opening his hands out.

"I know that you were in the army. But I'm curious as to how you came to be so…" Uncomfortable about prying, I stopped myself.

"Rich?" Aidan asked. "I played the stock market and won." He snorted. "Sounds clichéd, but that's what happened. I had a spell of luck. With the profits, I bought real estate. After the 2007 crash, plenty of houses came available at bargain prices. I developed some. Others, I turned into affordable accommodation for those in need, mainly women from abused backgrounds." He paused and finished his wine. "After a few years, my wealth built. And now, well, here I am, trying to seduce my PA." He raised his eyebrows.

"I'm impressed by all your charity work," I said.

He filled my glass with wine. I needed it to still my frantic heart. His hand brushed my cheek, leaving a fiery stain. He turned to face me again. "I have such a desperate need to kiss these lips." His thumb touched my bottom lip. When he withdrew, I ran my tongue over it. Aidan's lust-filled eyes became heavy again.

Placing his arm around my shoulder, he drew me close, his body, hard and accommodating at the same time. We fit so well.

Our eyes met and then our lips. At first his lips were cushiony, moist, and tender, then burning passion took over and his tongue parted my swollen lips. He groaned into my mouth as his hand slid over my thigh.

The heat from this exchange charged straight to my sex. I ached for his touch. My body pressed hard against his. Aidan undid the knot of my sarong. All the while, our lips remained locked as our tongues snaked together suggestively.

His lips travelled down to my neck, devouring my tingling flesh. Aidan smelt of the sea and raw male, so tantalizing I was breathless. The strap to my one-piece slid off. He kissed my shoulder and beyond, leaving a trail of sparks.

Aidan pulled down my swimsuit, releasing my heavy breasts. My nipples were so hard they hurt. His eyes devoured me as he caressed my breasts. Aidan growled as he cupped them. "My God, you're magnificent, Clarissa. You're every man's dream." He ran his hand across my nipples. His mouth followed, sucking and teasing them with his tongue.

I just melted into his arms. The sensation transmitted straight to my sex, which was now dripping wet. Sticky with desire, I was too weak to stop. I wanted all of him. Pain, ache, whatever—it would have been more tormenting not to have him.

"You're so shapely, pure female." His voice resonated in breathy desire. Unable to get enough of my heavy breasts, Aidan helped me out of my one-piece.

He stripped off his T-shirt. I did what I'd been dying to do forever, and that was to run my hands up and down his rippling torso, so soft and hard at the same time.

Aidan had his hand on his waistband. I knew what was to follow, and the anticipation was so extreme that I almost hyperventilated. He lowered his shorts.

He had a huge erection. I was not experienced with penises. I recalled Tabitha saying that anything from seven inches up was yummy. Aidan's was greater than that, I was sure. I wanted to devour it with my eyes. I wanted to touch him, but having never held a man's penis before I was out of my depth.

Aidan's eyes held mine. I was sure he recognized hunger in my gaze. When his hands slid up my inner thigh, my breath hitched. He parted the lips between my thighs and with his finger rotated gloriously around my clit. We'd suddenly become very intimate. But I was too aroused to stop him. If anything, I encouraged him by opening my legs wider. Not that Aidan needed encouragement.

A rough and ragged breath left his parted lips. With two fingers, he went somewhere nobody had ever been: he entered me.

I expelled a sharp breath.

"Am I hurting you?" he asked, struggling to talk.

"No, it's okay. Don't stop," I whimpered.

"Good, because you are very wet, and I really don't want to stop," said Aidan, his voice sounded strangled.

He lowered to his knees, and his tongue took over. I squirmed. "Do you want me to stop?" He looked up at me. My pubic hair against his face made him appear mustached, almost making me laugh.

"It's just that I should have a shower," I said. It was too late. His tongue ignored my concerns and fluttered masterfully over my clit. Oh my—it was beyond exquisite. I melted into the soft leather sofa and surrendered.

My muscles went into a spasm, and my toes squeezed from the torturous pleasure.

Aidan persisted, determined to see it through, much to my delight, for I was seriously swollen as an orgasm brewed.

Waves of vibrating heat rippled through me. I found myself moaning uncontrollably. Then I just let go, and the eruption overtook my body. Such heated delight. My pelvis rose to meet his feverish tongue. Aidan continued to suck, flutter, and tease. I was ready to stop at that, but he was on a ravishing rampage.

Then another wave built, even more threateningly pleasurable than the last. I'd only ever had one orgasm at a time, but I now hurtled towards another, even more intense than the first.

The walls of my sex went into frenzy as Aidan's fast-moving tongue ravaged me steadfastly. I cried out and pushed my pelvis into his face, losing myself in a fierce wave of heat.

Aidan took my trembling body and held me. His lips glistened with my climax. "You are so responsive, and you taste sublime," he said, wiping his mouth.

Then, insatiable for my breasts, Aidan's hands were all over me, his mouth sucking, teasing my nipples which were drenched in his saliva.

Two orgasms had done little to assuage my appetite for Aidan Thornhill.

My hand trembled, more from anticipation than shyness, as I stroked his thick and long penis. It throbbed just like my heart. Aidan groaned. "I need to be inside you." His devouring eyes were heavy with lust.

I let go of him, and in a pathetically thin voice, murmured, "I haven't been with a man before."

Aidan pulled his head back and stared at me, wide-eyed. "Do you mean you're a virgin?"

His bewilderment was so acute I had to look away. I felt ashamed.

Aidan, meanwhile, shook his head in disbelief. "But how? I mean you're twenty-one."

All the heat had drained from my body as I stared down at my feet.

"You're also the most beautiful woman I've ever seen, ever touched." Aidan ran his fingers through his hair.

"It's just that…I've never met a man I liked enough. Not until…" I needed a drink. I grabbed my sarong and covered myself. "Do you mind if I have a glass of water?"

"Yes, of course." Aidan pulled up his shorts.

He grabbed a small bottle of Evian from the fridge. "Do you want it in a glass?"

I shook my head. Aidan unscrewed the bottle and passed it to me.

After I took a long, thirsty sip, I said, "I'm so sorry." I peered up at Aidan. "It doesn't mean that I don't want to, however."

Aidan kept running his hands through his hair. It must have been a nervous tic. "Do you want me to be your first?" Aidan's intense gaze penetrated so deeply it was as if he could read my soul. "My need to have you, Clarissa, defies words, but having said that, I seriously don't want to pressure you."

Our eyes met. The hunger I felt for Aidan was reflected in his deep stare.

Spellbound, I went to Aidan and fell into his arms.

He lifted me effortlessly. Aidan's sweat-infused scent penetrated like a drug as my head burrowed into his warm neck. He carried me down the stairs and into the plush bedroom.

CHAPTER EIGHTEEN

Crisp white sheets caressed my tingly flesh. Aidan pulled down his shorts. I couldn't help but drink him in. His rod-hard penis curved up to his belly button. The anticipation of being penetrated made me creamy and sticky.

Aidan clasped me in his strong arms. We fitted so well together. Skin on skin, he stroked my hair. He pulled away and played with a strand of my hair that was lying against my breast. "You're exquisite. I couldn't take my eyes off you last night at the gala." He kissed me tenderly. He undid himself from my hold and stretched over to the drawer to get a rubber.

I gave a staggered sigh. "Are you sure you want this?" he asked, caressing me.

As a response, I opened my legs wide.

Aidan stroked my swollen bud. The pleasant ache returned. It hadn't really left. He placed his two fingers at my entrance, and they slithered in with little effort. Aidan's breath became heavy. "How is that? Am I hurting you?"

"It feels nice," I purred.

"You're so moist—dripping, in fact. You're extremely beautiful, Clarissa." He removed his fingers and sucked them. "Your flavor is addictive."

Although I winced at the grossness, I still found it erotic. He kissed me again. His lips burned into mine.

Aidan pulled away. "The last thing I want to do is hurt you. You must tell me to stop if it's too much."

"Uh-huh," I replied. Words were stuck back in my dry throat. Blood charged through my veins as his fingers fluttered over my bud. Within only a few sublime flourishes, the orgasm arrived. That was how inflamed I was.

"That's it, sweet baby. I love that you're so sensitive and responsive." He buried his face in my breasts, making a meal of my nipples again.

Love-making was more tantalizing than I could have ever imagined.

Aidan ripped off the plastic from his rubber and fitted himself in readiness. I couldn't help but watch. His cock made my mouth water.

He ran his thumb across my bottom lip. "I wish I had the right words to describe how stunning you are." His hands slid down my body, over my hips. "So beautiful," he whispered. His fingers entered my wet sex, and he hissed. "Oh…my angel."

To avoid crushing me, Aidan shifted his weight onto his strong arms. The sinews and veins were so alluring—my fingers luxuriated over his bulging muscles. I imbibed every bit of him. Sea and sex, his scent undid me. If it could have been bottled, I'd have sprayed it around my bed at night.

Aidan groaned into my kiss as we clasped each other. His penis pushed imploringly against my leg.

My hands moved down his hard torso. Every smooth contour of his muscles rippled under my curious fingers. Down his rock-hard thigh they crept. His breath hitched. Anticipation deepened. The closer my fingers got to his cock, the quicker his heart raced against mine.

Aidan's pulsating penis fell into my hand. A stretched rasp fell from his lips as he parted my legs. "Direct me in," he said, hoarse.

I placed his broad shaft between the lips of my sex. Such was the need to experience him that any remnant of fear had vanished.

Slowly, I guided his thickness into me, one inch at first—the stretching was so extreme it hurt. Aidan's body trembled. Tortured, his face contorted. Or was that ecstasy?

I could tell, instinctively, that Aidan wanted to penetrate deep and hard. But his concern for my wellbeing was stronger.

Flexing my pelvis, I took him in deeper. His large hard balls hit my palm. With a gentle push he inched deeper, while his unsteady breath resonated through me.

Aidan gritted his teeth, stifling a roar.

Oh my, it was indeed painful. Like a knife. My eyebrows drew in sharply. Witnessing my reaction, he stopped. "No, don't, please," I whimpered. My pelvis tilted towards him, and Aidan entered deeper.

Just like mine, his heartbeat increased. A primal growl escaped his clenched jaw as Aidan reached the full depth of my sex. With extreme care, almost tentatively, he moved in and out.

As I stretched around his hard cock, the pain disappeared and became pleasurable. The friction from his thrust generated a pleasurable burning sensation. Spasms started to shiver through me. I was clenched tightly around him.

"Are you okay? You are exceptionally tight," Aidan whispered.

"Yes," I uttered in breathless whisper. "I'm sorry if it's difficult."

"Clarissa, words cannot describe how you feel. You're every man's dream. You're my dream."

The thrusting increased in speed. I held onto his firm, round butt, which was as tactile as the rest of him. My thighs wrapped around his athletic legs.

A slow, long breath left him. "Oh my God, you feel good—too good." His movements built in rhythm. Aidan's breathing was so ferocious it penetrated through my flesh. The friction between us was divine as thick creamy waves engulfed me.

"I can't hold on. I have to come." Aidan's voice struggled, his face contorting. Jaw clenched, his head fell back. In a wild rush, he exploded, crying out my name with a primal roar.

He fell into my embrace panting. Aidan held me tight as he regained his senses.

"I'm sorry that was too soon. I've never felt anything as perfect as that. You're addictively delectable," he said, stroking my cheek. He pulled back his head so he could see my face. "How was it? Please tell me it wasn't too painful. I hope I didn't bruise you."

I was so overcome with emotion that I almost laughed for some crazy reason.

Aidan puckered his brow questioningly.

"At first it hurt. You're extremely big," I said, back to awkward Clarissa. "But it became really pleasurable after I got used to it."

"You divine angel." Aidan continued to caress me gently. "Next time, I won't come as quickly. I need you to come with me," he said, devouring me with his hooded blue eyes.

"I've already orgasmed three times, Aidan," I said. He kissed me deeply and slowly. In his arms I remained as I drifted off.

When I opened my eyes, Aidan was on his side, staring at me. "I hope I didn't wake you."

"You didn't," I said, rubbing my eyes. "Have you been awake long?"

"I haven't slept." He reached for a glass of juice and passed it over to me. "Here, would you like a drink?"

I lifted myself off my elbows and took the glass. The juice went down well. I was really thirsty.

"Finish it. I've already had a few," Aidan said.

"So why haven't you slept? Did I keep you awake?"

"You did," said Aidan with that adorable lopsided smile of his.

My brows shot up. "What—do I snore?"

He laughed. "No, silly." He tapped my nose. "I needed to keep looking at you. You're as beautiful asleep as awake, if not more so."

I fell into his arms. Aidan's warm lips softened into mine. Slow and drugging, the caress of his mouth set my body aflame, melting me like chocolate. His tongue traced my swollen lips and entered my mouth.

Within an instant, Aidan's need became fierce. His hands were all over my heavy breasts, groaning into my mouth, his lips hot and fiery. Meanwhile, pushing against my thigh, his cock pleaded to be stroked.

The desire to devour him suddenly swept through me. I travelled down the bed and placed the wide head of his velvety cock into my mouth. Salty arousal dripped onto my tongue while his hands were filled with my breasts.

Veiny and rod-hard, he stretched my mouth to the limit as my lips moved up and down.

Aidan pulled away. "No. Not this way," he said, tracing my lips with his fingers. "I love your sensual lips on my cock so much that I won't last. And I haven't got all day to fuck you. If only. Before I leave this morning, I want my cock to make you come." He took me into his arms.

A powerful reminder of lost innocence, the few drops of blood on the sheet made me recoil. Aidan held me tight. He whispered something inaudible while caressing me. "My darling girl," was all I heard.

His warm breath on my cheek, Aidan said, "You're a goddess." His ravenous tongue supped on every inch of my prickling flesh, leaving a trail of electricity all the way to my sex. There he teased and fluttered over my swollen clit until I came ferociously into his mouth.

I lay there, ready, legs wide open, dripping in arousal. He grabbed his primed, sheathed cock. This time, it slid in with no piercing pain, just a deep stretch that was so overwhelmingly satisfying that I moaned all the way.

"Clarissa, you'll be my undoing," he whispered into my ear, trembling with lust. He moved in and out. I was so inflamed and sensitive that the friction was sheer ecstasy. "I want to go hard, but I don't want to hurt you," he stammered.

"It's okay. Please do," I rasped.

Oh, how he filled me. With pure animal grace, Aidan ploughed into me. My pelvis moved up to meet his. His deep penetration sent electrifying shudders through me. My heart raced so fast I was lost in a dizzy haze. Each time he re-entered the heat intensified.

Spasms, tormenting and endless—I lost control. His big cock was on a ravaging campaign. Pure heat burned into me. While his hungry hands hadn't left my breasts, his mouth travelled away from my tumescent lips and feasted on my nipples. He bit me gently and I gasped in delightful agony.

Aidan's groans became growls as the room resonated with the primal cries of a couple lost in the throes of pure, raw passion.

Glued together by sweat, we were all flesh. My sex clenched tightly. I hurtled beyond the point of return, collapsing in a gush of pure heat. Then, without time to bask in that, another orgasm brewed as he relentlessly slid in and out of me.

The slow eruption began. It was like nothing I'd ever experienced in my life. Commencing with glowing stars shattering behind my eyes, a wave of swelling heat blasted me. With each hot wave, the swell grew in slow, toe-curling, time-stretching ripples. I surrendered, and my senses tumbled out of control. A stretched gasp left me. My nails sank into Aidan's sticky flesh. As he stretched the last vowel in my name it sounded as if he was plunging into a deep well.

We held each other tight. Our hearts beat in unison, taking quite some time to land back on earth.

When Aidan's breathing returned to normal, his gaze was so all-consuming I thought he was about to say something. But he kissed me with feverish tenderness instead

CHAPTER NINETEEN

I sat up naked against the cushions, only because Aidan wouldn't allow me to dress.

Aidan handed me a cup of coffee. "I hope that's okay. Are you hungry?"

"No, the coffee is fine. I can grab something later."

Semi-dressed himself, Aidan's naked torso was a serious turn-on as I sipped on the delicious cup of coffee. "Do you need something?" I asked, watching him walk about combing back his hair with his hand.

He kneeled by the bed. "Yes—you."

Good answer! I pulled back the covers and tapped the bed, my thighs sticky from our last round of sex. *Or was that lovemaking?*

"What a sight," he said. As his hands caressed my breasts, I noticed his erection pushing against his shorts. "I can't—I have to go." Aidan stood up. "You can stay. Finish your coffee."

I jumped out of bed. "No, I'll come with you. I won't know how to get the boat started otherwise," I said, tying my sarong around my waist. "I suppose it's only about two hundred meters back to shore, I could swim."

Aidan laughed. "You're adorable." He brushed my cheek. "It's not a difficult swim, I grant. I've seen you fly in the water, sexy mermaid. I'm sure you can manage it. But I don't want you to."

"I could do it with ease," I said defensively.

He held me again. "I can get Linus to come over." His eyes moved up and down my body. "Although… come to think of it, I wouldn't want him to see you in that see-through sarong." He ran his hands along my thighs.

"I'd prefer him not to see me either."

Aidan tilted his head, a faint smile forming. "Are you ashamed of being seen with me?"

"Of course not, but this is a little tricky," I said, heading for the upper deck to retrieve my one-piece. "Have I got time to dress?" I asked. "I'm naked under this sarong."

Aidan squeezed my bottom cheek as he followed me up the stairs. "I've noticed, and I want to fuck you so much that I'm having trouble moving."

"You're insatiable." I laughed.

"Around you I am. I wish I didn't have this damn meeting."

"What time's your flight?" I asked, pulling my swimsuit up.

"Anytime I want. It's my plane," he said casually, as if everyone owned a plane. "It's just that I have to be there by eleven o'clock. I can get there thirty minutes late, however." Aidan stroked my tousled, just-been-fucked-hair.

"I must look a mess."

"You're even more incredibly stunning. I love your hair out and wild." He tucked a strand behind my ear and kissed me again. He took my hand and led me off the impressive yacht.

Once we were back to the shore, Aidan lifted me off the dinghy and onto the jetty. I could have just as easily stepped onto it. But he insisted, holding me longer than necessary with those strong, muscular arms. Aidan's eyes were on mine. As I caught a whiff of him my pulse raced and a throb caused an ache in my pussy—a delicious reminder of Aidan being inside me.

In what would have made a fantastic advertisement for anything relating to male products, Aidan's strong muscles flexed as he tethered the boat to the pier. Just to add to my already aroused state, he swept his golden-brown hair away from his handsome face. For someone who hadn't slept, he looked fresh, especially with that healthy tan. But best of all were Aidan's blue eyes that reflected the delicate turquoise sky and blue sea.

Arm in arm, we walked to the stairs. I stopped and turned to look at Aidan. "Do you want me to wait for a few minutes?"

Aidan frowned. "Why?"

How could he be so relaxed? "I just thought people might talk," I said, following him up the uneven rocky steps.

"Don't you worry your pretty head about anything," Aidan said with a knock-out smile. He took my hand again, and we ascended the rocky climb.

"I love these steps. They remind me of some ancient city in Europe," I said, panting from the steep incline.

"That was the first thing I thought when I walked down them."

When we arrived at the top, Aidan took me into his arms and held me so close that his heart thumped against my chest. "I wish I didn't have to go away."

"How long will you be gone?"

He exhaled slowly. "Two long weeks." From his pocket, he produced a phone and pressed a few buttons. My phone pinged. "I just sent you my number. Call me, text me, anything. Only keep in touch." Aidan stroked my cheek and kissed me again. His tongue entered my parted lips as a cogent reminder of his passionate claim on me.

I pulled away. "You better go. I'm holding you up."

"Call me." Aidan remained before me. I was the first to leave, carrying away an after-burn from his smoldering gaze.

CHAPTER TWENTY

We were seated at a fashionable café in the arts district. It was a novelty to be back there for a day, a contrast to the beach wonderland I now called home. Despite the grimy hustle and bustle of the city, it was fun to hang out with Tabitha, who was ebullient after I'd just bought her a pair of red jeans that cost an average weekly salary.

"So, Clarissa Moone, you're now a woman," said Tabitha, sizing me up. She looked around and whispered, "Did it hurt? Did you come?"

I rolled my eyes. "Subtle as always." I giggled. "A little."

As expected, Tabitha threw one of her impatient frowns. I had to laugh at her exasperation. "I'll take that as a yes. Is he well-endowed?" Tabitha raised an eyebrow.

My face fired up, and I grinned.

"Oh, he is. Mm..." said Tabitha.

"You're incorrigible, Tabs." I giggled. Her reaction reflected my exact sentiments. It sent yet another electrical charge travelling down to my deliciously aching lower region.

"Did you come with his finger, tongue, or penetration?" Tabitha was leaning in towards me on her elbows.

"All of that," I said with a tight smile.

"Wow, he's a super lover, then?" Tabitha persisted.

"I don't know what to compare him to," I said, sipping on my coffee, which burned my swollen lips, a reminder of Aidan's passionate kisses. "Suffice it to say that if all men made love like Aidan, I imagine those columns filled with complaints about men not satisfying them would no longer exist."

"Far out...he was that good." Tabitha was starry-eyed.

"Uh-huh." I sighed. "Beyond anything I could have ever imagined."

"Wow...how many times did you do it?"

"Four," I answered, grinning.

"In one session! Fuck, Clarissa, was he on Viagra?" She laughed.

I shook my head. "Isn't that normal?"

Tabitha's laugh was so loud everyone's attention turned to our table.

"I hope they didn't hear," I whispered.

"It's not normal. The guy has stamina, lucky you. And he also hit your G-spot. He's not only hot but a sex god too. You really hit the jackpot, babes."

"It may be the only time. I can't get too attached." A sudden cold knot formed in my tummy at the thought of being a one-night stand.

My phone pinged, making me jump. It was Aidan. My heart leapt to my mouth. It was only four hours ago that he'd left, and he was messaging me already: *Hi...thinking of you (haven't stopped). I arrived on time. XXX Aidan.*

My huge smile piqued my nosey girlfriend's interest. She attempted a glance at the screen. "Who's that?"

With "haven't stopped" circling around and around in my head, I passed her the phone.

"Shit, he's got the hots for you, Clary." Tabitha's excited, high-pitched voice summed up my feelings. She passed me back the phone. "What are you going to say?"

I shrugged. "I don't know. What would you suggest?"

"Tell him that your pussy's throbbing and can't wait to have him inside of you again." Tabitha's green eyes danced with mischief.

"You lascivious woman you," I said, shaking my head.

"And make sure you don't intimidate him with your antiquated words."

"He likes intelligent women," I said.

"I know, send a photo of yourself," she said, grabbing my phone.

"Do you think?" I asked, wondering how I looked.

"Yeah, I do. Here, let's undo that braid and have your hair loose." Tabitha unraveled my hair and arranged it so that it framed my face. Then she undid the top buttons of my blouse to expose some cleavage.

I protested. "That's taking it too far, just my face. Damn, I don't have any make-up on. And I have slept little."

"Oh, be quiet. You look gorgeous. You have that just-been-fucked glow about you. Now, lean forward, elbow to the side so we can see that cleavage." She held the phone and clicked away. "Smile seductively. Think of him taking you, making your toes curl."

"You're too much, Tabs."

"Come on," Tabitha said. "Just think of how he felt inside you the second time."

I curled my lips.

"That's perfect." Tabitha clicked again and again.

She studied the shots. "That's the one. Your smile is angelic, not slutty. But then he sees that knock-dead cleavage and, well…" She passed it to me. My cleavage was plunging in that photo, which wasn't hard to do with my boobs. But I liked the shot.

"Okay, I'll send that," I said.

Noticing my hands trembling, Tabitha grabbed the phone. "Here, I'll do it." With typical deftness, she sent it off.

"I should send a text."

"Just did that," Tabitha said with a cheeky grin.

"Shit, Tabs. What did you write?"

Tabitha passed me the phone, laughing. "God, you should see your face. You've got it bad. I didn't write anything. Here, do it." She passed me the phone.

After staring down at the screen for a while, I wrote: *I'm so glad you got there safely. XXX Clarissa.*

Tabitha reached over to look at what I'd written. She rocked her head to and fro. "Hmm…a bit tame, but I suppose it's too soon for sex banter."

"I'm not a sex-banter kind of person, Tabs," I said, exasperated more with myself for being artless in this game of seduction.

"I can see I'll have to train you." Her green eyes twinkled. "A man like Aidan will need some of that, I'd imagine."

I exhaled sharply. Tabitha was right. Aidan was a sex god. How the hell could an inexperienced girl like me handle that?

"You'll have to go on the pill. As soon as possible— today even." Tabitha pushed buttons on her phone.

Before I could respond, I heard her say, "Hello, are there any appointments available this afternoon?"

I glared at her. She was making me an appointment. That was Tabitha— impatient and bossy. I shook my head and rolled my eyes.

She hung up. "Two o'clock. That's ideal. You start today, and by the time he returns, you can go au-naturel, skin to skin. That's after he's shown you a blood test clearing him of STDs."

"What? I can't ask him for that," I whispered.

"It's common practice, Clarissa. Everyone does it these days," said Tabitha patting my hand.

"Tell me about your new boyfriend," I said, taking a forkful of the yummy chocolate cake. It slinked down and made my stomach grumble with approval. I was so hungry despite having had a hot breakfast, three hours earlier.

Tabitha's face lit up. "He's tall, dark, and handsome. You know my tastes." She arched a brow. "And he likes to eat pussy," she said, fanning her face and giggling.

"Gross, Tabs. Too much information," I sang. "I'm really glad you've given Steve his marching orders, though." I wiped my mouth after polishing off the cake.

"Keep this Saturday night free, Clary, because it's Josh's birthday."

CHAPTER TWENTY-ONE

Aidan

"Aidan, if you want to maximize your bottom line, then we need to take the company off-shore."

"I will not sack the local workforce, Jacob. We've had that discussion before. And who says I want to lift the bottom line, anyway? That's your mantra."

My business advisor removed his thick-lensed glasses and rubbed his eyes. "But, Aidan, the company is not making any profit." He tapped his spreadsheet.

"It's not losing either," I said, taking a sip from my fourth cup of coffee, which was making me jumpy.

"The company only just broke even," he countered.

I glanced down at my watch. I had another three meetings that day, and my eyes burned from lack of sleep. "Jake, now listen. Thornhill Holdings are doing well in all our other interests. Our portfolio of real estate is going through the roof, especially in New Orleans. The low-cost housing development has yielded millions in profits. The solar farms are the next part of that equation. And by using local workers, the love goes around. Don't you get that?"

"You're too new-age, Aidan, with this karma obsession of yours. I can see that you could make a considerable profit with Solarm. But using locally sourced materials and labor will drag up costs."

"We're going around in circles," I said, not hiding my annoyance. Jacob was an astute man, who, having guided me wisely over the years, had helped make me very rich. "You know my philosophy—help those in need while making money from acquisitions that don't cause undue pain to local communities. The biotech investments are going through the roof, as are the medical marijuana stocks you so wisely advised me to pump millions into. We're sitting pretty, Jake. If Solarm is breaking even, then that's a decent result."

My phone lit up. I glanced down, and smiling back at me was the angel that had stolen my senses and ability to concentrate. Her wide brown eyes were so innocent, yet so seductive. Blood charged through me again as I lost myself in that face. And those luscious tits spilling out—fuck, my cock lengthened. "Will that be all for now?" I asked.

"Sure. We'll catch up soon."

I watched Jake close the door behind him and took a deep breath while stretching out my arms. My next appointment with Brad, my attorney, wasn't for another thirty minutes.

I couldn't stop looking at Clarissa's face. Her eyes were so mesmerizing it brought it all back. I thought about how she felt in my arms with those soft voluptuous curves. The memory of being inside of her caused my cock to thicken again.

I'd broken every rule in the book. *Never fuck an employee. Never fuck a virgin.*

But I'd lost my head. Her beauty had drugged me. That blue gown, her grace, her voluptuous body. And to add to that impossible list, she was sensitive, intelligent, and cultivated.

I'd wanted her from the moment I saw her on the beach. Those shapely long legs, her full breasts, those succulent nipples that stretched out provocatively from her swimsuit, making my cock ache and go rock-hard in an instant.

I couldn't take my eyes away from my phone. It was her eyes that captivated me the most—innocently sweet, yet full of desire and promise. Her black, wild hair led me to that pouting cleavage. I licked my lips, remembering how her tits had fallen all over my hands. My balls were blue from the memory.

Two weeks was way too long. I needed to hold her sooner. I ran my finger over the image of her ravishing lips. My aching cock pushed against my trousers as I relived her drenching cunt, so tight that my senses were starved of reason. And her rapturous moans when she came. I'd been somewhere no man had ever been. That did my head in on so many levels.

My obsession to have Clarissa had started the moment I saw her through the tinted glass in that tight-fitting skirt. Even her modest buttoned-up shirt had done little to hide her delectable body. And that thick black hair swept up in a messy bun, her swanlike neck, those full fleshy lips, and my God, those large brown eyes.

I transferred Clarissa's photo onto my laptop and was about to reply to her message when my phone rang. It was Bryce. What was I to say to him? We had such a complex relationship. Had it been anybody else, I would have fucked him off ages ago.

I picked up the phone. "Bryce." I kept my tone cold and professional.

"Aidan, look, man, umm...I'm sorry about the other night. I'd been drinking, and well, your new PA is scrumptious, even though she's become a ballbreaker."

"Ballbreaker?" My fists clenched.

"She set up this new system. I'm meant to report all my expenditures. It's time-fucking-consuming and shitting me." Bryce sounded as if he'd been drinking again—not unusual, considering he was an alcoholic.

"That was my idea, Bryce. The losses are running into the thousands at the expense of programs. I can't talk now. I'll be back in two weeks."

"Are you in New York?"

"Yes." I hoped Bryce wouldn't offer to catch up. The last time, he'd stayed at my apartment, and I had to put up with his erratic, wild behavior.

"Why don't I fly down? We can hang out. There's that Jacqueline babe, remember—the one with the big tits?"

"I've got too much going on," I said, keeping my tone patient despite being pissed. "And about Clarissa—I don't want you going near her." My voice went up a decibel.

"Why? Do you want to fuck her, or have you already?"

"Listen Bryce, I'm losing it here. You're out of control. I know about your gambling habit and that you're stealing from the fund."

"You can't get rid of me, and you know it. I get it she's a fucking goddess...that body, those tits, those big eyes."

"Listen, you fucker, you stay away from her. I've got to go." I nearly threw my phone against the wall in frustration. I had to rid myself of this jerk.

The buzzer roused me out of my troubled state. "Mr. Thornhill, Brad Russell is here."

"Thanks, Jane. Just give me five minutes and then send him in... oh, and can you get me some lunch?"

I put down the phone and stared at the million-dollar view of Central Park. I'd chosen the apartment, which doubled as an office and home, for its knockout view. Disinclined towards confined spaces, I needed an open view of trees and nature, which this apartment delivered. My timing had been just right for the coveted penthouse suite in Fifth Avenue. It had been love at first sight when I walked into the lobby of the 1926 building, with its marble entry and art deco designs.

What message could I send Clarissa? My stomach was a knot of nerves. Bryce had unhinged me. I took a deep breath and wrote, *Thank you for the photo. It's beautiful. You are beautiful. Aidan.*

I picked up the phone. "Jane, can you make a Skype appointment with Kieren Tyler? See if he can fit me in after four today. Thanks."

Boy, did I need a session with my psychologist. He was the only person, apart from Greta and my dad, whom I could turn to. My feelings for Clarissa would have to remain a secret from Greta for the moment. I didn't like it. But I'd promised my aunt, after that regrettable tangle with Amy, never to mix work with pleasure.

Clarissa was something entirely different. She'd gotten to me. I'd never experienced that before. I'd never had this unquenchable desire for someone. From that first day on the beach, I was under her spell.

CHAPTER TWENTY-TWO

The session with Brad went seamlessly. The ensuing meetings were brief and straightforward. Tomorrow was the big day. I was about to embark on a major project, leasing land from retiring farmers in order to install wind turbines and solar panels. Renewable energy was a deep passion of mine, which to date had yielded some unexpected profits, especially from my investment in battery-operated scooters and cars.

"Jane, can you come in for a moment?" Apart from Greta, Jane was the jewel in the Thornhill Holdings crown. She ran everything single-handedly from New York. She was forty years old, and I suspected she was gay. That didn't worry me. If anything, it was a refreshing change.

In the beginning, after my army days, I'd enjoyed the sport of fucking. My appetite was as healthy as any young man's. But one day I woke up to myself. Suddenly I found women trying to pick me up irritating. Perhaps I was old-fashioned, but I had developed a more subtle approach to mating. It was intelligent conversation that mattered most, and of course, breathtaking beauty like Clarissa's didn't hurt.

Jane entered my office, dressed in her usual gray corporate skirt and white shirt. She never veered away from that look, which I appreciated. I liked my employees to look the part.

"Jane, can you arrange a large bunch of roses. Uh..." *What should they be? Red...for passion? Or pink...a gentler, sensitive approach?*

"Make them red. And make sure they're fragrant. Spare no cost." I scribbled out the details and handed them over.

I gleaned a faint smile. This was a first. Jane took the slip of paper and nodded. Good, professional as usual. The problem was at the other end. Would there be questions at the estate? The envelope was marked Private. At worst, Greta would assume that Clarissa had an admirer.

All these potential issues brought to light the cumbersome nature of this romance. I'd have to deal with it somehow because to discontinue was not an option.

"That'll be all for today, Jane."

I poured myself a whisky and called Kieren, my psychologist. He picked up straight away. "Hello, Aidan. How are you?"

"Well... you know. I'm calling you."

"I take it you're in New York. How's all that going for you?"

Not one for small talk, I said, "I've met a girl." I leaned back in my chair. I preferred his LA office with that impressive aquarium that always put me in a calm frame of mind. Instead, I had his placid face on my laptop.

Kieren was a quiet, even-tempered man who never rushed me. He had been my shrink after I left the forces, and I'd never strayed. Being middle-aged, he was paternal without being patronizing.

"That sounds like a healthy development," said Kieren with a gentle smile.

I sighed. "Hmm…I suppose it is. Only Clarissa is my new PA. She only started two weeks ago." I cleared my throat and moved my head to ease the tension in my neck.

"Oh, and you're worried it's a repeat of the Amy incident?"

"In many ways, I'm not. Clarissa is nothing like that. Amy threw herself at me. She was drunk, and I was vulnerable. I didn't desire her like I do Clarissa."

"Clarissa is a younger woman?"

"She is. Not that that's the reason why I'm…she's graceful, gentle, a beautiful woman whose virginity I took," I said, surprising myself at the last admission. I released my clenched, sodden palms.

"Was she drunk?" he asked in his tranquilizing monotone.

"No. I mean, we'd had wine. I spoke to her at length about it. Clarissa wanted me to be her first." My voice cracked. "She's so desirable... this is a first for me, Kieren." I paused to steady my breath. "I've never felt like this before."

"When did it happen?"

"Last night," I said, wiping my brow.

"It's very recent, then." He leaned back in his leather seat. "Tell me, what are your emotions now? Regret, longing, or the dread of having to face her?"

"Longing. None of the others," I murmured. The answer came quicker than a heartbeat. "That's the thing. My need to see her is overwhelming. And I'm here for two weeks…" I stopped myself, realizing how weak, even stupid I must have sounded.

"It does seem like you've fallen for this girl. That's not strange. Attraction, desire can be so intense that it sweeps one away. It happened to me. It's a totally natural and healthy reaction."

I collected my thoughts. There was much I wanted to say. How was I to say it?

"Tell me, are you scared of losing her?" As usual, he'd nailed it.

I sighed. "Yes. I won't be seeing her for two weeks. And I keep wondering if I've unlocked something in her." What I really wanted to say was that Clarissa was so wet, so turned-on that I may have unleashed sexual need in her. Out of respect for Clarissa, I kept that to myself. All I could do was remind myself that the sexy angel who'd moaned in my arms as I entered her was a shy, unassuming, gracious girl.

"You need to learn to trust your judgement more, Aidan. She's warm and good-natured, you say. She's also inexperienced with men. And although you unleashed passionate yearning in her, I'm more than certain she won't be running off to another so soon. In fact, I'm sure she's as smitten as you are. You're a handsome, sought-after bachelor."

"But where to now? The thought of dating her excites me. But I don't want to hurt her. I don't want to give her false expectations."

"What's the worst thing that may happen here, Aidan?" he asked, removing his glasses.

I considered his question for a moment. "That I lose myself entirely— that I remain this unhinged and out of control. I can't get her out of my mind," I said, reaching for the bourbon.

"That sounds like someone who's scared of falling in love," said Kieren with a faint smile.

I didn't respond. I pondered the love concept as I'd often done. "Yeah, well…you're aware of my views on that." I tried to do away with the cynicism but failed.

"It comes down to fear of abandonment, loss of control. Love comes with many commitments—commitments you're frightened you will fail to meet. Perhaps it's to do with your father not sticking around."

"I disagree, Kieren. I don't blame my father. Mom was a groupie. It was a casual encounter. And even if Dad wanted to hang around, my mom was a train wreck. Still is. And I don't understand why that would enter my thinking where Clarissa's involved. Since she's nothing like my mother."

"That's right. She's nothing like your mother. From what you say, she's loyal, gracious, and potentially an ideal match for you. Time will only tell if that's so."

"But you know my views on marriage," I said, frustrated. I combed my hair back with my sweaty palms. It was getting too long. I brushed it away from my collar. But I also recalled Clarissa running her hands through it, declaring in her sensual, breathy voice that she loved long hair on men.

"Is that mainly due to your nightmares?"

Taking a deep breath, I replied, "How is someone meant to put up with the cries, the sweat-drenched sheets?"

"Are you also thinking about Jessica?"

A shiver ran up my spine at the mention of my ex-fiancée—my old control-freak girl-friend. Now, that had been a bad choice. We were introduced at one of my earlier gala evenings. Being new to the tycoon label, I'd been impressed by her old-money pedigree. She was also well-educated and quick-witted, which were her finer points. But I just couldn't stomach her bossiness and spoiled-brat behavior, not to mention her addiction to cosmetic surgery.

"I dodged a bullet there for sure," I said, regretting the metaphor as it brought back the reason I had a shrink in the first place. "News is she's back, circling around."

"Oh? And how do you feel about that?"

There was that question again. Fuck, if my over-active, sleep-deprived brain could find the answer to that, the real Aidan Thornhill might finally reveal himself. "I haven't given it much thought, to be honest, only…" I pushed my hair back from my face.

"Only what, Aidan?" He sat forward, facing me.

"Not sure, Kieren. I suppose… I hope she doesn't resurface. I heard she's back in LA. But getting back to what we were saying earlier, I can't compare the two women. I wasn't gaga about Jessica the way I am for Clarissa. It is completely different."

"The right woman will heal. Love is healing. She'll be understanding and patient. These days, there's more awareness of post-traumatic stress disorder suffered by ex-soldiers. Parasomnia is more common than you think. It is treatable. If need be, there are sleeping pills you can take to de-activate the REM cycle, thus defusing the nightmares. I've mentioned that before."

"I'm hardly likely to make a suitable partner," I said, my typical pessimism resurfacing.

"I actually think you'll make someone a brilliant husband and father. You're reliable, patient, and generous—perfect attributes."

I exhaled long and hard. "I don't know. I'm broken in many ways."

"You're improving all the time, Aidan. You're not the same young, wounded man I first encountered six years ago. You've come a long way."

I pictured the shaking mess that had been me at twenty-five—defensive, volatile, hating shrinks. Now, I couldn't imagine my life without him. "But it still leaves me with the dilemma of what to do with Clarissa. She's my employee, and an excellent one at that. Probably the best we've ever had. I'm messed-up over this, Kieren."

"It's simpler than you think. Enjoy getting to know her. Go with the flow. Don't over-think it. And by all means, never say never," he said, concluding our session.

His was the voice of reason, and as with all my sessions with Kieren, I walked away calmer. The knot finally left my chest. "Thanks for fitting me in. I'll see you back in LA."

I closed down the screen and headed up to my bedroom. It had been a busy day.

CHAPTER TWENTY-THREE

Clarissa

"You can't go back to Malibu to get your charger, Clary. I'll let you borrow my phone if you need to make a call," said Tabitha, zipping up her new red pants. She was still dressed in her bra, the silk blouse I'd gifted her earlier that day dangling from her hand.

"But what if Aidan's trying to contact me?" I said, staring glum-faced at my dead phone.

"God, Clarissa. He's texted you twice a day, which in my book adds up to one very keen man. It won't do any harm to leave him hanging for one day." She raised a well-plucked eyebrow.

Tabitha buttoned up her blouse and turned to inspect her butt in the mirror. "What do you reckon?"

Tabitha was shining. Her new boyfriend had brought a glow to her cheeks. Her green eyes were clear, and her long blond hair was full of bounce.

"You look amazing, Tabs," I said, tucking a hanging ribbon back into her new blouse.

After she stepped away from the mirror, I popped myself in front to check out my new cotton, floral, vintage-inspired dress. "I'm not sure about this dress, Tabs. It's shorter than I'm used to wearing," I said, tilting my head to one side and studying myself.

"Nonsense, you have the best legs."

We'd arranged to meet Josh, Tabitha's new boyfriend, in the arts district. As we entered the quirky venue, I checked out some murals of women's faces. Distressed and unfinished, the walls made the converted warehouse seem more like someone's studio than a bar. Subdued lighting, from recycled lamps acting as pendant lights, created a relaxed ambience.

Having turned up fashionably late, Josh, who was there with a friend, waved over to us, and we joined them at the table.

Josh held out his hand. "Nice to meet you, at last." He had an engaging bright smile. I took his hand. Despite doing my utmost not to study him too closely, I got a good first impression.

Tabitha slid next to him, and they hugged. It was so natural between them. They were clearly into each other, and Josh was just as Tabi had described: tall, dark, and handsome. His sincere, besotted gaze directed at Tabitha told me he was a legitimate potential partner. I liked that, considering the jerks and losers that Tabitha had a tendency to attract.

"This is Cameron," said Josh, pointing to his blond pal.

I greeted him with a faint smile. Cameron's face lit up, not hiding his immediate interest. I cringed. I hoped that he didn't assume I was up for a little action. Like some good-looking men I'd met, he seemed confident. No shyness, no self-doubt, he looked me straight in the face as if to say, "I'm all yours, and you're a babe."

The only seats available were double-seater sofas, which suited the besotted lovers, who were almost on top of each other. I settled on the other with reluctance. With his undressing eyes on my cleavage, Cameron appeared to have claimed me.

Eek. I'd warned Tabitha earlier that I didn't want this to be a double-date. But with little other choice, I sat next to Cameron, endeavoring to maintain a cool distance. His attention, meanwhile, was so unwavering that I cast Tabitha a "what the hell?" look, hoping that Josh didn't think me a snob. Not that I had anything to worry about, since his eyes hadn't left Tabitha.

Dressed in a tight blue T-shirt that set off his blue eyes, and with Celtic tattoos entwining his curvy biceps, Cameron was hot. Maybe, if Aidan hadn't stolen my heart, I might have even gone there. But Cameron couldn't compare with Aidan. How could anyone?

In fact, Aidan never left my thoughts. Aided by his heart-pumping texts, I kept reliving him, body and soul. So extreme were the sensations whenever I recalled how he felt inside of me that I even had to replace Toy Boy's batteries twice!

As I indulged in yet another of my Aidan moments, I caught Cameron's attention pitched at my breasts. They were pouring out of my new dress, which I adored because of its empire bodice and flattering, tulip-shaped line. White with red roses, it was so feminine and adorable. Still, I regretted wearing it. I'd had Aidan in mind when I bought it. But in this instance, with a seriously turned-on guy next to me, it sent out all the wrong messages.

Cameron kept inching closer. With every attempt I made to move, he responded by creeping back, bordering on comical. This was one very determined guy. I imagined he didn't take no for an answer.

I appreciated the break from his advances when he rose and rubbed his hands together. "What can I get you ladies?" Cameron's eyes started on my face and ran down to my cleavage again. And from where he hovered he had an excellent view.

"I'll have a coke, thanks," I replied.

He frowned. "Nothing stronger?"

"No, I'm good. Just coke, thanks."

Cameron did not hide his disappointment. I figured he wanted me drunk so that I'd spread my legs.

When he directed his attention to the lovers, Tabitha replied, "I'll have bourbon and coke, thanks."

"Another beer," said Josh, who hadn't spoken much. He appeared a quiet man, well suited to loquacious Tabitha, whose chattiness made it hard to get a word in.

Tabitha extricated herself from her boy's hold and stood up. "Back in a minute. Off to the powder room." She flicked her head, beckoning me to join her.

"What's your problem?" Tabitha asked, half whispering as we headed for the unisex restrooms.

"Nothing. I just don't want to give Cameron the wrong impression. He's trying to hit on me, and I'm not interested," I said.

"Yeah, okay, but stop being a snob."

There were no gender-specific restrooms, which was off-putting. Call me conservative, but I liked my restrooms segregated. I let Tabitha enter first. "Does it stink of male urine?" I asked, standing at the door.

"It smells of lavender, and it's really clean. You're so nineteenth century. Get with the times, girl."

Tabitha leaned into the mirror and reapplied her lipstick. "What do you think of Josh?"

I studied my plaits in the mirror, wondering if I looked too girly. "He seems lovely. And he's really crazy about you, Tabs."

Her pretty face brightened. "Do you reckon?"

I touched her cheek with sisterly affection and nodded. "I feel good about this one. But I'm not sleeping with Cameron." I pointed my finger at her.

"I've got it. Aidan Thornhill is one hot tamale, but just in case…"

"Just in case, Aidan drops me?" My throat tensed.

"Let's not do this, Clary. Anyway, Cameron's a hottie. And you never know. If Mr. -Sex-God-Tycoon doesn't work, then…" Tabitha stopped talking and put her arm around me, adding, "I'm just looking after my best friend, who has now become a woman." She played affectionately with my plaits then noticing my long face, added, "Why don't you call Aidan on my phone? Here." She handed me her phone.

"I haven't got his number."

"Well, then, relax. And let's have a fun night. Aidan has been sending you flowers and gifts every day. He won't lose interest just because you don't answer one text. Anyhow, you look so sexy in your little dress. You're driving Cameron crazy." Tabitha giggled, pulling a wicked expression.

I poked my tongue out at her.

Cameron's stare burned into me as we walked back to our places. As soon as Tabitha sat down, she wriggled into Josh's arms, and they kissed passionately.

"Hey, you two, get a room," said Cameron, laughing as he jumped up for more drinks. He eyed my glass. "Can I get you a shot of something?" When I shook my head, he fixed his stare at Josh, who nodded with enthusiasm. They were obviously out for a big night.

Cameron walked away with an unabashed swagger, his stride easy and confident.

When he returned, he nearly sat on top of me. Sliding away, I rolled my eyes at Tabitha. She returned a 'behave' with a puckering of the brow.

"So, what do you do, Cameron?" I asked.

"During the day, I'm a builder. At night, I'm a DJ," he said, all smiles and looking pleased with himself.

"It sounds like a busy life," I replied, searching for banter.

"I hear you work for the mega-rich Aidan Thornhill," Cameron said, raising an eyebrow.

I could not help wondering why he'd given me that look.

"I do," I answered curtly.

"He's a ladies' man, I hear, and a weirdo." Cameron lounged back with his arm around the back of the sofa, above my shoulder.

I stiffened. "What do you mean by that?"

"Word gets around." He met my questioning gape with a smug expression. "A friend of my mom's worked in the kitchen at his Malibu estate. He's well-known for fucking his staff and breaking their hearts."

A hot flush raided my face. "Did this friend of your mother's see this happening?"

"Not so much. But word got around. You know how folks are." His eyes had a sleazy tinge when he smiled. *Ick.*

"They could've been making it up," I said.

"My, aren't you his little champion for Thornhill," he said, grinning.

"He's kind and generous," I said, defensively. "What do you mean by him being a weirdo?"

He shrugged his broad shoulders. "For one, his gala nights—he gives all of it away to charity. But rumor has it, he's only doing that to dodge paying his taxes. And he accepts large wads of cash from the many women scouting for super-rich husbands, only to snub them."

That insight didn't faze me at all. In fact, it made me want Aidan more, if that were possible. However, the rumor about seducing female staff sent ice dripping through my veins. "That's not that weird."

Meanwhile, unable to resist her bit, Tabitha said, "Aidan Thornhill is at the top of Clarissa's people list at present. Nothing short of devil-worship would turn her against him."

Cameron grinned. "There's a whisper that he arrived at his wealth in questionable ways."

"How do you know so much?" I said, not hiding my exasperation. Cameron seemed determined to paint Aidan as a rogue. *He's jealous*, I reflected. How could he not be? Aidan was not only the sexiest man alive, but he was also wealthy.

"You're the only one that doesn't know much about him, Clary" chimed in Tabitha.

"Fuck, yeah," said Cameron, nodding. "He's the talk of LA."

I wanted to hear more about my mysterious boss turned lover, but I refrained from asking. I stared grimly at my feet while Cameron downed another shot. He pointed at the remaining shot. "Are you sure you don't want one?" His eyes were a little glassy. Having downed three shots, along with a few beers, he had to be slightly drunk.

"I don't normally drink heavy liquor," I said.

"What then, champagne? Wine? You can't sit on soda all night. That's not much fun." Cameron cast a wide white toothy grin.

Tabitha's face lit up with excitement at the mention of champagne, her beloved word. "Let's get bubbly, Clarissa. We're not driving, and you don't have to work tomorrow."

Finding it difficult to resist Tabitha, I agreed. That girl could get me to do almost anything. Only I was not going to have sex with Cameron. Aidan would be a hard act to follow. And he wasn't going anywhere if all the roses and regular text messages were anything to go by.

As it turned out, having a few champagnes worked a treat. I stopped thinking about my dead mobile phone and even laughed at some of Cameron's crude gags, even if he did fail to get the message by continuing to come on to me. His desire to bed me had become so blatant that he didn't even try to hide it.

Tabitha whispered, "Cameron's got it bad for you, Clarissa. You're giving that just-been-fucked vibe, babes."

I rolled my eyes and scowled.

"Here you are, a top-up." She held up the bottle of bubbly and filled my glass. "Later, we can go dancing. We'll go to that cool, jazzy club you like, the one where everybody looks like they're out of a 1960's film set."

Tabitha was, of course, referring to my preferred nightspot, Purple Haze. I loved it for the sixties and seventies music if not the interesting, eccentric characters.

My lips curled. "Let's. I'd love to dance." We nodded and clinked glasses.

The next half hour was spent playing a game of cat and mouse with Cameron. He would move up close—even after I told him I was seeing someone—and I'd move away.

Then things got interesting.

When Tabitha's eyes burst out of their sockets, I naturally assumed she was, as usual, being over-dramatic about something she'd seen, like someone dressed in the same outfit as one of us, or a guy she might have had casual sex with. But before my next breath, she knocked Cameron out of the way and was in my face. "Hey, don't look now, but I think Aidan's heading towards us."

I turned regardless. It was Aidan!

My jaw dropped. What was worse, I'd turned so abruptly that Cameron's arm slipped from the rim of the sofa and was now positioned around my shoulder.

It all happened within a matter of seconds. Before I had time to adjust my seating position, Aidan stood before me.

His eyes shifted from me to Cameron and back again. I sprang up from my seat and stumbled. "Mr. Thornhill," I stammered. "What brings you here? I thought you were in New York."

Aidan's eyes drew me in like magnets as he ran his hand through his hair. Living up to his most eligible *sexy bachelor* moniker, he looked impossibly handsome—casual in jeans and a white, loose linen shirt. An aura of power radiated off him.

"I had to come back for business." Aidan's eyes rested on Cameron again.

I kept shifting my weight from one leg to the other, while pointing to the seats occupied by my cohort. "Um… this is my friend Tabitha, her boyfriend, Josh, and Cameron," I said, wishing that Cameron would crumble to dust.

If looks could kill, then Cameron would have died. Aidan returned such a chilly stare to his imagined competitor, it made my veins freeze. He obviously thought I was romantically linked to Cameron. *Hell.*

Meanwhile, having been ignored all evening, suddenly our corner had become the focus of interest. The busy bar was almost at a standstill. Aidan's presence had cast a spotlight on us.

Aidan regarded my acquaintances with a quick sweep before returning his burning gaze to me. I must have resembled a startled creature in headlights. Speechless, I dug my nails hard into my palms.

"Have a good night," Aidan said.

After he extricated his attention away from me, Aidan cast one final cursory glance at the group, nodded, and walked off.

From jelly to concrete, my legs barely supported me as I watched him move away with ease and elegance.

Tabitha sprang up and whispered into my ear, "Go after him, for God's sake. He came here for you. Hurry!"

Although she managed to revive me a little, my body was heavy, almost drugged from the Thornhill spell. All wide-eyed and imploring, Tabitha pushed me out, and off I went to look for him. To add to an already sticky predicament, the patrons were all still riveted, watching our little corner as if it were a soap opera. Conscious of all that attention, I took relaxed steps. All the while, my heart thumped away because I wanted to run. But I managed to remain cool until I got to the door, after which I bolted to the parking lot.

Aidan was nowhere to be found. I pivoted on the spot, trying to locate him. It was incomprehensible how Aidan managed to disappear with such haste. As I remained glued there, the champagne churned away in my stomach, making me nauseous.

With frustrated resignation, I'd turned to go back when a husky voice penetrated through the back of my head.

I turned, and there stood Aidan, swinging keys in his hand.

CHAPTER TWENTY-FOUR

Aidan

In a bid to settle my racing heart, I leaned against a wall in the darkest corner I could find. My reaction surprised me. Seeing that blond dude's arm around Clarissa made me lose control. My fists were ready to punch his fucking smarmy face. I wanted to kill the jerk. How the fuck could Clarissa have moved on so quickly?

As I remained there, indecisive and swamped by emotion, I suddenly caught sight of Clarissa standing in the parking lot. My body released its tension. Seeing her in that tight little floral dress, her tits spilling out, and shapely, slender legs that I wanted to part and run my tongue over, made my anger evaporate in an instant.

Her luscious lips were open, and she was almost panting, a reminder of how she looked when I first entered her. My cock twitched. Even from a distance, she had that power over me.

My anger resurfaced. While this irrational, greedy need for her gripped my cock, my mind roared, *Who's that guy?*

"Lost something?" I asked, doing my utmost to remain cool—a technique I'd learnt from the army. *Never show emotion.* In love, I wasn't sure if that was the right tactical approach. But then, I'd never been in love. I was out of my depth. And was I in love, or just desperately in lust with this addictive girl?

Her wide brown stare had that bone-melting, lost look. "I... I wanted to say hello away from everyone." Clarissa's breathy and uncertain tone only added to her charm. I so wanted to hold her in my arms. She shook her head. "What are you doing here? I thought you were in New York."

You didn't answer my fucking texts. I remained enigmatic. It would make me seem a control-freak if she knew that I'd flown in just to see her.

"I had to come back for a last-minute meeting," I responded.

"Gee... that's a coincidence. You were in there all the time?" Her brow lifted sharply.

It felt horrible lying to her. I shook my head.

"Is that your man in there?" I snapped.

Her forehead puckered. "Cameron? Oh God, no... I only just met him. He's a friend of Tabitha's boyfriend. And against all my knowledge, they set up this date."

"He seemed close," I said, recalling the douche-bag's arm around her.

"Yeah, I know. He's super keen. But..." Clarissa smiled, and her pretty face lit up. I wanted to hold her so much. Instead, I settled for her soft little hand.

"Listen..." My eyes did a quick survey of the parking area and instantly caught a few people watching us. "Why don't we go somewhere, away from this? I'd love to hang out with you," I said, touching her warm, soft cheek.

"I'd love to. Only..." Clarissa glanced over to the entrance of the bar. "I have to tell my friend. Do you mind if I run in, and say goodbye?"

"Tell you what"—I pointed to the back of the venue—"I'll wait for you there. That's where my car's parked."

Clarissa didn't walk—she glided. I could have watched her all night, especially in that little dress, even if it was a bit too revealing for my liking. *For my eyes only.*

"Were your friends okay?" I asked when she came back, opening the door to my SUV.

"There were questions. But I managed to make something up," she said with a little smile.

I put my hand around her tiny waist to help her up. And her dress lifted. When I saw her red panties, my cock hardened.

Clarissa turned and gave me one of those girly, half-innocent, half-seductive smiles. *Phew.* I wanted this girl badly.

"Where would you like to go?" I asked.

Clarissa shrugged her shoulders.

"Are you hungry?"

"No. But if you want to go somewhere to eat, I'm good with that."

I reversed the car. "Why don't we go back to the coast? I'm dying for some sea air." I glanced at her. "Are you into that?"

"Sure, why not?" Clarissa sat back, looking uneasy. "You mean Malibu?"

"Is there a problem with that?" I asked, driving towards the Pacific Coast Highway.

"No. Only that I drove the electric car to my apartment. I was planning to visit my dad tomorrow."

"Easily solved." I smiled. "I'm flying out again in the morning. I'll drop you off."

"Okay, as long as it doesn't put you out. At least I'll be able to retrieve my phone charger."

"So that's why you didn't return my texts?"

"Yeah, I'm sorry about that. I left it back at the cottage." Clarissa crossed her legs. Every little move Clarissa made was erotic. I placed my hand on her naked thigh. The electricity ran up through my arm and all the way down to my aching cock. Boy, did I have it bad.

It was a perfect night. I was so glad to be back. New York was too hectic for me. I loved the coast, and the starry sky was magical.

As soon as I stepped out of the car, the salty air smacked my face, and in an instant, I was refreshed, my spirit and soul replenished.

While inhaling the energizing night air, I caught sight of an anxious Clarissa perched against the car. "What's up?" I asked, taking her hand.

"I'm worried that Greta will see us and Melanie and…"

I placed my finger on her soft lips. "Hey, no-one's around in the main house. After hours, it's my private space."

"What about Greta, Linus, Melanie, all the people I'm used to seeing about?"

"For starters, there's no security inside the house. I can look after myself." I nodded, and gave her a reassuring grin. "Greta lives separately at the back. Melanie doesn't work here anymore. We do have a new servant. She's around. But she's signed a privacy clause. This time, any gossip will lead to legal action. I take my privacy seriously."

Her eyebrows drew in sharply. "You got rid of Melanie?"

"She was caught stealing and talking too much. Worst of all, she gossiped to the media. Melanie knew the rules."

I went to plug in the SUV for the morning commute. When I returned, Clarissa hadn't moved. She still seemed worried about something. I took her hand. "Come on, then. I won't bite. Or do you want me to?" I said playfully. She tilted her head and smiled. Holding onto Clarissa's waist, I wanted to draw her in and kiss her badly, especially after I caught a whiff of her jasmine-infused hair. But there was still some tightness in her frame.

After I opened the front door, Clarissa took a step back. She was really on edge by then.

"Are we going in this way?" she asked in a whisper.

I took her into my arms and kissed her. She was so warm, soft, and moist that my mouth wanted to plow right in. But her moody state directed me otherwise. "What other way is there?" I said, brushing her cheek.

"My contract… I thought I'm not meant to be here." She looked freaked out.

"Hey, Clarissa… this is my home. I make the rules."

She was somewhere else and didn't seem to hear me. "I really love my job, the cottage, the estate, the beach, everything." Clarissa sighed. "And I signed a clause that stated under no circumstance should I enter the house after working hours. I will lose my job if I do."

"Consider that void as of now," I said, kissing her hand. "You can enter this way anytime you like. I'll even tear up the contract and write a new one. This time, I'll put in a few extra clauses."

"And what might they be?" Clarissa asked, arching an eyebrow.

I held my chin and contorted my face pensively. "Let's see, now. Whenever she's around her boss, she must wear low-cut blouses with buttons and sexy underwear, though preferably none."

She tapped my arm playfully. "You're a shameless reprobate."

Ah… that was better. Feeling lighter at last, I opened the door and bowed. "After you."

With an air of unself-conscious sensuality, Clarissa stroked the marble sculpture of Venus.

"Don't you look the natural here. Soon as I saw you, I knew you would be an excellent fit."

"You make me sound as if I'm a fixture," said Clarissa with a note of scorn. Instead of a joking grin, she had an earnest mien.

Shaking my head, I said, "Clarissa, that wasn't what I meant."

She didn't respond. Talking about emotions was not my strong point. If anything, it tangled me up.

I walked up the stairs and turned on the lights while Clarissa remained below, watching. She appeared to be waiting for something.

"Come on. No ghosts—the coast is clear," I said, attempting to lighten her mood.

"Did you really watch us that day?" Clarissa asked, joining me on the landing.

"Yes," I replied, ill at ease. "As soon as you appeared, I knew you were the one for the job." I smiled gently while playing with one of her plaits.

"Why me?"

I placed my arm around her waist and drew her into me. "Call it instinct." Clarissa needed more. I could see it in her face. "I wasn't looking for a girlfriend if that's what you're asking. God knows that was the furthest thing from my mind, Clarissa. I was looking for someone down to earth, who didn't pout every time she was around me. Not that I mind you pouting." I brushed her plump cherry lips with my thumb.

A subtle smile touched her lips. Clarissa lowered her eyes. "Why were you there tonight?"

Because of you. Because I can't get you out of my mind.

Even though I had this coming, it was becoming intense. "I'd dropped in to see someone." My neck muscles tightened. I hated lying.

"What— at the Escape? You know someone there?" Her eyes widened.

"No…" I stopped and turned to face her. I took her hand. "I came looking for you."

"What?" Her face contorted in shock. "How did you find me?"

"I tracked your phone."

She took a moment to answer. "You stalked me?"

"Look, I know it sounds bad, but…" I needed a drink. "Let's go up."

She remained glued to the spot. Her spooked expression was harrowing.

"Clarissa… I got worried. We'd been communicating every day, and then suddenly, nothing."

"Did you come all this way from New York just to see me?"

I froze. It did seem extreme. Where was my inner strength? "No, Clarissa, I had a meeting, and while here, I thought I'd look for you. I just wanted to see that you were all right, that's all." I pushed hair away from my face. "I'm a tad overprotective."

I kissed her hand, and her face softened. Her body relaxed, and she let me hold her hand. My stomach unknotted. One thing was for certain: Clarissa had knocked me out of my comfort zone.

CHAPTER TWENTY-FIVE

"I've never been down this end of the house before," said Clarissa as we climbed up to the second floor, still holding hands. The softness of her palm and the heat from her petite hand generated electrical currents through me.

When we landed on the second floor, I asked, "Would you like a quick tour?" Clarissa, absorbed in the artwork, glanced up at me. She looked flushed as she always did when staring at art.

I loved her creative spirit.

"I would love that." Clarissa smiled.

Knowing of her father's literary background, I directed her to the library first. Her surprised delight made the room even more special. Her eyes swept about the room. "Wow... this is incredible." Clarissa ran her finger over the spine of a gold scrolled book. "It has that distinct smell of old books."

I just stood and watched, thrilled at seeing Clarissa overjoyed.

"Oh my God—Celtic scroll. How magnificent." She peered down at a glass table housing the medieval text. "Did you buy this at an auction?"

I shook my head. "The whole collection came with the house. I fell in love with it. The former owner, a famous 1930's Hollywood producer, was an avid collector of original editions and rare books."

"And he sold the entire stock to you? It must have cost a fortune," she said, sounding all breathy and sexy. "Do you mind if I touch it?"

Only if you let me touch you.

"Please. You can borrow one if you like—I don't mind. I love the idea of them being read, enjoyed."

"Why didn't he auction them? I wonder," Clarissa said.

"It was a deceased estate. The son had debts up to his ears. He wanted an easy transaction, a quick sale."

Her eyes danced with amusement. "Ah... the prodigal son." She giggled, sending a warm buzz through me.

Just seeing her perched over the glass table, those glorious breasts spilling out, leaning on her slender arms, put my mind in a haze of desire.

"Consider this room open access to you and your father. Twenty-four, seven. In fact, I have a proposition."

Clarissa looked up at me, her eyes glistening with interest. I could have eaten her, she was so ravishing.

"I need these volumes catalogued. My insurer has been on my back for a while now. Do you think your father would be interested?"

Her mouth dropped open.

I added, "With compensation, of course—a proper contract befitting a professor of his standing and a little more."

Clarissa hadn't blinked. Her rosy, full lips parted, all moist, crying out for my mouth. "That would be amazing." I noticed her eyes misting over.

I held her. "I didn't mean to upset you."

"You didn't. It's just that this would be such a wonderful gift for my father. He's been struggling for a while. And it would be a dream job for him. That is… if you…" She pulled away from me. I needed her back. Her soft body had become an addiction.

"If I what? Anything—just come here again." I took her in my arms again.

"Would he be able to take his time and read as well? You wouldn't have to pay for that, of course."

I laughed, my heart spilling over. "You're a kind and caring daughter. I hope my daughter one day has a heart as big as yours."

Our lips finally met. My need for Clarissa was so intense I had to avoid crushing her. With much reluctance, I undid my hold. "I'll never leave this room… if we continue doing this."

"My father would love that job. I noticed you had *Bleak House*. It's one of his most cherished books." Her face filled with wonder. She was such a pure soul.

"Come on." I crooked my finger. "Let's get a drink."

Clarissa paused and pointed at a door. "What's in there?"

"Just some toys," I replied dismissively. The night was leaving, and I needed this girl in my arms, naked.

Clarissa's natural curiosity filled her face. "I'd love to have a look." That luscious smile had me capitulating in a flash.

"Just keep looking at me like that, Clarissa, and you can ask anything of me," I said, brushing her cheek.

When I turned on the light, the space with wall-to-wall guitars came alive.

"Do you play?" Clarissa approached the wall, where every single model of electric guitar ever produced was on display. On the ground were even more guitars in hard cases.

"A little," I said, sighing. The talk of music always produced the same result: frustration.

"You do?" Clarissa tilted her head, looking impressed.

"I'm not that good. My father"—I pointed to a framed photo of him— "is the musician."

Clarissa studied the image of my younger father with a guitar on his lap. "It's a fantastic shot. He looks like you," said Clarissa with surprise in her voice.

"Well, he is my dad."

My legs locked as Clarissa continued to study the picture. "You sound sad," she said.

"I'm not." I painted a smile.

She studied me closely. I sensed she was too intuitive for bullshit. "I'd love to hear you play." She stroked the machine head of the guitar standing up. It was such a sensuous gesture my skin puckered.

"You chose my most revered, the Ferrari. You exude fabulous taste, Miss Moone."

"Ferrari? Is that what it's called?" Clarissa's lips curled with amusement.

"No. It's a name I made up for it. It's all shiny, red, and living up to its fine appearance. The guitar is a fiery little monster."

Clarissa giggled. "That's so cool. I'd love to hear you play it."

"One day," I said, taking her by the hand. I wanted to leave the room.

She remained fixated on the guitar as if she was trying to learn something from it. It was strangely moving. "I still don't get why you're sad." Clarissa looked up at me.

"I didn't think I was." My chuckle was tight. I lost myself in her large brown eyes.

"Why didn't you want to enter this room?"

"Because I missed my chance at doing something I love. Doing it well, I mean." I sighed. I didn't want to do this now. Our power had shifted. She was in control. And for some twisted reason, I desired her more for it.

"But music is eternal," she murmured softly.

I shut the door to the room. "That's profound," I said in a weak voice. Clarissa had hit a nerve.

I flicked a switch, and the lamps in my bedroom all lit up at once. It was a massive space, taking up the entire area of the top floor.

"Oh…" Clarissa sighed. "How splendid." She turned about, and her dress flared out.

"And that is even more so," I said with a smile. The time to play was nigh. My emotions had already had more airing than was comfortable. I needed to suckle on those nipples, which provoked me as they pushed out of that eye-catching floral dress.

I headed to the bar and opened the fridge. "What can I offer you? Wine, champagne, beer? Something stronger?"

She shrugged. "What are you having?"

I opened the fridge and grabbed a bottle of Sauvignon Blanc. "How's white wine sound?"

Distracted by my busy space, Clarissa nodded. "I so like the color of the walls. Not quite turquoise but not pale-blue either. Nice."

"I'm glad you like it. I only just had it repainted. It was a pale lemon before."

Her eyes settled on the painting facing my bed. "You moved the Godward from the ballroom."

I passed the glass of wine to her. "Yes, well, I had to have it in here. She's you."

Clarissa turned and looked at me. A line formed between her eyebrows. "I've got the same hair, I suppose." She examined the painting.

"You're more beautiful. But the other night when you were asleep, I realized how alike you were, especially with your hair out." My eyes seared into her. "Only you were naked." I lifted her heavy plaits. "When do we undo these?"

Clarissa's lips curled gloriously as she let me unravel her hair. After that, she ran her fingers through the waist-length black hair.

As she stood before me with waves in her hair, I shook my head. "Clarissa, you'll be my undoing." As I took her into my arms, she molded into me effortlessly. Our lips met. Hers felt hot, moist, and soft—pure sensuality. When that word was invented, they had Clarissa in mind.

I tried to take things slowly, but when I felt her tongue, my need went up a gear. My hands ran up her smooth, naked legs. Her panties were so wet I hissed. I waltzed her to the bed, and we fell onto it, entwined.

I released her so I could remove my jeans.

All the while, Clarissa watched me. Her eyes travelled down to my hard cock. She bit her lip, and her eyelids grew heavier.

"We need to get you naked," I said, finding it hard to speak from the anticipation. I lifted her dress and nearly swallowed my tongue when I saw her soft flesh primed for the taking. Her breasts were barely covered by a red lacy bra. Clarissa allowed me to remove her tiny panties. Oh my.

Her heavy tits fell into my hands. My heart felt like it would leap out of my chest. Her erect nipples had me salivating. I sucked on them, played with them with my tongue, her body undulating as her breathing becoming heavier.

I pulled away, and she glanced at me imploringly. She didn't want me to stop. Good, neither did I. "I must show you something," I said, so aroused my legs were weak.

A sheet I'd placed by my bed fell into my hand. Life was too short. I could not deprive myself of skin on skin with this little angel.

Clarissa frowned. "It's a blood test. Why are you showing me this?"

"It proves that I'm STD free." I removed the document from her hands and held her again. "It means, gorgeous girl, that I can feel you properly," I said, caressing her heaving breasts. "You mentioned that you started the pill, a week ago. Are you protected?"

She nodded sweetly.

Our lips met again. She opened her mouth suggestively, her velvety tongue wet and ready. She was pure sex, unconsciously so.

My fingers travelled down her soft thigh. She opened her legs for me. The image would never leave me: her eyes shut, lips open, nipples erect. Hungering for her musky earth flavor, I needed to make a meal of her cunt. When my tongue landed on her swollen clit, I felt her flinch. Her legs stiffened by my side.

"I probably should shower," she murmured softly.

"You're not going anywhere. You're like a rose," I muttered, my head still buried low.

She was slick and sticky to my touch. I fluttered my tongue over her swollen bud and felt her pelvis rise gently. She gyrated, her moans vibrating through her. My tongue rotated, licked, and devoured, supping on her creamy nectar. Her juices flooded my mouth. As she scaled the throes of deep pleasure, my tongue was relentless. I wanted her crazy and desperate. Clarissa's agonized legato moans were pure music, my prize.

I entered her through a thick, creamy slick. One finger first. "You're so tight, my angel." I entered her with two fingers. "How's that? I need to fuck you badly, but I don't want to bruise you."

"It feels really nice," she purred.

I held my heavy cock in my hand. There was hunger in her smoldering dark eyes, breaking me. I would not last.

One inch at a time, I entered her. And my, she felt incredible, my groan reflecting every little inch of bliss. Blood raged through me. Fighting the urge to thrust hard, I eased.

"Please, don't stop," she whimpered. The need in her voice impelled me to enter farther. As I did, Clarissa widened her legs and clasped onto my ass, impelling me to fill her. Her moans strengthened.

"Are you okay?" I asked, struggling to speak. Her wet cunt strangled my impatient cock.

"Yes," she rasped.

I pushed in as far as possible—not balls deep, she was too small for that. Even so, the pleasure was so extreme that my breathing became heavy. I pulled out slowly and then pushed in again. Clarissa vacuumed me up with her tight little muscles.

Her panting increased. With each entry, the heat, her creamy sex devoured me. Our breathing merged into one tormented sound. I was losing myself in her. My little supple goddess had her legs wide apart, urging my thrusts to accelerate.

Within barely a minute, I shot out and filled her in what seemed an endless deluge. An entire week of fantasies flowed out of me. Skin on skin, the sensation, indescribable. Blood coursed through me, my heart banged hard against my ribcage, as I cried out her name.

To avoid crushing her, I rolled Clarissa onto her side. For the first time all week, my muscles slackened.

"I'm sorry I came so quickly. I didn't make you come," I said, pushing a strand of ink-black hair away from her face.

"I orgasmed." Her eyes held a wicked smile.

"Why, Miss Moone, I think you enjoyed that," I said, stroking her cheek.

"I did. Only…"

"Only?"

"I could go again," she said, looking up at me, eating me with her passionate wide gaze.

"I may need a few moments," I said, tapping her dainty nose. Normally, it would take me a while to harden after fucking. But with the need in her eyes, her mouth-watering hardened nipples, the way her long black hair fell provocatively over her white breasts, Clarissa had my cock under a spell.

"I can take you in my mouth if you like," she said girlishly. Now, that clinched the deal—I was rock-hard.

"That would be something else." I ran my finger over her cushiony soft lips. "Only, my cock needs to be inside you again."

CHAPTER TWENTY-SIX

Clarissa

Aidan's thick cock expanded in my hand. I was barely able to hold it. The veins vibrated on my palm. The memory of having his cock in my mouth had made me steamy all week. It was so irresistible, I slid down the bed.

Aidan stopped me. "I want to come inside of you again, Clarissa," he said in a raspy voice that sent a pleasurable throb whirling through me.

The greedy need for more orgasms swept through me. Although his silky tongue had taken me to a place I never wanted to leave, it was his hard, imploring penis that sent me to an erotic version of nirvana.

Was this what they meant by a deal with a devil? If so, I'd landed it, given that these moments of sheer bliss were worth any potential heartbreak. Then again, were they? Whichever way, Aidan Thornhill had certainly taken possession of my body, heart, and soul.

My legs wide, Aidan's expert touch sent me over the top again. He made me orgasm within seconds of circling my engorged clit. Toy Boy was incapable of that, and no fantasy could compare with Aidan.

I guided his velvety-hard length. The anticipation had me almost hyperventilating.

While I placed him inside of me, Aidan's big blue eyes burned into me. "I love you taking control, Princess."

The stretch was so divine I shivered with pleasure. His slow, almost tentative entry robbed me of air.

Our eyes locked. The fire between my legs was so intense that I involuntarily contracted around his hard cock. Waves of sensation ran through me. A growl vibrated up through his ribcage, out of his mouth and into mine. His tremulous muscular frame sculpted into me as he clasped me tight.

Aidan's eyes filled with fragile longing as his cock slid in. In that blue, devouring stare, I saw the sky. Or was I flying?

A tentative push and then he penetrated deeply. My pelvis flexed up to meet his insistent movements, and I gripped his firm, hard butt. Aidan's greedy hands were all over my heavy breasts. His cock was so hard it threatened to tear me in half.

I wanted it to hurt, to ravish me.

Aidan's golden-brown hair was tousled from my restless hands. His lips were half-opened, his gasps increasing in volume.

Electrical impulses sent waves of heat, raw and primal, into my sex. He moved quicker and harder, the friction from each thrust hot and intense— like the blending of sweet and sour. Pain and pleasure married.

My muscles unraveled as I submitted to the pure bliss of taking him whole. Aidan had metamorphosed into a wild, sexy beast, his face red-hot. Coated in lusty desire, his darkened eyes threatened to ravage me entirely.

I clasped on tightly to his strong, muscular arms as we built up to a ferocious tempo. Driven by pure need, he pounded into me, his heavy balls hitting against my clit. A threatening eruption grew with each thrust. One wave of warm, liquid delight after another grew in strength. The faster and harder he fucked me, the more frenzied became the spasms within until it became so unbearable I had to let go. And off I went, one warm impulse after another, each time more intense. Starved of air, I felt a rainbow of color dissolve into me. I levitated while the room spun around.

My God, this was one hell of a drug.

Meanwhile, back on earth, I'd swallowed Aidan whole. My legs clasped around his muscular thighs, my nails digging into his strong shoulders. My cheeks were dampened with tears. It was pure and raw, incomprehensible emotion. And even more perplexing was my chest, heavy with love.

Aidan was about to be swept away, his remote, but devouring gaze told me so. His jaw tensed, face contorted, and the cry of a wolf reverberated from him. The whole room vibrated with "Clarissaaaa." Then pure heat charged up, filling me with a hot torrent of semen.

Our bodies, sweaty and sated, breathed together as one.

"Clarissa, I've never experienced anyone like you before." Aidan's throat was thick with emotion.

Just as overwhelmed, I'd lost my ability to speak. Apprehensive that should my mouth open, tears would explode, I remained silent in his arms. Aidan pulled away and gazed into my face, brushing my tear-soaked cheek.

His kiss was so tender it was almost chaste.

When I woke, Aidan was tangled around me. Although he radiated so much heat, I was reluctant to leave his arms in case of waking him. Mouth agape, Aidan was in a deep sleep. Even like that, his hair messy and those captivating eyes hidden, Aidan was still devastatingly handsome.

In the meantime, there was plenty to distract me. Casting my attention upward, I was entertained by swirly cornices with carved angels' faces. Painted white, they stood out against the pale-teal ceiling, which was a shade lighter than the walls.

Splashed in daylight, the grand room, replete with adorable objects, seemed to come alive.

None of that could keep me away for too long, no matter how awe-inspiring, as my eyes returned to Aidan. His strong body, those shapely arms capable of lifting me effortlessly, and his movie-star looks made him the prize-winner in that beguiling room.

The guitar in the corner only intensified my attraction. I had a weakness for creative men.

Aidan moved in my arms. "Good morning, Princess." His eyes were clear and so turquoise blue I was rendered breathless.

"Hi," I said, moving out of his arms.

"Where are you going?" He pulled me back, and I settled in again. Our bodies melded together so comfortably, I never wanted to leave. "What time is it, my angel?"

"I don't know," I answered.

Aidan regarded the gilded French clock sitting over the fireplace. "Holy shit!" He sprang up. "It's nine. I've got to be in New York by midday." Running his fingers through his hair, Aidan said, "I've never slept this late before. I don't normally sleep much at all."

He caressed my arm, making my skin pucker. "Tell me, did I talk in my sleep?" Aidan looked serious suddenly.

"Not that I'm aware of," I replied.

"I wish I didn't have to leave." Aidan leapt out of bed. It was jarring. I missed him instantly.

Aidan's masculine fluidity was nothing but eye-candy. All lean muscle, a six-foot-two hunk of perfection. My gaze followed him as he looked out of the French doors.

He was comfortable in his nakedness, his cock semi-erect. Aidan turned and regarded me. The sheets were off me, which I'd arranged on purpose. I wanted to seduce him. It worked. His eyes became hooded, and his mouth-watering cock lengthened.

"Come and have a shower with me." He picked up the receiver of his phone. "Can I have two coffees, some fresh juice, and whatever's just been baked? Good... yep... in fifteen minutes... fine."

He hung up and approached me, his eyes twinkling with playful intent. He ran his hand up my leg, and his lips met mine. It was instant heat. "Come here, my little beauty." He balanced me in his strong, muscly arms.

I'd never been in such a roomy shower before. Aidan held me as the water cascaded over us. His needy erection pushed against my leg. "God, I wish I wasn't in such a hurry," he said, squeezing my bottom and running his hands up and down my body. Stopping at my breasts, he licked his luscious lips and went on to ravage my nipples. I was like jelly and as sticky as tar.

Aidan's fingers settled between my legs. He parted my aching pussy and entered with his finger, hissing. "You're so ready and juicy."

He towered over me. *How was that going to work?*

Aidan turned me around, his hands on my breasts, his heart beating between my shoulder blades. "Can I take you hard?"

"Yes," I whimpered. My butt was against his stomach. He entered me in one push. "Clarissa..." He shuddered. "Your pussy is addictive." He pushed deeper. It was pure fire. His heavy balls thudded against my cheeks. It was so erotic I simply rippled into his hard body. He leaned in very close. The words "fucking exquisite" bounced off my cheek.

The hot water, the urgent pounding, his fingers working magic on my clit, made me come so wildly my cries echoed off the tiles. At the same time, what started as a strangled groan grew so intense in volume that Aidan sounded as if he was dying. My name stretched out of his lips as a torrent of hot cream gushed up in me.

After our senses had returned, Aidan chuckled. "I guess we better do what we came here to do." He squirted some divinely fragrant body wash on a sponge and washed me.

He was in his own world as he cleaned every inch of my flesh. He need not have washed my breasts as thoroughly as he did.

When it was my turn, I did the same, except for his penis and heavy balls—I left that to him. Despite a hankering to take him in my mouth, I knew that he was on a tight schedule, so I abstained.

The knock at the door sent me off to hide in the bathroom. Aidan laughed. "Hey, where are you going?"

I didn't know what annoyed me more—the attractive new maid or that Aidan answered the door with only a towel covering him from waist to knees.

As she wheeled in our breakfast, I noticed with major dissatisfaction how sexy she was. Confident and swaying her well-shaped bottom, she went all gaga-eyed at her new boss. I needn't have worried about being spotted because she ignored me entirely.

It was all flirty smiles. Boy, did I miss Melanie. My stomach churned away. I was green with jealousy. How could I not be? Aidan casually pranced about half-naked, looking like a sex god in his barely-there towel, those mouth-watering, rippling pectorals all golden, with a smattering of golden hair, crying out to be touched.

To add to my angst, Aidan's towel hugged him precariously. The thought of it unravelling was enough to make my breath hitch.

"Thanks. It's Susana, isn't it?"

She nodded, sashaying about in her tight-fitted jeans and low-cut blouse. She wasn't as busty as me, but rather annoyingly she had a very curvy, wiggly butt.

Her eyes travelled from Aidan's face to his body. When Susana smiled, all heavy-lidded and coquettishly, she had an expression that said, *I can't wait to fuck you,* causing my hands to fist.

"Just put everything there," said Aidan, pointing to a table out on the balcony.

After she left, I said, "She was flirting with you, Aidan." I zipped up my dress.

"I didn't notice." Aidan smiled innocently. He was either acting oblivious to protect me, or he just couldn't see how he had affected her. Stroking my hair, Aidan said, "In any case, I'm not into blondes."

A dark cloud had drifted over me, nevertheless, reminding me how vulnerable I was.

"Oh, my princess, you're jealous." Aidan shook his head, and a lopsided smile formed. "You have nothing to be jealous about. I like my girls to have long black hair and large brown eyes." His finger trailed over my lips and then travelled down to my cleavage, burrowing in between my breasts, sending my pulse pumping. "She's nothing like you. No-one is." Aidan had turned serious. "And no-one has been where I've been. I've never had that with a woman before." He held me tight.

I was helplessly lost in him.

CHAPTER TWENTY- SEVEN

Aidan drove faster than I liked. After my mother's accident, I was paranoid about being a passenger in a speeding vehicle. But he also demonstrated proficiency and confidence as a driver, so I soon released my white knuckles.

"Why did you ask me if you'd spoken in your sleep?" I asked as we drove speedily along the busy highway.

Aidan shrugged. "I've been known to be a noisy sleeper."

This abridged response failed to answer my question. I recalled the tightening of his jaw when he'd asked me earlier. I didn't want to push.

Having turned on some music, Aidan entertained me by singing along with the Doors. With his hand on my thigh, along with the occasional eye-twinkling glance, he knew all the lyrics as he sang along with "Come on Baby Light My Fire."

The ordinary, almost shabby appearance of our apartment block, particularly after the opulence of Aidan's world, made me recoil.

"Would you like to come in?" I asked, hoping Aidan would decline.

He brushed my cheek. "No, beautiful girl, I really have to hurry along. My pilot will be waiting for me." He held me. "Our time together has been too short. We can spend next weekend together." Aidan pulled away. "That's if you want to."

"Of course," I said, releasing the car door.

"Wait." Aidan jumped out of the car. He raced to my side and opened the door. Before I could speak, Aidan lifted me up and onto the sidewalk.

"How chivalrous," I said, my heart all aflutter.

"You're very light." Aidan tucked a strand of my hair behind my ear. "I'll call you. Make sure you have your phone on." He hugged me.

I stood by the curb watching my new lover drive off. Asking myself if this was real, my body answered with a resounding yes, as a delightful, addictive ache rang up my legs.

After I entered my apartment, I headed for the fridge to grab a juice from the fridge. "Where's Josh?" I asked Tabitha, who was slouched on the sofa.

"He had to go to work."

"What, on Sunday?"

"That's what I said," responded Tabitha, all long-faced.

I touched her arm. "What's up Tabs?"

Her hair was unusually messy. She really had the blues. "I just feel so alone."

"Why, because Josh is working on a Sunday?"

"My life's going nowhere, Clary."

I looked at the clock. "Hey, let's go to Sammy's for coffee and cake, and then you can come with me to visit Dad."

"Coffee and cake sounds yummy." She sprang off the sofa in a flash. In typical Tabitha fashion at the mention of an outing, life suddenly brightened.

"I'll pass on the lunch, though. I've got a few things I should be doing," said Tabitha, combing her hair.

Reverting to the old me, I dressed in a modest, floral shift, and slipped on my flat pumps. Tabitha entered and sat on the edge of the bed. "Aidan's nuts about you, baby."

She watched me in the mirror brushing my hair. "I reckon he came looking for you after you didn't return his texts."

"He said he had some business there, but he also confessed to tracking me down."

Tabi's green eyes sparkled keenly. "Shit, stalking as well. Wow, Clary, he's really got it bad. But your phone had a flat battery. How did he do it?"

Good question.

"No idea. He's a man of great means, so I suppose he's got his ways." I twisted my hair into a bun and clipped it down.

"You didn't ask him?" she asked.

I shook my head. "I wanted to pick his brain. I suppose his big blue eyes and those searching hands of his led me astray."

Tabitha laughed raucously. "I thought he was going to knock Cameron's teeth in. The air was so thick with testosterone. It was very entertaining."

"Entertaining? I'd hardly call it that." Softening my tone, I asked, "So do you think he's into me?"

"Fuck, yeah. It's written all over him. And why shouldn't he be? You're one hot babe. You looked very sexy in that little dress of yours. Poor Cameron's heart was broken after you left. He was bereft."

My phone pinged. "Probably Dad. We'd better go," I said, getting my phone out of my bag. My heart jumped. The message was from Aidan: *I'm already missing you. XXX Aidan.*

My face must have given it away because Tabitha asked, "Let me guess— Aidan?"

I nodded. A wide smile stretched my face.

"See? Told you he's got it bad," Tabitha chanted. She pulled one of her silly faces and made me laugh—a throwback from our younger years. Tabitha loved to pull faces, often behind a superior's back, leaving me alone to face that person. We used to kill ourselves laughing afterwards and I always forgave her.

We'd had different reactions to the deaths of our mothers. Tabitha didn't handle her mother's death to cancer well, hiding her sorrow behind a guise of rebelliousness. I hid mine in books and playing mother to my distraught father.

CHAPTER TWENTY-EIGHT

My father headed straight for the glass cabinet. A startled expression filled his face. "It's original Celtic scroll." His voice was filled with more emotion than I'd recalled in some time.

When Greta showed us the guest room earlier, I was relieved to discover that it was on the ground floor. Then the realization hit me: my father would spend much of his waking time in the library. What if my screams travelled while I was in the throes of an orgasm? *Oh, hell.*

And then there was Greta. I had developed a close relationship with her. How would she take to my sleeping with Aidan? It was all too complicated for my overwrought mind.

After settling my father in, I decided on a walk around the grounds to empty my mind. I had invited my father, but he was lost in library wonderland as if it contained some time-shifting magic. Something told me he might never leave that room. I would have to remember to ask Aidan if his room was soundproofed.

My beloved old elm tree caught my eye, and I decided to pause there as I lowered my sex-drugged body to the ground. Was innocence simpler? Yes. Was it better? No.

A whiff of sea air hit my face. I inhaled it deeply. It only ever took one puff to feel restored and empowered. Strange really—I could conquer everything when surrounded by nature. My insecurities kind of dissolved.

Thoughts drifted off with the wind as I pulled at the grass. The delicious throb between my legs kept activating memories of how Aidan felt—something I kept reliving over and over again. Then, without warning, I cried, releasing salty tears like the sea-air circling around me. I'd become fragile and needy. Aidan had dug that deeply into me. I no longer recognized myself. I smelt him on my skin. I felt him filling me deeply by rubbing my thighs together.

Heavy panting woke me out of my Aidan-filled reverie. I glanced up and saw Rocket. "Hello boy." I patted him as his tail wagged enthusiastically. He seemed so happy to see me, his dark eyes ebullient and loving as ever. "Where have you been hiding?"

A young man ran up to me and said, "Sorry about that." He was about my age. His eyes fired up when he saw me. "I'm Roland." He held out his hand.

"I'm Clarissa," I said, rubbing Rocket's white chest.

"Oh, you're the new PA, aren't you?" Roland had smiling blue eyes and sun- bleached hair.

I nodded. "Are you employed to look after Rocket?"

He chuckled. "Amongst other things. I'm the gardener mainly, although I've been away on a surfing trip. I normally live at the back."

"Oh, like me. I'm in the cottage behind the kitchen."

"Makes sense. That's where Amy used to live."

"What was she like?" I asked brazenly. Curiosity trumped any discretion I would normally have exercised.

"She was okay, I suppose. A bit high-strung." Roland sat down on the ground.

"You knew her well, then?"

"You could say that," said Roland in a grim tone.

"Oh, were you together?" I asked. He nodded.

"For a while, but then she had a fling with Aidan."

"That must have hurt."

"It did. But Aidan was her prize catch. She didn't consider that he would just use her. You know he's a bit of a ladies' man?" Roland picked at the grass. He looked up and studied my face. Was he trying to warn me?

"He lured her, then?" I asked.

"No. Aidan's not like that. He's actually a good person. She got drunk and ended up in his room. She was kind of sexy. It would have been hard to resist her."

Ouch. That was extremely jarring. Ice filled my veins. Oh, why did I have to go there? Like a true masochist, I persisted nevertheless. "So did it keep happening, this thing between with her and Aidan?"

He shook his head. "No. It was one night only. From what I heard, Aidan tried to calm her down. Amy was a mess." Roland sighed. "After that, she lost her job, mainly because she made such a scene."

I nodded.

"And then Aidan's fiancée entered the fray and..." He chuckled.

"Fiancée?" My eyes bulged out of my head. "He's got a fiancée?"

"Last time I heard." Roland stood up.

I wanted to ask more questions, but figured I'd already probably pushed my limit.

The rest of the day was a blur. When I joined my father for dinner, at his urging, I was as pale as a ghost. Although he was off in literary la la land, my father did still notice. When he patted my hand, I felt such a lump in my throat, I had to leave, claiming to have a headache.

In any case, Greta was there fussing over him. And Dad looked very fetching in his hounds-tooth jacket with leather patches and silk scarf.

As soon as I arrived back to the cottage, I flicked up my laptop and went on a search, googling Aidan Thornhill's fiancée. Within a click, I was staring at a leggy redhead standing intimately close to him. Her eyes were on him while he had an aloof expression. *Shit.*

She was gorgeous in a confected way—tall and slinky. How was it we didn't find this out when Tabitha went on her googling mission? I suppose we didn't ask the right questions.

My heart froze. Tossed from such a high, I was now crawling on my stomach in a dark, cold place.

I jumped when my phone buzzed. It was Aidan, so I sent it off to voicemail. He didn't leave a message. It rang again. This time, I turned my phone off.

The following day, I was in the office. I'd hardly slept. Nevertheless, grateful for the distraction, I worked like a maniac, tallying up the accounts for all Thornhill Holdings' charities. I was too nauseous to eat. Boy, I had it bad.

Around mid-morning, the office phone rang, and I answered it. At the other end I heard a husky, "Clarissa." It was Aidan.

"Oh… hi," I replied, trembling.

"Why haven't you left your phone on? I've been trying to call you all night. And this morning… I'm going to have get you a few phones, I think," said Aidan, not hiding his annoyance.

That riled me. I hadn't slept, and my emotions were raw. "When were you going to tell me about Jessica Mansfield?"

There was silence at the other end.

"That's what I thought. Look, Aidan, thanks for everything. I love my job. So I'll find a way to get over…" I couldn't say it. My voice cracked. Tears threatened to crush me.

"It's not what you think. I've left her. I left her before we got together. It's just not public record yet."

"Apparently, you're a ladies' man," I said quietly.

"Who the fuck has been filling you with this shit?"

"Aidan, I can't talk now. I hope you'll let me keep my job."

"Don't be ridiculous. Of course, the job's yours. Don't do this, Clarissa."

"I have to get back to work." I could barely speak. My voice was swamped by the threat of tears. I hung up quickly. My hands shook.

By day's end, I'd finished the entire accounts. Considering they should have taken me a week to complete, Greta looked both impressed and perplexed. She intuited something was wrong.

Greta, on the other hand, looked prettier than usual with her hair down and sporting a feminine blouse. She was also unusually buoyant. Blessed with Aidan's blue eyes, she was looking very attractive.

Before heading back to the cottage, I decided to drop in on my father. Not surprisingly, I found him in a leather armchair, lost in a book. It was such a moving image that tears welled up.

My father peered up over his spectacles. "Hello, Clarissa." He smiled and appeared well rested. It had been awhile since I'd seen him looking so well.

I entered the library and hugged him.

He studied me, and a frown developed. "Are you all right, sweetheart? You don't seem well." My father placed his book down carefully on the walnut table.

"I'm okay, Daddy," I said, mustering the strength to avoid crying. I tilted my head towards his book. "Poe. You're reading Edgar Allan Poe."

My father's dark eyes glowed as if he'd encountered something metaphysical. "Oh, it's wondrous. A first edition. I can't put it down."

"American Literature. I would've thought you'd be obsessing over his Dickens collection, particularly *Bleak House*." I ran my eyes over the extraordinary collection, housed in dark, wooden shelves.

"I'm getting there, love. It's one huge, splendid banquet. I don't want to stuff my face too quickly." He chuckled. My father's mirth thawed the ice from my chest.

I hugged him again. "It's so great to have you here, Daddy."

"Oh, I'm in heaven, my angel. I'm in heaven."

That same night, at nine o'clock, a bang came to my door. Just having showered, I'd planned for an early night. But with desolation hanging like a cold, dark cloud, I resorted to watching television instead.

I opened the door and stuck my head out.

Aidan stood there in the dark. "Please let me in."

Reluctant to make a scene, I let him in. Dressed in a transparent shift, I hugged my body. He'd seen it all before. And anyway, this way I would inflict agony.

It worked. His smoldering eyes, all needy and dark, supped on me.

"I flew over after my meeting." Aidan pushed his hair back nervously. "Clarissa, I needed to see you, to explain." He took my hand. Electric sparks radiated off him. My skin tingled. My need was ferocious.

"Aidan, I can't do this." I stepped away from him. His touch had my heart hollering to lead him into the bedroom. "I'm too fragile for this."

"It's only you I want, Clarissa." His rasp transmitted through my flesh, making my legs liquid.

I hugged my breasts. My nipples pierced the backs of my hands. Aidan's eyes grew so heavy with tormenting lust he had to look away.

Finding it hard to stay away for too long, however, his eyes met mine again. There, I saw pain, raw and unhidden, reflecting my own state.

"I should've told you about my engagement to Jessica. But I'm no longer with her. I ended it last month. It's just that the media haven't been informed. Something I should've done. But I hate that circus." His clenched jaw relaxed, and his eyes softened. "Clarissa, I'm not good with words. But I want you so much it hurts."

Helplessly, I fell into his arms. Welcoming him, my lips parted. Aidan plunged right in and kissed me. It was tender at first. Then his silken tongue took me, all feverish and starved, while his needy hands caressed my breasts.

I craved his touch desperately. Moisture dripped between my legs as his hard, urging cock pressed against my thigh.

Snapping out of my drugged state, I pulled away. "No, I can't do this, Aidan. You have to leave."

CHAPTER TWENTY-NINE

Aidan

She drew me into her soulful eyes. Seeing Clarissa like that—semi-naked, hair hanging provocatively over her full breasts, and not wearing a scrap of make-up, just a natural, cock-swelling beauty, left me gasping for air. Words stuck in my throat. The ache was unbearable. Clarissa's persistent refusal to meet my gaze broke me.

I left, severely dejected with the urge to cry out like a lone, desperate wolf.

The next day was extremely busy. I was back in New York. Solarm was up and running. I'd arranged for a company in Germany to train locals the craft of solar-panel building. After that, they would install them in areas of need. Any leftover energy generated would be sold off, thus paying for itself.

My phone buzzed. It was my mother. She'd been ringing all week. As always, I tried to avoid her. My bitter and twisted mother was, as usual, drunk and high on weed.

Bankrolling her lifestyle, I'd bought her a comfortable home. But she was permanently unsatisfied, and always hounding me.

I picked up her call. "Hey there," I said, trying to sound welcoming despite the heaviness in my head. The last thing I needed was to listen to her gripes.

"At last, you picked up. Don't think that just because you pay me every month that somehow releases you from filial duties." My mother slurred her words.

I looked at my watch, it was only one o'clock in the afternoon. "You sound hammered."

"What do you expect? I have a heartless son who never comes to visit me. I'm so lonely…"

"Look, I'm busy. What's up?"

"I'd like a visit from my one and only child." She raised her voice.

Cringing, I wondered if I'd been dropped by a stork; my mother seemed so foreign to me. I'd tried tenderness over the years. That only made her worse. I also tried the best psychiatrists money could buy, but my mother refused to attend.

"I'm in New York all week. I'll be back on the weekend. I'll come by then," I said. The thought of doing so froze my soul.

"Yeah, yeah, heard that before… listen, I need more cash."

"What happened to the ten grand I deposited two days ago?" It wasn't the money. It was her drinking, her drug habit. I had two of them to carry—Bryce, who was bleeding me through gambling, and my profligate mother.

"Yeah, well, so what? I want to go to Vegas," she said petulantly.

"Okay…" I sighed deeply. "I'll deposit more cash today."

"Hey, by the way, I heard from Sharon. You know that bitch pedophile's neighbor."

I gripped the phone. "Stop calling her that. Her name was Jacqueline. And I was a consenting seventeen-year-old." My knuckles were white from rage. That was all it took—a few minutes of conversing with my mother—for the beast to be unleashed.

"Whatever… anyway, do you remember her?"

How could I ever forget her? It was Sharon's big mouth that exposed the relationship I was having with my schoolteacher.

Jacqueline, my busty teacher, had been one very desirable woman. Even though she looked younger, she was twenty-seven when I was in her class. Wearing low-cut blouses, she'd often pick up the chalk at my feet. It was hard not to be seduced. I lost my virginity to her. I was tall for my age. And she quickly became insatiable for my larger-than-usual-cock. Or at least, she kept reminding me of that. She also gave me my first ever head-job. For a boy from a messed-up household with a heavy weed-smoking-drunk parent, Jacqueline Howard was like an angel from heaven.

That was, until her nosey neighbor got involved and caused a major scandal. Jacqueline lost her job. Her brute husband, a violent, son of a bitch, beat her to death. Hence, I left home and joined the army.

"What about her?" I asked.

"She told me that John Howard's been released."

I stiffened. "What, already?"

"He's served fourteen years," my mother responded dryly.

"For the sadistic slaying of his wife, he should have got life."

"He's after blood. He's after you, Aidan."

"Well, I don't give a fuck. I can defend myself." The pulse at the side of my neck thumped hard. "Look, I've got to go."

My lungs expanded out slowly as I exhaled a stuttered breath. This situation called for more security. And Clarissa would have to learn of my checkered past. The thought brought bile to my throat. How could a pure soul like Clarissa accept someone with such a fucked-up history as mine?

Barraged by monsters from my past, I jumped when my phone vibrated.

"Kieren," I said, placing my legs up on my desk.

"Aidan, how are you?" His baritone calmed me instantly.

"I've been better."

"Tell me what's happening."

I let out a deep breath. "Clarissa, the best thing to happen to me in ages, if not ever, has pushed me away."

"Oh... I'm sorry to hear that. Was it too much for her? Is she frightened?"

"You could say that. She heard I was still engaged and that I'm a ladies' man," I said.

"You didn't tell her about your recent engagement?"

"No. We hadn't got to that stage. I mean, we've only been together twice. During that time, there wasn't a lot of talking."

"Yes. You mentioned that it had been very passionate." He paused. "I take it she hasn't given you a chance to explain yourself."

"What, about being a sex addict?" I said full of self-loathing.

"Aidan, don't beat up on yourself. You had much to deal with. At least you didn't succumb to drugs and liquor like many PTSD sufferers."

"Hmm... I fucked half of LA instead," I said, sighing deeply.

"Was it that many?" he asked, trying to make light of it.

"Don't know. I lost count. It disgusts me. How can an angel like Clarissa accept someone that fucked-up?"

"But you've changed. That's what counts."

"I have. There's been no-one since Amy. And even then, I didn't feel like being with her. She was naked in my bed, and I was drunk. Bad excuse, I know."

"I remember. You were hard on yourself over that. And did you tell Clarissa about your engagement to Jessica?"

"No. Another huge fucking failing," I blurted, frustrated. "I should've gone to the media with an announcement. I just didn't want to upset Jessica.

She's over in England. Rather naively, I thought nobody would notice." I peered over at my bottle of bourbon. Although it was earlier than usual for a drink, I needed something to remove the edge. "Hang on a minute, Kieren." I got up and poured myself a generous measure and returned to face the screen.

"Give it time, Aidan. Remember, you rushed into it. Maybe start again. You know, ask her out on an official date. Take it slowly. Get to know each other the old-fashioned way. During which, tell her about your addiction, tell her about your tour of duty and what happened. That's a big story, Aidan. Few would survive, let alone become successful and benevolent contributors to society like you have. Clarissa is sweet-natured. She'll understand. Chemistry doesn't just disappear like that. If anything, it makes two people's love stronger."

"John Howard's been released. Word has it he wants my scalp. It will be a feeding frenzy for the media. Oh, fuck..." I exhaled. "There's no way Clarissa will want me after that."

"You were a seventeen-year-old boy, a man almost. Your teacher had a notorious predilection for younger male students. There'd been others. It came out in the hearing. I followed it. You did what any red-blooded, hormonally charged young man would do. She was an alluring woman. Aidan, you have nothing to feel bad about."

"But she'd still be alive if I hadn't gone there, Kieren. That's the part that tears me apart."

"Aidan, her husband was a murderous alcoholic. He was beating her up all along. Police had reports of previous dealings with that household. I imagine it was probably a time bomb waiting to go off. You can't take responsibility for a seriously dysfunctional marriage."

"Aren't we all responsible for our actions?"

"Yes, but by learning and understanding why we acted in such a manner, we grow. That's what you've been doing, Aidan. At the time, your sex drive was high, and all your partners were consenting. I can't see anything warranting censure. In any case, you've stopped this behavior. I believe you're now cured of your sex addiction."

"Yes, six months without. And it's the last thing I want. Except for Clarissa, of course. I'm on fire when I think of her. Since being with her, attractive women don't even register. And that's how I know..."

"How you know what?"

"That what I have with Clarissa is unique and special." My voice carried a note of heavy frustration.

"I'm convinced you'll be able to repair this, Aidan. Tell me, how have you been sleeping?"

"The best sleep I've had in years was in Clarissa's arms. I could have slept all day. I've never slept as well. After Afghanistan, that is. Normally, my nightmares are a menace. That's one of many reasons why I broke off with Jessica."

"From what you said, Jessica wanted you to seek help."

"Which is exactly what I'm doing, wouldn't you say?" I sniffed sarcastically. "She wanted me to visit one of her own doctors. It always had to be her way. Jessica was a very stubborn woman. It was never love. I know that now, especially after Clarissa. No woman compares to Clarissa."

"Do you think that's because you were her first?" Kieren asked.

"There's no doubt that's special, very much so. With all the others, it was just sex. I've scaled unimaginable heights with Clarissa. This is what making love should feel like, I imagine. It's almost spiritual."

"In Eastern mysticism, making love is a way of communing with the higher forces. The out-of-body experience from the orgasm facilitates this."

"That sums up exactly how I feel with Clarissa." I sighed, pausing for a moment. "I had a terrible nightmare last night."

"The same theme? Afghanistan?"

"Yep, extremely intense. My cries woke me."

"Tell me about it."

I poured myself a two-finger shot of bourbon and gulped it down. "This time there was more detail." I cleared my throat. My palms gripped the glass.

"Are you up for sharing it with me? Or would you prefer to wait until you visit the clinic?"

"No. I need to talk." I squared my shoulders, and my bones cracked. "Ben— my buddy, a brother in many ways—took a bullet meant for me. He pushed me out of the way. I should have died. I just can't stop wondering why he did it."

"Yes, we've spoken about that. It's the ultimate sacrifice, one that justifies the hours of reflection. However, you don't have to weigh yourself down with a lifetime of guilt. You're a generous person, Aidan, and as with most givers, you're not good at receiving. And life is the ultimate gift."

"I know all this, Kieren. It just doesn't fucking make sense. Our instinct is to survive, surely."

"I agree. But war changes things. That's why the survivors of war often spend the rest of their lives trying to make sense of it. Aidan, soldiers often protect their own men, even at their own expense. Both World War 1 and World War 11 records show heroic acts, where men took the blast in order to protect their mates."

"I've read lots about it too. I've had to. I needed to understand." I pushed my hair back. "I needed to know I was not alone." My mind went dark, desolate. I wanted to cry, but didn't know how to. The closest was when Clarissa closed the door on me. A tear fell down my cheek. Trained in stoicism, I wiped it away quickly. On a deeper level, I suspected that by indulging in the profound grief I carried, tears would drown me. And a strong, tough man was meant to withstand pain. The Special Forces had drummed that into me.

But in the dark of night, all that tough-guy shit evaporated, and I became a fucking mess.

"You mentioned your nightmare was more detailed. Can you tell me about that?"

I swallowed deeply. "I relived it. Ben's eyes"—my voice cracked— "pleading for someone to put him out of his misery. I begged him to let me carry him to safety. But as he struggled, he argued that it was better to have one man alive than two dead. He begged me to shoot him. At first, my finger shook so hard I couldn't fire. But his face, those haunted eyes—he was so crippled with pain. Fuck." I took a deep breath.

"This may seem strange to you, but you made a brave choice. The pain would've been unbearable for Ben. What was your option? To wait there while he bled to death, waiting for the evacuation unit, and risk being shot as well? It was an open field, I believe."

As always, Kieren spoke sense. "Last night he came to me, Kieren. It was so fucking lucid." I shook my head in disbelief. "It was like there was a ghost in front of me." My hands trembled.

"Do you believe that he was truly there?" he asked.

"I don't know. How can I? I don't believe in ghosts," I said almost to myself. "He said something I can't forget."

"And what was that?"

"He told me he hated his life and that he joined the Special Forces because he wanted to die doing something for his country."

Kieren took notes. "Did he ever mention his desire for suicide before?"

"Never," I replied.

"So why tell you now?"

I took a deep breath before answering. "No idea. He always kept things to himself, although we were close—especially in times of combat."

"Tell me about that."

"He'd often ask me what was the cause? What were we fighting for? It wasn't something I could answer. In truth, the situation was confusing. Even those in charge were vague."

"To take out the Taliban, I believe."

"Yes. But then we were also doing deals with the Taliban. Considerable wads of cash were being handed over." I stopped. This was classified information.

"I've heard about these transactions. Same thing happened in Iraq. They pay for a peaceful passage for their men. Not an unusual practice, just not spoken about."

I exhaled. My head was heavy. "Sorry, Kieren. I'm wiped out. Can we do this later? In your office when I get back?"

"Aidan, try to rest. Remove these events from your thoughts until we speak again. Take care."

CHAPTER THIRTY

Clarissa

The rest of the week went by quickly. I made sure the days were filled so there was no room for contemplation.

Bemused by my incessant industry, Greta said, "At this rate, you can have the whole of next week off."

Despite being perplexed about my nervous energy, Greta wore a permanent smile. Her freshly tinted hair was down, and she was looking younger than ever. I suspected it was for my father's benefit. They got on so well. It was heartening. My solitary dad deserved a woman like Greta. And I noticed, much to my joy, that he liked the attention, not to mention the excellent meals.

When I could lure him away from the library, we'd take pleasant, long walks around the grounds—that was, when he wasn't going for beach walks with Greta. I'd never seen Greta in leisure mode. I was happy for both of them. I wasn't sure if it had turned romantic. I was happier not knowing. I couldn't get my head around my dad being that way inclined. Not that I was prudish anymore. How could I be after what I'd recently been up to?

Greta was such a good woman. Her initial officious bearing had gone. She was so generous and caring. I recalled Aidan describing her more as a mother than an aunt, and any mention of his actual mother sent him into a dark mood.

There was so much I didn't know about Aidan. Still, I couldn't erase from my mind the expression on his face when I kicked him out. His magnetic blue eyes had been filled with sadness, despair, and frustration. It was a new man standing in front of me. He was broken. The image haunted me. Each time I thought of it fresh tears erupted. My eyes were puffy. Although it had only been a few nights since I'd seen Aidan, it seemed more like a month. I missed him profoundly. He'd taken a part of me away. I drifted about like a shadow.

As it was Friday, I decided to head for our apartment. I needed to see Tabitha. We hadn't spoken since the weekend. Therefore, she wasn't aware of my break with Aidan.

It was bumper-to-bumper traffic, so I switched on the radio to pass the time. And just to further rip at my cold spirit, "Moon Dance" came on. That was one of Aidan's favorite songs, one he'd played on the yacht. Memories flooded in. My throat thickened with emotion. I recalled Aidan singing along with it. He sang in tune, really well in fact, and even swayed a little. I recalled my amusement and arousal as I watched him.

Tears poured out. I hoped the other drivers couldn't see me. I was sure that my face was contorted with grief, something sunglasses couldn't hide.

Aidan hadn't even tried to contact me. That hurt. Why wasn't he fighting to win me back? Maybe he'd moved on after fooling me with his purported passion for me. But the memory of the despair in his eyes contradicted that line of thinking.

The tears just fell and fell, I should have cried myself dry by that point. My pillow at the cottage was drenched.

How gray life was without Aidan. I wanted rain, not sunshine. Even the weather annoyed me. It should have been sympathetic to my grief. That was how deranged I'd become. I'd lost my mind to love.

When I walked through the door of our apartment, I found Tabitha painting her nails and the TV blaring.

"Hey, Clary," she said, smiling brightly.

"Hey there. What's happening? Is Josh here?" I looked about the place. It was unexpectedly clean. I assumed that was Josh's doing. He was not only an amiable guy, but a clean freak as well. That was a godsend, considering Tabitha's untidiness.

"No, he's gone for a weekend with the boys. Fishing." Tabitha tapped the sofa. "Sit down. I'll get us a wine." She jumped up.

I turned down the TV.

"I'm pissed with you," Tabitha said, handing me a glass of chilled wine. "No calls. You can't be that busy."

"Sorry, Tabs, it's been a hard week." My voice was shaky. I was fighting back tears.

A look of concern pushed away her frown. "Why, what's happened?" Tabitha sat close and faced me.

"I broke it off with Aidan." I took a large gulp of wine.

"Huh? Why?" She had that expression of disbelief she got whenever I did or said something radical.

"I found out he had a fiancée."

"Holy shit." Tabitha's mouth dropped open. "How did you find out? I mean, there's nothing in the media about it. We looked, remember?"

"We didn't look closely enough, it seems. Anyway…" I sighed. "I confronted Aidan about it. He said he'd broken off with her but didn't make it known officially because he didn't want to upset her."

She shook her head and opened out her hands. "What's your problem? That sounds reasonable enough."

"It was the bit about him being a ladies' man. That's what upset me." I held my head in my hands.

"Well, I'm not surprised. He's a hottie. Girls throw themselves at him all the time. You dropped him because of that? Seriously?" Her brows were knitted.

"I'm frightened of being hurt. I'm just too sensitive for this kind of thing. And I've really fallen for him, Tabs. It all happened so quickly. The calls, the flowers, his inability to stop touching me…" My voice thickened with sobs.

Tabitha grabbed a handful of tissues and passed them to me. "Shit, Clary, you're still young. We're both still young. I mean, even if it doesn't last, the experience would still be amazing—multiple orgasms, non-stop cunnilingus…"

She was trying to make me laugh. Instead, I winced. "It wasn't just the sex. Even though, yeah"—I sighed ruefully— "it was amazing. Not that I can compare it to anything."

"Well, let's just say that a yummy, fat nine-inch penis and someone who gets off on having his tongue inside of you, in my estimation, is ten out of ten even if it is short-lived."

"Tabitha Hendry, you're a sex maniac." A smile chased away my tears. Through talking, even if it was crude, my pain had eased a little. As usual, Tabitha had made me blush. I had forgotten how much detail I'd divulged. It would have been impossible to keep anything from Tabitha.

"I never measured it, you know," I said.

We looked at each other and giggled. The wine had kicked in. The tightness in my chest dissipated. And for the first time all week, I felt almost sane.

"You will just have to win him back." Tabitha went to get us a refill.

"How? And do I want to, Tabs? I'm not like you. I'm too sensitive for this game of casual sex."

"Are you implying that I'm not? Holy shit, you've seen how inconsolable I get over every fucked-up relationship," said Tabitha, pulling a long face.

"Sorry, Tabs. You're right. We're both fragile. But you're more of a risk- taker than me, I suppose."

My phone beeped, making me jump.

Tabitha's face lit up with excitement. "It's probably him. Quick, check it out."

I burrowed into my busy handbag and grabbed my phone. When the screen lit up, Aidan's name flashed in front of me, and my heart did a somersault.

"Is it him?" Tabitha asked.

Unable to hide my delight and fear, I nodded, peering down at his message: *I'm heading back tonight. Will you be there this weekend?*

"Well, what's it say?" Tabitha asked, standing over me, hands on hips. I showed her. "Call him. Don't text. Tell him you'll be there tomorrow. That you're going out with your friends tonight. That will make him wonder a little."

My mind went into a spin. How could I call him when I could barely speak? "I don't know, Tabs. I can't just be friends with him. Not after what we've experienced. Just being around him makes me go all gooey," I said, rolling my eyes at such a stupid expression. I joined Tabitha in a laugh, which helped ease the tightness in my belly.

"Don't be friends." Tabitha gesticulated. "Like, as if you're going to talk about Monet. For God's sake, Clary, this guy is nuts about you."

"He loves art," I protested. "Do you really think I should call him?"

Wide-eyed, Tabitha nodded emphatically. "Hell, yeah."

I kept gazing down at his message, trying to glean some hidden meaning. It was really my way of stalling for time while I built up the courage to make the call.

"Just do it, Clarissa. Tell him you'll see him tomorrow. Go to the beach. Wear a skimpy bikini. We'll go shopping for one now. Then we'll drop in at Sammy's for dinner. Come on—it'll be fun."

"All right, but I need to do it alone, away from you. You'll make me laugh." Anxiety tended to make me giggle at all the wrong moments. And wide-eyed Tabitha, with those ridiculous expressions she pulled, would be dangerous.

I sat on my bed. My hands trembled while dialing his number. He picked up straight away.

"Clarissa," he husked. That voice sent a million shivers through me.

"Hello." My mind had gone blank.

"Where are you?"

"I'm at my apartment."

"Oh, not at Malibu?" He sounded disappointed.

"No. I'm just doing a little shopping and then going for a meal with Tabitha, the girl who you met the other night."

"Oh, right? Just the two of you?" he asked.

"I suppose so."

"You suppose so?"

"We might catch up with her brother, Johnny. He's an old friend," I said, recrossing my legs for the umpteenth time.

"Are you staying downtown all weekend? Can I meet you there somewhere?"

"If you like… I mean, I thought of returning to the cottage tomorrow."

"How about if I catch up with you later on tonight then? There's a venue I'd love to take you to. It has live R&B music. What do you think?"

His voice had my lower regions gushing. I would've agreed to a gig where they performed scratching on a blackboard just to see him. How could one resist a man who sounded like that? "Okay, that sounds really cool. Where shall we meet?"

"Send me a text when you've finished your meal. I can swing by and pick you up. Is that good?"

"Yeah, that's good," I said, unable to stop smiling.

"Speak to you soon, then. I look forward to it."

"Yes… me too." I put down the phone and headed for the bathroom.

Drenched with sweat, I turned on the shower taps. Tabitha's sage advice ran through my mind. Age was on my side. And Aidan was about experience and fun. My heart, meanwhile, would have to learn to cope.

As hot water cascaded over me, massaging, and unravelling my tight muscles, I questioned whether I was doing a deal with the devil.

Not surprisingly, when I got out of the shower, I found Tabitha poking her head in my closet. "What did he say?"

"He's going to pick me up after we've had our meal. He wants to take me to a live R&B venue," I said, staring at the green dress that Tabitha had in her hand.

"I think I'll wear that." I stroked the silky chiffon fabric with affection. It was another of my mother's dresses. She'd bought it in London—Carnaby Street, no less. And I loved it to pieces.

"You don't think it's too vintage?" asked Tabitha, going through my closet. She pulled out a little red dress. "Now, this speaks of sex."

"Oh, Tabs, please. I want to be myself. And I love this green dress. He needs to take me as I am. Vintage dresses and all."

"I suppose. And it is your color."

The green chiffon dress had a full circle skirt. As I spun around, it floated in the air. Tilting my head from side to side, I studied myself in the mirror. The double layer of green chiffon cascaded elegantly from my waist. It had a fitted bodice, no sleeves, and was cut low enough so that my cleavage spilt out a little. It suited my mood. And the bottle green matched my dark hair and pale complexion well.

The night was hot, so I kept my legs naked. To finish it off, I found a pair of gold sling-backs, also from my mother's collection.

"You look fantastic, Clary," said Tabitha, dressed in jeans and the silk floral blouse I'd recently gifted her. Unlike me, she loved contemporary clothing, especially tight-fitting jeans. Since she was blessed with long, slender legs and a svelte, model-like, figure they suited her brilliantly.

"What are you going to do with that mane of yours?" she asked, grabbing my hair and experimenting by twisting it into a bun.

"Maybe a ponytail."

"What about the plaits? They looked so girlishly sexy the other night."

I opted for the ponytail.

After Tabitha insisted, I let her do my make-up. Nobody applied eyeliner like Tabitha. Deft with color and applications that required a steady hand, she would have made a fabulous make-up artist. But the drifter who was my best friend lacked the ambition for that.

Now that I made a decent wage, I paid the entire rent for our apartment and stocked the cupboards. I imagined Josh, who was doing well financially, would do his bit as well. He seemed to enjoy caring for Tabitha. I just hoped that she wouldn't sabotage it by getting back with Steve, knowing that unhealthy appetite she had for older men.

CHAPTER THIRTY-ONE

"Hey, these red ones are really cool," said Tabitha, holding up a pair of bikinis for me to try on. My eyes bulged out at the price tag. "Wow, $400 for such little fabric." I held them up. They were so skimpy. "Tabs, I can't wear these. I might as well go naked."

"Get with it girl, he'll never want to leave you. There's no-one like you, Clarissa, with that Natalie Wood face and the sexiest body on earth."

I tilted my head and smiled. Tabitha was my greatest fan. "I just hope that Josh knows how lucky he is with a Grace Kelly look-alike." I wasn't exaggerating. Tabitha Hendry could have auditioned for Hollywood movies.

"He knows. He's so cute." Tabitha smiled.

After I tried them on and complained that they were half the size of my already very brief panties, Tabitha tut-tutted. "You're buying them. It's your color. Come on. I'm starving."

As we made our way to the register, I watched Tabitha pausing at a floral bikini. "That's adorable. Do you want it?"

Tabitha looked at the price tag and raised her eyebrows. "I love it. But I can't expect you to keep buying things for me, Clary."

"Go try them on, Tabs."

She bit her bottom lip. "Are you sure?"

"Of course, I'm sure. Hurry. I'm starving as well." It was the first time all week that I'd actually felt hungry.

After I gave my credit card a good workout, we left carrying our little parcels. With Tabitha holding onto my arm, we giggled at silly things as we made our way to Sammy's.

Although the place was full, Johnny still managed to find us a table. His face lit up when he saw me. Tabitha's brother had always had a thing for me. He was two years older, and although he was a masculine version of Tabitha— all golden hair and striking green eyes—I'd never felt the desire to be with him. He was too much like an older brother.

"Haven't seen you for a while, Clarissa. How are you?" he asked.

"I'm good." I noticed he was looking quite muscular. Having always been a skinny boy, Johnny had suddenly become a man. "Have you been working out?" Eyeing the Celtic tattoo around his bicep, Johnny nodded and smiled shyly.

"What can I get you?"

I looked up at Tabitha. "What are you having?"

"Mm… nothing too fattening so that I can do justice to my new bikinis." She chuckled.

"I'm starving," I said. "Let's not worry about that. Nor should you, Tabitha Hendry. You're supermodel thin. I feel like lasagna and salad, and a bottle of Sauvignon Blanc, the best you have."

"Lasagna sounds delicious. I'll have the same," said Tabitha.

Johnny managed Sammy's. And despite the fact the restaurant was busy, he found time to sit and have a beer. I suspect it was really so he could hang out with me.

When Aidan arrived, he found the three of us huddled together, having a laugh over old-time antics. I had been so ravenous that not only did I finish my pasta, but I also polished off a piece of chocolate mud cake, all washed down with two glasses of crisp white wine.

Johnny had his arm around my seat. For anyone who didn't know us, it would have appeared intimate.

Tabitha tapped my arm. "Aidan's here."

I turned, and a wide smile filled my face. The wine had dropped any reserve. As he glided towards me, the whole café stopped what they were doing. All eyes were on Aidan. Such was his presence.

Wearing jeans and a loose-fitting blue silk shirt, he moved with elegant, self-assured ease. Focused directly on me, he seemed oblivious to everyone around him.

A surge of blood raced through me. "Hi," I said, feasting on his deep-blue eyes. Five days had been like a lifetime.

"Hey." His low husk echoed. Standing by our table, he nodded at Tabitha and cast a passing, albeit cold, glance at Johnny.

Aidan's body language spoke of someone claiming what was his. And more than happy to hand myself over, I stood up. "I'm ready now unless you'd like to stay for a drink."

"No, I'm good." Aidan put his arm around me. Tabitha was all smiles.

"You've met Tabitha from the other night. And this is Johnny, Tabi's brother."

Aidan shook Johnny's hand. His smile never quite made it to his eyes. Johnny, likewise, sized up his competition.

"So, you're ready, then," Aidan asked.

I collected my bag with my shopping. I bent down to Tabitha and pecked her on the cheek.

"Now, don't behave," she whispered.

I touched Johnny on the arm. "Catch you soon."

He returned a gentle, if slightly sad, smile.

When I stepped out onto the busy street, my green dress fluttered in the breeze.

"You look spectacular. That's your color," said Aidan, who had not taken his eyes off me. Taking me by the hand, he led me to his car.

"Thanks. It's a dress that belonged to my mother," I said, floating on cloud nine. The heat emanating off his hand inflamed me.

I noticed all eyes were on us. It was a busy night with crowds amassed in the streets.

"Aidan, you draw an audience everywhere we go."

He sighed. "Yes, I know. It's a pain. But it can't be helped. I don't want to have to hide. Does it worry you?"

"To be honest, it's not something I've ever experienced before."

At that moment, someone stood close and took a photo with their phone. "I think we're being snapped," I said.

Aidan seemed unfazed. "Hope it's a good shot. I'd like one of you in that dress." An expression of need filled his gaze. The intensity burned as before. Nothing had changed except a hint of suffering within those blue eyes. Just like me, Aidan had not handled our break well it seemed.

"Tell me about that guy Johnny. He's in love with you. I can see that," Aidan said, as we were approaching his car.

"I've known him since the age of five. He's like a brother. We've been nothing but friends."

"He wants more. That's obvious." He helped me up onto the seat. His hand around my waist was intimate and affecting. Aidan's eyes had hijacked my senses again.

Aidan jumped in and closed the door. He turned towards me. A serious expression claimed his face. "Thanks for seeing me. I can't tell you how much this means to me." He touched my arm gently.

"It's hard to stay away," I said with a tight smile.

Aidan touched my cheek tenderly. "By the way, just in case you haven't noticed, I'm a jealous guy. The thought of you being with someone just does my head in." Aidan appeared so lost. I could see that our separation had hurt him.

Good.

Tears pricked at the back of my eyes. Despite doing my utmost to resist, my eyes misted over. "Oh, Aidan..." I shook my head. "I'm not interested in anyone at all, only you."

"Are we good, then?" he asked, his brows meeting.

"Yeah, we're good," I said, swallowing. "I'm just scared of being hurt. And I know nothing about you."

Aidan stroked my hair. Tingles travelled throughout my body. His touch was so gentle yet intoxicating. "I'm in the same boat, Clarissa. I can't stand the idea of anyone touching you, having you."

"You're the only one, Aidan. And to be honest, I don't want anybody else."

Aidan leaned in. In full view of interested onlookers, Aidan took me in his arms and kissed me deeply. I liquefied into his arms. Stars swirled in my mind. Aidan's scent of subtle cologne and masculinity transmitted through me, ramping up the heat.

His lips were soft and burning hot. My mouth parted, and his fervent silky tongue slid in. A firestorm raged between my legs. I wanted him then and there. Blood coursed me as his sweet tongue ravished mine. Sighing into my mouth, his fingers crept up my leg. The craving ache and anticipation of his touch overwhelmed me.

"You're so soft," he rasped.

Although our bodies begged to remain close, we separated. If we had continued to feel each other, it would have been sex in the car. All gushy and sticking to the seat, I took a deep breath and tried to calm my raging hormones.

"I've got opaque windows. But with that lot hanging about..." Aidan sounded frustrated.

"We've got all night, Aidan."

Aidan's eyes glistened with delight. "Mm... I'm one lucky man." His mood deepened. "When you returned my text and called me..." He ran his hands through his hair. "Colors returned. I thought I'd lost you." He appeared vulnerable and insecure. Something had broken him. I could see that.

"Aidan." I touched his face. "I feel the same."

His eyes softened tenderly. "Well, then"—a faint smile chased away his furrowed intensity— "that's all that matters."

Aidan started the engine. "I'd like to take you to a special place. I've never taken a date there before. I'm known. They may make a fuss when they meet you. You don't mind?"

Wow.

"No, but I'm seriously curious. I can't wait," I said, giggling stupidly. In truth, I was so weighed down with emotion that some light relief was desperately needed.

CHAPTER THIRTY-TWO

We pulled up at a venue on Venice Boulevard. Painted bright red, its name Red House fitted perfectly.

Aidan jumped out of the car, and helped me out. Although I could've managed alone, I loved his strong arms lifting me up like a ballerina. His eyes were on mine, devouring me. Gender equality notwithstanding, I'd developed a deep fondness for chivalry.

Staring at the long line snaking around the building, I said, "Looks like a popular venue."

A sudden gust of wind blew my skirt up, exposing my tiny panties. It was lingerie Tabitha had insisted I purchase during a shopping spree, referring to it as *tarting* me up. Aidan's heavy-lidded gaze showed that it had worked.

His eyes sizzled. "Mm… very nice indeed. But only for my eyes." He held my skirt down and kissed me suggestively on my neck.

Phew, steamy. Our mutual need had become more ferocious by the minute.

"Let's go around the side entrance." Aidan took me by the hand.

He pressed numbers into a keypad by the door and two security guards welcomed us. "Hey, Aidan. Good to see you, buddy," they chorused. Their attention drifting over to me, they looked surprised.

"Wayne." Aidan nodded. "Jake, how are you?"

As we walked away, Aidan whispered, "They're two guys I was in the forces with. All my security guys were in the army. Men I served with, all buddies, like family."

"Like Bryce?" I asked.

"Yeah, only Bryce is a rogue. He's got some issues."

I shook my head. "One day, you'll explain why you have him there."

Aidan ran his fingers through his hair. My, I'd missed seeing that. "One day soon. I promise." He touched my face affectionately while his eyes turned a pale shade of grim.

Mystery had taken grip again, but I had to let it go. My heart demanded it.

We entered a dressing room and found a musician with head bowed down, tuning his guitar. He looked up, and his face lit up instantly. "Aidan." He put down his guitar, and they hugged.

I noticed a similarity between them. After they separated, the older man acknowledged me with a welcoming smile.

Aidan said, "Clarissa, I'd like to introduce my father, Grant."

My shock must have showed, because both men grinned. My eyes switched from one to the other. "Pleased to meet you," I stammered.

Grant was an older version of Aidan. The similarity was unmistakable. He was also very much like Greta.

"Have you been on yet?" Aidan asked.

"We've done one set." Grant's eyes skimmed my face again. "We're going on again in a minute."

At that moment, a woman with long red hair entered. A little older than Aidan, she was attractive in an earthy, bohemian way. Dressed in a velvet purple dress, she had one of those contagiously warm natures that put one at ease. When she saw me her eyes lit up.

"This is Sara, my father's partner," said Aidan. "Sara, this is Clarissa."

She hugged me. Smelling of sandalwood, Sara reminded me of a 1960's hippie.

"It's a delight to meet you, Clarissa." Sara lifted the top layer of my green dress. "What a stunning little number. It looks genuine."

"It belonged to my late mother," I replied, noticing a twinkle of admiration in Aidan's eyes.

"You'll fit in real well here, then," said Grant. "The Red House is very retro." He chuckled.

Aidan seemed at ease, almost boyish, in this relaxed, familial environment. I hadn't seen this side of Aidan. Around his father, he was very respectful.

"We should get out there," said Sara, grabbing her flute.

"Yeah, sure." Grant was unpretentious and handsome, like his son. I liked him. They were also the same height. The resemblance as they stood side by side was striking. It gave me a preview of Aidan in his early fifties. *Hot.*

"Has Clarissa heard you play?" Grant asked Aidan.

"Not yet," Aidan replied, sending me a shy smile.

Grant's face lit up with glee. "Tonight's the night, then."

"I'm not sure about that, Dad," muttered Aidan.

"I would love to hear you play." I had to raise my voice in order to be heard. The spacious room was bursting with noisy patrons. And the band hadn't even started.

Predictably, all the female attention was on Aidan. I, too, had my own audience. Aidan claimed me. With his arm around my waist, he drew me close. His warmth radiated through me. And once again, I was light-headed, drugged out on Aidan.

Even in a ghetto, I would be having the time of my life. Close and hot, with Aidan by my side, I didn't need anything more. Not that the Red House was run-down. If anything, it was highly sophisticated.

"What can I get you?" Aidan asked.

"I'm not sure. What should I get?"

"What do you like? Bourbon, gin?"

"Gin and tonic, then," I said.

While Aidan went off to get the drinks, I made my way to the restroom, worried that our earlier steam session had messed up my hair, particularly because there were so many eyes on me. But then, maybe the bright-green dress had more to do with that. Considering that most of the girls wore tight blue jeans, I stood out.

The mirror revealed nothing too shameful. My eyeliner was still doing what it had been designed to do. If anything, it was a little smudgy underneath my eyes, but flatteringly so, rendering my eyes wide and sultry. My complexion was rosy from the anticipation of having Aidan inside of me. In truth, I was in a permanent state of arousal.

My hair, however, was another story. The sad excuse for a ponytail was half undone. I'd met Grant and Sara looking like I'd been through a windstorm or a session of steamy coupling. I was sure they figured it was the latter. Aidan hadn't hidden his feelings towards me at all.

The fact he'd introduced me to his dad was profound. It was still sinking in as I undid the ponytail and let my hair out.

I loved the room. The stage was draped with cascading red-velvet. The rest of the space, covered in bordello-style wallpaper, was reminiscent of the barrooms in the Wild West.

In acknowledgement of celebrated blues artists, there were black-and-white framed photographs of famous African-American musicians, along with signed album covers. My favorite aspect of the décor, however, was the sheet-music wallpaper behind the bar.

Aidan chatted away with a broad, solid man. He looked like a security guard. They were laughing about something when Aidan's eyes shifted towards me. The room emptied suddenly. It was just us. He was ravaging me again with that smoldering gaze. The guy he was talking to turned to see what had drawn his friend's attention. He said something to Aidan who, having not taken his eyes away from me, just nodded in a trancelike way.

I stood by his side, and he drew me in close. In an open display of affection, he kissed me on the cheek. Who would have thought a peck on the cheek could be so erotic?

"I love your hair out, Clarissa. I cannot tell you how much you're driving me crazy." His eyes had that heavy, lust-filled look.

Aidan ran his hands down my hair. Despite demurring, with a thousand eyes watching us, I could do little but succumb to the sheer bliss of Aidan's closeness.

I imagined being the envy of every woman present, with their unwavering attention blatantly directed at Aidan. How could they not feel that way when he had jeans that hugged his athletic body perfectly and a face that Hollywood producers would've leapt over pits of vipers to sign up?

Aidan Thornhill was pure male in every sense of the word. And as he stood behind me and pulled me in close, I felt his desire, hard and ready.

"What do you think of this place?" asked Aidan.

"I love it. It's so Victorian bordello, very sensual. I love the velvets and satiny textures. It's a triumph. I could live here."

Aidan laughed. "Well, I don't know about letting you live here. But you, darling girl, have got impeccable taste."

"Does it belong to somebody you know?" I asked, recalling him pressing the security code earlier.

"You could say that." Aidan smirked.

"Well?" I said, shaking my head.

"This is my place, Clarissa."

My lips parted. "Oh… its charming, Aidan—all the pictures and the design. The sheet-music wallpaper is marvelous. Did you get a designer?"

"Not really. I designed it." Aidan had that adorable off-center, uncertain smile. I'd learnt to recognize that expression, which appeared whenever Aidan admitted to an achievement. I sensed that being a humble person, Aidan felt pride deeply, but not in a boastful way.

"You have a great eye, Aidan. You surround yourself with so much beauty," I gushed.

"Nothing as beautiful as you, you're the masterpiece, Clarissa." Aidan held me tighter. My face hurt from smiling too much.

CHAPTER THIRTY-THREE

Grant Thornhill had the exemplary blues voice. His throaty rasp seemed infused with cigarettes and whisky, or at least that was how it sounded. His body bent back slightly as he twanged his guitar. Confidant and very capable, Grant was the consummate performer. With Sara on keyboards, along with a drummer and a bass guitarist, the music was visceral. Then again, everything about that night seemed raw and emotive.

I enjoyed the blues, especially how the bass worked through my ribcage. Grant was an accomplished musician, plucking his dark chords with deep emotion. And Sara's melodious harmonies blended effortlessly. They were a tight and well-practiced band.

Aidan stood behind me, and with his arms around my waist, he was enticingly close. He felt divinely hard against my butt. And as he moved to the music, it was almost obscene. I prayed nobody could smell my desire, because I was dripping with it.

When Aidan asked me to dance to the slow ballad, I responded with a puzzled frown.

"What's wrong? You don't want to?" Aidan asked.

"I do, only it's slow," I replied.

"All the better," said Aidan with that chocolate-melting smile.

He led me onto the dance floor, placing one arm around my shoulder and another around my waist. My cheek rested on his shoulder for a slow and sensuous dance.

I suddenly discovered another magical aspect of the past: the waltz. Aidan was right—the slower the better. I had never waltzed before. And Aidan was an excellent partner, confident and capable with no clumsy moves. I don't even recall feeling my feet on the ground, we seemed to glide.

When the song ended, Grant said, "Thanks for coming, folks. This is the last number and I'd like to call my son, Aidan, up for a little jam."

Aidan shook his head. "No."

I was in his ear in an instant. "I would love you to play, Aidan. Please."

The audience was with me, clapping keenly. "I think you have to," I said with an encouraging nod.

He brushed his hair away from his face and rolled his eyes. His face flushed, he finally agreed. Aidan's innate sensitivity made my heart dissolve.

I saw him whisper something to his security mates, whose attention thereafter was directed at me.

Aidan picked up a green electric guitar and waited for his father to plug him in. Then, with a harmonica in his mouth, Grant started the song. Side by side, father and son made for a powerful and moving image. The rhythm so hypnotic my body swayed.

Ripping into a guitar solo, Aidan was a rock god. He had an immense presence on stage. And his playing, oh my, I hadn't expected it, but Aidan was a consummate musician.

The place went wild. My heart flipped with each explosive strum of that sexy-sounding guitar. Talent was supposed to be an aphrodisiac, and Aidan had plenty of it to add to his already supreme sexiness.

His solo was heartfelt. With eyes shut, while biting his bottom lip, Aidan looked like he was in the throes of a musical orgasm. Or did I read sex into everything to do with Aidan?

My face and body ached. I was overdosing on his sheer animal allure.

A thorn in my side was the pest who wouldn't take no for an answer. After I refused to dance with him, he grabbed my arm imploringly. And despite being in deep musical concentration, Aidan's expression hardened. I noticed his eyes move over my head. Within a breath, a security guard, the one Aidan had spoken to, came over, and after a few words, my admirer crept off with a disappointed scowl.

Aidan played the guitar as if making love. His pelvis flexed against the instrument. I had to fan my face. In fact, the whole room by then was awash in female hormones. I'm certain I wasn't the only one heating up down south.

Their tuneful singing melded brilliantly. Aidan's eyes never left mine as he sang along. The ballad spoke of pain. I wondered what he was telling me. I was the only one there suddenly. Unable to close my jaw, I thought to myself, how did I—an art history major with very little to show for it— end up with such a man?

After performing an encore to rapturous applause, the set came to an end, and the patrons cleared out.

Aidan and I sat with Grant and Sara. While Aidan slid off to have a chat with his ex-army buddies, Grant sat next to me.

"I can't tell you how it feels to see Aidan looking so happy. It's the first time in ages, if ever I've seen him like that."

Ever?

"Oh?" Questions suddenly lined up in my busy mind.

"Aidan hasn't had an easy life. His mother was, and still is, a raging alcoholic and not a pretty one at that." He smiled grimly. "The army broke Aidan."

"He hasn't spoken about that much," I said.

"Why doesn't that surprise me?" said Grant almost to himself. "Aidan doesn't speak to anyone about that period in his life. When my boy returned from Afghanistan, not only had he changed physically and mentally, but he also brought back a demon."

"One reads about the shock of war. *Shell shock* it was called in the olden days. I guess it's still the same."

"It sure is. Not that Aidan has fessed up to anything. He doesn't speak about it at all. But there's something going on." He took a sip of his drink and rolled a cigarette. "Do you mind if I smoke?"

I shook my head.

"Anyway, this is a first. I can see he's crazy about you. I've only met one woman, and he never brought her here, mind you." Grant took a puff of his cigarette. "I met his ex by sheer accident. I've never seen Aidan as relaxed as he is with you." His eyes, just like Aidan's, glowed with sincerity. I could see the love he had for Aidan. "And by the way, all that gossip about Aidan changing women as often as his underwear is absolute bullshit. I can see you're a sensitive girl." He smiled gently. "I'm sure that's what my boy sees in you. And one thing's for sure: Aidan has changed since I last saw him. When he made money, Aidan had lots of girls around. While many of his army buddies abused liquor or drugs to deal with the aftermath of a vicious campaign, Aidan got his escape from chicks." He raised his eyebrows. "But he's changed, especially after Jessica."

"After Jessica?" I asked.

His eyes did a quick sweep of the room. "Let's put it this way. Aidan got involved for all the wrong reasons—some irrational need to tie the Thornhill name to old wealth. Not that he's ever admitted that. I think it's because he wanted to remove attention from his dysfunctional upbringing. I'm not too proud about that, mind you." His mouth twisted. "But in those days, career and touring came as natural to me as breathing did."

"The life of an artist is complex," I said gently.

"Yeah, sure is." His mouth turned up at one end, just like his son's. "Aidan's made running away from his past a lifetime habit." He paused and regarded me with familiar intensity. Like father, like son. "Maybe one day he'll reveal to you what's holding him down. He sees a shrink."

"Oh, right?" I recrossed my legs. "You mentioned Jessica."

"She brought with her a lifestyle foreign to Aidan. He changed, or at least, he couldn't be himself. That's when Aidan built this place—not only to keep me from touring, but so he could escape Jessica." Grant chuckled. "They didn't look good together. One can always read people's relationships by their body language. It came as no surprise when Aidan ended it. It was a relief."

"Was she that bad?" I sat forward, keen for all the gritty detail.

"She's attractive, to be sure." Grant's face softened. "Not like you, of course. I've never seen Aidan with anyone as strikingly beautiful as you. Jessica was alluring in a manicured way. Aidan described her as bossy, controlling, and someone who whined a lot."

Grant paused and took a sip of his drink. "When he broke it off, she left the country. It created a rift with some of the families around Malibu. Not that Aidan cares about that." Grant's focus suddenly shifted away from my face to above my head.

A hand landed on my shoulder. I turned to find Aidan there, his eyes narrowing suspiciously. "You two appear to be in a deep and meaningful conversation." He settled down by my side.

"Just learning a little about Clarissa, that's all," said Grant, giving me a subtle wink.

Aidan leaned in and whispered, "Are you ready to go?" He touched the nape of my neck, sending a shiver through me. I nodded.

As we stood to leave, Sara said, "You'll both have to come over for dinner soon. How about this week sometime?"

"I've got business to attend to. I'll be out of town this week. And there's an auction." He looked at me as if that activity involved me. "Let me get back to you. Probably the week after." He kissed her on the cheek.

Judging by his relaxed manner and familiar tone, it was clear that Aidan liked his stepmother.

"Okay. But make sure you do. I'd like to get to know this little sweetie." She kissed me on the cheek.

Grant whispered, "It's been a delight meeting you. Take care of my boy. He's more fragile than he makes out." He hugged me, and they left.

CHAPTER THIRTY-FOUR

It turned out that Aidan had an apartment not far from the Red House. Not in the mood for driving, he suggested we stay there. I was fine with that. Even a garbage dump would have been acceptable as long as Aidan was there.

"Sara's friendly. I'd enjoy meeting them for dinner," I said.

Aidan had his arm around my waist as we sauntered along. Although he'd had a few drinks, too many to drive, he didn't show any signs of being drunk. I sensed Aidan held his liquor well. Like my father, who was also partial to a drink or two, Aidan never slurred his words or stumbled about.

"She's a vegan. She cooks these colorful, elaborate meals." Aidan laughed. "I always have to grab a cheeseburger on the way home."

I giggled. "I'm the same. I tried to do the vegetarian thing at college, but I got so iron deficient I couldn't get out of bed."

Aidan turned and regarded me at length. "There's so much I have yet to discover about you, Clarissa Moone. I'm excited at the prospect of doing just that." Aidan smiled radiantly.

"That makes two of us. There's much I don't know about you, Aidan Thornhill."

"I must say, you were pretty thick with my father there. I'm sure you weren't just talking about the weather."

"He told me that philandering was your way of dealing with the aftermath of Afghanistan."

Aidan stopped walking. His face contorted. "What?"

"Well, those weren't his words, but..."

We stopped at an apartment tower across from the beach. It was such a magnificent night. The fresh, breezy air had sobered me up, because unlike Aidan, I was a little drunk.

"We're here." Aidan swiped a card over the double glass doors.

It was a very modern building with a marble-floored entrance. The walls were filled with giant canvases of contemporary abstract art, very much like the corporate buildings downtown.

"We'll continue this later," said Aidan in a serious tone.

We were alone in the elevator. Aidan held me. And as I stood against the wall, he pressed against me, his lips ravishing mine. Like mouth sex, his tongue took possession. I was putty in his hands as his fingers crept under my dress. He squeezed my bottom before running his hungry fingers up my thigh, settling on my cleft. "Oh God, you're wet, my little princess," Aidan said with a heavy breath.

When the elevator stopped, Aidan extricated himself from me. I was a little disappointed. I wanted to have hard, quick sex against the wall just like in the movies.

On my wavelength, Aidan said, "As much as I'd love to ravage you right now, a comfortable bed is more fitting for what I plan to do to you."

Yum. With that engorged erection throbbing on my thigh, all my muscles below my naval clenched in excited anticipation.

"This is your other home," I said, standing by the full-length window. With nothing but the sea and sky in view, the room's dimensions seemed infinite.

"It's one of my homes. I have a few. I grew up around Venice Beach, so I'm fond of this one."

"Are you really that rich?" I asked.

"Uh-huh." Aidan took me in his arms. "Would you be with me if I wasn't?"

I pulled away. My brows met furiously. "What do you think?"

Aidan laughed. "You're even sexier with a pout. Come here, Princess." He crooked his finger.

"There's so much I don't know about you, Aidan," I said, sitting next to him on the sofa.

"What do you want to know?" He kissed me on the neck.

"Why did you leave your fiancée? Do you plan to use me?"

Aidan pulled away and frowned. "Shit, Clarissa."

"Well, you asked." I rose and moved about the large room.

Despite being more contemporary than I was used to, the room had many tasteful and attractive objects to absorb, namely, the enormous canvases of seascapes and abstracts. They were masterfully created, textured and painted in oils. And as with everything Aidan surrounded himself with, I was impressed.

Aidan grabbed two small bottles of Evian from the fridge. "Do you want a glass?" His face had softened, dropping that anguished look from a few moments earlier.

"No, I'm good."

Aidan undid the cap for me and handed me the cold bottle.

I took a long sip. It was so refreshing and worked wonders for my pasty, dry mouth.

Aidan removed his shoes. Even his bare feet turned me on. "I left Jessica because I didn't love her. I wasn't attracted to her. For starters, our tastes diverged on everything. She liked modernist minimalism, and you're aware of what I like." Aidan's lips curled up on one side.

"But different tastes are interesting," I said.

"I wasn't attracted to her. Simple." Aidan's eyes had that searing, carnal glint. "Clarissa, I've never met anyone like you before. I'm new to this."

"So am I," I said softly.

Aidan took me into his arms. I buried my head in his neck while he stroked my hair. "I'm crazy about you, Clarissa. I thought of little else. When you pushed me away last week, I lost it. I couldn't concentrate. I've got a lot on my plate as well." He sighed. "I had it so bad. I needed a session with Kieren just to get through the week."

"Is he your psychologist?" I asked.

He nodded slowly. "Did my dad tell you?"

"He mentioned that you had one, mainly for issues related to the army."

"Fuck." Aidan pushed his hair back.

"There's nothing wrong with that. Everyone's got a therapist these days. It shows that you're trying to become a better person."

"Do you want me to become a better person?" he asked.

"I like you the way you are. It's just that I don't know you that well."

He approached the sofa again and sat close. He stroked my face, his blue eyes drilling into me. "That makes two of us."

Lost Aidan was just as magnetic as confident, unsinkable Aidan. If anything, his vulnerability made me want him more.

Emboldened by liquor, I reached for his trouser button. With my eyes firmly on his, I undid his zipper. His hooded gaze ate into me. He lowered his pants and stepped out of his boxers.

Aidan stood before me. My breath hitched. I forgot how long and thick his penis was. I became breathless with anticipation. As I took it into my hand, it dwarfed my tiny hand. He grew steel hard, the veins pulsating in my palm.

He murmured, "Careful. I'm not going to last."

Aidan lifted me up and carried me to the bedroom, placing me on the bed. He unzipped my dress. "I've been dying to remove this charming little number. My cock's been aching all night, thinking about it."

When he unclasped my bra, he growled. His eyes filled with hunger. "Oh my God, Clarissa. Each time is like the first time. How can someone be so fucking sexy?" His hands ran up my body, his eyes darkening with lust. "You steal my breath away."

Aidan took my heavy breasts into his hands. He groaned heavily, his eyes never leaving my face. As he took my ripened nipples between his moistened lips, an electrical impulse travelled straight to my sex. I turned to liquid.

He pulled down my panties. On a campaign to devour me, he buried his head between my thighs. Tingling and electrifying, his tongue masterfully stroked and rotated softly over my swollen clit. An extended sigh left my parted lips. Aidan's two fingers entered and stars exploded before me.

His hard, hungry cock was next. I ached as my legs opened wide. My eyes half-closed, my body burned. Aidan wiped his creamy mouth on the back of his hand before ravaging my mouth, his tongue, flavored in my cream, plunged deeply—a rehearsal of what his cock was about to do.

Pressing urgently against me, his erection fell into my hand.

I directed him into my sticky entrance. The thick, wet head entered slowly. The stretch was so intense it stole my breath.

"Are you okay?" Aidan struggled to speak.

"Uh-huh," I whimpered.

Aidan's heart pounded hard against my ribcage. "My God, you feel amazing."

We moved slowly, almost tentatively together. Aidan was being careful. He didn't want to hurt me. All the while, his fervid gaze pierced me. A glint of vulnerability burned through. The deeper he entered, the more I could see in his eyes this burning need to possess me. In response, I drowned Aidan in my desire.

My nerve endings had become increasingly sensitive. With each thrust I soared higher and higher as I gripped his firm butt. His hard body fitted so well with mine.

I flexed my pelvis to meet Aidan's penetration, which had grown deeper and harder. My toes curled tightly. The walls of my sex contracted wildly. The friction, the intense stretch of his rampaging cock set off a series of hot waves.

Spasms came in rapid succession. I relinquished gripping, and an overpowering swell grew with increasing intensity. My core tightened from the immense heat. My drugged body took off, gliding through jewel-like constellations, fireworks erupting in my mind. As my nails dug into Aidan's curvy biceps, a stretched, uncontrollable moan came out of my lips.

"That's it, Princess," Aidan gasped.

Undergoing his own eruption, Aidan's body trembled in my arms. Hot cream spurted, filling me. We tumbled in a wave together, Aidan holding me as he cried out my name.

We remained clasped together waiting for our senses to return.

"I'm sorry I came so quickly," said Aidan. My head rested on his firm, undulating chest. His pounding heart vibrated through me.

"There's no need to apologize, because I had two orgasms."

"I love being inside of you. I've never known a woman who feels like you do. You've bewitched me, Clarissa. You have such a responsive pussy."

"Is that a good thing?"

Aidan laughed. "Hell yeah… you're a dream, my little angel. I love your innocence." He kissed me. "Although you're a natural when it comes to…" Aidan paused. "That's the best bit." He trailed his finger around my moistened lips.

"A natural when it comes to…?"

"I was going to say fucking. But it doesn't seem the right word to describe what I meant."

"I don't mind. I love fucking you too. I never imagined it would be this enjoyable. Consider me a willing student." I giggled.

"My princess, I don't have to teach you anything. You're doing just fine." Aidan's vivid blue eyes softened. "This is new for me as well, you know?"

"How so?"

"It's the first time I've ever made love. With all the others, it was only fucking." Aidan played with a strand of my hair. "Your flavor is so addictive.

Your exquisite pussy is so pure. No one has been there." Aidan whispered. "Nor will they if I have my way."

What???

Even though it was all too soon, my heart exploded with such ferocity that hot blood raged through me.

That was the moment I dropped my guard and fell head over heels in love with Aidan Thornhill.

As my eyes travelled down to his half-erect penis a carnal thirst swept through me to drink him dry. I went to go down on him and Aidan said, "You don't have to, my princess— really."

"You don't wish me to?" I asked, peering up. I licked my lips in readiness. That did it. His cock stiffened without me touching it.

"Well, of course... I love it. I love your full, soft lips... ooh." He closed his eyes as I took him. It didn't take long for him to grow rock-hard.

I moved my pursed lips up and down. My tongue fluttered along his veiny shaft as his hard balls fell into my hands. Aidan's hitched breath told me I was getting it right. Cream fell onto my tongue. I tasted us. It was so erotic.

His enormous cock made my jaw ache, but I kept going anyhow. I loved tasting his arousal. I took him so deeply I nearly gagged.

"I will not last," he said hoarsely in a bid to push me away so that I wouldn't have to swallow. I ignored Aidan and continued anyway. Then a few moments later, with his eyes closed and jaw clenched, a cry of agony echoed from his ribcage. Aidan emptied his salty hot release into my mouth.

Aidan took me into his arms. His heart thrummed into my ear. "Where did you learn to do that?"

"With you. You're my first, remember?"

Aidan looked deeply into my eyes. "What, not even having these mouth-watering tits devoured?" He fondled me again.

"No," I said. "Sad, isn't it?"

"Not sad, just fucking bamboozling. Were all the guys you met gay?"

I laughed. "No. But I've never met one I was attracted to until..."

"Until me?" Aidan's fleshy lips curled divinely. "I'm one lucky man, that's for sure." Shaking his head in disbelief, he murmured, "Words cannot explain how that feels."

CHAPTER THIRTY-FIVE

Aidan

It was ten o'clock in the morning. I'd never slept that late before. How long had I slept? The last thing I recalled was Clarissa giving me a blowjob that sent me off to heaven. Where was she?

I dragged myself out of bed. My cock was hard, which wasn't unusual for the morning—it had a tendency to ache for sex first thing, especially since Clarissa arrived.

Dressed in nothing but a bath towel, the goddess was in the kitchen, making coffee. I stood by and watched. I prayed she'd bend over. Boy, I had it bad.

She smiled. "Good morning."

That face. Those glistening brown eyes, that soft black hair that sat just above her pear-shaped ass—Clarissa was a gift from the gods. After all the women I'd been with, I'd never met someone so pure in heart and soul. Just hearing her speak penetrated deep to my core.

Every gesture was unconsciously sensual as Clarissa brushed her hair from her face with that delicate hand. I could still taste the musky flavor that oozed from her when she came in my mouth.

She snuck a peek at my hard cock. He twitched in approval. Oh God, that expression— uncertain, yet aroused. What an honor to have watched Clarissa turn into a woman whilst in my arms.

For someone who liked to be in control, I was terrified of the power Clarissa had over me. I needed to be with her, in her, around her. It was like conquering Everest, only better. That was how I'd felt after Clarissa responded to my text the day before. After a week of desolation, I soared so high that in a rare display of emotion, I nearly hugged Greta, who probably would have reciprocated given she had a thing for Clarissa's dad.

"I made you some coffee. I wasn't sure how you like it."

"Black is fine," I said, entering the kitchen, I dropped her towel. Clarissa giggled. Her laughter could lift a fog, turn dark into light.

I pushed my hair back. Fuck, those tits. I'd always loved big breasts. But I didn't like boob jobs. Clarissa's were soft and firm, her nipples rosy and puckered like delectable raspberries. And the way her tits bounced about delectably, falling into my mouth when I fucked her—my heart skipped a beat thinking about it.

"Good morning, beautiful," I said, kissing her luscious lips. Clarissa had the softest lips, not pumped up like some ridiculous cartoon character. Recalling them around my cock, I nearly came there on the spot.

I pulled away. "Let me look at you."

Clarissa blushed, even after everything we'd done together.

Leading her by the hand, I said, "Let's have a shower."

After checking the temperature, I invited Clarissa in. I held her in my arms. She was about one foot shorter than me, which suited me fine—I loved petite women.

The water cascaded over us. I wanted to take her hard, but I had to prepare her. So I got on my knees. How I loved her musky earth scent.

Clarissa held onto the tiled wall, whimpering and quivering. I gripped her thighs and breakfasted on her sweet release as she flooded my mouth.

I stood up and kissed her swanlike neck. "Do you mind if I enter you this way?" I turned her around so that I faced her behind. "I don't want to bruise you, but I'd love to fuck you hard." My heart landed in my mouth. It was like we were fucking for the first time again.

"I'd like that," she said with a breathy voice.

That did it. I plowed into her.

Her moaning was music. She was so wet and hot. That super-tight, responsive pussy clenched my cock. It didn't take long at all. In fact, I only had to enter a few times, and I shot into her hard. I'd never come so quickly and intensely. Never one to cry out in sex, suddenly I'd become a crybaby.

"Hey, I didn't get you off. That was way too hot. I lost all control," I said, turning her to face me. I held her.

Her beautiful face flushed. Her eyes had that glint of arousal. "It's fine. Maybe we can have another go soon." She licked her lips.

Aah… She wanted to blow me. This girl swallowed my cum as if it tasted like chocolate. That thought alone made my cock bounce up. With her hand on my cock, Clarissa was a natural. She knelt down and moistened her luscious lips, then she took me deeply.

It was so hot that my cock went steel-hard in an instant. Instead of letting Clarissa finish me off, I lifted her up. And for round two, my balls pounded her firm, pear-shaped butt, my cock making a meal of her slick little pussy. This time, I made sure Clarissa climaxed so hard that her honeyed moans echoed off the tiles.

"Do you like pancakes?" I asked while toweling my hair.

"I love them," replied Clarissa with a wide, amiable smile.

Her hair stacked high in a bun, Clarissa looked sophisticated. Although I loved her hair out and wild, her hair tied up showed off her long swan neck. She looked radiant.

"I know a great place within walking distance. What you do think?"

Clarissa glanced down at her dress, frowning.

"Is there a problem?" I asked.

"I'm overdressed. You know, the morning-after type of thing."

"Clarissa, it is the morning after." I laughed.

"Yes, I know. But I'm not dressed for it. This is a little out there." She touched her dress.

"I love that dress. But I don't like you feeling uncomfortable..." I thought about it for a moment while my body screamed out for pancakes. "Ah... I've got it. There's a dress store a few doors down. How about we go in there? You can buy something suitable."

Clarissa nodded. "Okay then. Why not?"

One could not avoid, it seemed, the devouring regard of the entire male population as we moved along the sidewalk. An uncomfortable tightness, something I'd never experienced before, settled in my belly. While oblivious to the stir she caused, Clarissa floated along. She did not have a femme-fatale bone in her body, which suited me fine. I was predisposed to jealousy, and if it was unleashed, I became highly combustive.

After we were seated in the busy eatery, all eyes were on us. Although accustomed to it, I hated it.

"Everyone's staring," Clarissa said, leaning forward and whispering.

"Tell me about it. This is the land of gossip and speculation. They've been on my back for a while now. Jessica saw to that," I said in an icy tone.

"How so?" Clarissa asked.

The waiter arrived with our order. After he left, Clarissa said, "You were about to tell me about Jessica."

And there I was, hoping Clarissa had forgotten the subject. "There's not much to tell. Only that Jessica always made sure that cameras rolled whenever we were public." I raked my fingers through my hair. "One of her many annoying traits."

Clarissa raised a brow. "One?"

I sighed. "When I moved into the estate, I wanted to wash off the stain of my impoverished past." I paused for a sip of coffee. "So, I mixed with the well-to-dos. Jessica came with that. I should've just gotten a publicist. That would've been more expedient." I didn't want to do this.

"In what way did she annoy you?"

"She wouldn't take no for an answer. We were like chalk and cheese, different in a grating way. No pun intended." I smirked, and Clarissa returned a wry grin.

Clarissa leaned on her elbow. That delectable cleavage had my cock pushing hard against my jeans. How could someone do this to me? I just wanted to fuck this girl all day and night.

"There's not much to tell other than that the paparazzi and all of this unwanted attention started with her and hasn't abated. It's so not who I am, Clarissa. I'm a private guy." I smiled tightly.

"How did she take the break-up?" asked Clarissa.

"Not that well. I suppose I ruffled her ego. Jessica never showed much emotion unless she was pissed. The relationship was one major, stupid mistake."

Clarissa touched my hand, and my whole body fired up. Her limpid eyes kindled with sympathy, almost emasculating me. I didn't do pity well.

"Hey, people do this all the time," I said. "They have relationships that don't work for whatever reason. You're an anomaly, a rarity, one of those flowers that botanists spend their entire careers looking for."

Clarissa's face brightened into a wide smile. "How beautiful, what an amazing thing to say."

Good. Let's move on.

The food arrived and not too soon—my appetite was huge, as was Clarissa's. For one so petite, Clarissa had a hearty appetite. I loved watching her eat. Even that turned me on. And when jam dropped onto her cleavage, I wanted to lick it off. I used my finger instead. Reading my arousal, Clarissa responded with a girlish giggle. I spent the rest of the meal hoping that jam would spill down Clarissa's cleavage again, childish though that was. I'd never had that much simple fun before.

CHAPTER THIRTY-SIX

Clarissa's apartment tower looked even seedier in the cruel light of day. I didn't like her living in this bum area known for drug dealers and lowlifes. I sighed with relief when Clarissa said she'd return to the estate that same afternoon. I wanted her out of there. But how could I tell her that? I'd only known her for three weeks.

"It's Tabitha's birthday today. I promised to lunch at Sammy's," said Clarissa.

"Where we met last night? Do you hang there much?" I asked, picturing that good-looking dude all over her.

"Johnny, Tabi's brother, runs it, and we like it there."

Clarissa seemed so young. Was this the same girl who'd dangled her heavy tits in my mouth as she mounted my cock? I wanted her badly right then. My needy hand moved up her leg. Clarissa stared at me seductively, encouraging my journey up her dress.

Oh, holy shit. She wasn't wearing panties.

"Clarissa," I exclaimed, my cock pushing hard against my jeans.

"Aidan?" Her lips curled.

"You forgot to wear your panties. You were like this at the diner. What if a wind had lifted that pretty dress?" The notion both terrorized and thrilled me.

My fingers crept between her lips. Oh, she was wet. I caressed her clit. Clarissa's heavy-lidded gaze held me captive. Fortunately, I had tinted windows.

I pressed a button to make the windows opaque, designed for moments like this—only I'd never had a moment like this. My finger fluttered over her bud.

"Can anyone see us?" she asked, in a breathless, about-to-come voice.

"No. In any case, if one was to be caught in flagrante delicto, this would be the place to do it."

Clarissa laughed. I bent down and opened her legs wide. I didn't know if it was the thought of doing this in public during broad daylight, albeit with tinted windows, or the exhilaration of observing Clarissa unfold like a rose, but my cock throbbed so hard it threatened to erupt.

Clarissa tangled her hands in my hair. Although it was borderline painful, I didn't mind, especially when Clarissa squirted into my mouth. I'd never experienced a woman ejaculating before. Now, that was a serious turn-on.

Trancelike, her dainty hands reached into my boxer shorts. Wet and ready, my cock sprang up. Clarissa licked her lips. Driving me crazy with anticipation, she lowered her face onto my lap.

Oh, those soft, full lips. Clarissa moved up and down with her mouth, her tongue licking me as she sucked. Exquisite torture. I needed to be inside that tight, wet pussy.

I pushed back the seat to make room for Clarissa to sit on my lap.

"Are you sure no-one can see us, Aidan?" she asked in that cock-swelling, soft voice. I shook my head.

Straddling me, Clarissa used her toned thighs to lower slowly onto my cock. *Ooh.* In a moment, that would remain with me forever, I unbuttoned the dress, which I'd chosen for its buttons. Her tits poured out. "This not wearing underwear will have to be a regular feature, I think," I said.

Clarissa giggled. While she bounced up and down, I supped on her erect nipples, making a meal of them. It didn't get better than this. My cock was in so deep in this position.

"Slowly, my darling." An explosion was imminent. Blood raged through my veins. "I need you to come, Clarissa." My face contorted. I struggled to speak.

The walls of her sublimely tight pussy closed around my cock. It was tighter than ever, the friction immense. Stars shot before my eyes while Clarissa moaned in agonized pleasure. Her spasms increased, strangling my cock.

"That's it baby. Come for me," I said, struggling to speak. Clarissa released, flooding me, which set my own fiery deluge off. I gave a body-shuddering groan as my hot sperm emptied into her.

We held each other, waiting for our breathing to steady. Clarissa, all weightless, had her legs clasped around me, her wet cheek against mine. Rather disturbingly, I almost cried—something I'd only done once before in my life. And that wasn't due to a mind-blowing orgasm. Was this how true love felt?

Clarissa buttoned up her dress and moved over to the passenger seat. I opened the glove compartment and passed her some tissues.

Unable to take my eyes off her, I watched Clarissa, whose hands were under her dress. It fired me up again.

"Clarissa, stay with me, please," I said, surprising myself. I had work to do, but that could wait.

She turned and studied me, looking perplexed. Her cheeks glowed, and her eyes luminescent, her lips slightly open. "It's my friend Tabi's birthday. She's expecting me."

"Tell her you'll catch up tomorrow. Take her shopping on me," I said, getting out my wallet.

She touched my arm. "No need for that. You're already paying me over and above my contracted wage. I can afford it."

"Then give her a quick call and hang with me all day," I said with a cajoling smile.

"What will I do about the car?"

"I can call one of my guys. He'll pick it up."

"But the keys are upstairs in the apartment," said Clarissa, her brow puckering.

"Easily done. I'll call him now. He'll be here in five minutes."

With those doleful eyes on me, Clarissa grabbed her phone.

"I need to be with you today," I whispered into her ear, leaning over to kiss her. She flashed one of her knockout smiles. And I was a goner.

"Hey, Tabs. Listen, sweetie, I can't make it. Aidan's going away tomorrow, and we want to hang out. I'll swing by in the morning, and we can go shopping. That's if..." She looked over at me. "If I can get the time off work."

I nodded. *You can have the whole week off if you want.*

"There'll be someone coming within the hour to pick up keys for my car." Clarissa listened without a murmur. This friend seemed too dependent on her for my liking. And I hated all the guys that came with Tabitha. Everyone wanted Clarissa. How could they not?

I picked up my phone and pressed the number for the head of my security team. "Hey, Evan. How's your day? Look, I need you to do me a favor if you don't mind."

After I finished the call, I turned to Clarissa. "Tabitha relies on you a fair bit."

Clarissa tilted her head. "I know, but we've been together since we were five. We grew up in the same area. We're close."

"I get that. It's healthy to have a close buddy. I just don't like her brother's needy eyes all over you."

Clarissa brushed my face with her soft hand. "Aidan, I've known Johnny for a long time. He's like a brother."

"Incest is more common than you think," I said churlishly.

"Where to? Venice Beach? We can hang there and watch a film. Or go down for a swim, cook a meal. What you do say?"

Indecisive as ever, Clarissa shrugged.

"Unless you want to go back to Malibu?" I asked.

"No. Venice is fine. It's private."

"You don't feel comfortable sleeping with me at Malibu?" I asked, starting up the engine.

"I do, but…"

"But?"

"There's Greta, my father…"

"Their rooms are nowhere near my space. It's soundproofed, anyway. Your dad is only in the library during the day. And that has a separate entry. I, too, Clarissa, am a very private person."

"That's a relief. I love being on the estate," said Clarissa enthusiastically.

"But you prefer the apartment?"

"For today, yes." A gentle smile painted her face, which, as always, affected me like a sea breeze on a hot day.

"Do you spend much time there?"

"Only when I go to the Red House. Mostly, I'm at Malibu. It's my sanctuary."

"It's glorious." Clarissa sighed.

"I love hearing you sigh," I said. "Your breathy voice makes me hard."

Clarissa blushed, making me even harder.

"When I first visited the estate, it reminded me of Lake Como, in Italy. One of those massive villas one sees in magazines," said Clarissa.

"The architecture is based on the Italian model. That's what attracted me to the house in the first place," I said, entering the expressway.

"What was your favorite part of Europe?"

I puffed out my cheeks and blew out slowly. "Prague, Paris, Madrid... all were spectacular. But I have to say Italy really did it for me. The art is just mind-blowing. Venice is like something out of a fairy-tale. The whole of Europe had that vibe, really. Especially after the brutality of Afghanistan, the contrast was extreme. Europe with its spectacular, unimaginable art seemed so civilized and refined."

"You're inspiring me to go," Clarissa gushed.

"Don't say that. I'm not ready for you to go."

"Not yet, of course, but I will one day."

"Yes, with me," I said, sneaking a quick glance. She looked at me earnestly, with her brows squeezing in. "What's that look, Clarissa? Am I coming on too strong?"

"A little." She looked down at her hands. "But I like it," she said in a tiny voice that I had to strain to hear.

CHAPTER THIRTY-SEVEN

The wind threatened to reveal Clarissa in all her glorious nakedness. I held her dress down as she giggled infectiously. I smiled more than ever. For someone known to be serious, my facial muscles ached.

I'd re-entered civilian life as a shadow. That probably fulfilled my original motivation for going to war, which was to lose myself. But my spirit also perished— a spirit that Clarissa, through her touch, soft voice, and beauty, had restored.

We stopped off at the supermarket and picked up food. Even something as mundane as shopping was fun with Clarissa gliding along by my side. When she reached for a packet of crisps, noticing that we were alone in the aisle, I let my hands creep up her legs. The fact she was without panties had been driving me crazy from the moment we entered the busy store. She turned and cast me a frown, which was quickly chased away by a giggle.

"I can't help myself, and nor can you it seems, you wet angel," I whispered.

"I'm always like that around you, Aidan," Clarissa responded in girlish softness, sending my cock into a frenzy.

Noticing another person enter the aisle, I stopped and wiped her arousal on my jeans. My petulant cock throbbed for round three as I hurried Clarissa along.

I insisted Clarissa choose all the toiletries she needed. As she reached for the cheaper brands, I redirected her to the more expensive versions. When I handed her a body-wash, Clarissa balked. "Aidan, that's thirty dollars too much."

"Do you know how much I earn in an hour?" I asked.

She shook her head. Her hair fell around her face in such a captivating way. Each time I looked, her beauty increased. Then there were Clarissa's many expressions. Although on the reserved side, those large eyes and that expressive elfin face always had something to say even without uttering a word.

She was like a sunset that improved with each viewing.

"The last time I looked, I made fifty thousand an hour," I said.

Her mouth dropped open. "Holy cow, that much?"

I laughed. "I know it's crazy. It shocks me at times."

We grabbed enough to keep us in store for the night and morning and headed back.

"Tomorrow, I fly out again," I said as we entered the apartment. "This time, it's Germany for two weeks." My tummy tightened. I hated the idea of leaving Clarissa that long. "That's why I needed this day with you."

"What's in Germany?" Clarissa sat on the sofa and kicked off her shoes. Starting at her dainty feet, my eyes travelled up her legs. That she was not wearing panties had become an obsession.

"I'm going there to study their solar farms," I said, pouring two glasses of juice.

Clarissa took a glass and sipped. "That seems like a passion for you." Her eyes showed no concern that I'd be away for two weeks. Hell. Did I want her more than she wanted me?

Clarissa stared at me expectantly. I realized she'd asked me a question. "Sorry, I just can't concentrate, knowing you're"—I ran my hand up her leg— "not wearing panties."

She giggled. "Aidan, you're a sex maniac."

"I'm not normally," I said defensively.

"I'd just like to know more about you, and what you do, what drives you. You fascinate me, Aidan— that's all." A cheeky little grin formed. "But I do also like being touched."

My mood heightened, while my cock grew hard at the way she emphasized "touched."

"I'm a fan of renewables, to answer your earlier question. I want to gain insight into best practices so that I can develop farms here—mainly for those folks at the bottom of the food chain—so that they can access clean and cheap energy."

Clarissa's face filled with admiration again. "That's such a noble ambition. But why Germany?"

"Because they have the best systems in the world. For a country not known for sunny weather, it's now generating an impressive amount of energy. Solar is the major contributor, although there's wind and hydro in that mix as well. My plan is to get with the team over there and learn how to replicate their model."

"Did you study engineering or the like? You seem so knowledgeable."

I shook my head. "Dropped out at sixteen—not something I'm proud of, mind you."

"Hey, some of the most brilliant people in history were not formally educated. Knowledge is everywhere. In any case, colleges don't make us intelligent. They equip us with knowledge so that we can work. Intelligence is innate." She paused. "I met some dumb people at college."

Clarissa's sardonic tone made me chuckle. "One year spent in Europe gave me time to think, read, and absorb. That's where I formed my love of art."

"I love that about you, Aidan," Clarissa crooned. "You're one of those unique beings who can be anything he wants to be." She smiled so sweetly my heart went to liquid. "Why didn't you pursue music as a career? You're very talented."

"How many compliments can a man take?" I said, pushing back my hair.

"Did your mom or dad encourage you?"

"My mom was all over the place. And Dad toured all the time. When he was around, he taught me to play. And I suppose he encouraged me. But if anything, his lifestyle discouraged me from pursuing music as a career. Dad was always broke and frustrated. It's a very competitive industry, and the type of music we're into is everywhere. I needed to become independent. That's why I joined the army. It was the only career where I didn't need a college degree."

"What do you mean by your mom being all over the place?" Clarissa asked.

Now we were on a slippery path. I hated talking about my childhood. I did not like airing my dirty linen around Clarissa. She was too pure for that. The only dirtying belonged in the bedroom. Not her soul.

I shrugged. "She was a hippie, smoked a fair bit of weed, and drank too much. Not a fit mother. But that's okay, I managed. It made me independent. I learnt how to open cans of food at the age of two."

"Oh my God, that's terrible, Aidan."

"Clarissa. Let's not do pity. I hate it." I dropped my gruff tone and added, "I'm here now. I'm rich. I'm with the most beautiful girl in the world. I wouldn't do anything different, because I wouldn't have met you otherwise." I stroked her cheek.

Clarissa fell into my arms. *Ah… that's more like it.*

"Are you hungry?" I asked, wiping my mouth after feeding off her juicy pussy.

"Yeah, for you," she said.

Good answer.

I entered her hard. "I don't want to bruise you baby. Tell me if it's too much."

Her mouth covered mine, her lips feverish, her tongue whipping into mine. She was on top of me, which was fast becoming my preferred position, with her delectable breasts dangling in my face. Her hair out and wild, Clarissa rode me hard. She was a fucking natural in the bedroom. Her appetite for my cock nearly brought tears to my eyes—particularly when she swallowed hard, licking her lips as if she'd tasted something delicious.

"Can we make it a rule for no more underwear when we're together?" I rasped, making myself heat so badly that I was about to erupt. Normally, I could fuck long and hard. But with Clarissa, it was so overwhelming that it didn't take long for me to fill her.

Clarissa's moans built. Her pussy contracted in sharp spasms, sucking my dick in deeply. Even her cries were erotic. Her nails dug into my arms, her tits on my face.

Oh… it didn't get better than this.

Our release joined forces into one mighty, ceiling-hitting explosion.

Waiting for my breath to regulate, I stroked her curvy back. She had the type of shapely butt that made a man sigh. "Where did you come from?"

Clarissa cast one of her enigmatic grins. "From a pair of eccentric parents."

"Hmm… you too." I sniffed.

"Well, maybe not like your mom and dad."

"Tell me, why did you pursue art history?" I asked, realizing that so far, all the talk had been about me.

"My mother introduced me to art as a child. She was into painting. I suppose my love of art started there." Clarissa glided gracefully over to the window. It was a stormy day, and the clouds were gathering at speed. In the background, lightning pierced the dark-gray sky. "I love storms. Especially here with this view."

I nodded in agreement. It was a marvelous view, all sea, sky, and nothing else, just as I liked it, just as I needed it.

"Did you study art?" I asked, recalling her impressive sketch.

"For a while I did. But I decided that art history would at least get me employed somehow. To be a successful artist these days requires business skills and money, and I'm not that person. I'm not ambitious, nor am I that driven. At least with art history, I can teach one day if need be." Clarissa sat down next to me.

"You undersell yourself," I said, turning to face her. "You're driven, I believe. We loved what you did for the fundraiser. You're a hard worker, Clarissa."

"I found it really enjoyable."

"Would you like to paint full-time?" I asked, thinking about the space downstairs at the estate that could easily be converted into a studio.

"Yes. One day. I'm not in a hurry. I sketch. I enjoy that. We'll see."

"You're a remarkable girl, Clarissa."

She sat by my side on the sofa. "And you, Mr. Thornhill, are a remarkable man." Clarissa combed away a stray hair from my face. Her soft, moist lips melded sublimely with mine.

Each time we kissed was like the first.

"Aidan?"

"Yes." I stroked her hair, as she rested in my arms. It was the most relaxed I'd been for a long while. I couldn't recall a more perfect day.

"Why didn't you introduce yourself when you were with Rocket in the garden and at the beach?"

"Because I was smitten," I said, stroking her arm.

She frowned. "Why would that stop you from introducing yourself?"

"Good question. I suppose I wanted to see how you reacted on neutral ground. How you were with me as an ordinary man."

"You were far from ordinary, Aidan." Clarissa raised an eyebrow. "So did I pass the test?"

"Although there was no test, you would have passed one with flying colors," I said. "I loved how you and Rocket got on. I loved the fact you were so down to earth. And holy shit, in that swimsuit." My eyes burned into her. Clarissa had her shapely legs up on the sofa, and her dress had ridden up. My cock lengthened again.

"My spinster one-piece." Clarissa giggled.

"You didn't look like a spinster to me." Her dress, still unbuttoned from our last steamy session, invited my greedy fingers in as I fondled her heavy breasts. I sat with her on the sofa and teased her nipples.

"That's Tabi talking," said Clarissa with her breathy getting aroused voice.

"Tabi? Oh, your housemate—or ex-housemate if I have my way," I muttered.

"Your way?" Clarissa's brow puckered.

"I want you with me, Clarissa," I said, surprising myself. I hadn't expected to do this so quickly.

When she didn't respond, I asked, "You don't like the idea?"

"I do… I suppose in a way I'm already there in the cottage." Clarissa leaned forward, and I could see her tits completely. Christ, this girl was killing me.

"It's just happening so fast. It's brilliant how it is."

"Yes, sure…" I stroked Clarissa's cheek. I didn't want to frighten her by my need to possess her. "What was your impression of me, then?" I asked, changing the subject.

"I thought you must've been the gardener." Clarissa chuckled.

I grinned. "A gardener?" I thought about this. "Hmm… you know, I relate more to being a gardener than a billionaire."

"What do you want to do with all that money?"

"I don't know. Just keep setting up funds so that I can help those in need. And spoil you rotten. It's brilliant being rich."

"That's what attracts me the most to you, Aidan—your kindness." Clarissa's emotion-filled voice penetrated to my soul.

"What, not my animal charms?" I said, smiling.

Clarissa giggled. "I thought you were a hot, sexy gardener. And whenever I went out for my walk, I hoped I would run into you."

"Now, that turns me on," I said, running my hand up her leg. "Clarissa…" I looked into her eyes, my own eyes heavy with need. "You're so delectably wet."

"That's because of how you're touching me."

"I like the way you touch me," I said, circling her swelling clit with my finger. Clarissa reached into my unzipped pants and played with my cock. "We're like two over-sexed teenagers who can't get enough of each other," I said, my voice thickening from arousal.

I loved Clarissa about to orgasm. She got this look in her half-closed eyes, her mouth agape and her whimpers sweeter than any music I'd ever heard. Just as I felt her clit pulsing, I entered her with two fingers, and she trembled, squirting cum on my fingers. "That's it, baby. Yes," I murmured. I lifted her off the sofa and carried her into the bedroom for round four.

CHAPTER THIRTY-EIGHT

The view stilled my mind as I stood by the window. I watched the ever-changing blues, and soul-lifting turquoise sky that was at times tranquil, while other times, wild and unexpected, just like my emotions.

My eyes shifted to the painting of the reclining woman. Clarissa entered my thoughts. Not that she was ever that far from them. I recalled the tingly feeling I got when setting eyes on the painting at Sotheby's. Paying higher than its value at the time, I had to have it.

I'd always been a sucker for women with long black hair and brown eyes. The need for the painting superseded mere indulgence. Never would I have predicted that I would find myself in the arms of its double.

Having not picked up a book since Europe, I decided to visit my library. Clarissa had inspired me to read again.

It came as no surprise to find Julian Moone there with his head buried in a book. Seated in a recliner, he looked the part in his cravat and gentlemanly attire. It was like stepping back in time and gratifying to see the room being enjoyed.

Julian peered up over his horn-rimmed glasses. "Oh, you must be Mr. Thornhill." Placing the book down, he started to rise.

"No, stay there, please." I approached Clarissa's father and held out my hand. "Pleased to meet you."

Julian took my hand and nodded. "Likewise." He had that familiar uncertain smile. Like father, like daughter.

"Are you enjoying the collection?" I ran my finger over one of the gold- scrolled spines.

"I'm in heaven," said Julian. "You have an impressive collection here." He got up and directed my attention to the mahogany desk, where a ledger sat. "The catalogue is coming along very well. I'm recording everything by hand. And Greta…" He paused, his face looking flushed suddenly. "Ah, Greta suggested I photograph the entries and pop them into digital format." He smiled faintly. "Or at least, she'll show me. I'm not good with technology." His dark eyes reflected a hesitant nature, another family trait.

I opened out my hands. "Work it as you like, Mr. Moone. I'm just excited that the library is being used." Shifting gears into personable mode, I asked, "What are you reading?"

"Please, call me Julian." His eyes lit up. "Nathanial Hawthorne, *The Scarlet Letter.* You have a fine collection of early American literature. I can't wait to get into the Henry James' first editions. All unexpurgated. Mind you, the man would've done well to trim some of his prose." He laughed.

I responded with a chuckle, not because I knew anything about this subject, but more because his laugh was infectious. Just like his daughter's. I instantly warmed to him. There was such joyful eccentricity with Julian. He reminded me of some of the characters I'd met in Europe.

"I came in for a book to take away with me. I'm off to Germany for two weeks."

"Oh..." Julian wrinkled his brow, deep in thought suddenly. His eyes rested on the dark wood shelves. "I suppose you won't want a heavy hardback in your luggage," he said with hand on chin.

"That won't be a problem," I responded, careful not mention I was going in my own private jet. This was hardly the time to flaunt my obscene wealth.

"Well, then," he said. "Have you got any book in mind, an author perhaps?"

"Not sure. I'm interested in war history, I suppose."

Julian's eyes fired up. "Ah. Right, then..." He regarded me. "You were in the army. Clarissa mentioned something about that."

I nodded.

"Which unit?" Julian asked.

My body stiffened. "The Special Forces." I didn't want to talk about that.

Julian's face was brimming with interest. "The elite squad, I take it."

I nodded.

"Impressive," Julian replied. I relaxed again. He had a calming, avuncular quality. "Did you read much while deployed?"

"I did."

"Which were your favored books?"

Without giving it a thought, I replied, "*Les Misérables* and *War and Peace.*"

Julian's eyebrows shot up. He nodded in approval. "Door stoppers. They're major works. Extraordinary books, in fact. If somebody were to ask which books edify and enrich while challenging moral concepts, I would direct them to those two."

I smiled. My head officer, an avid reader and well-educated man, had spoken similarly on their virtues.

"So, war history, then," Julian reflected. "How about Ernest Hemingway?"

Before I even opened my mouth, Julian had a copy in his hands.

I took the book *A Farewell to Arms.* "That should work," I said, adding, "I'll probably take one other."

Julian's eyes sparkled. He was enjoying this. "What about *A Tale of Two Cities* by Dickens?"

"Sure, if you recommend it."

"It's about the French revolution. Taking into account you've read *War and Peace,* I think you may find this enjoyable." Julian had it in his hand before I had a chance to reply. He knew his way around the collection almost supernaturally.

I received the book with gratitude. Then, clearing my voice, I announced, "I probably should mention that I'm seeing your daughter." This wasn't easy, but the last thing I desired was that Julian heard it from another source or encountered an image of us kissing on the streets of LA. Which would surely surface sooner or later, considering I hadn't hidden my passion for Clarissa.

"Oh, right, yes..." he said, shifting his glasses. I'd thrown him a curve ball.

"I was hoping for your blessing." My muscles tightened.

Julian opened out his hands. "As long as Clarissa is happy, I'm happy." His voice had a tinge of hesitancy about it.

Unable to leave it there, I said, "You sound concerned."

"Clarissa is a sensitive girl." Julian paused to reflect. "She was never the same after her mother died. Before that, she was an excitable, bubbly child, full of drive and joyful creativity. Very much like her mother, who was equally remarkable—that's where Clarissa gets her beauty." His eyes drooped wistfully at the mention of his late wife. "When my wife died, Clarissa was eight. For one whole year, she didn't speak. The shock was that extreme."

Shit.

"Anyway..." He sighed slowly. "She eventually snapped out of it, and one day she just talked again. But something in her had changed. Lately, I've seen a glimpse of that little girl—the bubbly, excitable child." He looked at me, a faint smile forming. "Now I know why."

My chest finally filled with air. "Mr. Moone, I mean, Julian, I have no intention of hurting your daughter." *How can I? I'm fucking head over heels...*

"Mr. Thornhill..."

"Aidan. Call me Aidan."

"Clarissa's been a model daughter." Julian brimmed with parental pride. "In that, she's never given me cause to fuss or worry. On Saturday nights, instead of pestering me to let her out, which I would've allowed, of course"—he chuckled— "she preferred to stay home and either paint, read, or watch a classic movie with me." Although Julian struck me as the stoical kind, his voice was thick with emotion.

"You have some reservations, Julian?" I asked.

"Only that my daughter is young for her years, due to this lack of experience."

"Julian, I have no intention of hurting her. My feelings are genuine. That's her charm—Clarissa's pure heart and spirit. I just want you to know so that we can be together without sneaking around."

"Yes, yes, I can see that, Aidan," he said. "And you have my blessing. I only told you this because Clarissa is as fragile as a rose in the hot sun."

I exhaled slowly. "Love makes us all a little vulnerable, Julian."

Julian held onto his chin pensively, nodding slowly. "Quite so, Aidan, quite so." Pain glistened in his eyes. It was obvious that Clarissa's mother remained deeply etched into his soul.

I left the library lighter knowing that I'd made my connection with Clarissa official. Julian's shared insights made my desire for Clarissa even stronger—if that were at all possible, considering how much I already wanted her. As I sat staring at my empty suitcase, with my head in my hands, all I could think of was how Clarissa would take me once she learnt of my past.

Eight-year-old Clarissa, taciturn and frozen, entered my thoughts. A childhood interrupted by trauma. I'd confused that lost expression for innocence. It explained the silent treatment, the insecurity, the sad glint in those doleful eyes. Having witnessed animation leave my best friend's once expressive eyes, I knew how it felt to lose someone close. That dark, veinicing moment still haunted my sleep— his lifeless eyes staring at me so lucidly was suffocating.

A knock at the door made me jump. Such was the muddle of contemplation besieging me.

"Sorry if I startled you," said Greta as I stood aside to allow her passage.

My aunt had totally shed the serious persona I'd come to recognize. Apart from the change in clothes, she'd colored her hair, taken to wearing make-up, and was generally in a gay mood. Although I found this rather baffling, I was nevertheless pleased.

As my father's twin, Greta was the mother I should've had. She had cared for me with the intent of reversing the neglect I'd suffered as a young child.

"I'm just packing. I have to leave soon." I glanced down at my watch.

Greta's eyes fell on the two books I was about to pack away. "You've been to see Julian?"

"Yep. I picked up something to read. He's a knowledgeable man." I opened my closet and selected my warmest winter jacket. "He's a calming influence, much like his daughter."

"Aha…" Greta lingered. I could tell she wanted to say something.

"So, Greta, what's up?"

"I spoke to Grant earlier." She shifted nervously. "He mentioned you introduced him to Clarissa, and in his words, you were all over her."

"And?" I asked, shrugging.

"Aidan, she's a lovely, gentle, and sensitive girl. I don't want to see you hurt her. I've grown rather fond of her."

Despite being annoyed at the assumption that I would hurt Clarissa, I was touched that Greta cared so much for her. Instead of giving her any stay-out-of- my-life bullshit, I kissed Greta on the cheek. "We're good, real good. I've never felt this way before." My eyes went misty.

Oh Christ, tears? No! I'm tougher than that.

"She's not like the others. That's plain enough. I just needed to understand," said Greta.

I exhaled a slow breath. "She sure isn't like the others." I combed back my hair. "I'm in there for the long haul, Greta. I mean it."

We regarded each other silently. A very faint smile grew on my aunt's face.

"She's the best event organizer we've ever had, Aidan. I'd hate to lose her."

"You will. I've got other plans for Clarissa." I kissed Greta on the cheek. "I better get cracking. See you in a couple weeks. I'll stay in touch." As she was about to leave, I added, "Oh, and Julian Moone's a decent man." I smiled and raised my eyebrows.

Greta responded with a blush and a rarely seen wide smile.

As I snapped shut my luggage, I was already missing Clarissa. I'd only dropped her off at the cottage two hours earlier. My lips had devoured her. And Clarissa had ended up pushing me out the door, giggling. God, I wished I could record that giggle. It was such a turn-on.

CHAPTER THIRTY-NINE

Clarissa

Roaming around the cottage in a haze, I'd lost count of how many times I'd entered my bedroom. I was facing two weeks without Aidan.

Would he come and say goodbye? He'd already done that one hour earlier when dropping me off. Another good-bye was highly improbable, and it was ridiculous for me to even want that. This need I'd developed for Aidan was frightening. He'd become an addiction.

My swimsuit dangled in my hand. I was off for a swim to clear my head. Opting for my sensible one-piece, I left the red skimpy ones on the bed.

A knock came at the door just as I was about to change. Wrapping my sarong around me, I went to answer it.

Aidan stood before me, dressed in beige chinos and a linen shirt that was fluttering in the breeze. My eyes went to his shapely pectorals covered with a sprinkling of hair. With that panty-wetting smile, Aidan's eyes darkened when he noticed the skimpy sarong covering my otherwise bare body.

I stepped away from the door and let him in. My heart was beating fast, which was crazy considering I'd only seen him one hour earlier.

"I've come to say farewell. I didn't do it properly last time," said Aidan, his lust-filled eyes moving up and down my body.

Before I could speak, Aidan took me into his arms. My sarong had come off. A growl vibrated off his chest as his hands ran up and down my body.

"I wish I could take you with me." His mouth was on mine, groaning as he cupped my heavy breasts. I heard his zipper, and my core clenched.

"I can't leave you alone, Clarissa. Why aren't you coming with me?" He pulled away. He looked fragile suddenly. Aidan was suffering as much as I was.

My heart was full. "I have to get the gala together." I bent down to pick up my sarong.

He stopped me. "Don't. Let me look at you." His hands crept up my leg.

Oh, how I wanted him to take me again and again.

"Clarissa, my little angel, you're so ready," he rasped. His finger circled my clit, and I started to writhe against his hard body.

Aidan waltzed me to the wall, and draping my leg over his curvy, veiny bicep, he penetrated deeply into me. "This will be quick," he said hoarsely. His large, hard cock stretched me so divinely I expelled a hungry moan.

It was wild and hot. His lips on mine, devouring me, making me lose control as fireballs mushroomed before me. I gasped, while Aidan shuddered and groaned through a jaw-clenching release.

When our breathing stilled, I unraveled from his tight hold. "Aidan, you really should go."

Aidan combed back his hair with his hands. "I'll call you." He kissed me and left.

Just as I watched Aidan moving away in the distance, my phone buzzed.

I pressed the button. "Hi, Tabs."

"First you miss my birthday lunch. And now you don't deliver on the breakfast you promised."

"I'm so sorry." I sighed wearily. "This thing with Aidan is intense. He's off to Germany today. That's why he wanted to spend the day with me. I'll make it up to you."

"It's cool, Clary. I get it. You're with the hottest guy in the universe. I would've done the same. You wouldn't have seen me for dust." She chuckled. "But listen, something's happened. I really need to see you desperately."

"What?"

"Can we meet?"

I looked at my watch. It was eleven. "I'll meet you for lunch in an hour."

By midday I was sitting at a vegetarian diner with Tabitha. I figured I needed something healthy after all the hamburgers and yummy junk food I'd eaten recently.

After we ordered, I faced Tabitha, who was quieter than usual. "So, what's happened?"

"I've left Josh." Tabitha's eyes evaded my imploring gape.

"Why? I thought you were crazy about him. And he's a really decent guy."

"That's the reason." Tabitha bit into her nails.

"You're not back with Steve, are you?" I was so perplexed I sounded like a scolding mother.

"No way. I'll never go back to him." She paused. "Josh was too gushy. You know me. I need tension." Her eyes kindled playfully.

"You're a fucking nut-job," I said, sipping on my juice. "Why are you like this, Tabitha? Are you determined to be a masochist?"

"No, I'm not, and anyhow, I've met someone." She peered up at me, a wicked smile forming on her lips.

"What? So soon!"

Tabitha raised a brow.

"Shit, Tabs. You met him and then dumped Josh?"

A glint of guilt coated her big green eyes. I could tell she'd had hot sex. Tabitha had a post-orgasmic glow about her.

"When did this happen? Because we were meant to have lunch together, Josh included. And that was only twenty-four hours ago."

She laughed at my incredulous tone. "Oh, Clary." She touched my hand. "I'm so glad you're here."

"Come on sister, cough up." Our dynamic had shifted. I'd become the pushy one. Aidan had inspired me to be more confident. Or perhaps, I was finally growing up.

Unable to remove the smile from her face, Tabitha sipped on her coffee. I had to admit, it was the most excited I'd seen her ever over a guy. And I'd seen many come and go in her four years of boyfriends.

"You're partly responsible," said Tabitha.

"How? Stop being all mysterious."

"God, Clary. You're not yourself. You're all fired up. What's got into you?"

"You have," I said, swallowing my food. "I really liked Josh. He was such a kind-hearted guy."

"He just didn't make me come," Tabitha said dryly.

"Well, it's not all about orgasms. There's got to be other things that matter. A compatible love match can't be predicated on how many orgasms your lover gives you." My voice wavered. This wasn't any easy argument.

"Says Miss Multiples can't get enough of Mr. Nine Inch Penis." Tabitha glared at me with a sardonic smirk.

"Point taken, but surely, we can't measure love solely by orgasms?"

"We sure can. Or at least, I can, and Evan—oh my God, Mr. Nine Inch Penis too."

Tabitha sighed and fanned her face at the same time.

I had to laugh. Tabitha had one of those expressive faces that cracked me up. "Okay, so the man is well-endowed. Goody for you."

"And goody for you," Tabitha said, tapping me on the nose.

"Is this, 'If Clarissa can do it, so can I'?"

"Partly." She played with her fingers.

Tabitha was competitive to a fault. I couldn't hold that against her. She'd missed out on much as a child.

"But you said Josh gave amazing head, made you happy?"

"I made it up. He didn't make me come once." Tabitha's voice was louder than it should've been. We noticed the women at the next table turning to stare.

Tabitha looked at me and giggled. She didn't give a damn. That was what I loved about my friend, even if her behavior at times was cringe-worthy.

I lowered my voice. "What, not even with his tongue?" My face heated.

"No, he doesn't eat pussy, Clarissa. He doesn't like doing it." Tabitha sniffed. "Now, can you imagine me with a guy that doesn't like fellatio?"

The women at the table turned and looked again. Tabitha sent them a charming smile as though butter wouldn't melt in her mouth. I had to cover my mouth to stop myself from laughing. The women, looking mortified, directed their attention away quickly.

Aidan and his insatiable need to taste me entered my thoughts, which caused a sudden rush of desire, making my sex, still deliciously sore from his surprise visit, ache.

"So how was I responsible? And who's Evan?"

"He runs Thornhill Holdings security. He's Aidan's right-hand man, a buddy from the army."

I winced. "How the hell did you meet him?" I didn't know if I liked the sound of this.

"He came knocking at our door yesterday morning. Just after you called in sick…" I was about to correct her. "Sick from love," Tabitha added.

"Anyway, I answered the door wearing my little kimono, you know the one." She raised an eyebrow.

"Shit, Tabs, you didn't there and then, did you?"

Tabitha chuckled. "No way... what do you take me for?"

"Rhetorical question, is it?"

Tabitha rolled her eyes. "Anyway, I mentioned it was my birthday, and he asked me out for dinner and I accepted."

"But what about Josh? Did you go out to lunch with him? Is that when you dumped him?"

"I called him and told him it wasn't working."

"You broke it off before you'd been with Evan?"

Tabitha nodded.

"Were you, or I should say *are* you that confident this will go somewhere?"

Her eyes lit up. "I'm surer than anything. He couldn't stop touching me, even after we'd fucked. And he's already sent me a text. One gets a feeling about these things."

I reminisced about my first time with Aidan on his yacht. Although I was generally a pessimist, Aidan's unceasing affection made it hard to imagine he was faking it.

Tabitha cupped her chin. "Evan is so hot, Clarissa, I mean hot. I've never felt this way before, and four orgasms. He made me come while being penetrated. Something I've never experienced." Her eyes glazed over. "To be fucked well adds up to falling in love, in my book. And let no one tell you otherwise," Tabitha said loudly enough that the women at the next table had become engrossed in our conversation. Never one to shy away from the limelight, Tabitha was having a ball.

I was bewildered. "Hang on, your first orgasm being penetrated? Are you serious?"

"Yeah, and don't you gloat just because you hit the jackpot."

"I'm not gloating. But what about all those nights I heard you crying out while the bed sounded like it was launching off?"

Tabitha stared down at her hands ruefully.

"What, you were faking it?" My voice went up a decibel.

Our audience, having been listening closely, had schadenfreude etched on their heavily made-up faces. For some twisted reason, they were extracting joy from Tabitha's deep shame.

Tabitha's lips drew a tight line. "Not proud of it." Her face brightened. "But… Evan." She fanned her face with her hand. "Wow, I'm so in love. He's hot."

"This is too soon, Tabitha. You only got with him last night. Aren't you being a little hasty?"

"Nope. He's available. He's super-hot. He makes me come by the bucket-loads."

I winced at that image. "Please, Tabs, I'm trying to eat."

She giggled.

"But what about Josh? He was practically living in the apartment and paying for your upkeep. You'll definitely need a job now."

"I've got that sorted. Evan needs a receptionist. He offered me the job."

"You'll be working together as well?"

"And how's that different from your situation?"

Touché. I smiled faintly, conceding defeat.

As our audience was leaving, Tabitha smiled in their direction. They regarded her awkwardly and hurried off. I looked at Tabitha, and we giggled.

After I paid the bill, I asked, "Do you want to go shopping? Aidan has set up an account at Victoria's Secret for me."

I might as well have told a child she could have unlimited candy. Tabitha's eyes boiled over with excitement. "God, yeah." She took me by the arm. "Let's go right now. An account, you say?"

"That's right. After he put a pair of my panties in his pocket to take away with him to Germany, he mentioned it."

Tabitha stopped and looked at me. "Fresh ones or worn ones?"

I reddened. In a little voice, I replied, "Worn."

A wicked smile pushed away her frown. "Love it. Like a dog-owner who gives his pet a piece of clothing so that the creature doesn't fret." Tabitha's eyes danced with amusement. "I hope you gave him the tiny ones I made you buy and not your white cotton spinster briefs."

Still digesting the analogy of the dog owner, I spluttered, "There's nothing wrong with cotton undies. They're eminently more comfortable. I've even got a pair on now." I stood defiantly with hands on hips.

Tabitha grimaced. "Ick."

"You're so shallow, Tabs."

"Ha… and loving it," she said, using her Maxwell Smart voice.

CHAPTER FORTY

We dropped all the shopping bags on the sofa and collapsed. It had been an exhausting afternoon. I'd spent my entire monthly wage in one afternoon. I bought two very expensive, must-have summer dresses for myself, and a slinky green wraparound dress for Tabitha to wear on her date with Evan.

Unaccustomed to spending Aidan's money, even if he was ridiculously wealthy, I needed Tabitha's constant reminder to reassure me that it was okay.

For Tabitha, I purchased one negligee, two pairs of panties, two bra and panty sets and a garter and nylons. For myself, I purchased bras and panties, along with a couple of very skimpy negligees. After picking my jaw off the ground at the obscene prices for such scant pieces of fabric, I drifted over to the cash register. The sales assistant, whose mood lifted when she noticed my unlimited credit, welcomed me with an obsequious smile. From that moment on, she tripped over herself to serve me.

"Tabs, this was over-indulgent, you know."

Tabitha poured out two glasses of coke and handed me one. "Balderdash. We're only young once." She gulped down her drink. "That's better. Now the fun begins. Let's do a photo shoot." She rubbed her hands together.

"What do you mean?"

"Just that—a photo shoot. We'll create fourteen images, one for each day Aidan's away. You can send one daily," said Tabitha, bubbling with excitement.

Uneasy at the notion of being photographed semi-naked, I said, "I don't know, Tabs."

"Get with the times, girl. Sending suggestive pics to one's lover is so now. It will keep his eyes on you and not the frauleins."

I hadn't thought about that. We hadn't even discussed exclusivity. Aidan hadn't really given me cause for jealousy. And he did seem oblivious to other women when we were out. Even before we got together at the gala night, Aidan's eyes were constantly on me. Nevertheless, the thought of a woman in Aidan's arms made my stomach tighten. I quickly jumped on board with the scheme.

I heard a cork pop. Tabitha opened the Prosecco we'd picked up on the way home and handed me a flute filled with chilled sparkly. Crisp, cold, and pleasant, the bubbly was just what I needed after a hard day's shopping.

"Okay, then, which should I model first?"

A white tiny lace bra swung in Tabitha's hand. "Let's start with this little sexy number."

I took the bra and matching panties with pink ties at the sides for ease of removal.

Tabitha's mobile buzzed. As she read the screen, her face brightened with excitement. Her green eyes sparkled. "It's Evan. He wants to see me tonight." She went to her bag of goodies. "I can wear my new lingerie." Tabitha pulled out a red lace bra.

While I waited for Tabitha to upload the images to her computer, I kept reminding myself this was not uncouth. There were times where I had to refuse to comply with Tabitha's directions which bordered on being pornographic, especially at the suggestion that I pose with legs apart. Nevertheless, Tabitha acted as a consummate professional by ensuring that background colors and moody lighting blended harmoniously. I was taken aback by her approach and attention to detail. Was this the lazy Tabitha I knew? I'd finally stumbled upon an ideal vocation for her.

"You look so cave-woman with that bush of yours, Clary," Tabitha said, leaning on her palm, studying her work.

I nearly spilt my drink. "What?"

"You may need an appointment for a Brazilian." Tabitha raised an eyebrow.

"Aidan happens to like it untouched. He doesn't subscribe to this obsession with pre-pubescent hairlessness. He thinks pubic hair is sexy." I was getting steamy thinking of Aidan's feverish touch.

"Then he's a cave-man as well." Tabitha chuckled. "Hopefully, he won't grow a beard."

I shuddered at the thought. I did, however, love his permanent shadow. I particularly enjoyed the gentle scraping between my thighs. I found that definitely a turn-on.

Aidan had only just left, and I was missing him. How was I going to last two whole weeks? With a heavy heart, I peered over Tabitha's shoulder at the computer screen.

"These are amazing, Clary. You're seriously photogenic. Shit, you could make a fortune if you wanted to."

"Let me see," I said, trying to push her out of the way.

Although I normally struggled when seeing pictures of myself, I had to admit they were tasteful shots. Tabitha had done a superb job. The photos were not cheap, only sensual.

"Wow, Tabs, they're super. This is what you should be doing."

"I love this one especially." Tabitha pointed to one with me in a red lace bra and garter with nylons. I was perched on a fluffy sixties dressing-table chair that had belonged to my mother, my hair up in a messy bun.

"Your expression is seriously boudoir," she crooned.

"Are you saying I appear slutty?"

"A little slutty, just enough. Not in the whore sense. You've just seen him naked, and you've gone all froofy."

"Froofy? Is there such a word?" I asked.

"Smoldering, then." Tabitha sniffed.

The images were indeed special. I was glad Tabitha had talked me into the shoot. "I might need to get drunk before sending them," I said.

"Send one now. Go on... the white one. Let's start all virginal," said Tabitha, winking.

"They're hardly virginal, Tabs," I said, flicking through the many images again. "These are fantastic. You should become a photographer. I mean, the way you've dressed the background and the choice of light is very professional."

"It was only my phone camera."

"Fuck the false modesty, girl. You're talented," I said, channeling Tabitha's kick-ass attitude.

My phone buzzed, waking me up. When I saw it was from Aidan, I woke quickly. "Hi." I tried not to sound too sleepy.

"Did I wake you?" asked Aidan with his toe-curling husk.

"No... it's okay. How was your flight? Are you in Germany?"

"Yep. It was all good. It improved a lot when I received that photo you sent me," Aidan said hoarsely. "You're delectable."

"Tabitha suggested I try on some of the lingerie we purchased today. And she photographed me while we were at it."

"Are there more?" Aidan sounded aroused.

"Yes. I'll send you another tomorrow," I said softly.

"How many are there?"

"One for each day you're away."

"I can't wait." He sighed. "I love hearing your sexy, breathy voice. I'm missing you madly. Next time, you're coming with me."

"I'd like that."

"What's that noise?"

"That's the neighbors. They've got bad plumbing," I said.

"Where are you?"

"I'm at my apartment."

"Why are you there?" Aidan didn't hide his annoyance.

"I had a few glasses of bubbly for the photo shoot and was too tired to drive, so I crashed here. It's still my place," I said, a little disturbed by his controlling tone.

"Is Tabitha there with her boyfriend and his friend?"

"No," I replied, trying not to giggle. Aidan was being ridiculously jealous. "I haven't seen Cameron since that night. He's not in the habit of coming here. I'm alone. Tabitha's out with a guy…" I stopped there. This was not the time to tell Aidan that my best-friend was sleeping with his right-hand man.

"I hate you being there, Clarissa. Shit… the security, or lack thereof. Anyone can get in. Your door's flimsy. And there are lowlifes living there."

"The neighbors aren't that bad," I said. "There's old Tom next door. He's a lovely old man, wouldn't hurt a fly."

"Old Tom could be a pervert who drills holes through walls." Aidan sounded more serious than I would have hoped.

I giggled. "Oh, Aidan, that's ludicrous. He's not like that. The man can barely move. Tabitha and I do his shopping to help. He's nearly ninety. And on the other side, there's Hilary. She's got lots of cats and keeps to herself."

"I've never trusted old women who live with lots of cats," said Aidan earnestly.

"Seriously?" I had to squeeze my lips together.

"I worry about you, Clarissa. I don't like you living there, especially in that neighborhood."

"Aidan, I've lived here for ages. Nothing's ever happened. Anyhow, I can look after myself. I did a course in self-defense last year."

"You did?"

"Yeah, so you better behave." I deepened my voice.

Aidan laughed. "What are you wearing?" His soft, bedroom tone was back, much to my relief.

"Not much." I didn't think he needed to hear that I was in my far-from-sexy worn cotton nightie.

"I like the sound of that," he rasped.

My stomach tightened. Were we about to do phone sex? "Hmm…" I was at a loss for words.

Aidan chuckled. "Don't worry. I won't get you to breathe loudly down the phone. Maybe we can do a bit of Skyping while I'm here. What about tomorrow this time?"

"Yeah, sure. How am I to dress?" I wasn't sure if that was a requirement.

"Glad you asked. Anything with buttons," Aidan replied in a low voice thick with desire.

Blood pumped down below my navel. Aidan was pure sex, even over the phone.

"I'm sure I can arrange something, Aidan," I purred.

"You sound hot, Clarissa. I'll go crazy. Two weeks is way too long."

"Can't you cut it short?"

He sighed. "No. There's too much to do."

"I hope you don't get so desperate that you…" Hell, I was sounding like a jealous maniac.

"Clarissa, I don't do desperate," Aidan responded churlishly.

"Sorry, I didn't mean to…" My face heated up.

"I'm very monogamous."

"I shouldn't have mentioned it."

"I'm glad you did." Aidan softened his tone. "I'm so connected to you, Clarissa, that the thought of you with another man would rip me apart."

"I don't want anyone else, Aidan."

"That's music to my ears." There was a pause. "I have to go, Clarissa. Hey, that photo was exquisite. I can't wait for the next one. I'll let you get back to sleep. Tomorrow this time, we'll Skype, okay?"

"I look forward to it, Aidan. And it's lovely to hear from you."

"Dream about me, beautiful girl," rasped Aidan.

CHAPTER FORTY-ONE

The day was a blur. The gala was the following weekend, the same day that Aidan would be returning. By popular demand, my design was to be replicated. Apparently, word had gotten out, and tickets were sold out by the following Monday. It was not only a great vote of confidence for me, but it also meant that the preparations for the event would be a breeze.

Balancing a tray of food prepared by Will, I headed for the garden to meet my father. As usual, it was sunny. In fact, the weather always seemed perfect. It was as if nature was in step with my mood. And with the gentle breeze swaying the languid branches, I felt loose and serene.

"How are you, Papa?" I used the endearment I'd adopted as a teenager, after having made a personal vow to replicate all things French.

"I am full of joi de vivre." My father had such a handsome face when he smiled. I hadn't seen him like that since my mother was alive.

"And so am I, Daddy," I said, embracing him.

"Look at this place." His arms swept about. "It's a veritable paradise."

"Isn't it just. I've started sketching."

The pleasure in his face nearly made me cry. We'd been through so much. And at that moment, as we regarded each other brimming with optimism, it seemed as if we'd won a celestial lottery.

"I brought enough for both of us," I said, placing the tray on the iron table.

"Not hungry, Cheri. I've never eaten so much food." He laughed.

"Nor I. I'll have to be careful. I'll get fat," I said, regarding with guilt the full plate of pasta staring at me.

"You could use a little more weight, darling. You're actually looking skinnier," he said, removing his horn-rimmed glasses.

"There's heaps here."

"No, seriously, I'm not hungry. Don't let me stop you. Please eat," he said, with a gentle nod.

As I swallowed a forkful of pasta, my stomach groaned in appreciation. I was hungry. I'd had no breakfast because I'd slept in and had to rush to work.

"How's the cataloguing going?" I asked, chewing away.

"Awfully well. Charging through it. Love it. The best job I've ever had—left alone to muse over a most wondrous collection of books. It's hard to fathom how vast and varied it is. I'm told an eccentric film producer in the 1930's was a committed collector. He did a fine job too." He sipped at his tea. "Greta tells me that Aidan has also bought a few original editions at various auctions and estates so that it keeps growing. She even intimated that I may be asked to do some procuring." My father's eyes glowed with childish wonder.

"Oh, really?" I said, overcome with a swelling of respect for my handsome lover. "I wasn't aware that Aidan bought books as well. I suppose it makes sense. He's a keen buyer of art."

"Does he do the buying, or has he an advisor?"

"No. Aidan goes to the auctions himself. His cultural education came the pure way. One year spent in Europe visiting galleries."

He nodded, looking notably impressed. "Then he's got impeccable taste. I haven't observed anything past 1930. Not one skerrick of post-modernism anywhere."

As I chuckled, I decided not to mention that Aidan's apartment in Venice had more than its fair share of modernist art.

It was a joy hanging out with my dad, marveling at the flowers, butterflies, and abundant bird life. My dad had always been a calming influence on me.

"Doesn't it seem like we've travelled back in time, sitting here?" I said.

"Indeed, very European. There's an original Brueghel here, you realize."

"I know. I spotted it on my first day at work," I said, recalling my sense of wonder.

Against a background of insects and birds buzzing, I finished off my lunch.

After I wiped my mouth, I said, "I've heard that you and Greta..." My face heated up. This was not an easy subject for us.

"Yes, we're together," my father replied with a shy, tight smile.

"You look really great, Daddy. It's the best I've seen you in years. And I like Greta. She's a good woman."

"She likes you too." In a rare show of emotion, my father's eyes had a watery film. I hugged him as my eyes misted over. I wanted to tell him about Aidan, but wasn't sure how to broach it.

"Dad, I need to tell you something also," I said self-consciously.

"If it's about you and Aidan, darling, I'm already aware," he said, reaching into his jacket pocket for his pipe.

My brows met. "Did Greta tell you?"

"No. Aidan did," he replied dryly.

"He did?" My voice hit a high note. I collected myself. "He mentioned you had suggested a couple of books. That's all."

"Yes. And he slipped me an excellent bottle of single malt. He's a lovely man. Very handsome." My father nodded. "You'll make a striking couple."

"Well, let's not jump the gun, Daddy. I mean it's early days." My heart pounded anyhow.

He smoked his pipe and looked out at the grounds.

"What did he say exactly, then?" I asked.

"Not much, only that he was crazy about you and that he'd protect you." He regarded me warmly. "That's music to a father's ear. Especially coming from someone like Aidan," he said, pausing for another puff. "He's a decent man, has a kind heart. He's been through a lot."

"Did he speak about his days as a soldier?"

He nodded slowly. "He did a little. But I could see it in his eyes. I gleaned the same haunted expression as in my brother's eyes after Vietnam."

A shiver ran through me. I'd seen it too. Tossed about in an undertow of emotion, I was flooded by pity. My heart hurt all of a sudden.

"Are you all right, love?" He touched my arm.

"Sure, Daddy. Everything's fine. How could it not be?" I glanced down at my watch. "I'd best be getting back. Got a fair bit to do."

In truth, I needed to be alone with my thoughts for a moment. I hugged my father.

"Let's do this again," he said, smiling brightly.

"Yes, of course, Daddy. It will be like old times. Only our living arrangements have somewhat improved."

He kissed me on the cheek. "Don't worry about anything, my petite belle. I'm sure your mother would approve."

When I returned to the office Greta was there. She greeted me warmly. "Did you enjoy your lunch?"

"It was yummy, thank you. The pasta was amazing. Will's cooking will be my undoing." I touched my tummy.

She pulled back her head, frowning. "You're very slender Clarissa."

I smiled.

Greta hovered. "Did your father mention that we've been spending time together?"

"He did, Greta, I'm so pleased for both of you. It's the best I've seen my father since my mother…" Unsure how much father had actually revealed of his earlier life, I stopped myself.

Her face softened. "Thank you for telling me that." Her earlier frown faded into a faint, uncertain smile. I'd seen the same tentative glint in Aidan's eyes, and in his father's. The Thornhills were a sensitive lot.

Greta switched back to business mode. "Oh, by the way, Bryce Beaumont is on the warpath. You may get a call. The account's overdrawn again."

"So what do I say if he calls?" A shiver ran through me at the thought of dealing with Bryce.

"Tell him I'm waiting to hear from Aidan," Greta said, shaking her head. "He's hopeless."

"Why does Aidan put up with him?" Yet again that question.

"He threatens to cause trouble for Aidan, something that happened in the army. Instead of dealing with it, which is what I've suggested, Aidan keeps Bryce close by paying him off." Greta's response brought with it a dark cloud.

Suddenly, my lunch sat uncomfortably in my gut. Hell, talk about vicissitudes. One moment, I was soaring high in a seemingly endless turquoise sky; the next, I was scrambling on barren ground clutching at crumbs of information.

"Oh," Greta said as she was leaving, "should I arrange for the stylist to organize a gown for the ball?"

"I'd go shopping, only…" This was sticky. I'd spent all my monthly allowance. Greta tilted her head. "Only?"

Paranoid that I was emulating Bryce's vampiric habits by taking advantage of Aidan's generosity, my stomach knotted. "If the stylist can do it again, that would be helpful. The blue gown was heavenly."

As always, Greta's intuition was sharp. "Did you get the credit card that Aidan issued for you?"

I shook my head.

Greta approached my desk. "There's an envelope somewhere." She rustled through the in-tray. "Oh, here it is." She passed it over.

I tore open the envelope, and a credit card fell out. "Oh…" I looked up at Greta questioningly.

"It has no limit." Her tone was matter-of-fact. "If you want to, you can pop out anytime this week and go shopping for that gown. That's unless you want the stylist. It's your call."

"Oh… okay. I see," I stammered.

"And Clarissa, I've never seen Aidan happier. He's a generous soul, sometimes to a fault. Aidan would want you to have the best. He *can* afford it."

My mouth opened, but nothing came out except a thin "Thanks."

CHAPTER FORTY-TWO

Aidan

Blood coursed through my veins as I stared at the image Clarissa had sent me. She was dressed in red lace and posing on her stomach. Despite her mouth-watering curves it was her face that fired my cock, which had gone rock hard.

I needed to feel her in the flesh. This was torture.

We'd Skyped every night. That night had been particularly steamy. My voice was captured in my throat as she unbuttoned her shirt, and instead of a bra, Clarissa appeared naked. I had to undo my jeans. The ache was so severe my balls had gone blue. Heavy-lidded, Clarissa had that erotic glint in her eyes.

The phone buzzed, startling me.

Down to earth with a thud—it was Bryce. I was worn out after another huge day. There had been long meetings where I had to grapple with technical jargon that was tantamount to learning a new language. It had been stimulating nevertheless. Maybe I was atoning for my misspent youth, because I had become a serious knowledge junky.

I took a long slug of bourbon. Bryce brought the wild beast out in me. I just wanted to pummel the bastard. "Bryce."

"How are the German girls? I hear they're wild over there." Off to a crude start as usual.

"Haven't noticed," I replied coldly.

"Can't say I'm surprised. That Clarissa's one fucking hot chick," he said, making it sound as if he'd seen her naked. I wanted to kill the fucker. My knuckles stretched to the limit.

"Listen, you sleazy prick, I don't want her name passing your greasy lips."

He laughed. My involvement with this devil dressed up as a man grated on me day and night. Something had to give. This would not continue.

"I need some cash. Greta's holding back. And another thing—your sexy little girl turned up a few weeks ago with an accounting system I really can't be bothered with. There are better things to do with my time."

"Yeah, I can imagine," I replied sarcastically. "Hanging around slot machines and late-night card games can be a time-consuming." I exhaled deeply. "The fund is being starved too quickly. I hear that the clubhouse is run down. The gala nights are there to bankroll the charity and ensure that everyone receives proper care. The facilities are for those in need. You're aware of that. You're the fucking CEO. The charity is not there for your gambling and cocaine habit, Bryce."

"I take sniff and like to gamble. At least it eases my PTSD. You can say you're giving me charity as well." Bryce chuckled.

"I think I've given you at least one million, over and above the generous wage you're paid. It's got to stop. The only money you'll have access to from now on is your wage. The club's finances will be handled at our end."

"That's fucking unfair."

"I have nothing further to say on the matter."

Bryce puffed out smoke. "We'll talk about this again. In the meantime, can you tell Greta to put some funds into my account by tomorrow?"

"It won't be much. Start exercising restraint. This is the last time."

"I haven't told you this yet, but apart from being the only other person who knows about Ben, I know how you got your first million."

My chest tightened. Stolen of breath, I struggled for air. It was lucky that we were on the phone because had Bryce been in front of me, I'd have given the game away. "You've got no proof."

"Oh, I have proof all right. Remember Johnno Boy?"

I sat down. "What about him?"

"I know about the safety deposit key. And that it was missing. Johnno was there when they searched Benji's locker, Aidan."

Clearing my throat, I replied, "It has nothing to do with me."

"Then how did you get all that cash to go to Europe for a year, not to mention the windfalls on the stock market? It's public record. Everyone knows you made your money on stocks. I'm only telling you this because we're sewn at the hip. And you owe me big time, Aidan, so make that call to Greta. I want a hundred thousand deposited into the fund. The place needs a little renovating. Some of the guys have offered to paint it."

"They can bill us direct. In the meantime, I'll instruct Greta to deposit ten thousand into your personal account. After that, you're on your own. I want you out, Bryce," I said, raising my voice.

"Aidan, don't forget you could do time with the information I'm holding."

"You're full of shit, Bryce. I've got to go." I cut the call.

As I poured another drink, I relived the event that had catapulted my life from that of an ordinary, if dysfunctional, nobody to a billionaire who couldn't go anywhere without the glare of the world.

Exhaling a slow, long breath, I resumed staring at Clarissa's photos. I flicked to my most cherished image: that bashful smile, her full breasts spilling out of the tiniest white lace bra, those succulent, rosy nipples piercing through. My cock throbbed so hard that Bryce had perished from my thoughts.

Now that my nightmares had returned, I was reluctant to sleep. Only in Clarissa's arms did I sleep peacefully. Was she in communion with an angel spirit who had a purifying effect on my jaded soul? For a non-believer, this was crazy. But my frayed mind needed something to believe in because in the dark of night, away from my busy life and Clarissa's embrace, I was a crumbling mess.

I glanced down at my watch and decided I need another hit of Clarissa on Skype.

"Hey, baby." I sat up in front of the screen. Clarissa had her hair out looking bone-meltingly ravishing.

"Aidan, I didn't expect another call."

"I just needed to see you, hear you again."

Clarissa's smile flushed me with warmth. "You don't seem yourself. Has something happened?" she asked.

"Bryce is causing trouble again."

"He's a bad sort. Why not give him his marching orders?"

"It's complicated," I said, combing back my hair. It had grown so long. I needed to cut it. But I loved the way Clarissa tangled her fingers through it while in the throes of an orgasm.

"Tell me about it." Clarissa sat forward.

Normally, I'd have gone straight into dirty speak, but my soul ached too much to go there. "I probably shouldn't have called again, Clarissa. I'm just a little adrift."

"I'm glad you did. You can ring me anytime and talk to me about anything, other than"—her lips curled— "sexy things, although, I do like that too." She spoke all too deliciously.

Just one little twinkle in those brown eyes, and my cock twitched. "Yeah, well. It's hard not to be aroused seeing you, Clarissa." I took a sip of my spirits. "My life seems so fucked-up."

"Is it about your days in the service?"

I nodded slowly. "Uh-huh... tons of skeletons in the cupboard. Not that they're all from my army days. I already had a few stacking up. Now it's overflowing." I laughed nervously.

"Aidan, I can see it in your eyes. I've learnt to recognize it."

My brow creased. "You have? Am I that messed-up that I'm wearing it on my sleeve?"

"No, not all. Aidan, you're no more messed-up than me or Tabitha."

"I don't know," I said, combing back my hair, which kept falling back on my face. "Hey, would you mind if I get a haircut? Would you still like me?" I chuckled.

"I'd like you even if you were bald, although I hope you won't shave it off. I love it long ala sexy rock star."

"Hmm... okay, maybe just a trim, then. I'd hate it if you cut your hair."

"I won't be doing that anytime soon," said Clarissa with a cute smile. "Anyway, back to what we were talking about. You never told me why you joined the army." Clarissa adjusted her position. I could now see her upper body, which distracted me as always.

"That blouse has no buttons, Clarissa." I purposely tried to sidestep the question.

Ignoring my saucy digression, Clarissa said, "Tell me, please."

I rubbed my eyes. "To run away from my crazy mom."

"I know that bit. There seems to be more. You're carrying something heavy, Aidan."

"Education. I joined the army for the education," I said tentatively, hoping Clarissa wouldn't ask about my earlier school life.

"But isn't it all about combat training?"

"It's much more than that. We were encouraged to read books. Development of the intellect is just as important as learning about combat. I learnt to read without distraction. We studied philosophy, psychology, social studies, anthropology… to be honest, that was the best part."

Clarissa nodded sympathetically. "I get it. Away from your mother, you could concentrate. It also explains your super intelligence."

My brow wrinkled. "I wouldn't say I'm super intelligent. Not like you. Just being around you compels me to excel. I want to shine for you, Clarissa."

"Aidan, you do shine. You're an amazing musician. I can talk to you about any book or work of art. You're one of the brightest men I've ever met, other than my dad, of course."

Her warm voice caressed my soul. All the earlier tension had simply evaporated. My body felt loose again. "I'm so glad I called you. There's nothing quite like Clarissa magic." I grinned.

"You're not wiggling out of it yet, Mr. Thornhill," she said authoritatively.

"Do you know how sexy you sound with that bossy tone?" I smirked. "Tell me, are you into leather?

Clarissa laughed. "Oh, Aidan, you're such a reprobate."

"Only around you. You bring out the beast in me," I said, leaning back in my chair. "Clarissa, I'm better for having spoken to you. Only one more day, and I'll be back. Why don't we pick up on this then? I'd prefer to see you in the flesh. Not that I'll want to do much talking."

"I suppose so." She sounded disappointed. "I'm open-minded, Aidan. You can tell me anything. I want you to know that." Her eyes shone with sincerity.

"Then, being so liberal minded, how about removing that pretty blouse of yours? Just to help elevate my spirit to the max."

Clarissa did just that. Oh fuck, she wasn't wearing a bra. My cock thickened. My breath hitched. "Rub your nipples for me, baby," I said, my voice trapped in my throat.

She did, and they hardened. It was enough to make a grown man cry.

"Oh my, Clarissa, you've grown." My breathing became heavy.

With her heavy-lidded gaze oozing, Clarissa licked her lips, and that sealed the deal. "Does it turn you on as much as it does me?" I asked, hoarsely.

Clarissa bit her lip and nodded demurely. How could she at once look so innocent and sexy?

"Your turn," said Clarissa, her voice deeper, needier than usual.

I pulled my head back. "My turn? What, my chest or my cock?" I don't know why I was shocked. Clarissa was, after all, doing it for me.

"Both," Clarissa asserted.

I unbuttoned my shirt. "I can't imagine this being a turn-on." I laughed.

"From where I'm sitting, it is."

"Are you touching yourself, Miss Moone?" I asked. My heart was beating hard. Were we about to do this?

"Not quite." She was back to her little, shy voice.

I sensed it was too much and wanted to leave it there.

"What are you doing?" she asked.

"I'm about to blow you a kiss good night," I replied.

"What happened to the other?" she demanded.

I stood up. "Look at what you do to me, baby."

Her eyes had gone all lusty. "I can't wait to feel you, Aidan."

"Clarissa, I would ask you to do the same, and I can't tell you how erotic that would be. But I don't want to cheapen this moment. My feelings for you are too profound for that."

Clarissa's eyes moistened. She cleared her voice. "I wouldn't mind so much, only it seems a little gross."

"Oh God, no. It's far from gross, Princess. Your pussy's exquisite." I sighed deeply. "But not now. I'm already seriously turned-on."

"We can't have that," she said playfully. "You may need to seduce a sexy German girl."

"I'm monogamous to a fault, Clarissa. I'd never do that. Just like I hope you'll never."

"I'd never dream of it. You're my first, Aidan. I'm not like that."

"That's music to my ears, Princess, as is your wispy, little voice." I blew a kiss. "Till tomorrow, beautiful girl."

Clarissa pursed her lips and kissed me back.

CHAPTER FORTY-THREE

James, my driver, stood waiting for me. The day was hot. Germany had been much milder than LA, even in summer.

Not a keen flyer, I felt relief to be back on the ground. I'd slept after taking a pill to knock me out, something I often did on long flights, especially this time as the prospect of seeing Clarissa had wired me up.

The gala ball flashed in my mind. I'd planned poorly, given that I was not in the mood to socialize. A quiet night with Clarissa would have been preferable.

My impatience to get back home was heightened by the congested freeway. "It's ten o'clock Saturday morning. You'd think they'd all be either breakfasting, jogging, shopping or doing something other than driving."

James laughed. He was an army buddy like everyone who worked for me. "How was Germany?"

"Inspiring. Their renewable energy programs are light-years ahead."

"Is that so?"

I nodded. "And without the sunlight we get. Imagine that."

"Is it cheaper?"

I exhaled. That was a big question for me. "It will cost a fair sum to set up. But once it's running, the energy is free except for running costs, which means the general upkeep of equipment. Don't have to buy coal or oil. Or dig earth, drill ocean beds, or even fight wars over it." I snorted.

"Don't we know about that," said James icily.

I nodded, maintaining my silence. Politics was not my choice topic.

"So the consumer won't pay much or anything for energy, then?" James asked.

"That's the intention. The plan is to build renewable energy farms—a mix of solar panels and wind turbines in areas with little employment and lots of open space that's deemed useless. After I get there, it won't be useless." I smiled, feeling excited as I always did when mulling over my project's life-changing potential.

"Aidan, that's so impressive. That will make a difference. Energy is really expensive."

"It will also clean the air." I pointed out the window at smog-blanketed LA.

"What about here? Are you going to set some up in California, considering the sun?"

"The deep south is more in need. There's already quite a bit happening here. Although looking outside at the moment, the air's dirty. But that's more to do with cars than energy."

"That's the next step, isn't it? I know we're driving an electric car, but it would make a difference if everyone was in one."

"You bet." I paused to reflect. "For starters, there needs to be a battery that lasts longer and takes less time to recharge. The batteries available now are a bit of a turn-off for most people." I stretched my arms and yawned. "It's coming. I met an engineer in Frankfurt who, in conjunction with some students here, is working on a nanowire battery capable of recharging itself. No more stopping and recharging. When that becomes a reality, it will be a major game-changer."

"That gives me much hope." James glanced at me. His handsome African-American features brimmed with respect. "I worry about my grandchildren. That's if I ever have any." He chuckled.

"What about you, Aidan? Are you planning to have a big family?"

"I haven't given it much thought." My stomach tightened.

"I wasn't much into the idea myself, but when Natalia came along, my heart grew so big I…" His voice cracked. Wow, this giant of a man was about to cry.

I touched his bulky arm. "You'll make a fantastic father, James."

"And so will you, Aidan. Look at how you care for everyone—the club for the veterans, the women's shelters, the lost dogs' home."

"I don't know. Helping others is one thing, but bringing up a life is another."

"With a good woman, it's nothing but a joy," said James.

"Maybe so." I visualized Clarissa holding a baby. The thought suddenly terrorized me. I didn't want to share her. "To be honest, James, I cringe at the thought of it. I have no idea on how to be a father. I wasn't exactly exposed to a nurturing family environment."

"Mine was pretty fucked-up. Drugs, liquor, violent dad," said James. "But I tell you one thing." His black eyes shone with determination. "I will make a difference, just like you are already making a difference to so many people's lives."

I touched his arm affectionately. "You're a good man, James."

"And you, bro"—James pointed his long, dark finger at me— "apart from being the most handsome dude in the whole of LA, have a brilliant mind, a heart bigger than the whole of California, and an ear like a mother-fucker."

James played the bass guitar and would often pop into the Red House to jam with me.

I laughed raucously for the first time in two weeks.

At last, we were heading along the scenic ascent to Malibu. As soon as the deep blue sea came into view, my body relaxed. I unwound the window. The salty air caressed my face and entered my lungs. Ah… elixir, body and soul. Yes, so good to be home.

"It's another perfect day in Malibu." I sighed, dreaming of a swim, with Clarissa bobbing up and down in the water. My cock stirred.

"Isn't it? Wouldn't want to live anywhere else. I love the place," said James with that white, toothy, infectious smile of his.

"I'm with you there, man," I said, matching his smile.

After showering and unpacking the gifts I'd bought Clarissa, I threw on a pair of shorts and a T-shirt. I took off with a hurried step. My heart was beating as excitedly as that of a teenager about to kiss the girl he'd been pining after for a whole season.

But first, I had to visit Rocket. I loved my dog. His bark rang in the air as I headed to greet him. Whenever I travelled, he lived at the back with Roland, Will's son, who I was pissed at for telling Clarissa I was a ladies' man. That rumor had been passed around by Amy, so technically it wasn't really Roland's fault, but it still annoyed me. And were he not Will's son, I would have fired him, which would have been a pity because Roland was great with Rocket.

My loving pet came bounding towards me, leaping up and licking me with wild doggy abandon, his dancing brown eyes full of love.

"Hey, buddy," I said, patting and hugging him in the way one does a dog. He was my best pal. I'd rescued him from our dog shelter. His sad, take-me-home eyes were too much for me to resist. He'd been with me for five years. Most nights, I had him in my room. I found his company calming, and he kept me sane. But since meeting Clarissa, I had spent little time with him.

I didn't have the heart to leave Rocket, so I let him follow along at my heels as I made my way to see Clarissa, certain she wouldn't mind.

I turned the corner, and saw Clarissa sitting under the old willow, sipping coffee with her father. I paused. They were laughing about something. It was heartwarming to have both of them together, not only because the library had become a thriving environment, inspiring me to buy more rare editions, but also because I'd made this charming, well-spoken man seriously happy.

As I watched them together, my heart spilled over with joy. Clarissa had her bare feet up on the other chair. Her slim, shapely legs were out on glorious display. And her hair in a braid fell seductively over— *sigh*— her voluptuous tits.

Julian wore a cravat. I loved his style, so old-world and elegant.

Rocket was the first to charge.

"Aidan," exclaimed Clarissa glancing up at me. A gorgeous smile lit her face. She patted Rocket. "Hello, Rocket."

Julian nodded warmly and held his hand out. "Comfortable flight, I trust?"

"Yeah, it was fine. Thanks for asking." My gaze headed straight over to Clarissa. How could I not? What an angel.

While Rocket and Julian bonded, Clarissa giggled away. The scene would stay etched in my memory; it was such a natural, perfect moment.

"Who does he remind you of, Dad?"

"He's just like Huxley. I've met Rocket on numerous occasions. We've even been down to the beach together, haven't we, boy?"

After Julian patted Rocket, he rose. "I'd best be getting on. I've got a few things to do before the big night." He glanced over at his daughter, smiled warmly, and saluted me.

"I'm so glad you'll be making it to dinner tonight, Julian," I said.

He raised an eyebrow. "It was considerably difficult to get out of, with not one, but two women coming at me. I'm not one for pomp and ceremony normally." He grinned.

"We share that, Julian. I'm not too keen on crowds myself," I said.

Julian's focus settled on my bag. "Gustav Klimt—*The Kiss*." He looked over at Clarissa and raised his eyebrows. "Did you tell Aidan you were a fervent admirer of Klimt?"

All wide-eyed and filled with wonder, Clarissa shook her head. "No, he doesn't know that." I handed her the bag.

"Did you go to the Belvedere Museum in Vienna?" Clarissa's tone was filled with envy.

"Yes," I said. Her far-reaching knowledge of art always impressed me. "I did a quick detour to Austria. I visited it once before and was so struck by the art that I had to go back and get you something from there." I glimpsed at Julian, who was watching Clarissa as she unpacked the gift.

Clarissa lifted a huge book. "Oh my, Aidan. It's tremendous," she cooed. The gift sat heavily in her arms. "Look, Dad."

"How marvelous. It must have the entire collection," said Julian, holding his chin and looking professorial.

"Oh, and I got you something as well, Julian." I dug into the bag and brought out a cellophane wrapper with a silk cravat.

Julian's eyes widened in gratitude. "Oh, how choice. You shouldn't have."

"It was too irresistible. I passed a shop that specialized in cravats, and I popped in. Thought of you, of course, and then"—I looked over at Clarissa—"I picked up a few for myself."

Her smile widened. "I can't wait to see you in one," she enthused in that girlish, knee-weakening voice.

"I have to go." Julian touched my arm. "It's very elegant. I'll wear it this evening." He bowed his head respectfully, knelt to pat Rocket a final time, and left.

Clarissa, meanwhile, had opened the book and was marveling at the images. "How did you know that I loved Klimt?"

I shrugged. "I just guessed, I suppose. Anyway, there are more gifts."

She peered up. "Oh, Aidan, you've already spoiled me with this." She opened the show bag, reached in, and pulled out a T-shirt with an image of *The Kiss*. "I love it. Oh, I love it." She hugged me.

As much as I wanted to take that hug further, I needed her to find the rest of her gifts first. "Keep going."

She frowned. "Really?" Her little hand burrowed in and brought out an attractive wooden box that had a Klimt painting etched into it. "It's fetching, Aidan." She put it down on the table.

"Open it," I said.

Clarissa's excited face lengthened. She looked afraid. I had to smile. What was she expecting?

Clarissa's jaw dropped. "Cartier..." She opened the velvet box. "Oh my God, Aidan." Her voice had gone up in pitch. She held her mouth. "They're not real, are they?" The diamond chandelier earring glistened brilliantly in the sunlight.

"Clarissa, I'm not so cheap that I'd buy fakes."

She stared incredulously at the magnificent classic earrings. Aware of Clarissa's predilection for vintage designs, I went for that style. They also happened to be the most attractive, despite the overly friendly assistant trying to steer me towards a more contemporary style.

"Aidan, I can't accept these. They must've cost you a fortune. I've never owned anything like this. I mean, they're breathtakingly stunning to be sure." She peered up with those large brown eyes that were driving me and my cock mad.

"You will accept them, because for one, they won't go with what I'm wearing." I lisped making myself sound ridiculously effete.

Clarissa's frown faded, and she giggled wildly. *Ah, that's better.* Her peals of infectious laughter registered immediately with my groin.

"Let's go into the cottage. You can try them on for me." I stepped up onto the patio and took Clarissa gently by the arm.

Her eyes were still on my gift. "I'm sorry, it's messy, Aidan, I haven't..."

Before she could say anything else, I had her in my arms, holding her close. "I've been dreaming of this." I sighed. "I've missed you, Clarissa."

"Me too." Clarissa ran her tongue over her full lips.

That did it. My lips met her soft, warm mouth. I wanted her so badly that it was hard to be tender. Instead, my tongue searched hers and entwined with the full force of my out-of-control libido. Her cheek burned against mine.

My hands ran down her undulating waist to her firm soft thighs. I felt her curvy bottom. My cock was as hard as steel. I wasn't going to last. I pulled down her shorts. Her firm, voluptuous bottom fitted into my hungry grasp. My heart pumped wildly. "You're not wearing panties, Clarissa," I said, gasping.

"I was hoping you'd drop in, and"— her voice was silky and soft— "I remembered your request." She giggled again, and that was it. I lifted her up and led her to the bedroom. She was as light as a feather.

"I'm sorry it's a mess."

"I couldn't give a shit, Clarissa." I placed her on the bed. "Just come here and take that top off for me, please. I need to look at you." I could barely speak.

She lifted her top, and I exhaled a jagged breath. "You've grown. Is that at all possible?" I caressed her swollen, soft breasts.

"I'm about to get my period. They always tend to swell up," she said softly.

I undid my fly and dropped my shorts and boxers in one go. Clarissa lifted off my T-shirt. I loved her newfound confidence. Clarissa's eyes lingered on my erection. The way her eyelids grew heavy with lust unhinged me. She was becoming a glutton for sex. *The more insatiable the better.*

"Can you see what you do?" I said, holding my cock.

Clarissa's eyes were so seductive. I opened her legs and hissed. My mouth watered. Her pussy was wet, and equally needy as my cock.

As I joined her on the bed, Clarissa's hand went straight for my cock. "Careful. I may not last," I whispered into her ear.

Our lips crushed. We were equally famished. Her scent was earthy with a hint of jasmine. I hungered for her breasts after having fantasized about them for two weeks. And as I fondled them, my cock threatened to shoot. My tongue ran down her neck to her nipples. I teased them with my teeth and tongue, and Clarissa writhed beneath me, whimpering.

My hands ran down between her round thighs and landed on her swollen clit. Her whimpers grew louder.

"My delectable girl," I rasped. "I have to eat you first. Get you wet and ready. We don't want this pretty little pussy bruised."

Clarissa opened her legs wide, encouraging me, as my tongue rotated around her bud. The stickier she became, the louder her moans. It didn't take long before Clarissa's tormented whimpers bounced off the walls as she flooded me with her musky cream.

"You're like honey." I wiped my mouth and kissed Clarissa, whose mouth was wide and equally needy.

Clarissa, with my guidance, sat on top. That gorgeous face, those full bouncing tits. She slid onto my erection, her eyelids lowering. My slow groan resonating in primal pleasure.

Ah… I'd experienced nothing like Clarissa before. This was lovemaking that every man dreamt of.

"I hope I'm not crushing you," murmured Clarissa.

"You're super light, baby," I gasped, barely able to speak from the sheer bliss of her drenched pussy clasping on tight. "I love you on top."

I had to use all my control because I wanted to shoot. But first, Clarissa needed to orgasm with me.

As she leaned in towards me, her breasts fell into my mouth. My heart pounded so hard it hurt. After two weeks of unabated arousal, I was on a rampage to ravish.

Clarissa's vaginal walls contracted around my inflamed cock. Her movement was frenzied. The sheer friction robbed me of my senses.

What a moment. Clarissa's nipples were in my mouth, my hands kneading her breasts. "Am I hurting you?" My voice was strangled.

"I like it," Clarissa said. Yes, she loved me fondling her tits. Clarissa loved my cock ripping into her as well, if her contorting face was anything to go by. Agonized ecstasy echoed out of her parted lips.

"One can only dream of a pussy like yours, Clarissa."

"I love feeling you inside, Aidan."

"Did you think about me doing this?" My thrusts increased, and the friction burned deep.

Clarissa's moans grew in strength. "Yes."

"Did you touch yourself?" I asked, about to lose it completely.

"Yessss…." Clarissa's pussy contracted in frenzied spasms, taking me with her. I shot so hard and deep that I thought my head would burst. It was lift-off. The heat was so intense that time stretched, as did my growl. I had never experienced that kind of orgasm before.

Clarissa fell into my arms, and together our hearts beat in wild harmony.

"That was something else. It just keeps getting better," I said, trying to catch my breath.

"It does for me too." Clarissa sighed.

"I didn't hurt you, did I?" I asked, caressing her cheek.

"A little, but I like it." Clarissa smiled so sweetly that my cock hardened again.

I drank in her beautiful face.

"What?" she asked.

"You get this look after coming, Clarissa. There is a tinge of shyness mixed with a hungry, turned-on glow. It socks it right to me."

"Socks it right to you?"

"Yeah. Haven't you ever watched *Laugh-In*?" I asked, tickling her tummy.

"Ah…" Clarissa pulled away and giggled. "Don't, I'm ticklish." She sat up. "Yes, I have. I love the sixties, remember?"

"I do. I remember everything about you, Clarissa Moone."

I pulled her into my arms. My cock thickened, and we were ready for round two. She licked her lips while gazing heavy-lidded at my cock. This girl had a penchant for fellatio. With those full, soft, and sensuous lips, how could one complain?

How erotic to see the semen dripping off her lips, like a hungry vampire, Clarissa wiped my creamy release from her mouth. She sat up, looking pleased, and deservedly so because that was one hell of a blowjob. I wanted to stop her so that I could enter her, but Clarissa insisted on going all the way.

My fingers explored below. "Now it's your turn."

"I can't. I have to work. We have guests arriving tonight, remember?" Clarissa tilted her head.

I followed her into the bathroom. "Delegate. Get others to help. Let's stay here. We can go to the beach. I'm hanging out for a swim. Then we can have lunch and then…" I wiggled my eyebrows.

She slapped my shoulder playfully. "You're incorrigible, Aidan Thornhill."

Clarissa turned on the taps and stepped into the shower.

Compared to the double-sized showers I'd become accustomed to, it was a tight fit. Nevertheless, I followed her and held Clarissa as the water cascaded over us.

"I can't do any of that today, Aidan, as much as I'd love to." Her eyes sparkled flirtatiously. "I could show off my new bikinis."

My cock stirred. "You've got new bikinis?" I hissed.

She nodded with a girlish smile.

"I hope you haven't worn them already. In public, I mean. You're a well-developed girl."

Clarissa laughed. "You're so possessive."

I slid my hands over her wet breasts. "I have a right to be. I'm sure you wouldn't want me flaunting it around horny girls, would you?"

"No, I wouldn't." Clarissa sighed. "But I have little control over that. Every time we're out I notice girls' eyes feasting on you."

"I haven't noticed," I responded dryly.

It was a half-truth. There'd been a few occasions where I'd been blatantly groped. LA was teeming with assertive women. A part of me liked that kick-ass attitude, but not for love-making. I admired it in business, but initiating sex was another thing. I'd never been aroused by women who threw themselves at me. I cringed at the thought of Jessica, my ex-fiancée, who was overly confident and vain. *Give me grace and sweetness of nature any day, if only for the languid sensuality that comes with it.*

I massaged body wash over her body. Hard again, my needy cock pushed against her leg.

"Turn around. I'll do your back," I said, rubbing myself against her butt. My cock needed to take her addictive pussy this way. As my fingers crept between her lips, I felt her heat. "Mm, that feels sublime," I said. My fingers dripped with her desire.

"Oh…" Clarissa purred a stretched moan. Yielding to my beseeching erection, Clarissa stopped talking about all the things she needed to do. Much to my delight, she seemed to love this as much as I did.

"Ah…" I drew a sharp breath. "Do you want it hard or gentle?" I said in a barely-there voice.

"Hard." Clarissa gasped.

Good answer.

Clarissa's soft, curvy butt squished against my balls as I entered her in one exquisite push. She sucked my cock with her tight little pussy. The pleasure bordered on unbearable.

With blood charging through my veins, my thrusts increased. Driven by pure lust, each penetration created a raging fire. My hard body pressed against Clarissa's soft and undulating form. Her voluptuous ass danced provocatively against my ravaging cock.

My heart threatened to erupt as her heavy breasts filled my insatiable hands. The build-up was agonizing. I could feel Clarissa sucking my cock in deeply. She shuddered. Her moan turned into a stretched wail. Her pussy had gone into a spasm, taking my cock with it.

A tormented growl escaped my lips as I shot long and hard.

"Fuck, Clarissa, what are you doing to me? I didn't know I had so much jam."

Clarissa fell into my arms, all soft and supplicating, panting into my neck. "Me too, Aidan."

"Yes, you wet little angel."

My heart unfurled. I wanted to tell Clarissa I loved her, but I stopped myself. It was too soon, even though I knew that nobody else could make me feel this way. I'd never been so aroused before. And my heart had never been so certain.

CHAPTER FORTY-FOUR

Clarissa

I kissed Aidan goodbye. His lips, swollen from feasting on me all morning, left a moist, sex-infused imprint.

"Are you sure you don't want to come down for a quick dip?" Aidan asked, rubbing Rocket on the belly.

Putting aside the three orgasms I'd just experienced, that handsome face had me gaga. Aidan's unshaven face accentuated his full lips, and those deep turquoise-blue eyes, *phew*—they really stole my breath away.

I shook my head. "My day's too full. I've got the hair stylist coming to deal with this." I lifted a tangled, wet strand of hair.

"I love it wet and hanging in your face." Aidan's off-center grin faded into an earnest frown. "There's one thing I insist, Clarissa."

I frowned. "What's that?"

"That you're on my arm greeting the guests when they arrive. I want you by my side," said Aidan, gazing deep into my eyes.

My eyes widened. "Are we ready for that? I mean, to tell the world that we're together?"

"Don't you want that?" Aidan's eyes narrowed.

My heart punched my head out of the way. "Yes, Aidan, of course I do."

The tightness in his face faded. Aidan's lips curled divinely. "Good. We'll meet… what time are the guests arriving?"

"Seven o'clock in the garden. Like the last time."

He nodded. "Have you got the same musicians booked, inside and out?"

"As instructed," I said in a business-like tone.

"You're not just a drop-dead beauty, but our best PA ever as well. It will be sad to lose you." Aidan pulled an enigmatic grin.

My brow lowered. "What?"

"We'll talk about that later. Only promise me one thing." Aidan's tone returned to serious. "Promise me you'll wear the earrings. They look stunning on you." He ran his finger up my neck. "I'm dying to see you wearing them," Aidan husked with knee-weakening tenderness.

I hugged him and whispered, "I'll wear them. And look forward to them quivering against my neck when you fuck me."

Aidan's mouth curled up at one end. "When we make love, you mean."

"Yes, that too."

I watched Aidan glide off. Man and dog, it was such a heartwarming sight. Aidan moved with a leisurely, self-assured gait, his calves muscular and lean. I exhaled slowly. He certainly was six foot two of mouth-watering masculinity.

My phone buzzed. It was Tabitha. I didn't have time, but I picked up anyway.

"Hey, Tabs." With one shoulder hunching the phone against my ear, I moved about, getting ready.

"Hello, old friend." Tabitha sounded morose.

"Oh… Tabi." I chuckled at her theatrical tone. "I'm sorry. I've been so flat- out busy. I've spent the morning with Aidan. Can't talk for long. I will make it up, promise."

"Hmm… heard that before. Anyway, guess where I'm going on Monday?" Tabitha's mood had shifted to exuberant.

"Where?" I asked, lifting the earrings out of the velvet box.

"Hawaii," she sang.

"Oh, wow. With Evan?"

"Yes… for two glorious weeks. Can you believe it? He's got a little apartment there. Clary, I'm so, so in love," she crooned.

"And I'm over the moon for you," I enthused. "Tabi, I want to ask you something."

"What?"

I exhaled slowly. "Aidan has just gifted me a pair of Cartier diamond earrings."

"You're fucking kidding me." Tabitha screamed. I had to hold the phone away from my ear.

"No, I'm not. It freaked me out, to be honest. Are they worth much, do you think?"

Tabitha squealed. "Cartier… hell, yeah… Tell me, are they studs or single strand?"

"No, they're chandelier, with lots and lots of diamonds— quite heavy." The earrings collected the light shining through the window. I'd never witnessed anything so luminescent before.

"Oh my, Clarissa. You've been blinged," she shrilled.

"Blinged? What sort of word is that?" I mixed my words amongst giggles.

"Bling. Get with it, girl. This is the twenty-first century. They'd be worth at least fifty thousand if not more. I can google if you like."

"No, don't." I sighed. "What am I to do?"

"What sort of question is that, you wild child? They're yours, take them. Hello. You're fucking a billionaire."

I winced. "Tabi, that sounds obscene. It's more than fucking. I think I'm in love." My voice cracked. After being in Aidan's arms all morning, having mind-blowing sex—or love-making, as he insisted on calling it— and receiving a ridiculously expensive gift. And then following that—Aidan's request for me to accompany him that night. My tears just tumbled.

"You've got it bad, Clary," she said gently. "It sounds like you've had a few toegasms. That's enough to make any grown woman cry, not to mention diamonds."

I laughed and cried simultaneously. "Toegasms? Oh, Tabs, you're wickedly hilarious." I sniffed, ripping a tissue out of the box. "I'm so glad you called. Where would I be without your sage, if ribald, advice?"

"No idea what ribald means. I take it's something to do with dirty-talk."

"It sure does. I've got to go, Tabs. Hey, let's talk tomorrow."

"No chance of a catch-up?" she asked. "Hey, by the way, you haven't told me what you're wearing tonight. Go on, tell me you've got an Oscar de la Renta so I can borrow it sometimes." Tabitha laughed. "One with a slit right down to your belly button, robbing every man of his senses and ability to move."

"Nothing of the sort. In fact, you'll go crazy when I tell you." I was unsure how my dress would be received that evening, despite loving it.

"Let me guess: something vintage?"

"You know me too well." I picked at my unpolished toenails, reminding myself they needed painting for my open-toed shoes.

"Well, then, put me out of my misery and tell me," said Tabitha impatiently.

"It doesn't even have a name or a brand. I think it may be a homemade job," I said, hearing Tabitha bristling in the background. "It's silk, turquoise, 1950's, I'd imagine, with a lace empire bodice and silk chiffon layers that fall elegantly to my feet. The only problem is I have to wear skyscraper heels because I haven't had time to get it shortened."

"Turquoise is a yummy color. It's very you. I want photos, selfies, anything with you and Mr. Perfect on your arm. Speaking of which, have you googled Aidan lately?"

"No, I never do. Why?"

"God, Clarissa, what universe do you live in?" Tabitha sighed. "I'll send you the link. There are a few snaps of you in the green dress with Aidan on your arm. They're fabulous shots. I only just stumbled on them."

"You're kidding." I was suddenly curious as hell. I checked the time. "Email it. I really have to run. Ta-ta. We'll talk soon."

CHAPTER FORTY-FIVE

Everything was in full swing. Preparations were flowing. In director mode, Greta pointed over to where things needed attending. I crept up, head bowed, mouth in a tight smile. "Greta, I'm…."

She shook her head, not giving me time to finish. "It's all under control. The lighting was kept intact from the last function. There's not much more to do."

Greta glanced down at her watch. "I've got to get my hair and face done. Can you keep an eye on the table arrangement?"

I nodded, and Greta smiled brightly.

Was this the same woman I'd met five weeks earlier? Greta's blue eyes reflected a glint of hope and optimism. Just like me, she seemed excited but scared. We were two women in love.

"Leave it to me, Greta," I said, steadying my voice and in business mode. "I'll also check the garden and make sure everything's in place."

Just as Greta was about to leave, I asked, "Are you wearing your hair up or down?"

"Down. Why?"

"Good. Dad's always been a sucker for long hair," I said with a smile.

Her lips curled. Greta touched my arm. "I know."

After I'd made sure everything was in place I went off to get ready.

Transformed into a beauty salon, my office reeked of hair lacquer and other noxious perfumes all designed to make me delectable. I imagined needing paint-stripper to remove the makeup, or vigorous sweat-inducing sex, the thought of which made me heat up.

From zero to extreme in three weeks, I'd turned into a sex maniac. Post-coital endorphins certainly beat any happy pill available to humankind. The sensation between my legs was relentless, with each throb setting off a delicious reminder of my well-endowed lover.

In his heavy Italian accent, Mario asked to see the dress I'd be wearing. I held the dress up against me. And after a few moments of switching his studious eye from dress to me, he suggested a goddess hairdo. He lifted a fistful of hair, then twirled and bunched it on top while leaving some to hang over my shoulder to one side. The hairdo was just a rehearsal, but I loved it.

"With your longish face and neck, this will work very well." Mario squinted into the mirror, studying my face.

I had been transformed. Mario had captured something masterful. Classical in design the hairstyle matched my empire-line dress. The cherry on the cake was the pair of earrings, which set off the whole outfit magnificently. As I studied myself in the mirror, it was obvious that no other jewelry could compete with them. So instead, I tied a thin black-velvet ribbon around my neck.

My cleavage ballooned out of the empire bodice, making that cut at once feminine and sensual. *Go, Jane Austen.* Although the hips and lower regions got a little lost in the cascading silk, there was a hint of curve when one moved.

I leaned into the mirror and studied my face. The make-up seemed exaggerated, all eyes and lavishly painted red lips, a bit pouty. But Mario insisted we go dramatic. In that effete Italian accent of his, he crooned, "You have divine eyes and lips, the window to the soul and to the promise of"—he kissed his fingers— "passion."

I squeezed my lips tight in order to suppress laughter. Mario was such a cliché, albeit a lovely one. His florid description of his beloved Italy was so engaging I almost stopped thinking about Aidan for an hour.

With shoes in hand, I descended the stairs, reproaching myself for not practicing walking in them earlier. The last thing I needed was to stumble. Overlooking the fact it could be fatal, I was more worried about the humiliation of it all.

As I sat on an ornate chair at the bottom of the stairs to do up my shoes, a familiar deep husk vibrated through me. "Do you need a hand?"

I looked up and my jaw dropped. Before me stood a man who took my breath away. Aidan, likewise, devoured me with his eyes.

Before I could answer, he'd knelt down and finished the job of buckling my shoes. "Shouldn't this happen at the end of the night?" Aidan grinned, testing to see if they were too tight. When he finished, his hand slid up my calf, sending the butterflies in my tummy deep down south.

"That's only if I'm running away and lose a shoe," I retorted. "And there are two reasons why that won't be happening."

Aidan's brow twitched. "Two?" He cocked his head. "Let me guess: no stepsisters to get away from."

"That's a third reason."

"Now you've got me curious." Aidan's impossibly blue eyes twinkled playfully.

"For one, I can't run in these shoes, and for two, dressed as you are, Mr. Aidan 'Drop-Dead-Gorgeous' Thornhill, you could be the very devil, and I'd still be the one undoing that silk cravat at the end of the night."

Aidan laughed. "Well said."

He helped me up off the Louis XIV chair. "My only regret so far this evening is that I didn't watch you descending the stairs. Clarissa Moone, you're a goddess."

I wobbled a little. How the hell was I meant to walk, let alone glide along gracefully? "I'm having a hard enough time standing, Aidan." I giggled.

"Don't worry, I've got you." Aidan kissed me on the lips. "They're stilts, all right. I didn't even have to bend down to meet your face." He brushed my cheek affectionately. "And what a gorgeous face that is."

He lifted one of the silk layers of my dress. "This is a sensational dress." Aidan touched my earrings. "When Cartier designed these, they had you in mind." He leaned over and kissed me. That was it. I was seriously swooning.

Aidan wore a sky-blue jacket, tailored to perfection, capturing his broad shoulders masterfully and the color setting off his magnificent eyes. Beneath the linen-silk jacket, a white silk shirt hung elegantly over his manly chest, while the cream-colored linen pants fell elegantly from his waist. If that wasn't enough to make me want to faint, the turquoise cravat with tiny burgundy polka dots had me gasping for air.

"Aidan, you look like you've just stepped out of *European Vogue*. I'm almost expecting a little sparkle when you open your mouth." I chuckled.

He laughed. "Now you're being ridiculous." He held me. "Are we ready for showtime?"

"I suppose." My voice was unsteady.

"Hey, it's only a charity event. We're not meeting the Queen."

"Strangely, that wouldn't make me as nervous. Perhaps only having to curtsy would pose a problem."

"For me, it wouldn't, not with that low-cut dress of yours." His eyes shone flirtatiously.

What was a girl to do? For one, take the arm of the sexiest man alive.

As we descended the outside stairs, I used stomach muscles, something I'd learnt from my childhood ballet classes, to help me balance. With my arm entwined with Aidan's, I miraculously floated along—only to be awakened from my dream as cameras flashed in my face.

Aidan whispered, "I hope you don't mind. They're an annoyingly necessary feature."

"I don't mind. It just looks like we're a couple," I replied.

"Isn't that what we are?" Aidan asked, pausing to look at me.

"If you say so, then we are." My voice wavered.

It was so overwhelming, with people staring and whispering. I had to keep reminding myself to appear natural as my eyes zeroed in on a tray filled with glistening glasses of champagne. Fortunately, the waiter came straight to me. Taking a glass with a trembling hand, I quickly took a sip.

It was a repeat performance—not only the entertainment, but there were guests from the last function as well. This time, many of the husband-seekers had men attached to their arms, although as I looked about, I did notice a cohort of scantily dressed girls. Their eyes skimmed over me before settling on the prize: Aidan.

With my arm locked in Aidan's we moved about the crowd. It was such a perfect evening with a pink-orange twilight that made the clouds look like balls of fire. The grounds were in full bloom, and birds chirped along to the gentle, undulating sounds of violins. My preferred sensation, however, other than Aidan's cologne-infused male scent, was the salty, floral air that gently massaged my flesh.

"Aidan, you're looking as handsome as ever. And who is this magnificent creature?" asked an older woman.

"I'd like to present, Clarissa Moone."

She held out her diamond-laden hand. "How lovely to meet you."

"This is Marianne Kingsley, a novelist and a neighbor," said Aidan warmly.

I smiled. "Pleased to meet you."

"My, you are enchanting. You've also made every girl here green with envy." She chuckled. "I love your dress. It's so classic and feminine. Not like the crass excuse for dresses on display. I mean, none of that pouty flesh is real, is it?" Her lips curled derisively.

Marianne was so down to earth I liked her immediately. She lit a cigarette and directed her attention over to my father. "Hey, who's that gorgeous man?"

Aidan cast me a side glance. "That's Clarissa's father. I'm afraid he's spoken for."

"Oh, what a pity, all the handsome ones are always taken," she said, sighing theatrically.

Wearing a subtle grin, Aidan held out his hand. "I hope you have a pleasant night, Marianne."

We continued to greet so many guests that I had no hope of remembering their names. It was all a blur. I was already on my second glass of champagne, which was helping me relax, when Aidan exclaimed under his breath, "Fuck."

I saw a tall, attractive woman with long, chestnut, bouncy hair heading towards us. She could have been a model. And like the other Aidan hunters, she wore a dress with a slit down to her tummy, her bust ballooning out. The fact that her breasts didn't jiggle had me speculating that they were fake. I know if I wore something like that, mine would swing out of control. The dress was low-cut in the back as well, all the way to her curvaceous butt. She was very beautiful. My veins iced with jealousy.

Her unwavering attention was on Aidan. Upon arriving at our spot, she initiated a hug. Aidan's frame went discernibly stiff when she kissed him lingeringly on his cheek. By that stage, I was as green as her dress.

Aidan pulled away first. "Jessica, this is Clarissa Moone; Clarissa this is Jessica Mansfield."

While Aidan remained tense, Jessica stood close. Too close. Apart from a slight curve of her spongy lips, she regarded me with indifference for a moment. After that, Jessica ignored me.

"So how was London?" Aidan asked in a disinterested monotone.

"Oh, it was okay, a bit gray and cold. I missed sunny California. I missed the hunky guys," Jessica gushed. She looked at my dress and then back at Aidan. She stroked his cravat. "This is a nice touch. Color coordinated, I see."

Jessica turned to me suddenly. "That's an interesting dress." Her eyes checked out my chest. I wondered if that expression was envy, considering that my breasts were soft and real. *Miaow*.

"Thanks," I replied coldly.

"It's different," said Jessica, not hiding a mocking tone. Turning away and discarding me again, Jessica cast her attention back on Aidan.

"Aidan, I'm just going to chat with my dad," I said, unable to tolerate pompous Jessica any further.

Not as well-practiced at arrogance as Jessica, I nodded and left the two former lovers to chat before Aidan had a chance to respond. My chest was so tight I'd forgotten to breathe.

While performing the sexiest strut I could muster in my heels, I made sure I avoided the grass.

"Hi, Daddy." I hugged my father. He looked handsome in his linen suit. "You look so debonair, Papa."

"As do you, Clarissa. You're a masterpiece." His dark eyes were filled with so much love and admiration I wanted to cry.

Noticing a waiter with a tray of champagne, I asked, "Do you mind if I have one of those, please?" He came straight over, and we took a glass of bubbly each.

"I say, this is truly magnificent. It's a class event, honey. And you designed it all. I'm proud of you, daughter mine," my father said effervescently. It was not his normal demeanor. I put it down to nerves and liquor. Like me, he got rather excitable in new situations.

"Where's Greta?" I asked.

"She's dealing with some fellow named Bryce."

"Oh God, it just gets better and better."

"What is it, sweetheart? You seem a little flustered."

"Aidan's ex-fiancée is here. She's all over him, and she's beautiful." I bristled.

In his subtle way, my father took a moment to survey the situation. "Oh, the one in green, dressed like a prostitute."

I laughed. He sounded so old-fashioned. "Oh Dad, that's the latest fashion."

"It's horrible. All fake and out there. Leaves nothing to the imagination. Can't compare her with you. You're a beauty, Clarissa, classically and naturally so. Come the morning after, when all that make-up has gone, one would make a dash for the door."

I giggled. "Oh, father, I'm so glad you're here. I'm just jealous and frightened."

"Frightened of what, dear girl? Aidan is besotted. And why shouldn't he be? He's with the most beautiful girl here by far."

"You're only saying that because you're my father," I said, squeezing his arm affectionately.

Noticing my father peering over my shoulder, I turned, and met Aidan's eyes. How could one not be possessed by that gorgeous man?

"It's good to see you here, Julian," said Aidan, shaking my father's hand. "Love the suit."

"Thank you," my father replied. "You're looking rather continental yourself." He pointed at Aidan's cravat. "That goes brilliantly with Clarissa's dress."

Aidan smiled at me. "I had no idea Clarissa would choose that color."

I remained cool.

"Can you excuse us for a moment, Julian?" Aidan asked, taking me by the arm gently.

When we were away from the crowd Aidan whispered, "I didn't invite Jessica. I don't know how she bought a ticket. I'm seriously pissed."

"Why?" I asked.

"Because she's a notorious flirt."

"But don't all women flirt with you, Aidan?"

His eyebrows drew in sharply at my bluntness. Aidan studied me. "I suppose some do." He took my hand, and staring into my eyes, added, "Clarissa, it's you and only you I want. Jessica has this way of claiming people. Whatever her body language might suggest, it's you that I am here with. She's nothing to me except a pain in the neck." The last comment was muttered irritably to himself.

"I'm just overwhelmed by all of this attention. And"—I sighed— "I suppose the fact that she's so good-looking."

"Jessica's nothing compared to you," returned Aidan, eating me up with his intense eyes. "I've never met or been with anybody remotely like you, Clarissa." His voice filled deep with emotion. My legs weakened, and I fell into his arms.

I inhaled the smell of his flesh— an intoxicating cocktail of cologne mixed with male desire and tension— as I would an afternoon rose.

As we hugged, I spied Jessica watching us. Her eyes met mine. The bliss emanating from me must have been so blinding that her caked-on haughtiness hardened into resentment.

CHAPTER FORTY-SIX

Devina Velvet kissed me on the cheek, purring, "Sooo lovely to see you again, Clarissa." Her hand danced over the silk of my dress. "Now, that is one sublime little dress." With the projection typical of a singer, Devina's words travelled. I noticed Jessica stood within earshot. She'd joined the group of Aidan admirers, whose stolen glances and little whispers had been hard to miss.

"And that color is luscious," she went on. "It suits you. Anything would with the drop-dead figure of yours, girlfriend."

"Thanks," I said.

"Where did you get it? It's such a classic cut, and deliciously silk."

"I bought it on-line."

"Oh, one of those designer brands?" asked Devina.

"No, I got it from Vintage Rocks," I replied. The cat-club went to town, all cackling at my expense. And they didn't even try to hide it. In what was well-choreographed mockery, they stared at me, whispered, and then laughed.

"They sure made gorgeous dresses back then. You must send me the link." Devina's almond-shaped eyes gave a side glance at the giggling gal pals. Projecting her Southern husk, she added, "You're the belle of the ball, girlfriend. There's not one chick here tonight that touches you in the beauty stakes, and I love these little darlings." She pointed to my earrings. "Ooo... diamonds. A little gift from that gorgeous man on your arm?"

At first, I squirmed, not sure if I should divulge that information. But I couldn't help myself after the battering I'd been receiving. "Yes." I glanced at Jessica, whose smarmy expression faded into a glower.

Having discovered how tiring unwavering attention could be, I headed upstairs to my own private restroom for some respite.

Upon reaching the landing, I heard Aidan's voice. "What the fuck is she doing here, Aunt?"

"I have no idea, Aidan. She purchased a ticket like everyone else. We were swamped with requests. We sold out straight after the last event, and to be honest, I didn't notice a Jessica Mansfield amongst the names. I'd say she used an alias."

"I hope she doesn't drink too much and cause trouble. Revenge is written all over her conceited face, and she doesn't do *no*." He sighed deeply. "This is the last event, Greta."

"The final charity gala?" Greta's voice tensed. "But it raises cash for your causes. You're not planning to close them, are you?"

"Of course not. I'll never do that. There's too much need out there. It's what drives me."

"How will you raise money for them, then? The monthly expenses just keep increasing. And that's not only because of Bryce but also the rapid rise in need, especially at the women's refuge."

"I'll never abandon women, children, or dogs in need. I've got other plans. It's to do with art."

I walked past my office and pretended that I hadn't heard anything.

Aidan saw me, and his face lit up. "Princess."

"I just needed a little time in my private powder room," I said.

"You look fabulous, Clarissa," said Greta, touching my dress. "That dress is striking. I had one similar to that when I was your age."

"And you too, Greta. Blue really suits you. It brings out your eyes," I said, genuinely struck by how youthful and attractive Greta looked.

It also made me see how love brought out a glow that cosmetics could never achieve.

Greta smiled, touching my arm affectionately, and left.

Lust was written on Aidan's face as he stared deep into my eyes. My heart pumped so hard my senses dissolved to the floor. Before my mouth opened, I was in his arms. Aidan's hands were under my dress, moving up my legs and stopping at the garter. His response so primal he growled.

His fleshy, hot mouth crushed mine, parting my lips, his velvety tongue snaked feverishly around mine. Before I could breathe, Aidan's fingers had found their way into my panties.

Aidan's imploring erection pushed hard against my thigh. He unzipped his pants and lifted my dress. His hard cock pushed impatiently into me as he waltzed me against the wall. His need was so extreme, he ripped my panties. His breath rough and fast, he lifted my thigh and entered me with one thrust.

"Ooh... Clarissa. I'm addicted to you, to the way you feel. I love being inside you. You're so hot and creamy. I just want to eat you, as does my cock."

What followed was fiery, hard sex. Fueled by the earlier tension, the friction of his thick cock pounding into me had my nerve endings sparking off wildly. My skin was so sensitive that as his hand moved down my bodice to caress my breasts, my nipples pushed out hard against the lace.

His groans became more intense, blending into my own gasps. The build-up was like the crescendo to fire-works. My involuntary spasms made Aidan drive harder and faster until I couldn't hold back anymore, and a stretched moan escaped my lips.

"That's it, Princess." I slumped into Aidan's arms, tossed about, stars behind my eyes. I panted into Aidan's neck as his creamy release gushed in, drowning me in raw heat.

His jaw clenched, Aidan trembled in my arms, sighing my name as if starved of air.

We remained against the wall in each other's arms until our senses returned.

Adjusting my dress in the mirror I said, "No wonder the French refer to orgasms as *la petite mort.*"

Aidan combed back his hair with his hands and cast me one of his adorable lopsided grins. "Do you feel as if you're dying when you come?"

I nodded. "Don't you?"

He nodded reflectively. "With you, the release is extremely intense. I've never experienced it like that before."

"Likewise," I murmured. "Although, I must admit I have nothing to compare it with, other than…"

"Than… what?" Aidan cocked his head. "What haven't you told me?"

"As you know," I said, with a nervous giggle. "I haven't been with any guys, but I…"

His eyes enlarged. "You've been with women?"

I had to laugh at his stunned expression. "No…. my hands and Toy Boy."

"Who the fuck is Toy Boy?" Aidan asked, his face contorted with such intensity, I felt a shiver up my spine. He could be frighteningly jealous.

"Toy Boy is my vibrator. Lately, he's been relegated to the back of my drawer with *Middlemarch.*"

Aidan looked puzzled. "*Middlemarch?*"

"It's a book by George Eliot."

Aidan's lips curled wickedly. "So how do these"— he wiggled his fingers— "and this"— he licked his lips— "and that"— he pointed to his groin— "compare with Toy Boy?"

"There's no comparison. You, Aidan Thornhill, are a stud."

He held me again. "And you, Clarissa Moone, are the most arousing woman I've ever kissed, touched, fucked, and for the first time ever, made love to."

My heart melted. "What's the difference between fucking and making love?"

Aidan exhaled a slow breath. "Um… well, making love is when we're together all night, touching, kissing, licking, imbibing, swallowing, laughing, fucking, and our hearts swell to the point of no return."

"And fucking?"

"Just what we did then," he said. "Only…"

I shook my head. "Only?"

"With you, when I orgasm, it feels as though I'm emptying everything into you, my whole body and soul. So, I guess they're the same thing."

Good answer. "I love it when you take me hard, Aidan."

"I love it hard too. I'm just scared of hurting you," he said.

I hugged Aidan. "You did," I uttered in his ear.

Aidan pulled his head back to stare at me. "Why didn't you say something?"

"It's divine pain. The type that one can't get enough of," I said, arching a brow.

He kissed my cheek and whispered, "I liked you in the shower standing up with your gorgeous curvy butt all hot and wet against my balls."

"Now I'm getting all steamy again, Aidan."

He held me tight and kissed me passionately.

We'd taken a few steps when Aidan stopped. "Hey, I'm sorry about Jessica turning up like that. It's doing my head in, to be honest. She's a real piece of work."

"You're not the type of man a woman gets over easily, Aidan."

"Hmm…" Aidan took my arm, and his mood brightened. "As Bugs Bunny would say…"

"What's up, Doc?" I asked, puzzled.

"No." He chuckled. "On with the show— this is it." Aidan kicked his legs out like the rooster in *Merry Melodies*, and I lost it. I laughed like a hyena, so contagiously that we both entered the ballroom giggling like teenagers.

All eyes were on us, especially those of Jessica, whose face soured upon witnessing how easy-going and happy Aidan and I were together. Considering how serious Aidan often was, I imagined his merriment was a rare sight.

Bryce intercepted us. "Have you two been smoking weed or something?"

"No, Bryce, we haven't," said Aidan.

CHAPTER FORTY-SEVEN

Aidan was called over by an older male patron whom, he whispered, was a war-veteran. It touched me to see Aidan so respectful around older people. This was a gentle, kind Aidan. I recalled with distaste his smug, almost outright rude disregard towards my unofficial date Cameron and his dismissive attitude towards Tabitha and her date. But as Aidan started to reveal his true essence, particularly around people devoted to benevolent and lofty causes, I saw nothing but a gentleman.

Seated at our table were some of the people I recognized from the last dinner. Bryce was as troubling as usual with that salacious stare that rarely made it past my cleavage. *Eek*. Seated next to him was Jessica. A cold sensation settled in my gut. Nevertheless, I tried my hardest to ignore both of them. How she'd ended up at our table was a matter for Greta, I suppose.

Aidan didn't hide his displeasure as he headed towards the table. His soft gaze, directed at me, turned acidic when his eyes landed on Jessica. Instead of taking a seat, Aidan headed over to Greta and whispered something in her ear. He had that stern, scary look in his eyes. Poor Greta just shook her head and shrugged.

The food was predictably sumptuous. I was so hungry that I wolfed down my soup, silently oohed over the ridiculously fresh seafood salad, and ate my medium-rare steak as a vampire would her first meal of blood in a century. My body obviously needed replenishing after all the vigorous sex.

Aidan glanced over at me. "Haven't you eaten for some time?"

About to pop a potato in my mouth, I peered up from my plate. "I tend to eat a lot. I love food."

"I've noticed. And I love that about you. You're a rare flower." His blue eyes shimmered tenderly.

Unable to help myself, I glanced over and saw Jessica watching us. I couldn't understand why she was putting herself through this. It must've been torture. She was clearly still in love with Aidan. And he was not holding back on his display of affection towards me.

"It's Clarissa, isn't it?" asked the same man whom I'd spoken about art at the last function.

I glanced up. Despite recalling his face, which had reminded me of my father— whom he was now seated alongside— I couldn't recall his name. "It is. Wonderful to see you again."

"I don't think we were introduced last time. This is Dorothy, my wife. And I'm Rudi." His dark, amiable eyes beamed.

"Pleased to meet you," I said, putting down my utensils. I took a sip of my wine to help wash down the food.

"We enjoyed that little discussion about art at the last gala. In fact, we came tonight because of that." Rudi glanced at his wife, who nodded with matching enthusiasm.

Rudi allowed his wife, who seemed ready to erupt volubly, to speak. "We wish to invite you to our next soirée."

I nodded slowly. "That sounds very interesting. Is there a theme?"

"I'm glad you asked. We're hosting an evening of nineteen-century art." Dorothy spoke with a slight German accent.

"Oh," I replied. Aidan placed his warm hand on my thigh. I almost lost my train of thought as it seared into my flesh. "You're having an exhibition?"

"Not as such. We host soirées regularly. Aidan's attended a few," she said, regarding him with the fondness of an old aunt. Aidan returned an approving nod.

"That sounds very entertaining," said my father.

"It does. It reminds me of Gertrude Stein," I replied.

Most of the younger guests, including Jessica, looked lost at sea. Not Dorothy, whose eyes widened with excitement. "Oh, what a colorful character," she exclaimed. "We are passionate admirers, and of that era too."

"She was affiliated with Picasso," I said, glancing over at my father.

"And Hemingway," he added.

Rudi switched his attention to my father. "And that invitation extends to you, Julian." He regarded me again. "Your father and I have a lot in common it seems, in our love of English literature. Aidan has shown me his extraordinary library."

Returning to the subject of the soirée, Dorothy said, "We were wondering if you would speak a little on any artist that you admire from that era. We enjoyed listening to your insights at the last dinner so much that both Rudi and I thought it would be an honor to have you there."

My eyes reached out to Aidan, who cast me a reassuring look.

"I suppose I could," I said hesitantly.

"It doesn't have to be long, maybe half an hour at the most."

I thought about it for a moment. "Aidan made me a gift of the Klimt catalogue from the Belvedere in Vienna."

At the mention of Vienna, their faces lit up. Rudi said, "Oh, that would be spectacular. We've visited that gallery. What a joy that would be. Would you? I mean, we don't wish to impose on you. It's not for another month."

Aidan nodded. "I'll be here. I wouldn't miss it for the world," he said, focusing on me.

"Well, why not, then," I said. "I can turn some of the images into slides and talk about his seminal works." I smiled. "I do love him."

Dorothy clapped her hands. "That sounds glorious. We're hoping to have music from that period. And poetry." She regarded my father. "Julian may be able to help us there, we hope. You have got such a musical voice."

My father resembled me in his modesty, but Greta, beaming with pride, impelled him to accept.

"Maybe some T.S. Eliot? In my earlier college days, I trod the boards," he said, chuckling.

Aidan kept his hand on my thigh, burning a hole. When I accepted their strange offer, he squeezed my leg. I looked at him, and his eyes sparkled with admiration.

The night continued on gloriously. Devina had the guests enthralled, her hips swaying sensually in her slinky black-satin dress. The charismatic diva looked every bit the provocative chanteuse. With her bedroom husk, she introduced her first number, "The Man I Love."

Aidan, who had been chatting about his projects to Rudi and my father, turned to me. "I love this song. Will you dance?"

"I'd love to, only I don't know how to waltz," I said.

He took my arm. "Come, there's nothing to it. Just let me lead." Aidan took my hand and led the way.

It was so effortless being in Aidan's arms that even in my impossible shoes I floated along. My head fitted cosily into his shoulder. Thanks to my heels, I was the perfect height.

"You're a fantastic dancer, Aidan."

"And you, Clarissa, are very light and graceful, easy to lead." Aidan spun me around.

"Have you taken lessons?" I asked.

"My mother used to be a ballroom dance teacher, and when I was a young boy, she would get me to dance with some of her students."

That was so unexpected my brows hit my skull. "You're kidding?"

Aidan shook his head. "No, I'm not."

"There's so much about you I don't know, Aidan. Why have you never spoken of your mother?"

"Because she's not a good person, that's why."

"But she's your mother," I said, sensing stiffness in his body.

"That she is." Aidan held me tight again. "I'll tell you about her one day. Let's not spoil this memorable moment." He kissed my neck, and I forgot everything. His lips had that mesmerizing effect on me.

We danced and danced and danced.

Occasionally, we rubbed shoulders with my father and Greta, who, like us, had drifted off into their own romantic bubble. My heart filled with bliss. Were it not for Jessica, the night would have resembled a fairy-tale.

When Aidan wasn't in my arms or hanging close to me, he chatted about his renewable-energy project to any willing audience. While he was thus engaged, I left him to it and visited the powder room.

Soon as I opened the door, I recoiled at the sight of Jessica in the mirror.

A wry smirk grew on her face. "Oh, it's the belle of the ball."

Reluctant to feed into a bitchy standoff, I produced a tight smile.

"Have you been together long?" Jessica asked in a neutral tone.

"One month," I replied, reaching into my purse for my comb.

"The honeymoon period, Aidan's insatiable at this stage," she said, leaning into the mirror to fix her eye make-up. Her almond-shaped green eyes were very striking. With that thick red hair cascading down to her tiny waist, Jessica was definitely a stunner.

I remained quiet, my core tightening by the second.

"You're another one of his PA's, I believe." Jessica stared down at my cleavage.

Curiosity got the better of me. "What do mean by 'another one'?"

"Only that he's fucked most of you."

"You're lying. You're just jealous. It's written all over you." I sharpened my claws.

She snorted. "How old are you?"

"None of your business," I said, clasping my clutch-bag tightly.

"You don't know about young Amy?"

"I do, in fact. Aidan told me about her." I tried to maintain a cool tone.

She arched one of her thin eyebrows. "Oh, did he?" Her voice went up a register. "Did he tell you the bit about his fiancée being pregnant at the time?"

I froze. The blood drained from my whole body. "What?"

"Yes, that's right. Look shocked. Because it was pretty fucking shocking for me too," said Jessica bitterly.

"What happened to the baby?"

"Good question. I miscarried." With a twisted smile on her face, she added, "I found them fucking, and I ran out in such a hurry that I fell over, and that was it, the end." Although Jessica wore a blank expression, she was out for a scalp—mine.

It was working. My skin was suddenly infested with a swarm of creepy-crawly nasties, sending me into a meltdown. Beneath me, my legs were numb, useless even, as I clutched onto the basin for balance.

"I'm only telling you this because you're young. You could get any man you want—an honest, handsome, rich, untainted man. Aidan is a dark character."

"I get the impression you want Aidan back even after that."

She nodded. Her cold green eyes were determined and steely. "I do." She ran her hands down her slinky dress, adjusting her silicone breasts so that they jutted out as far as possible. "You see, Aidan and I are very similar in many ways." Her icy stare froze my heart. "I, too, fucked my teacher when I was sixteen." Jessica had a wicked glint in her eyes.

My eyes widened in shock. "What?"

"He didn't tell you about that either? Fuck, he told me on the first night we met. Just after I'd swallowed everything that big fat gorgeous cock had to offer."

I pushed past her and got to the cubicle just in time to vomit, disgorging everything. My soul included. I remained there until her heels clip-clopped out.

CHAPTER FORTY-EIGHT

I ran and ran and ran— into the dark of the night, with shoes dangling from my hands so that I could charge ahead unhindered. When I was out of sight, I fell onto the ground, face down, and cried like a baby.

My heart was beating against the ground so intensely that I didn't hear steps approaching. My despair was interrupted by a male voice. "Now, what have we here?"

Before I had a chance to look up, an arm was lifting me off the ground. It took a moment to focus through my teary, blurred vision, only to discover Bryce holding me.

I tried to break away from his tight hold, but he proved too strong.

"Let me go," I screamed.

"Not quite yet, my little lovely." His dark eyes were filled with sleazy intent. He locked one arm around me, and his free hand squeezed my breasts. "You're one very fuckable girl. These tits…"

He hurt me with his rough hands. I smelt liquor on his breath and was overcome by nausea. I screamed as he tried to kiss me.

Next minute, Aidan's voice rang loudly through the air. He grabbed Bryce and pulled him off me and proceeded to pummel him.

It all happened so quickly. For a moment, I remained leaden and shocked. But as I returned to my senses, I quickly realized that there could be a murder if this wasn't stopped. Aidan was smashing into Bryce with such force, I could hear bones cracking.

I ran into the kitchen and cried for help. Will came to the rescue and ran to the scene. Being a well-built man, Will was able to get Aidan off Bryce, who, coming off second best, had blood streaming down his face, and was clutching his gut.

After my repeated pleas, Aidan agreed not to involve the police. He tried to hold me, but I was cold and unyielding. I said, "Leave me. I need to be alone."

Aidan ran his hands through his tousled hair. His eyes filled with confusion as he gazed at me looking for answers. Just as he was about to say something, Greta turned up.

He took her aside and spoke to her. I could see her face lengthening in distress. I heard him instruct her to go back and act as if nothing had happened. He told her to tell the guests that he'd been called away on urgent business. He also asked her not to alarm my father. For that I was grateful.

I sat in the kitchen, my palms on my cheeks, peering down. "Do you think I can go to the cottage, please?"

Aidan looked lost and confused as he stroked my hair. "Yes, of course. I'll take you."

I stood up, barefoot and disheveled. My dress was stained with damp grass. "No. I wish to be alone. I don't want you there, Aidan."

He frowned. His stormy blue eyes were so intense I had to turn away. He was so beautiful. I wanted to forgive him and fall into his arms. I was in love, and weak.

"What were you doing there?" Aidan asked, shaking his head. "What's happened? Why do I get the feeling that something's happened to us?"

He held me, but I struggled out of his arms. "Let me go, Aidan, please." Tears streamed down my face. I took my earrings off and placed them in his hand.

Stunned and confused, Aidan said, "Don't do this, Clarissa." His distraught timbre penetrated deeply.

I ran away, too frightened to turn and look. I was certain Aidan remained watching me, for his energy burned into me.

The following day, I hurried back to my apartment. I couldn't face seeing anybody. I rang Greta and told her I was not feeling the best and that I needed the week off. I detected a note of concern in her voice, and was relieved that she didn't push for details.

My father was a different matter. In addition to the ten missed calls from Aidan, my father had left another five.

I opened the drapes to our dowdy apartment. Tabitha had been away for a day. The dishes sat piled up in the kitchen. I groaned when I saw them, cursing her loudly. I was, however, glad to be alone, being so despairingly traumatized, I couldn't bring myself to speak. Even though this could never compare with the loss of my beloved mother, the same heavy, debilitating cloud was back with vengeance.

I plonked myself on the sofa and called my father. He would've been too stressed out otherwise.

"Clarissa." My father's voice was filled with concern.

"Hi."

"Where are you, honey?"

"I'm at the apartment. Hey look, Daddy, don't worry. I'm okay. I need a little time alone to think things through." My voice was thick with emotion.

"Yes, of course. It's all happened so quickly, hasn't it? You're still young." His voice was gentle and understanding.

"I heard some disturbing things about Aidan. And I need time to process things."

"He's a good man, regardless of past misdemeanors. There aren't many that compare to Aidan," my father said soberly.

What had he learnt? "What has Greta told you about Aidan, Dad? Please tell me. Anything will help." Out came the waterworks again. I couldn't believe I had so many tears.

"Darling, she's told me little. Only that he had a difficult upbringing, and that his hedonist mother put his needs last. I saw Aidan last night and today. He's in a bad way. He begged me to speak to you on his behalf. Just speak to him, sweetie. He's a decent man, a kind man." Not one for interfering in people's private affairs, my father had stepped out of his comfort zone to champion Aidan.

"I'll talk to Aidan, but not today. I need a little time and space. I'll see you soon, Daddy," I said, my throat swelling with sobs.

Wallowing in gloom, I flinched at the knock on the door. I looked through the peephole and saw Aidan, keys jangling in his hands. My hair was a tangled mess, and I was dressed in an old tank top and shorts. I froze.

"Clarissa, I know you're there. I'm sensing you," said Aidan, raising his voice. "I won't go until you open the door, even if I have to stay here all night."

"Go away, Aidan. Not now," I said. Hoping the neighbors weren't in. We'd had a few of these standoffs in the past thanks to Tabitha and her tempestuous relationships.

"Just open the door. Talk to me, Clarissa. You owe me that at least. Please."

I took a deep breath and opened the door. I stood away, allowing him passage.

Although Aidan looked scruffier than I'd ever seen him, he was still ruggedly handsome, his hair tousled and wild, his dark-rimmed eyes so breathtakingly blue my heart did a somersault. He was dressed in worn, ripped jeans and an equally worn T-shirt that showed off his sinewy, well-developed arms.

My heart instantly started arguing with my mind, insisting that I fall into Aidan's arms and have hard sex against the wall. Instead, I remained icy and remote. My mind was winning.

Aidan stared at me for what seemed a long while. His eyes had that lusty glow, moving from despair to arousal in one breath. It was because I wasn't wearing a bra.

I crossed my arms. "Aidan, you shouldn't have come." My mind had gone haywire. The apartment, as disheveled as I, was not in a fit state for visitors.

"I changed my schedule. I couldn't leave without seeing you." He ran his hand through his hair. "I'm leaving tomorrow instead." Aidan did a quick sweep of the apartment. "Why are you here? I don't like you being here. There's no security door," he grumbled. "Just as I arrived, a bunch of guys were doing a drug deal downstairs." His tone softened. "If anything happened to you, I…" Under the light, the dark rings around his eyes were visible. I could see he hadn't slept.

He tried to take my hand. I pulled away. "I need time to be alone, Aidan." I combed back my messy hair.

"You've been traumatized, Clarissa. I can see that." Aidan voice was soft and gentle. "I hope you'll reconsider pressing charges against Bryce."

"I don't want to, Aidan. It would involve court hearings. And with you being such a prominent figure, it would turn into a circus."

Aidan sighed deeply. "You have a point. I'm so sorry about all of this. Clarissa, what made you run in the first place? I'm sure Jessica's involved somehow." Aidan cornered me with his dark-blue stare.

My mind went blank.

"Do you have anything to drink?" Aidan was pacing about like a restless tiger.

"Only cooking sherry," I said with an apologetic half-smile.

He grinned. "I'm willing if you are."

Ghostlike, I drifted off into the kitchen and poured some into a glass. Although I was about to abstain, I made myself one as well. My nerves needed something.

As I passed Aidan the glass, I said, "It will probably taste terrible, especially for someone like you."

Aidan's brow wrinkled. "Someone like me?"

"You know what I mean. You're used to the finer things in life." I took a sip of the liquor.

Swallowing the liquor, he winced. "It wasn't always that way, Clarissa. I lived in a similar set-up to this with my mother." Aidan remained standing, waiting for a response.

"Jessica told me everything," I said, staring down at my feet.

His eyebrows drew in sharply. "Everything?"

I nodded slowly.

Aidan cleared his throat. "You may need to elaborate. Lying comes naturally to Jessica. I wouldn't mind hearing which version of our fucked-up relationship she told you." His tone was cold and acerbic.

I exhaled a staccato breath. The sherry had at least steadied my palpitations. "Jessica told me she caught you in bed with Amy. And that the shock was so great it caused a miscarriage." I stared directly into Aidan's eyes. "She told me the child was yours." My voice broke up, and tears fell. I hated crying in front of people, especially in front of the man who had stolen my heart.

Aidan produced an unused handkerchief from his pocket and handed it to me. "Fuck. No wonder you ran." His shoulders slumped. He looked crushed. "Clarissa, now listen. It was not—I repeat *not*— my child."

"But how would you know that?"

"Because while Jessica was in the hospital, I ordered a paternity test." His voice grew thick with emotion. Seeing Aidan in such a state felt like cold fingers scratching at my soul.

"Can they even do that? And why?"

"Why?" Aidan's eyes widened in disbelief. "I'll tell you why: because Jessica can't go one night without having sex. She's an addict. I was away often during our relationship. She fucked half of LA, Clarissa."

"But how do you know?"

"Clarissa, this town is smaller than you think. And rich folk hang out in all the same places. And…" He finished off his drink. "She fucked Evan."

"Evan?" That was Tabitha new man. "He's dating…" I paused.

"Your roommate. Evan told me. He's smitten. He's also a close buddy. She'd better not fuck around on him."

"She wouldn't do that," I snapped.

Aidan rolled his eyes. "Come on, Clarissa. Your friend gets around."

My face reddened. "How do you know that?"

"By the way she checked me out," he said coolly.

"Aidan, even a cloistered nun would check you out."

His grave expression melted into a grin.

"Anyway, Evan's not that much of a buddy if he had sex with Jessica."

Exasperated, Aidan said, "Clarissa, to cut a long story short, at the time, Jessica told Evan we'd broken up. Please, will you accept my apology? I haven't slept all night. I've had the worst night of my life, to be honest." He rubbed his eyes.

"But it still doesn't exonerate you from cheating on Jessica, despite her loose ways."

"It should, because our relationship had ended. It's even on the record—posted in those silly gossip columns. I can get Greta to source them for you if you like."

Heaviness left my body. "No need, I believe you. Please don't involve Greta in this." I took a moment to process everything. "What about the school teacher? She told me you had sex with your school teacher."

"Fuck, she got in your ear, didn't she? No wonder you ran away." He touched my hand, his eyes glistening with regret. "I was sixteen going onto seventeen when she seduced me. She was beautiful and seemed younger than twenty-seven."

A cold, jealous stake ran through me. "Go on."

Aidan ran his tongue over his lips—unintentionally, surely, but it was still suggestive. My inner core fired up.

"What can I say? She seduced the shit out of me and"—Aidan sniffed—"I capitulated. Clarissa, my life was messed-up when she came along. Instead of doing drugs and liquor, like all my screwball friends, I had sex with my teacher."

"What happened to her?" I asked, biting into a nail.

"She's dead. Her brute of a husband killed her."

"Shit." I shook my head.

He exhaled slowly. "That's when I joined the army."

"Did you love her?" I asked.

He nodded. "I think I might've. I'd never known affection from a woman before. My mother had no interest in caring for me— only Greta." Aidan was staring down at his feet. "I suppose I'm too fucked-up for you now." Aidan rubbed his neck. His eyes met mine. He was shattered in a way I could never have imagined.

"You're not, Aidan," I said emphatically.

Aidan's eyes sparked up. "Will you come back, then?"

I wiped my eyes. "I need time before I can answer that. This has been a huge blow."

Aidan sat next to me and held me. My body melted into his. Our lips met. Soft and moist, his hot lips ate my mouth with hungry ferocity. My body started to unravel. But mustering every bit of strength, I pulled away. "Aidan, I need time. Please give me that. This has been so overwhelming. Give me some space."

"I've had the worst twenty-four hours ever, Clarissa. And that's saying something. Afghanistan wasn't exactly a walk in the park. I haven't slept at all." He combed through his thick hair with his fingers.

Oh God—I wanted to do that!

"I have to go away tomorrow until the end of the week. Please tell me there's hope, Clarissa." Aidan's voice was weak and tired.

I'd never seen his shoulders droop. I'd affected him that much. His face was drawn and unshaven but yet he still looked sexy.

I let Aidan hold me again, his strong arms around my waist. His needy hands moved down to my thighs. Despite dripping with sweaty arousal, I broke away. "We'll catch up when you return, Aidan. We can talk then."

"Is there hope, Clarissa?" Aidan asked, his panty-wetting gaze searing through me.

I nodded. A faint smile grew on my lips. I let him kiss me again. This time, his tongue slithered in and took me with such force that I pined for his cock to do the same. I pushed that primal need aside and extricated myself from his hold again.

Dejected, Aidan followed me reluctantly to the door. Holding the door handle, he said, "Please promise me you won't go out wearing those clothes."

I nearly laughed—Aidan sounded so old-fashioned. "Oh Aidan, I would never be seen like this. No one has ever seen me like this, except you and Tabitha."

He tucked an unruly strand behind his ear. "And will you promise me not to date another guy?" His eyes had a glint of insecurity.

"Aidan, you're kidding me, aren't you? My heart is filled with you," I said with resignation.

His brows knitted. "Then why are you kicking me out?"

"Because I need time alone. Because the pain has been so intense that I need to trust again."

"My darling, your pain is my pain." His bereft stare burned into my soul, and then he left.

I stood by the door, listening to Aidan's steps fade away. All the while, my heart screamed at me to call him back.

Resigned to a state of exile, I remained rigid on the sofa. Aidan's scent clung to the air while sensations from his desperate caresses possessed me.

CHAPTER FORTY-NINE

"What's your star sign, my lovely?" she asked, in a smoke-infused croak.

Incense and tobacco drifted through the air, threatening to make me sneeze as I shifted nervously in my chair. "Pisces," I answered.

The morning after Aidan's visit, I'd had an unshakeable urge to speak to someone. In many ways, I was glad Tabitha remained out of town. She would have just screamed at me to forgive Aidan in her typical race-through-life-head-on-fashion.

While I was out shopping for food, I passed a storefront. "Clairvoyant-Medium" was hand-painted on the window. Without thinking I rang the bell, and Mary answered.

She looked like anything but a medium. Disinclined as I was towards channeling angels that clinched the deal, and I entered.

In fact, Mary was very down to earth. She swore like a sailor, chain-smoked—much to my discomfort— and had a maternal, straight-to-the-point way about her.

After I handed over all the money I had on me, she sat me down and closed her eyes. For the first time in two days, my mind stilled.

Mary handed me a pack of standard playing cards. They were so haggard and overused that as I shuffled, I thought they would disintegrate.

"Cut them in three, love," said Mary, lighting another cigarette. "Mm… let's see. You have an excellent life ahead. But first, there's work to do. You must trust in life's many gifts. Let go of fear. The pain you suffered in the past will not be repeated."

Mary then handed me enormous cards with eye-catching geometric designs. I shuffled them awkwardly. They kept falling out of my small hands.

"Cut in three." Mary puffed smoke as she spoke.

As she turned over the first card I shuddered at the gloomy image of the Grim Reaper.

"Don't fret. It's in your past," Mary said without looking at me. She turned over another card, which depicted a woman in a shroud. "A woman died. She was close to you. She's now your guardian angel, my love—your protector, bringing you luck."

I sat forward. "Could that be my mother?"

"She passed away?" Mary tapped the death card.

I nodded.

She closed her eyes. "That's her indeed. I feel her presence around you. You have a very strong aura, my dear. I felt it as soon as you stepped in."

My body stiffened. How did she know this? Spooky.

The next card showed a king on a throne, holding a cup. "Ah… lovely. A water-sign man." She turned two more cards, one big cup and then another with many cups. "He's in love with you, deeply and with his soul. The best type of love."

Warm fuzziness swamped me. I had to remind myself to breathe. A cynical party-pooper chimed in, however, suggesting that Mary probably told everybody the same thing.

"Water-sign?" I asked. Aidan had told me his sign, but I'd forgotten.

"Pisces, Cancer, or Scorpio. What's your lover's birthday?"

"I'm not sure," I said, recrossing my legs. "We weren't together for long."

Mary studied me with her piercing dark eyes. "Were?" She frowned. "This is happily-ever-after love. I rarely get this configuration, to be honest." She turned another card, a giant radiant sun. She tapped the card. "Look at this. I mean, this is about abundance, love that is flourishing. No, my love, it has not ended."

"Maybe it represents a new person."

She shook her head. "No, it's in the present. This man is in your life, my dear. You are already with him. Look here: your heart is taken, as is his. It's so perfectly balanced. It sends a shiver through me." Mary cast me a smile before turning over another card.

A freaky image of a devil character appeared, followed by a body breaking out of a tomb. *Eek.*

"He's had a difficult past and is trapped by secrets. But he is a kind, generous soul. Always has been. His intentions have always been honorable. Others have wronged him. There's danger around him. His past is still casting a shadow over his area of happiness."

My heart was gripped. "Danger?"

"No need to concern your pretty head, he's protected enough. But there are those who wish to harm him. He must watch his step. You're in his area of protection. As long as you're in his life, no harm can come to him."

"And if I weren't?" I asked.

Mary's dark eyes scrutinized me. Her lips curled slightly. "That's not what I see."

I left Mary with my mind in a fog. I even forgot to buy food. Instead, I headed straight home and googled Aidan, hoping to find a date of birth. Frustratingly, there was nothing. But I did encounter images of us together. I was in the green dress while Aidan had his muscular arm protectively around me. His eyes radiated that recognizable devouring glint, and my face had a heavy-lidded, blissed-out expression, the look of someone drugged. Mm... yes, drugged on Aidan.

A long, wistful sigh escaped my lips. I couldn't take my eyes away from the computer screen. We looked so happy together. And photogenic Aidan was magnetic. His presence seemed to radiate off the screen. I saved the images for a screenshot.

For the next few days, I stared at the walls. My tears had finally dried. I was in zombie mode as I recalled over and over again Mary's predictions. In those words, I sought nourishment, and I seriously regretted that I hadn't recorded the session. Had I done that, I would have had the *happily ever after* bit on replay.

A skeptical muscle would twitch every now and then, however, dousing all hope by suggesting Mary had read the prediction from a script. But then, my soul kept asking my mind how was it that Mary had seen my mother's death?

CHAPTER FIFTY

It was Friday, and I was a million miles away when the doorbell sounded. I jumped up off the sofa. Could it be Aidan? The very thought of that impelled my heart to beat wildly. I headed to the door and stared through the peephole. Greta stood there, holding a box.

I opened the door. "Greta," I said with wide-eyed surprise.

"Clarissa, I hope you don't mind me arriving unannounced like this. Your father was worried. And so was I."

After I let her in, Greta said, "Julian was concerned you wouldn't have anything to eat, so I brought food." She looked around the apartment, which was tidier than when Aidan had visited.

"I probably should've called," I muttered, taking the box from her. "Thanks. It's very generous of you, as always."

In the box sat paper-wrapped burgers and two containers of juice. I placed it on the table. The aroma charged straight to my grumbling empty tummy. After having not eaten much lately, I was suddenly hungry.

"I haven't had lunch, so I hope you don't mind. I brought cheeseburgers," Greta said with her signature tight smile.

"I'll grab plates," I replied, heading for the kitchen.

The cheeseburger went down really well. We munched away silently and sipped on our juices.

"Aidan mentioned that he visited you here," Greta said, wiping her lips with a paper napkin.

I nodded.

"Aidan's a complex man. He always has been. But one thing's for sure, Clarissa: I've never seen him like this before. I've known him all his life. He didn't have an easy beginning. Has he spoken of his mother?"

"Aidan told me that it wasn't an easy upbringing. And that you cared for him."

"That's right. Patty was hooked, and still is, on pot and liquor. She was a groupie when younger. That's how she got pregnant. She was with Grant only once." She paused. "Grant, who was away touring most of the time, was worried about Aidan, so I stepped in. He moved in with me. It wasn't easy because Patty would come and drag him back with her. That happened all the way up to his teens."

"I see," I said, sipping on my juice. Tears welled up as I visualized young Aidan, bedraggled and alone.

"Anyway…" Greta sighed. "Aidan made a few bad calls. He then joined the army and worked hard. He was the top of his grade, a major in the Special Forces within three years." Greta had a sip of her drink. "The women, the choices weren't always good. But Aidan's never shied away from hard work. And he's one of the most generous of souls—the work that Aidan does for all the charities, as you know. And then, when you came along, Aidan was besotted. I tried to stop him due to your working relationship. But I could see what a perfect pair you made. Or I should say, make." Greta paused for a response, but I remained quiet. "I hope you can forgive him. Jessica was a mistake. And Amy threw herself at Aidan when he was vulnerable. I can confirm he'd broken up with Jessica. And…" She collected her breath. "I saw the DNA report. It was not his child. It was a horrible tragedy. But Jessica should never have been there. She's out to get Aidan. If she can't have him, then no-one else can. That's her approach as I see it."

Mulling over Greta's explanation, I remained silent.

"Anyway, we were hoping you might come back. It's your home now. We all want you to know that." Greta nodded reassuringly. "Your father would've come with me today, but he had to visit an estate. They're auctioning their entire hundred-year-old library. Aidan gave him an open checkbook. You can imagine your father's delight." She tilted her head and chuckled so infectiously I had to smile.

"I certainly can," I replied, breaking my silence. "Dad's in heaven. And he's also the happiest I've seen him since mother…" I stopped myself short of saying it. "And it's not just the books, Greta."

She smiled shyly. "Please come back, Clarissa." Greta touched my hand affectionately.

"The electric car has run out of charge," I said almost to myself.

"Then, I'll wait while you get ready. You can come with me. You can have the week off. In any case, the gala events have ceased."

"I heard. I hope it's not because of this."

She shook her head. "No. Aidan has a new scheme for raising money. He was hoping to have you on board." Greta drew a tight smile.

In my slow, hazy-minded way, I reflected on everything Greta had said. My heart and mind were at war. But this time, my heart had the winning edge. "Can you give me twenty minutes to pack a few things?"

Greta's body slumped with relief. "I can give you whatever time you need." She went to the box of goodies and removed a small carton. "It will give me time to eat this yummy cake. I bought one for you too, if you like." Greta opened the lid and showed me a mud cake. My stomach leapt with joy. I definitely had room for that.

"Yum," I said. "I'll pop the kettle on."

"Good thinking. I'll make the coffee." Greta followed me into the kitchen.

Having left Greta to it, I entered my bedroom and tied back my hair. I regarded the pile of clothes that had been grabbed in a hurry. I popped them back into my bag without bothering to fold them.

Fueled by adrenaline, my heart had taken charge and was on a mission. We didn't want that stubborn mind of mine stepping in.

As I dangled the one-piece, my eyes wandered over to my dressing table at the red bikinis with tags still intact. Discarding the one-piece, I packed the tiny triangles into my bag.

****

On our way back to paradise, we drove along the picturesque highway. The deep-blue sea, a soulful reminder of bliss, caused my throat to thicken with emotion.

I turned to Greta. "Do you happen to know Aidan's star-sign?"

"He's a Scorpio. The same sign as his father and me, why?"

Goosebumps and tingles rippled through me. My heart cartwheeled. "I just wondered." I smiled brightly for the first time all week.

THE END OF BOOK ONE.

Book 2 of Thornhill Series *Enlighten* will be available February 2018.
Connect with me on https://www.facebook.com/JJSorel/ or @JJ_Sorel

Made in the USA
Middletown, DE
19 March 2019